The Casebook of ‘

The Emperor’s Detec

By Peter K Los

PREFACE

Pichler’s abiding memory of the summer of 1870 was one of fear and confusion. And he’d been right to be frightened – it had so nearly cost him his life. But now as the end of the year approached, the successful conclusion of the affair of the fraudulent birth certificate had more pleasant connotations. The gratitude of the Emperor was one, his new role was another, but without doubt, Anna was by far the best.

1871 promised to be a quieter year – marriage and the start of his academic career, but after the summer he’d had, would this be enough for him? He had acted many parts in his life; farm boy, soldier, student, investigator and teacher. Was he the type to settle for the domestic life – would he even have the option?

Where would his new role as the “Emperor’s Detective” take him in the years to come? The great man had told him – “*I may have need of your services again*”. But would he? And even if he didn’t, would Inspector Hodža ever want to use him again? As the festive season beckoned, Klaus “K-P” Pichler wouldn’t have to wait long to find out.

Books by Peter Los
The Retribution Waltz Trilogy:
The Emperor's Detective
The Affair of the German Kaiser
The Swiss Experiment

The Casebook of "K-P" Pichler

Available from Amazon books in paperback and e-book.

TABLE OF CONTENTS

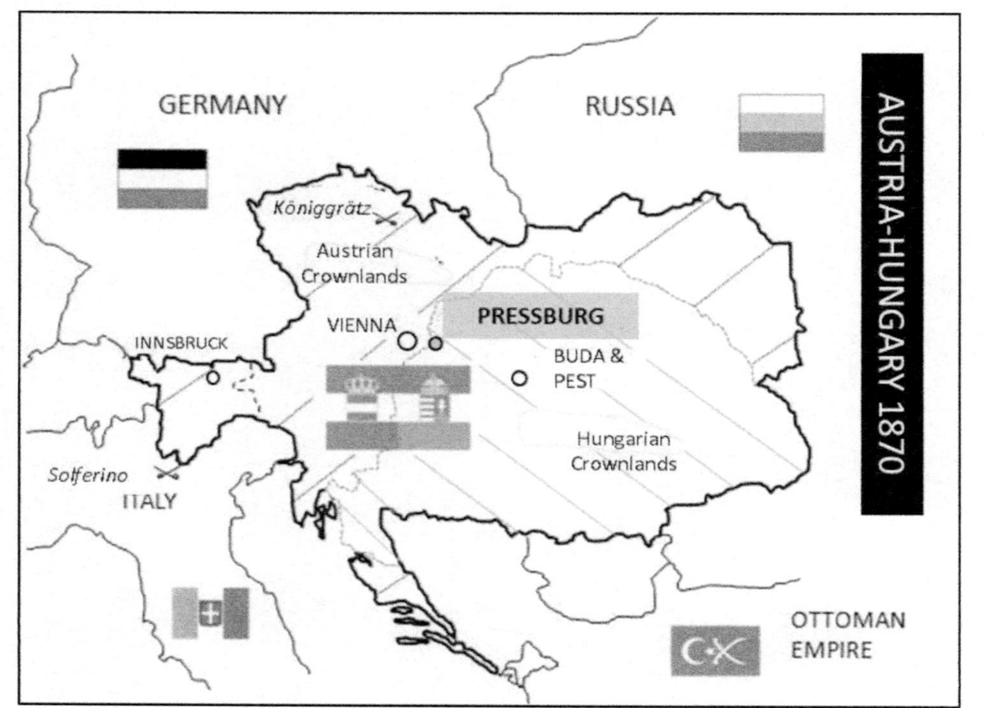
AUSTRIA-HUNGARY 1870
GERMANY
RUSSIA
Königgrätz
Austrian
Crownlands
VIENNA
PRESSBURG
BUDA &
PEST
INNSBRUCK
Hungarian
Crownlands
Solferino
ITALY
OTTOMAN
EMPIRE

THE NIGHT STALKER

Giuseppe Verdi – 1923

December 1870, the University at Pressburg:

Pressburg didn't have a university, at least not one it could call its own. Vienna, Buda and Prague all *did*, naturally. And to rub salt into the wound, they had had since the mid-fourteenth century! Fortunately a few of the forty or so Emperors since then had spread the jam a little wider. Pressburg was one of the beneficiaries. This made good politics – it pandered to local sensibilities at minimal cost. To those who worked within Pressburg's prestigious seat of higher learning – those who actually *did* any work, that is – it was the University of Vienna at Pressburg. To the locals, at least those few who paid the slightest heed to such lofty matters, it was the "big school up the hill".

Inspector Karol Hodža of the Pressburg police force was a regular visitor to one particular building within this "seat" of learning – "arse-end" he called it. The building was the "Department" of Applied Criminal Science. This consisted of just two rooms, and *one* of those was the basement. It had one Professor, no students and therefore no lecturers. The Prof in question was Professor Doktor Maximillian Kasselbaum, late surgeon of his Majesty's imperial army. Today, Hodža was content to just stick his head around Max's door to say hello. His target was to be found one floor below. The basement laboratory was known, for administrative purposes as U01, though "known" was putting it a bit strongly. The Dean, the Bursar and even the cleaners for that matter were infrequent visitors to this distant outpost of the University.

He immediately spotted his quarry. It was Kasselbaum's sole member of staff – a man of average height in his early thirties, Pichler by name. He sat hunched over a pile of papers and he did *not look happy*! He sat in one corner of the laboratory. Pichler was far too junior to warrant his own office or even a shared one come to that – not that there was anyone else to share it with.

'Cheer up, K-P you're getting married in a month's time!'

Pichler looked up in surprise, offered a wry smile and then pushed his chair right back in frustration.

'That's why I'm so tee-ed off, Karol.'

'And I thought you were in love!' responded Hodža with a stupid grin written all over his face.

'Thing is, I want to get on and enjoy life with Anna. I don't want to spend the next forty years, stuck here marking this load of old tosh. I wouldn't mind so much if the buggers actually took any notice of the copious comments I write.'

'They don't?' asked Hodža, struggling to recall his own school days.

'Mostly they just look at the mark and those are the ones who *have* to get a diploma at the end of it all. The sons of noblemen are just here to have a bloody good time, mainly drinking and seducing the ancillary staff.'

'Hang on, K-P. How come you've got so much marking to do? I didn't think you had any students.'

Pichler explained. Lecturers from a number of other departments had worked out that if they made applied criminal science a compulsory module, they could dump a heck of a lot of their marking. The "dumpee" in this case was one Klaus Heinrich Pichler, known to his friends as "K-P" – for reasons that are too complicated to go into here.

'So how many is "a" number of other departments?' asked Hodža.

'Chemistry, law, medical!' reeled off Pichler. 'I suppose I should count myself lucky that the Fine Arts department hasn't jumped onto the band-wagon.'

This last comment was accompanied by a fulsome laugh. He was a man who liked to laugh. With his recent past, it was a bloody necessity!

'Well ditch the academic life, K-P. Come and join Ján and me on the force. We're always on the lookout for bright young minds, or even not so young ones, in your case. And you are the "Emperor's Detective" after all.'

Ignoring that comment, Pichler handed the Inspector a sheet of paper. It was the very same one Max had pushed under his nose not ten minutes before. Hodža ran his eyes over it. Written on official university paper, it said "INTERNAL APPOINTMENT – LECTURER (DOCTORAL)".

'This is for the history department, K-P. What's that got to do with you?'

'No doctorate, no lectureship, simple as that,' said Pichler gloomily. 'And I'm not sure I can stomach any more studying.'

'But if you *were* to become a lecturer, wouldn't you have *even more* marking to do?' asked Hodža somewhat puzzled.

Pichler laughed at that idea and not just your common or garden laugh but a real belly-wobbler!

'Let me explain, Karol,' he began patiently. 'The grander the title, the more remote academic staff are from students. Senior lecturers see the little beggars only when cornered. Profs are always somewhere far more important than a lecture theatre. And Deans! Well, they wouldn't know a student if they bumped into one. Though I'd have to say the chances of that happening are pretty remote. They make sure of that!'

'No choice then, K-P. But look on the bright side. How many students are in your fortunate position? All those *little* jobs you get up to for the powers that be! Why don't you write these up as case studies? Of course you'll have to change a few names to protect the innocent. Maybe you'll have to protect the guilty as well... if he turns out to be a Count von "do-da". Then add a bit of academic flim-flam, you know the sort of thing better than me. Why not? You'll be Doktor Pichler by this time next year!'

Pichler smiled. It wouldn't be *quite* that simple. Max had had the same idea, but he said two to three years. But Karol was right. It didn't have to be *that* complicated either. It wasn't as if he was trying to discover a cure for cholera, you know, do something really useful! He was still smiling when the Inspector got down to the business that had brought him here in the first place.

'So by way of kicking off your thesis here's one case Ján and me could do with a bit of help on.'

***

It had all started three nights ago. Two "ladies" from the notorious Zigeunerplatz turned up at the police station at just after two in the morning demanding to see Herr Slota. Now that in itself, Hodža explained was extremely unusual. Such ladies wouldn't normally be seen dead in a police station. In fact *dead* was usually the only way he ever saw them, lying in the morgue, awaiting the attentions of the police surgeon. Ján wasn't on duty as it happened, "more on that in a minute", Hodža said. According to the desk sergeant, they were both terrified out of their wits. On being told Herr Slota wasn't available they turned and rushed straight back out into the night.

'I got the report the next morning and that evening I went round to Ján's. From the duty sergeant's description, he thought it sounded like Heidi and Helga. Apparently they're something of a "double-act", if you know what I mean, K-P. In any event they're usually seen together. Ján is the only policeman they'll talk to. It's like that! It's not the badge or the office – it's the *person* they trust.'

'So did he track them down and find out what had spooked them so badly?' asked Pichler.

'No, he didn't! Or more accurately he couldn't! He's in bed on doctor's orders, hurt his back lifting furniture which was far too heavy for him, the daft old sod. I've only one junior constable with time to look into this. He's far too green *and* these two wouldn't trust him anyway.'

'Can't you get anybody else in?' asked a surprised Pichler.

'Not unless my Chief approves it and he won't. And here I quote him – "not for these sorts of women!" So Ján suggested I ask you. There may be nothing in it of course. After all we know bugger all at this stage, but what with your, what do you call it?'

'Scientia autem deductio rationis,' replied Pichler with a slightly self-conscious grin.

'Smart arse!' responded Hodža, but kindly so. 'Let's just stick to good old Slovakian shall we! "Reasoned deduction". Good enough for you? Well, you use that and we'll see how far it gets you.'

Pichler had studied medicine, but he wasn't a doctor. He'd studied law, but he wasn't a lawyer. And he knew a lot of chemistry, but he wasn't a… you've got the picture. He was an all-rounder – some less charitable types would say "a jack of all trades and a master of none!" How best to describe him then? A detective yes, but one whose best tool was the one he kept between his ears. That, together with pen, paper and the determination to see the thing through to the end was what marked him out as special. Hodža's boss wouldn't use the word "special" – "totally unsuitable to work in *my* station" would be closer to the mark.

'I'll do it!'

'Thank God for that!' responded Hodža. 'Now I can't give you a warrant card or a temporary rank –

not that that would do you any good even if I could. But I *do* have something far more useful to give you!'

At that he pulled a single sheet from his top pocket, unfolded it and handed it over.

Helga and Heidi. Hear you've had a spot of bother, girls. Can't come me self – done me back in, so I'm sending this one. You can trust him just as if it was me. Call him K-P. He'll keep me in the picture. Look after yourselves. Herr Slota.

'He's added a few extra notes re: the girls on the back which might help you a little. And he gave me his night stick to lend you. He stressed *lend*, so don't you damage it!'

Pichler felt its weight – not *especially* heavy. Would it be much use, he wondered. He looked at the Inspector enquiringly.

'Make no mistake, my lad. These things can be lethal. Do NOT hit anyone anywhere near their head – you're likely as not, kill them. These are for disabling. Go for the shoulder or just below the knee. You might break something but you won't kill anyone. And one other thing, K-P – don't piss about with the blessed thing! If it looks like someone's about to have a go at you, then hit 'em as though you mean it. Always assume that they have a knife.'

The Zigeunerplatz, old town Pressburg, down by the river:

That evening was the start. He'd got there just after seven. The streets were mostly as dark as pitch, it being December. The Zigeunerplatz – not its proper name, just something the locals called it – was not known for the quality or quantity of its street lighting. Nor its pavements come to that and he tripped over numerous times during the evening as he walked the walk. Quite how these "princesses of the pavement" managed he couldn't really imagine. It was the poor lighting that made him wonder how anybody could have seen anything at first. However there *were* lampposts just not very many of them. It was under these that he would invariably find a woman or two. The more presentable ones stood directly under its beam, the less presentable ones off to one side. Asking for Heidi and Helga was pretty hard going from the start.

'Yeah, I'm Heidi and what was the other name you was after, Helva, weren't it? We can be any name you likes, darling, just so long as you'se got the where-wiv-all.'

She rounded off her "kind offer" by sharing a largely toothless grin with both him and her friend.

Moving smartly on, Pichler was beginning to wonder if he'd ever strike lucky. It would have helped if Ján had provided the names of the streets the pair usually worked. Perhaps he couldn't; perhaps there was little rhyme or reason to the way these women plied their trade. He was on his tenth attempt to find said ladies, each time going through the same pantomime, when…

'Oi! You two! Piss off!' said one of the two women striding aggressively towards Pichler and the latest pair.

'Piss off yourself!' replied one of them, though they quickly surrendered the lamppost to the newcomers.

'We've heard as to how you've been looking for Helga and Heidi,' said one of them, now that they had Pichler to themselves.

'He's a nice looking fella, ain't he, Heid,' said the one he presumed to be Helga.

'Young and all, eh Helg! So what can we do for you, me young lover. Fancy a threesome, do yer? It's our speciality,' said Heidi who giggled lasciviously across to her friend.

Slota's note hadn't told him that much, a brief description only. Both blond, both in their early twenties, both a good cut above the usual ladies who plied their trade in the Platz district. All in all, he had to say that they were nicely turned out. They even had most of their own teeth and some of these were still reasonably white. The reason? They'd come late to the profession after a career in service only ended by the deaths of their respective masters. Slota reckoned that they must have met up on the street and decided to "go into business" together. What their family names were, he had not the faintest. In fact he very much doubted that Heidi and Helga were even real – "stage" names more like.

'Herr Slota sent me – can't come himself, he's injured his back!' declared Pichler, handing them the note as he spoke.

They'd turned away towards the light, read it and briefly conferred.

'All right… so what's he look like then, lover boy?' said one, making no effort to conceal her suspicion.

'Short, stout, craggy around the face, usually seen in a much darned overcoat, speaks broad Slovak and terrible German. Kind when he can be, tough when he can't – and he is *my* friend!'

They paused, looked into each other's eyes and then into Pichler's. And they each held him there for some moments, during which time he moved not a muscle.

'So you're *not* the law then?' asked Helga.

'No!' There was nothing else he could usefully add.

'Good!' they both declared almost as one. 'We're going to trust you then. Nothing to lose have we? Don't suppose anybody but Herr Slota would give a shit about the likes of us.'

The story they told to Herr Slota's friend was a strange one indeed. It had happened just the once. That was the night that had sent them scurrying to the police station, scared witless, in search of Slota. It *had* started out normally enough. They'd been standing under this very lamppost, chatting away, waiting for punters. They knew they'd land their fish – they invariably did. "Best looking tarts in Pressburg, we are, ain't we Helg!" They already turned away a couple of rough types – they had their standards after all – when they noticed this fellow standing under the post on the opposite side of the street. "He must have blooming good eyesight", Helga told Pichler she'd said to Heidi at the time, and she beckoned him over. He didn't move. Half an hour later he was still there, so they decided to move on. It wasn't that they were frightened. He looked like he might be a "poly-man" and that would put off punters. Pichler took a moment to realise that a poly-man was what the ladies called a police officer. Pichler very much doubted that he could have been a "poly-man". The Zigeunerplatz wasn't somewhere the police were keen on patrolling in broad daylight in pairs let alone after dark on their tod.

'And so what happened next?'

'Well,' began Heidi, 'we'd only been at the next post-but-one along for a few seconds and he turns up again. Thing is, erm what's Herr Slota told us to call you?'

'K-P!' said Helga.

'Yeah, well you see Kaypah, thing is we never saw him approach, never saw him walk towards us, never saw him follow us. One second he was standing at our usual post way back there,' said Heidi, pointing as she spoke, 'and the next second he was at this one!'

'And always standing under a lamppost on the opposite side of the street?' asked Pichler.

'That's right! So there he was staring at us and we was starting to get a bit edgy, like. It was so bloody…'

'Creepy,' added Helga. 'And believe me, we see all sorts down here and we don't scare easy – wouldn't last long in this business if'n we did, would we Heid?'

'So you moved on again?'

'Not straight away! As Helg says we don't scare easy, so we both tried staring him out. Usually that's enough to send these sorts packing.'

'What do you mean by "these sorts"?' asked Pichler.

'Not really interested in doing business – too scared to do it. Just after cheap thrills that's all.'

'So what happened next?'

'He stares right back, didn't he Helg? And then his eyes turns red… glowing red… just for a second and then back to normal. God it gave us such a turn. We'd thought we'd imagined it, but then he did it again.'

'Did he move his hand to his face or...'

'Nah! He didn't move at all… arms straight down by his sides, legs together, standing fully upright – the whole bleeding time.'

'By this time, we'd had enough!' This time it was Helga who took over the narrative. 'Fuck this, I said, didn't I, Heid? Fuck this, let's get out of here. So we started to leg it. I looked over me shoulder and there he was, only he'd turned a bit so he was facing us directly, just as he'd done afore. Anyway, the bastard didn't move and he was still there the next time I looked back, only 'bout half a minute later.'

'By which time he *still* hadn't moved?'

'That's right, Herr Kaypee! So we slowed down and started to stroll like, didn't we Helg?'

'Yeah, even had a bit of a giggle to ourselves… saying what daft cows we were. Anyway he weren't there anymore and…'

'Then he was,' interrupted Heidi, 'steps right out, not two yards in front, only now his eyes were glowing like hot coals and his face… oh God his face… deathly white… like a corpse he was.'

'It *couldn't* have been the same man, not to have got in front of you so quickly. You said you'd seen him standing where you'd left him, not seconds before, and you'd run some of the way, what a hundred paces?' stated Pichler.

'But it weeerrreee!' The two women almost screamed this, so vehemently that he was in no doubt that it *was* the same man – at least in the minds of these two terrified women.

Their description, not surprisingly, was of limited value. The man wore a hooded black full length cloak, from which a red lining could be seen within the folded back hood. The hair they did notice, despite their terror, jet black with a pronounced widow's peak.

'And you've only seen this character the once?' asked Pichler.

'Too right! We've told the other girls 'bout it... advised 'em to work in pairs like us,' replied Helga.

'And are they?'

'Nah! They just laughed, said we'd been at the Schnapps... or worse. They're carrying on as before, the daft bitches!'

'I could ask around, amongst the other ladies, I mean,' said Pichler.

'Don't bovver yourself Herr Karpay. We's the only ones Herr Slota got to talk and that was after a lot of trying. The girls 'round here won't talk to poly-men. Nah, you come to us if you want to know what's happening.'

Pichler handed them what he hoped would be a suitable recompense for their time.

'Ooooo. That's proper handsome of you. Sure you don't want to...'

They both giggled at Herr Slota's friend and half-smiled as they watched him set off back to, they had little doubt, his nice wife and three kids.

Pichler's digs, the student district, Pressburg:

Pichler pondered what was known and what could be surmised. He was not dealing with a mythical creature of demonic origin, though *this* was exactly what Helga and Heidi thought. He wasn't going to ask them to confirm this, not wanting to stir up further panic in the Zigeunerplatz. The man was however definitely trying to convey that impression. Changing his eyes without moving his hands was simple enough. Paint his eyelids with luminous paint, close his eyes and "red-hot glowing coals" magically appear. But that gave him some insight into the man he was dealing with. Did he say "man"? No, men! There had to be two of them, he'd already established that. But painting eyelids with that kind of substance is bloody risky, even if somebody skilled does it for you. Get some of that muck in your eyes and well, a lot of pain and even blindness could be the result.

So that pretty much ruled out casual pranksters. He could just about imagine some of his own students dressing up in this way for a laugh. But not shaving their hair to give this distinctive widows peak, not if they had lectures the next day. Anyway, a tad lazy some of them might be but evil minded bastards they most definitely weren't. He'd occasionally have to have them in his office after some of the towns folk had complained to the university. Their usual explanation was – "we were just having a bit of fun, sir – no harm done, really there wasn't – won't happen again, sir". In mitigation they would usually plead an excessive consumption of alcohol.

That left one of two options, neither of which was particularly comforting, though one was marginally better.

"Escaped lunatic" he'd written, adding an "s" immediately afterwards. That wasn't in itself ideal but at least he ought to be able to wrap up the case fairly quickly. They'd almost certainly be local, so a trip to the city's asylum, find out who'd escaped, then report the fact to Hodža. His boss would be obliged to act, put some men on the job, round 'em up pretty damn quick and lock 'em away again – job done!

Second option – "Fanatics". He immediately crossed the word out and substituted the one he'd meant to use, which was "Fantasists". He then added "misogynists" followed by a question mark. Ah, now *that* was a problem. On the surface these men could be upright pillars of the community, with established positions and a settled family life. But underneath, as mad as a barrel load of monkeys.

But did they *have* to be mad, that is of the certifiable kind as opposed to just plain bloody weird? Pichler took down his dictionary and looked up the exact definition of chauvinist versus misogynist. The former, in this context anyway, applied to men who considered the male sex to be superior to the female one. At best, which wasn't saying very much, this could come down to as little as "don't you worry your pretty little head about such things, my dear – leave it to us men"!

At this he laughed out loud as he imagined himself saying such a thing to either Anna or God forbid Prof Maggie. He'd never get out of the room alive.

Patronising – yes, criminal – no! Misogynists though, they just didn't like women.

Could there be a fanatical element after all, a religious-based one perhaps? The only two victims so far were prostitutes, so maybe some extreme Christian sect could be responsible. If so it was probably one which considered the New Testament to be altogether far too liberal, as in too few "pillars of salt" and too much "mercy and forgiveness"! And that *could* mean women were involved as well as men, which didn't bear thinking about.

But was it only the two, Helga and Heidi? Would there be more? *Had* there actually been more already? Probably a "no" to that last one. The two women had already told him; they'd tried to alert the community. So what if they'd been pooh-poohed at the time. If any of the other locals had encountered his red-eyed "friends" since the warning, then they'd pretty soon have come running to Helga or Heidi and they would have got a message to him. And so far they hadn't! And if there were just two of these red-eyed monsters then two girls at a time was probably their limit. It was unlikely that Pressburg boasted an army of these madmen. So Pichler had arrived at his "best working assumption" so far.

But the plain fact was he had far too few data to go on, just the one incident as reported by Helga and Heidi. He briefly considered dragging himself around the Zigeunerplatz and making his own observations.

Pointless! The two "H's" had already told him that none of the other working girls would talk to him and the odds of him running into these… these… these what? "Midnight Lurkers" – yes! It was a bit melodramatic, but so far that's all they were. Oddballs who got some kind of thrill from scaring the bejesus out of women whose lives were already hard enough. So, "lurkers" it was then; but just short-hand for his personal use. If this ever appeared in an official report and Heaven forbid Slota got to see it, he could already visualise the Sergeant pissing himself stupid! So Scientia autem deductio rationis had hit the buffers, for now anyway. There was nothing he could do but await further developments.

The Pressburg Asylum, Dr Havelchek's office:

But there *was* something else he could do. He could eliminate… or otherwise as the police manual says the "loonies" option.

'No escapes, Herr Pichler. In fact we haven't had one since the early sixties. Is that what you were hoping to hear?' asked Doktor Havelchek, the asylum's director.

Pichler shrugged, which Havelchek took to mean "no".

'I'd half expected as much,' replied Pichler. 'All this red-hot coals thing and moving at incredible speed. It all smacks of trying to mimic some kind of supernatural being, far too elaborate for a lunatic!'

'Oh, you *think* so?' replied Havelchek. 'Hmmm! Do you have some time to spare? I have someone I'd very much like you to see.'

Doktor Havelchek's office was light and airy, a real pleasure to work in, Pichler thought. By the time the two of them had descended down five flights of stairs, the picture was very different. Thick iron bars replaced large windows and there was no furniture, save for a wooden bench and a bucket.

'We daren't let them have an iron bedframe. They'd have the springs off in the blink of an eye. You've no idea how many ways these demented souls can devise to end their own lives.'

Doktor Havelchek nodded at the warden or nurse as he insisted on calling the fellow that he could go. Pichler heard the man throw the bolt once he'd closed the door with them on the "wrong" side, leaving just the iron grid separating them from the figure that was curled up in the farthest corner of the cell.

'Come now, Herr Welbach. See, I've brought you a visitor.'

Pichler noticed that Havelchek had retreated to the locked door, as far away as he could get from the iron grid. He smiled back encouragingly, mouthing "don't worry". Pichler stood in a shaft of sunlight which emanated from a small skylight.

When he turned around he saw the figure was now pressed hard up against the grid. His face was deformed but not from birth. Both ears had been trimmed to end in a sharp point and there were strange symbols cut into both his cheeks and forehead.

'Herr Welbach…?' began Pichler.

'The Welbach creature is dead, long-dead! I have consumed his body and his soul is now mine.'

As he spoke, he stuck out his tongue, which to his horror, Pichler saw had been split into two forks.

'Come closer, friend,' said the creature.

Pichler didn't move a step. Welbach turned his back on his visitor and stepped away from the grid.

'Come closer, my friend. You have nothing to fear if your soul be pure.'

Picher took a cautious step forward. That was the trigger. Welbach hurled himself against the grid with such ferocity that he actually bounced off it. Pichler's panicked retreat was so fast that he bumped into Havelchek. In that fleeting moment, Pichler saw his wild staring eyes – his yellow eyes – as yellow as sulphur.

'Your soul be not pure… you must give it to me. Come closer… COME CLOSER… obey me, you must obey me… you must…'

Pichler hadn't heard Havelchek bang on the door, nor the sliding back of the bolt. He was only aware of two men bundling him out of that space and locking the door behind him.

Back in Havelchek's office, Pichler had recovered – a little – from the incredible scene he'd just witnessed.

'Would you like anything in your tea, Herr Pichler?'

Pichler nodded. Most of the people who'd just seen Herr Welbach answered "yes" to that question. Some went further. They just had the alcohol. Not that Havelchek was in the business of exhibiting the poor demented man to all and sundry. He only did so when it was absolutely necessary – and for Herr Pichler it *was* necessary – absolutely!

'How long has he been like…?'

'Oh, a decade at least.'

'Did he do all that to himself before…?'

'Yes, all except the eyes. We don't know what he put in them, but it happened two years ago. He'll be blind within the next year – nothing we can do about that. I'm sorry to subject you to that. I hope it won't give you nightmares. However I thought it was important that you should see it.'

'Thank you Doktor Havelchek. I had no idea man was capable of such abominable self-deception… or deliberate self-mutilation. Now I do!'

As he walked back towards his basement office, Pichler tried to imagine just how terrifying such a creature would have seemed to the two women. There they were far from any help, at night and without the benefit of a dirty great iron gate between them and "it". He *couldn't* imagine it!

He also had no doubt that without that gate the demented being would have torn him apart. So that posed a question. Was what the two "H's" had seen liable to be equally dangerous? And if so, what the hell was he going to do about it?

Once back in his office, he brought out his shiny new casebook and started writing.

Assume violent madman – for now. He underlined the last two words.

Possibility (1); permanently and grossly disfigured. Hence he'd be unable to pass as normal in everyday life. Corollary – he must hide away somewhere during the day – only come out at night. Limited number of hiding places.

Possibility (2); uses a disguise, e.g. the painted eyelid and wig. Corollary – could pass for normal in everyday life, so could be anyone anywhere in the City.

He put down his pen. 'Bugger!' he exclaimed out loud. Suppose it was possibility one? It got dark about five. The tarts would be out on the street, some of them were out all day, but the one and only visit had taken place after midnight. That made sense. Most of the locals who'd spent the evening in the drinking dens would be lying on their own beds, pissed out of their minds, or lying in the gutter, ditto. So there wouldn't be that many people out and about and that included the ladies of the night. So why were Helga and Heidi out and about? How much had he given them? Blimey, it was actually quite a lot, probably a much bigger fee than most of the women he'd encountered could command. But Helga and Heidi were as Slota had told him, quite a cut above the others; in fact he was surprised to see them on the street at all, rather than working in one of the higher class brothels. Why was that? And they worked as a twosome – why was that?

The home of Professor Margaret MacPherson:

Anna's aunt Emma's house on the Rösslgasse was temporarily uninhabited. Next Christmas he would be living there with Anna; this Christmas would be his last one as a single man. Anna was spending her last Christmas as a spinster with Maggie and he was going to cook the festive feast. He'd had so much on his mind recently that he'd forgotten all about it. This thing was all-consuming. No wonder Hodža's boss had been so reluctant to assign an officer to it. Understandable, given the paucity of data!

It was on the way to the Lubecks' Lebensmittel emporium, his shopping list in his hand, that it struck him.

'Of course! How could I have been so stupid?' he declared out loud, causing a startled passer-by to reproach him with a hard stare. The gentleman club's chucking out time was around midnight. This left said "gentlemen" one of two options if they felt the need to satisfy their carnal urges beyond the confines of the marital bed. They could visit a brothel but this would not suit those who wished to keep their nocturnal proclivities a closely guarded secret. This was nigh on impossible once you'd had to report in to the madam and then run into Wilhelm from the club and Albert from the office. No, much better to visit two street women, who were probably just as "clean" and as handsome as any others to be found in the city's establishments. Heidi and Helga could be relied upon to be discrete *and* they did threesomes. What "gentleman" could ask for more? So that answered the question – why were "H&H" out so late?

He left that thought hanging because Herr Lubeck was looking at him expectantly. Twenty minutes later, interspersed with much chat on the exorbitant price of herring and the health of the Emperor, Herr Lubeck had Pichler's order all boxed up. It only remained for the handing over of the necessary.

It was in fact quite a big box as befits a festive celebration for three so Pichler took a cab. He told the cabbie, "There's no need to hurry". He wanted to enjoy the ride, which he did every time he visited. Maggie's house was a single story, red brick building, ideal for a newly appointed lecturer of single status. It was one of a number of University "grace and favour" properties which were made available to new staff. Maggie had signed the lease fourteen years ago and could hardly be counted as new staff anymore. But such properties were some way from the University. This was no drawback for a hardy walker from the Highlands like Maggie, but was less appealing for a young man intent on enjoying the delights of the city centre. Years passed and nobody else seemed to want it. Professor Margaret McPherson timed her offer to perfection when the University was particularly strapped for cash. She persuaded the bursar to accept a sizeable one-off payment in lieu of future rents and so it became hers.

He knocked on the door – then he knocked again… and again, this time with vigour. Then he walked around the side into the garden.

'Oi, cloth-ears,' he shouted over the fence, which was no way to address his intended.

Anna looked up and smiled.

'Sorry, I was miles away. Did you get everything you wanted?'

'Certainly did!' was his somewhat self-satisfied answer. 'I'll put it on the kitchen table, shall I? It'll be best to leave Maggie to put it all away when she gets in.'

She was sitting on the garden swing, wrapped up in a thick fur coat, hat and muffler and as she gently oscillated back and forth, it was obvious – she loved every single second of it. Yes! Maggie had a garden!

'Scottish or Polish?' asked Anna, meaning was it to be fowl or fish for Christmas day?

'Fowl! Though, I've only brought the non-perishables today. I'll bring the bird from the bakery on the morning of the actual day,' declared her fiancé.

This house, you must understand was in the Scottish highlands, yes that one, the one two and a half thousand kilometres to the northwest. There was a garden feature that proved it every Spring; a diagonal cross of white stones which had bluebells planted in each of the four quadrants. Maggie's command of the languages spoken in this part of the Empire was so complete that most people thought she was Swiss or maybe Dutch. Nobody believed that "home" lay in the far north of that far away offshore island! Yet when she crossed her own threshold, she would invariably return, just a wee bit to her roots.

'Room for a little one?' he asked. She budged up.

'Maggie made me a Scottish breakfast this morning!'

'Which is what exactly?' asked Pichler.

'Fried egg and fried ham! Wonderful it was too.' Anna was silent for a moment while she pondered on this thought. 'You know, K-P, what with this lovely garden and that delightful breakfast, I think I've changed my mind. Perhaps I won't marry you after all. I think I'll live here with Maggie instead.'

'Oh, she'd *love* that,' he replied sarcastically.

She laughed. 'Oh, well, second best will have to do!'

At that moment, Pichler saw Maggie's face peering over the fence.

'Ach, I see yon vagabond's finally turned up. Left me to put everything away, has he? The rogue!'

Taking the hint, Pichler got off the swing. He'd need to know where she'd put the stuff… so he could do the business come the twenty-fifth. It was his way of saying thank you to Maggie for the past few months giving Anna somewhere to live – somewhere that wasn't the scene of her Aunt's murder just a few months ago.

Over tea they chatted about life and the living of it but at no time did he raise the subject of his case. In fact it didn't even cross his mind. Walking home some two hours later, he recalled an apposite "Max-ism". "Compartmentalisation, young Pichler. That's the key. When you're working, you're working – when you're not, you aren't. Got it?" Yes, that was the key to managing his life – good old Max!

He'd gone less than a mile from Anna and Maggie and that lovely garden before the case popped into his head once more. Those gentlemen in their smart clothes, leaving their clubs for he knew exactly where had filtered ever so gently into his thoughts. Compartmentalisation, you see!

Slota's house:

When he arrived at the laboratory early the next morning he found a hastily scribbled note on his desk. It simply said that he was to come to Slota's *immediately*. It was initialled "H". How did the two women know where he worked? He'd not said anything. Then it struck him; "H" for Hodža, not Helga, not Heidi.

***

Ján's wife Maria opened the door and she looked very upset. Pichler didn't even get a chance to ask how the old fellow was. Instead he was rapidly ushered upstairs to their bedroom.

'It was just Heidi who called around, about four-ish,' he began without any preamble. 'She got my address from the station. I told them that'd be all right if ever a Helga or a Heidi came asking for me. Never thought they would mind – never thought they'd go anywhere near the station, come to that,' said Slota.

'Is she still here?' asked Pichler.

'Noooo! Maria tried to calm her down but the best she was able to do was to get the girl to take a sip of brandy. I say a sip of brandy but it was actually a bloody big tumbler full which the poor moppet downed in one. Listen K-P, you should have seen her – she was scared shitless!'

Pichler's mouth dropped open. 'Tell me!' he demanded, which came out more assertively than he'd intended.

'Course I told her to wait here. I'd get you to go round and bring Helga back here with you and they should both wave a cheery farewell to the Zigeunerplatz. She simply wouldn't wear it. Of course, it's where all their things are, not to mention their money.'

'So what did Heidi tell you, Ján?' said Pichler, now more in control of himself.

The story he told Pichler was considerably more succinct than the version she'd told him. Every other sentence was interspersed with tears and pleas for him to help them. It wasn't the Heidi he'd come to know, that was for sure – he'd never seen her like this. It took three attempts before it was reasonably clear in his own mind and even then he could hardly credit it.

'Does that make any sense to *you*, K-P?' asked Slota, 'cos it makes bugger all sense to *me*. It's the kind of nonsense the "druggies" spew out but I know for a fact neither of the girls are addicts!'

'In a weird way, it confirms *one* of my various theories?' replied Pichler.

'Whhaaaattt!' demanded Slota. 'You mean you *actually* believe all that tosh?'

'I believe Heidi described exactly what she saw. I don't believe that her interpretation of events is remotely possible. I *do* know who I need to speak to – and I need to speak to him now!'

"Mad" Gabriel's office – the University:

The University of Vienna in *Vienna* was the most prestigious seat of learning within the Empire, of that there was no doubt. Some would even say within the Continent. The University of Vienna in *Pressburg* wasn't! While this lowly status might have been a disadvantage in every other way, there was one benefit. Less established disciplines which would give traditionalists in Vienna a severe attack of the vapours, could usually find a home in Pressburg. Applied criminal science, Pichler's own, was one such. This attitude also extended to research, the most extreme example of which was Doktor Gabriel Albescu.

The Albescu family home was near the city of Brassó in Transylvania, quite near to the Romanian border. Albescu's passion was the folk law of his people. The stories of the ancient inhabitants of his homeland region were hard to credit to the modern mind of the late 19th Century. Consequently though it was an area he had researched diligently, he kept his findings very much to himself. Even in the most ragged of feral packs, dogs will always look down on the runt and so it was for Albescu. He had few visitors to his office. Today was to be different.

Pichler had never met him before. He'd expected to see the stereo-typical mad-Prof. They did exist! Unkempt grey hair, dishevelled clothing, rambling speech and a complete and utter shambles of an office were their trademarks.

'Do come in my dear fellow,' said the good-looking forty-something man of above average height. He was dressed in a suit of clothes that made Pichler feel like a beggar. And his office was immaculate!

'Take a seat. I know it's a little early but I was about to partake of a small plum brandy. Would you care to join me?'

Too bleeding right I would thought Pichler after the listening to Slota's harrowing tale. He was grateful to see that "small" did not mean tiny.

'So what may I do for you?'

Pichler spoke uninterrupted for ten minutes.

'I see,' said Albescu once the tale had been told.

'Red eyes and a widow's peak on the first visit and a reptilian face complete with claws on the second. Tell me… was there a visit *before* Herr "Roten-Augen" appeared?'

'Not as far as I'm aware, Doktor Albescu!' replied Pichler. 'Should there have been?'

'Please call me Gabriel. I get so few visitors in my little den, that I feel we are already old friends. Are we not K-P? Oh yes,' he added on seeing Pichler's surprise, 'even in the depth of darkest Transylvania,' he said waving his hand around to indicate his little empire, 'your name is known. I like to keep tabs on all my fellow mavericks within the University. So tell me, are you interested in legends or myths? I presume you know the difference, do you not?'

'A legend is an unverified story that *could* be true, but probably isn't. A myth is a load of old hooey, usually involving supernatural creatures prancing about in the nude,' said Pichler.

'Not perhaps the most definitive of academic definitions, but in essence... you are surprisingly accurate. Myths it is then!'

Pichler nodded.

'Let me tell you a story. Are you sitting comfortably? Good. Perhaps a top-up? This is not for those of a nervous disposition,' said Albescu.

Pichler nodded and smiled at the same time. He was warming to Doktor Gabriel Albescu. Quite why he had acquired the epithet "mad" was completely beyond him.

'If we are talking about the myth I think we are, then there should be four visitations; the Test, the Revelation, the Judgement and the Sentence. I won't trouble you with the ancient names of these creatures – there are so many. Unless you speak Romanian…' Pichler shook his head.

'Well then,' Albescu continued. 'The Test is conducted by the principal. We may call him the "Soul-Saver". He represents good, God in his Heaven in later incarnations of the myth. In the test he will visit a young maiden and… put her to the test, hence the name. Is she pure or has she been corrupted?'

Pichler interrupted… 'Does the Soul Saver take human form?'

'Mostly! Some myths talk of a white stag, but mostly it is a handsome young man – to tempt the young maiden do you see? Why do you ask?'

'In that case, there might have been an earlier visitation before old red-eyes showed up!' answered Pichler.

'Very well! We now introduce the other creature in this fable called the "Night Stalker". He is the devil's creature. He may take a variety of forms, at least according to the literature, before revealing his true self. If the maiden is found wanting…'

'Found wanting by the Soul-Saver, you mean?' asked Pichler.

'Indeed! Odd isn't it, that good and evil should be in direct communication one with the other. However this is not unusual in this type of story. "Myths with a Moral", I call them. The Stalker makes his first appearance in the Revelation. Here he presents as an unearthly creature but his appearance is constrained, nothing too devilish. The red-eyes and the hair you describe would be a good example. The purpose is to send a message… a silent message to the maiden... repent now or there'll be worse to come.'

'And if she doesn't?' asked Pichler.

'And if she doesn't, the creature will appear for a second time to pass Judgement, this time…'

'In his true hideous form,' interrupted Pichler.

'You're really getting the hang of this, aren't you K-P? We must chat more often,' said Albescu with a broad grin on his face. 'Yes as you say. Creatures from the pits of hell often appear as snakes when they are not imps or little demons, that is. Your description of a green lizard fits nicely.'

'And finally?'

'And finally, K-P, our previously friendly Soul-Saver metamorphoses into the "Soul-Snatcher", that is God's avenging angel. He's still the same good looking young fellow he was before, but now he's an angel on a mission… to kick the poor benighted maiden down to hell.'

'Which happens on the fourth and final visitation, the erm… "Sentence"! Yes I can see this makes sense to a 8th Century peasant who's just got married to the village beauty. He'd want to be sure that what pops out nine months later is actually his. Perhaps the less good looking maidens were not considered to be at such high risk of temptation.'

Pichler went silent for a moment. Albescu let him think. Then came the question.

'How do you know all this stuff Gabriel?' he asked.

'Much of it appears in books written in the fifteen and sixteen hundreds which was long after the practice ceased.'

'What do you mean, the practice ceased? You can't be saying people actually did this kind of thing,' replied Pichler.

'Oh yes, I'm certain of it. You see the myth lives on in many forms. Years ago, when I was a lad back home, I saw this myth acted out on the stage, purely as entertainment, pretty much as I've described. Only there were two night-stalkers.'

'*Two*?' asked Pichler.

'Oh, yes. Well there had to be, do you see. A night-stalker can move very fast, faster than the human eye can see. So when they did this on stage they needed to use two actors – quite well done actually.'

A pregnant pause followed, followed by a "just as I thought" muttered by Pichler.

'What was that old chap?' asked Albescu, but there was no reply.

'My own research has indicated that non-supernatural versions persisted in more remote rural areas well into the seventeen century,' continued Albescu. 'Except rather than sending her to hell, the poor lady – who was probably entirely innocent – would be damaged goods and hence fair game for all the over-sexed menfolk in the village.'

'Seriously?' said a slightly stunned Pichler.

'Oh my word, yes! Most of the myths which have lived on are just an excuse for a bit of rumpy-pumpy in the haystacks. Was that helpful, K-P?'

'Extremely so Gabriel,' replied Pichler. 'I won't take up any more of your valuable time,' he added prising himself from his chair.

'Any time,' replied Albescu with a smile adding, 'no need to book!'

So there it was. The puzzle was now complete. Scientia autem deductio rationis had done its job. It was now time for "virtute non verbis" – action not words.

The Zigeunerplatz:

So only the fourth and final visit remained. Not by a black-cloaked, red-eyed man, nor by a green lizard this time but by the "Soul-Snatcher". Pichler's plan was simple, a one man job. No other choice! Go to the spot which Helga and Heidi routinely occupied (*if* he could find it again and *if* indeed it was their usual place). Wait across the street where the "Night-Stalker" was first seen, just as they'd described it on his previous visit here. And then… play it by ear. What else could he do?

There was no point arriving too early, so he planned to be there no earlier than midnight. This could turn out to be a complete fool's errand, him being the fool, so the fewer hours spent freezing his bollocks off, the better. He was as sure as he could be that this was the spot, but no sign of the girls. Then it struck him.

'Oh, you damned fool,' he said under his breath. 'The girls won't be on the street – not after their traumatic experience of the previous night.'

What an utter waste of time. What the hell was he thinking? Pichler was on the point of leaving for home when… hello… hang on…who's that?

The man strolling along was smartly attired in top hat and full-length coat, his cane striking the pavement at regular intervals. He stopped instantly on his arrival at the "girls' lamppost".

'You're out of luck, mate, they're not here tonight – try tomorrow,' muttered Pichler to himself.

Undeterred the man tapped the post three times. Its metallic note rang out loud and clear for some distance including up to the window beneath which he stood. In the gloom, Pichler hadn't noticed this window before. The man drew back his arm as if to strike the post once more. The noise of the window frame being slid upwards halted him in mid-strike.

'Fuck off! We ain't doing business tonight!'

'I'm sorry to hear that Helga, my dear, very sorry indeed. And I had something special in mind for you two lovely's tonight,' he purred.

'Oh, it's you, is it sir? 'Cuse me.'

The head ducked back inside. Snatches of agitated conversation could be heard even as far away as where Pichler stood, concealed within the shadows.

'Righty-ho, sir. As it's you. Give us a few minutes,' said the woman as she shut the window.

The man paced back and forth for about five minutes. He stopped the moment the door below the window opened – Pichler hadn't noticed that either.

'Ain't you coming inside like last time then?'

The man smiled. He'd already seen the cab appear around the corner and directed their attention to it.

'Ooooo! Are we going to a hotel tonight then, lover?'

Those were the last words Pichler heard as the man taking a girl on each arm headed towards the now stationary cab. Once there being the gentleman he was, he helped each lady to board in turn.

Pichler had seconds to decide. The man was the Snatcher and the cabbie the Stalker, of that he was certain. He was equally certain that their destination was no hotel. Once the cab had turned the corner at the end of the street, once it had started its journey out of the Zigeunerplatz, it would be lost. And with it Helga and Heidi, perhaps permanently so.

Two of them – could he take them both? God to have his old service revolver to hand! How could he get a message to Hodža and not lose them in the process? He couldn't – plain and simple. There was only one option and it was the most dangerous one.

The shelf mounted on the rear of the cab was, not surprisingly, free of luggage. He was able to hoist his arse onto it without making a noise, even though the cab was trotting by this stage. Long may it continue! If the cabbie decided to go for it, he might not be able to hang on.

It was now gone two. The night was still, not a breath of wind to stir the air. The only sounds were those of the horse's hooves clip-clopping along the cobbles and the squeaking of the axle which was badly in need of a good greasing. And there was one other noise; a series of mutterings and burbles emanating from the cab driver.

Pichler could hear these sounds well enough but they meant nothing to him. What was he speaking? Romanian perhaps? A wise man – Max as it happened – had a view on languages, as he did on most subjects.

'In this tower of Babel that is Austria-Hungary, K-P a man would do better to possess five hundred words of ten languages rather than five thousand words of just one.'

This was rich coming from Max. Apart from his native Wiener Deutsch, he possessed only a few hundred words of English. And most of the ones he did have he misused, most of the time. Still, that didn't make him wrong.

To have the Romanian for "Police" or "I'm armed" was what he needed now. His ability to discuss foreign affairs in Slovakian was about as much use as a chocolate coffee pot! On his to do list then, always assuming…

The Chapel of Saint Markus:

He recognised their destination even when he was a good three hundred metres from it. Saint Markus's had once sat in an area of slum dwellings and had been the only source of comfort to the poor souls who lived there. Forty years ago, in a rare outbreak of charity, the city council had pulled down the slums. Their intention was to provide better housing for the city's poorer folk. Forty years later, good intentions were as far as they'd got, managing only to de-consecrate St Markus's. Since then most of the above ground stonework had mysteriously disappeared, some of it ending up in the "better" parts of the city. So there it stood – a ruin in a sea of flattened brick, wood and glass with little to signify that it had once been a place of worship.

Pichler recognised the place from a visit he'd made four years ago. Recently arrived in the city, he'd gone to a letting agency to enquire about available digs. Initially the man was all charm and smiles up until the minuscule size of Pichler's budget had dawned on him. After successive "haven't you got anything cheaper?" the bastard said, "Well, Herr Pichler, I think I can save us both some time. The cheapest rentals in the City are to be found in the St Markus district. Here I'll show you on the map." Just as well Pichler wasn't the type to bear a grudge.

As the cab entered the demolition site, the ground became progressively rougher and rougher. Consequently it slowed up, at points coming to a complete stop. Pichler seized the opportunity to slip silently off the backboard and crouch behind a nearby pile of rubble. There were plenty to choose from. From there he watched the cab travel on a further couple of hundred metres. Two "lizard-masks" emerged from the chapel and went to meet it. Within seconds they were carrying the two semi-comatose women into the chapel to be followed by the man. The cabbie remained outside to hitch up the horse to a railing. Once done he reached inside his cloak and pulled out some items, some *green* items!

'Oh, shit! There weren't two of the buggers, there were *four* of them!'

Still he was here now. He'd do what he could – he could do no more.

Once the six of them had disappeared inside, he crept towards the chapel taking care not to spook the horse. He worked his way around the outside perimeter. There were places where the earth had been removed to reveal a good metre of the heavily cracked crypt wall. Emanating from several cracks were shafts of red light. Peering through one of these he discovered the source – three small braziers. It resembled a scene from Hell but then it was probably meant to.

Pichler went inside the largely demolished building. Standing on the chapel floor he found to his dismay that there was only one entrance into the crypt. A flight of steps led down to a wooden door. Red light broke from around the door edge, not because it hadn't been shut properly, but because it *couldn't* be. Time and the elements had warped the frame over the years. He opened the door no more than a thumb's width but it was enough to hear *only* male voices. Were Heidi and Helga unconscious or had they been terrified into silence?

He eased the door open another inch, hoping to God that the rusty hinges wouldn't betray his presence. He didn't notice that the voices had ceased the moment he'd begun to widen the door a little further. Before he knew it, the door was violently flung open. He was bodily hauled off both feet and tossed onto the hard, unforgiving floor of the crypt. He looked up to see the man towering above him. He was now bereft of hat and coat and wearing only a thin silk shirt unbuttoned to the waist. He also wore a superior expression as he stepped away from Pichler. His arm swept across the scene as he invited his "guest" to inspect his surroundings.

The three reptiles stood against the back wall, masked and gloved; all part of the fantasy. Next to them, tied to a vault column were Heidi and Helga. Their heads were slumped onto their chests but they *were* still breathing. Thank God, he thought, they are alive. At least they are being spared having to witness this nightmare. Pichler saw the brazier next to the column. It had two metal irons protruding from the burning coals – branding irons. He looked up at the man who nodded, and smiled, sadistically.

'They must be "marked" so that the Devil will recognise them as his own,' he declared.

He sneered at the prone figure before him. His smile vanished. His gaze turned towards the nearest of his creatures.

'Kill him!'

Pichler leapt to his feet, withdrawing his truncheon as he did so. The creature advanced, unarmed but with his claws out stretched. Pichler made a trial swing in a vain attempt to deter him. The creature advanced further. He was now within range. The truncheon began its upswing, ready to come crashing down on the head of this monster. It would have brained him but for a wooden rafter.

A new truncheon may well have just bounced off the rafter but this was not a new truncheon. It had seen many, many years of faithful service. At some point during its latter years, it had acquired a crack. Slota wasn't to know, he'd not used it in anger for some time. Had he known then he'd never have lent it to Pichler. The thing broke in two, with the end spinning off far across the crypt, leaving a short jagged-ended piece still in Pichler's hand.

The man laughed. The reptile halted momentarily. Pichler still clutching the now useless weapon looked around desperately for some other means of defence. There was none to be had! As he backed away, his other hand brushed against the red-hot brazier. He yelped with pain, nearly tripping over a coal sack. As he steadied himself his injured hand touched upon a handle – a coal scuttle handle! It was a forlorn hope, he knew that, but he had to at least try. Could he scoop some hot coals onto it and hurl these into the face of the creature? The man observed all this, quite unconcerned, even as the salvo of hot coals hit their mark. But then his expression changed as did Pichler's for the masked face of his adversary burst into flames. The creature screamed and made to rip off his mask. He clutched at his face with both hands, his gloved hands, and this attempt to smother the flames only fed them further. The wretched man writhed in agony as he sunk to the floor. His head, hands and now his upper torso were totally engulfed. There he lay until he expired after less than a minute of sickening contortions.

Pichler stared in amazement at the smouldering corpse. The mask, the gloves – both flammable. One down, three to go!

The man's expression of amazement had been replaced firstly by disbelief then horror and finally fury – a blind fury. Somebody was going to pay for this. That somebody was standing by the brazier. Like a maddened bull he backed up several paces slowly, menacingly. Pichler still held the handle end of the broken truncheon. He flattened himself against the wall, gripped the handle and braced himself for the charge. His wild-eyed assailant hit him at full tilt, smacking Pichler's skull back onto the unyielding stone wall behind. The man in the silken shirt paused, a look of pure astonishment on his face. He stepped back and glared at Pichler and then his gaze dropped onto his chest. There it was, just a few inches of handle now jutting out from his chest. The rest had pierced his chest wall and buried itself deep into the vital organs that lay beneath. He slowly slid to the floor, clasping onto the man who'd done for him until finally Pichler kneed him off. There he laid – his life force expended.

Pichler readied himself. The two remaining creatures would surely charge, surely want to avenge their master, but no! They stared at him, they stared at the prone figure in front of him and then… almost in slow motion, they collapsed side by side in a dead swoon.

First thing; check that the two corpses *really were* corpses. He'd been on a number of battlefields in his time and he'd never seen anybody look deader than these two did now – still better safe… There was a surprisingly small amount of blood on the "Soul-Snatcher". If Pichler were to remove the stake then that would surely change. But the terrified man he had been had gone, now replaced by the professional detective in him – preserve the scene at all costs.

Second thing; he untied Helga and gently laid her semi-conscious body on the ground. Heidi would have to wait a few moments longer. He needed Helga's rope. He bound the two lizard-creatures who still showed no signs of coming around, leaving their "fancy dress" in place. In the process of doing so he cast an anxious glance over his shoulder – just to make sure the Snatcher had not risen from the dead.

'Now you're just being a prat, Klaus Heinrich!' he said to no one in particular.

He soon had Heidi untied as well and both women were wrapped in the cloaks of their former tormentors.

The cab was only big enough for three – the two women then. Slota's place first, then onto Hodža's – no point going to the station – not at this time of night. Could the two live ones escape while he was away? What he wouldn't have given for two sets of police bracelets. Then he spied a heavy roof beam lying on the floor. He dragged it over and laid it across their legs, wedging it under a stone ledge at one end.

'Get out of that one, you swine!' Always been a belt and braces man, had Klaus "K-P" Pichler.

***

He'd expected to have to bang for ages in order to wake Maria and Ján so he was surprised to find the light on in the front room. Tapping on the window he was further astounded to be confronted by the sleepy face of Sergeant Slota. By the time he'd got back to the front door with Helga in his arms, it was already open and Slota stood by it, directing him into the same front room. Pichler raised his eyebrows as he passed him.

'Only way I can get to sleep at the moment. An hour in the armchair, then an hour on the floor – bloody back,' smiled Slota. 'Still it seems to be doing the trick!'

Pichler needed a breather by the time he returned with Heidi. A few minutes after he'd sat down Maria appeared, disappeared and reappeared again, this time with some blankets and cushions.

'Right off you go, old son. They'll be all right here.'

At Hodža's he did have to bang away for ages. God knows what the Inspector's neighbours made of this racket.

***

Surveying the scene, the Inspector nodded his satisfaction at Pichler. Even if he didn't know K-P to be an honest man, objectively, it was all pretty clear cut. There was no question. It *had* been self-defence. They hadn't stopped off at the station on the way there. Pichler didn't want to leave the "live" ones a moment longer than necessary, notwithstanding his precautions. He needn't have worried himself; they hadn't stirred one bit. It was left to Hodža to bring the cavalry, so he left after about half an hour and returned later with the "works" which in this case was two officers and the medical examiner. These he left to do their job and returned to the station, picking up the two women on route from Slota's. Pichler came with him. He was seated on the luggage shelf again only this time he didn't mind one bit; he even whistled as they trotted along.

Early the next morning, Pressburg police station:

'Thanks for hanging around to make your statement – you must be exhausted,' said Inspector Hodža. 'I'm just going to have a look at the two prisoners to see if they're fit to be interviewed. Do you want to tag along?'

Yes, Pichler was exhausted and he still had one more visit to make, but this was an offer he couldn't turn down.

***

The holding cells were two floors below Hodža's office. The front of these cells consisted of a metal fence, designed to facilitate observation at all times. The two men were being kept in the same cell, handcuffed to separate metal beds placed far enough apart to prevent any physical contact. Hodža put his finger to his lips as they crept silently along the corridor. The two prisoners were totally unaware of their approach.

'Look!' he mouthed to Pichler.

Pichler edged his head around the corner. Each man was rigid and perfectly motionless, staring fixedly into each other's eyes. And they were smiling, a rather sickly, unnatural type of smile. Then Hodža banged on the fence.

There was no reaction, none at all. They continued to stare, they continued to smile.

Hodža shrugged at Pichler as if to say, "Not much hope of a statement today is there?"

Then he spoke, loudly and distinctly.

'They're certain to hang, Sergeant! I'm convinced of it!'

Pichler was stunned. He turned to face Hodža, who winked at him. Inspectors never make this kind of prejudicial statement in front of suspects. Hodža noted his astonishment and answered him with a nod in the direction of the two men. So he looked.

There was no reaction, none at all. They continued to stare, they continued to smile.

There was nothing more to be gained here, so both men headed back to the Inspector's office.

***

'I must say,' continued Hodža, 'this is just about the strangest case I can ever recall in my twenty plus years in the force. What the ficking hell was the motive for one thing? And the way those two just fainted away. I can't explain it, can you?'

Pichler grimaced. If this case had taught him anything it was that trying to find a sane motive for the actions of the insane was itself a route to madness.

'You know Karol, I think I could give it a decent shot now but its better if you get it directly from a professional head doctor. I'm going to talk to Havelchek as soon as I'm done here. I'll ask him to come into the station to make a statement, if that's all right with you.'

'Most certainly it is. But it's strange though K-P that this should only involve these two girls. I mean there are any number of women working the streets around the Zig…'

Pichler interrupted him in mid-sentence.

'Sorry, I should have asked about Heidi and Helga earlier. How are they?'

'I'd say they've moved on from "petrified" to "dazed". I think making their statements actually helped in that respect. By the way I think you've achieved official "Hero of the Empire" status, assuming you *are* this Kaypee chap they insisted on praising to the hilt! Anyway they wanted to go back home, so I sent them in a cab not an hour ago.'

'That was good of you!' said Pichler with a smile.

'Well, good of the corpse actually… I used his, which has now been impounded.'

'Any idea who he was?'

'We don't know, K-P; not at this stage – we may never know. We can't be sure that he even owned the cab. He may have just hired it or stolen it. According to the girls, the only previous time he'd "used their services", he'd arrived on foot.'

Pichler nodded. 'That fits. He had to be known to them otherwise they'd never have gotten into the cab with him.'

'Yes of course,' replied Hodža, 'you saw all that didn't you! Well, I think that's about it, I'll let you get off to your bed.'

Pichler got up – the asylum beckoned, but then he remembered something from earlier.

'Karol, you were saying something about "why just Helga and Heidi" and I interrupted you. I think I can provide an explanation of sorts. You've heard the expression "all that glitters is not gold" of course.'

Hodža nodded – Of course, who hadn't?

'Well, these four were fantasists who became obsessed with an ancient myth. The essence of this myth involves testing out the purity of young and beautiful maidens. If you look at paintings of angels, you've got your work cut out to find an ugly one. It's the same with the devil's mob. You never find a beautiful portrayal of a demon.'

Hodža frowned.

'That's certainly a reasonable explanation,' replied the Inspector. 'Heidi and Helga are more suitable candidates than most of their fellow workers in the Zigeunerplatz. Yes I can buy that. I'm beginning to wish I hadn't asked though. Best to let that particular sleeping dog lie. It'll only confuse the Chief. Still I thank you for telling me. You've satisfied my curiosity if nothing else.'

'True enough, Karol but you might want to say *something* to him.'

'The Chief, you mean?' asked Hodža.

'Suppose they'd gotten away with it at the first attempt. They might have moved on to another City. Or they might have worked their way through the entire Zigeunerplatz until they got to old mother Schmidt, aged sixty-two. But my bet is that they would have moved up the social ladder in their search for beauteous maidens. Think of all the ramifications that would have had for the city. It'd be a major headache for the Chief!'

'Tell me, Herr Pichler. *Are you suggesting* that I should drop hints to that effect to my superiors in the vainglorious expectation that it would raise your own standing within the department?'

'Can't hurt!' smiled K-P, tongue firmly in cheek.

The Inspector smiled as Pichler left his office. The boy was learning and learning fast. Just as well he wasn't after his job.

The Pressburg asylum:

'The whole thing was strange Doktor Havelchek. Even now I'm not sure I understand what it was I witnessed in that cellar,' said Pichler.

'That doesn't surprise me in the least,' replied Havelchek. 'I'm a trained psychotherapist with twenty five years' experience dealing with such sad creatures and I'm not sure I fully understand it either.'

Pichler had no intention of "leading" Havelchek with his own theory, or of bringing the supernatural into this conversation. Havelchek was a man of science. Damn it all, *he* was a man of science. These "creatures" were men, as mad as Caligula maybe, but still *just* men.

'So you want to know why the two fainted and why they didn't seem to care that they might be hung. Tell me exactly what happened in that cellar and omit nothing!'

Havelchek sat back in his chair, pulled his pipe from his top pocket and started to idly dig out the residue from his last smoke. He also frowned but only because he was thinking how best to put this.

'From what you've told me, I suspect that they believed their leader to be invulnerable. Perhaps he'd convinced them that he had supernatural strength. He did man-handle you through the door into the crypt, you told me. It's not difficult to fool the simple-minded.

And he had his back to them when he impaled himself on the broken stake, so they only saw him fall to the ground. They never saw the extent of his injuries. I suspect that they shared some sort of telepathic or symbiotic link or had convinced themselves so. He fell, so they collapsed in sympathy.'

'And the smiling?' asked Pichler.

'Either they do not believe their leader is really dead or they're convinced that he will return from the grave. In any event in their minds, they are certain that they won't hang because he will come to their cell and save them!'

At Ján Slota's house:

Pichler left the asylum in an altogether more settled state of mind than he'd experienced since this cursed affair had begun. Perhaps this was why he was feeling far less wiped out than he had been earlier this morning, despite the lack of sleep. Talking to Havelchek hadn't changed a thing legally speaking but it was gratifying that the good Doktor had concurred with his own theory. It never hurt to have a statement from a medical man and hopefully that would shortly be in Hodža's hands. The downside was that this statement would be seized on by their defence as mitigation. The two loons would more likely end their days as guests of Doktor Havelchek. Pichler would have slept more soundly with them taking a short, sharp drop to oblivion, which in his humble opinion was what they thoroughly deserved.

Arriving at Slota's, Pichler got a warmer than expected reception from Maria, who saw herself as the guardian of her husband's recovery. He was directed to the sitting room where he found Slota ensconced in an armchair, propped up on several pillows.

'Well done, K-P, old son. Sounds like you did a first class job on this one,' said Slota. 'How are Heidi and Helga?'

'I'm not sure, but according to Karol they're in the same boat as you are. They're definitely on the mend, but not quite there yet. Anyway, they're back home, so I'm going to call around later.'

'I shouldn't worry too much. They're tougher than they look. I *hope* you're not going soft on them. What would Anna say?'

Pichler laughed.

'Phah! But seriously, I've rather come to admire them. To live the lives they live, even before all this happened *and* still keep a sense of humour, well! I'm not sure I could. Oh, by the way, I'm sorry about your night stick, Ján.'

'Don't worry. I've had it for years. I'm only sorry it decided to give up the ghost on you just when you needed it most.'

'Don't be Ján. It was that that saved my life!' replied Pichler with an appropriately broad grin. So he should smile. He knew just how accurate that was.

'Still, the Inspector tells me that you intend to write this up as a paper of some sort. For the University, I presume. What's it going to be called then? How about "A day in the life of dealing with some of the mad fuckers in this world".'

'I'll probably want to dress it up a *bit* more than that but you're not far off the mark.'

'The Inspector also tells me you're going to need a whole stack more of these… for your, what did he call it, your dessertitation. Well, I've good news for you on that front, old lad. There's no shortage of mad fuckers around here!'

Pichler was still smiling when he left Slota's house, one hour and one beer later.

Klein's Bakery:

'Right then, here's your ticket. Your goose'll be cooked and ready for you to collect any time after ten on the 25th. Don't lose it! No ticket, no bird – got it!'

'Thank you Herr Klein. By the way, you don't happen to have a smaller bird that's already been cooked, do you? I want one I can take away now.' asked Pichler.

'Thought you'd have enough of fowl, what with the size of bird you've ordered!'

'No, it's not for me!' he replied.

The Zigeunerplatz, mid-afternoon:

Pichler found their street, their lamppost and their window quite quickly – piece of cake in the daylight!

'Heidi, Helga. Are you there? It's Herr Kaypee.'

Nothing stirred. He tried again – not a peep. He resorted to small pebbles.

'Who the fuck's that?' screeched a young woman at the top of her voice as she thrust the window upwards. 'We ain't open for business til… oh, it's you. 'Ang about, we'll be right down.'

He could hear voices coming from the open window.

'Come on Helg, shift your fat arse, we've gotta a visitor.'

'Oi! I aint gotta a fat arse, yer cheeky bitch.'

The two ladies presented themselves on the pavement two minutes later. They looked considerably rougher than the first time he'd seen them. It might have been the daylight or the effects of their recent harrowing experience. But then none of us look our best when we've just been dragged out of bed, do we?

'I brought you something,' said Pichler. 'With best wishes for the festive season.'

Helga took the bird, raised it to her nostrils and drew in a long, gratifying sniff. 'Hmmmmm – yummy!'

Heidi took the paper bag which clinked – always a good sign in her book.

'Are you going to come back tomorrow... when we've had a chance to restore ourselves to our normal state of gorgeousness?'

'No. Tomorrow I shall be spending the whole day with a young lady and her friend.'

'Ooooooo! Get that Helg. Here's a man what likes a threesome.'

Pichler couldn't contain his laugher as he explained the situation.

'*Soooo*, you ain't *actually* married yet, eh? Well, it ain't too late, you know. We're both still single and fancy free so you could have either of us instead, if you wanted!'

'Or both!' added Heidi giggling as she did so.

'Well ta very much for the pressies and that, but why are you *really* here?'

'I just wanted to be sure that you were both all right, that's all,' answered Pichler.

That wiped the smirks right off both their faces. He cared! And that touched them, it really did.

'You can tell your young lady from us that she's one lucky cow!' said Helga, which snapped both of them out their unaccustomed reflective mood.

'Yeah, we are all right now, ain't we Heid? It's true we was badly shook up when we thought it was ghosties and goolies that we was facing. Once we knew it was *just* men though, we was fine. We know how to deal with men what give us trouble, don't we Heid?'

'Oh yeah! You knee 'em in the bollocks and I kick 'em on the way down'!

Christmas afternoon, Maggie's house:

'I've eaten too much and I've drunk too much and I enjoyed every *single* mouthful, didn't you Maggie?' asked Anna.

'Aye, I did that!' replied her host. 'I never thought he'd pull it off, but he did and washed up as well. I think you may well have a good'un there Anna. Just don't you go letting him slacken off, not now you've got him so nicely trained!'

Anna turned her head in the direction of her intended and listened. It sounded as though he might be asleep. Indeed he did have his eyes closed and had done since shortly after bringing them coffee. His own cup sat untouched.

'Ah, bless the child,' said Maggie. 'Let's go into the next room and leave him to sleep it off.'

But Pichler wasn't asleep, at least not quite. He was still thinking about his last conversation with the two ladies. Yes, they *were* going to be all right just as Slota had said they would. But he had to know. He had to be sure before he felt able to close the book on this one. Compartmentalisation is a grand idea in principle but it's important not to wear it out with over use!

THE CONTEMPTUOUS NOBLEMAN

The Late Autumn of 1871, Seefeld in the Tyrol:

The village of Seefeld lay around thirty kilometres north-west – as the crow flies – and six hundred metres straight up, from the city of Innsbruck. Getting between the two places could be a tedious business. The quickest method was definitely by crow. Carts would make the occasional journey to and from the metropolis to deliver essential supplies. Another option was the twice-weekly coach from Innsbruck to Garmisch which made a stop at the village. From Garmisch it was possible to visit far away Munich by train.

"Metropolis" might seem an exaggerated description of Innsbruck to those more used to the delights of Vienna or Munich or even Salzburg. But to the four hundred souls that inhabited Seefeld, the principal city of the Tyrol represented an entirely different world. Its pavements, street lights and trams were steps into the future which bore little relevance to their daily lives.

The hub of the village was the Gasthof Durstein, known by the locals as "die Bauernruhe". Strangely there was no sign to indicate its presence. But then perhaps not so strangely – tourists were not encouraged to linger. The "Farmer's Rest" did offer limited accommodation, though this was rarely ever occupied.

Like most of the villagers, Familie Durstein could not manage on just the one source of income. Come winter, the merry throng there to enjoy a beer and a chat would often need to raise their voices. They had no choice! The racket emanating from the Tyrolians Greys housed next door in the "Rest's" barn could be something quite appalling.

For some of the villagers, even Seefeld was "just too noisy and had too many damned people". For these people, whose farms generally lay on the outskirts of the village, contentment at the end of a hard day's work was not to be found at the "Rest". With all the jobs set for that day done and dusted, their beds were of far more interest. Happiness was heathy – and profitable – livestock. These hardy types asked for little more than that from the great "farmer" in the sky. Farm "Pichler" was one such.

Klaus Pichler hadn't been back to the family's farm since just before he was posted to Galicia. Ah, the fortress of Lemberg in Galicia – happy days. And they were – happy – eventually. Galicia was the most eastern province of the Austrian crownlands, bordering the Tsar's Empire – some twelve hundred kilometres east of Innsbruck.

Newly promoted Unterleutnant Pichler was due to be posted to the Serbian border, right up until the day before his departure. He couldn't believe it when he opened his orders. So there he was, standing on Lemberg station, not a word of Ruthenian and bugger all knowledge of the area. His platoon either couldn't or wouldn't speak German. Luckily for all parties concerned, all had a smattering of English. He'd picked some up in the army – his lot were all aspirant emigrants to the Americas. He could still recall the black looks he got from his commanding officer. Each platoon commander would call out the order "einen Schritt vörwarts", until it got to him. His "one pace forward" did not go down well – not at all well!

That was when? He had to think quite hard. Yes… it must have been 1865, a year after the Danish war. And a year before his unfortunate encounter with

Prussian artillery on the heights of Blumenau just north of Pressburg.

Anna and he had had to take a cab from Innsbruck station and it had cost an arm and a leg. Even that price required some considerable haggling. He'd telegraphed a week beforehand and asked Anton to pick them up. He said he couldn't, no reason given. No matter, they were here now.

The old place looked a bit different. What was it? The barn! Anton had built a new barn. Well that augured well; the farm must be doing rather better than he'd realised. He half expected to see both the lower and upper fields occupied by the herd. They weren't; they were empty. Still out on the Alpine pastures, no doubt! But Freddie should be in the paddock, nose in his hay-bag as usual. Freddie was only a year old when he'd left, so he should be in his prime now.

The greeting they received once they were inside the farm house was a little strange. Well perhaps not strange, more like… distant. Pleasantries were exchanged but he could tell from Anna's face that she was rather taken aback by this reception. Perhaps it was just the passage of time.

His mother sat at the dining table, a cup of tea in her hand that she was trying to offer – unsuccessfully – to his wife of less than a year. That had been the reason he'd finally bitten the bullet. Of course, he'd invited his mother and older brother to come to their wedding but they couldn't. It was the best part of six hundred kilometres. Anton wouldn't leave the farm for that length of time for any reason short of the end of the world. But then who was he to cast aspersions when it came to family? *He* was the one who'd walked away from the farm – and at the very first opportunity he could.

Anton would never understand or forgive this familial "betrayal". Nor would their father have done, had he still been alive. It wasn't that his younger sibling had opted for the army that was the problem. Anton himself was a reservist as was their father before him. No, the problem was in Anton's head. As a boy, Klaus had always followed his elder's lead, whether he wanted to or not. Anton wanted to be a farmer and therefore so *must* Klaus. He tried his best to explain, but neither Papa, Anton nor even his mother wanted to hear *those* words. Despite this, he continued to do all that was asked of him with as good a grace as he could muster. All the time, his father and brother were oblivious to his wishes. They had convinced themselves. He'd often overhear them telling each other – "don't worry, he'll grow out of it"!

Klaus looked back at Anna and his mother. The teacup and saucer had moved not a jot.

'I don't think mama has fully grasped the situation yet,' said Pichler junior with a wry smile.

Anton's only response was a barely perceptible curt nod.

'Mamaaa, you'll have to *place* it in Anna's hands!'

Frau Pichler looked up at the sound of her youngest son's voice.

'Oh, I'm so sorry my dear,' she said to Anna, her embarrassment obvious, 'how silly of me.'

'Don't give it another thought, mother-in-law. It happens all the time, back home!' replied Pichler's wife with her usual broad smile.

A cold silence descended. It wasn't the faux pas which now distressed the old lady. No, it was the realisation that this was no longer her son's home. He had another home – he had another life. He would *never* return home to share the farm work with Anton, not now.

Anton snapped out his stupor.

'Can't she see *at all*?' he asked, his tone devoid of any trace of empathy.

'Noooo. It was a childhood thing. But never a day goes by when she doesn't astound me with just how well she seems to manage.'

'She's Hungarian, isn't she?' Hungarian – almost a term of abuse this far west!

'Anton, you old Tyrolian diehard, she's *not* Hungarian. She's as much Slovakian as she's a Magyar. Come to think of it, the same could be said of me!'

Klaus wasn't sure his brother had heard any of this. He'd only momentarily emerged into the land of the living. Now he had returned to his stupor, perhaps even more deeply so than before. There was something weighing him down, that much was obvious – only one thing for it.

'Anna, mama, Anton's going to reacquaint me with the "Rest" in town. You don't mind if we stroll down for an hour before supper, do you?'

'You mean two hours, don't you? Well make sure it is no more, K-P. Your mother and I are making a Pressburger hotpot. You know that will spoil if it's left in the pot for too long!'

Anton merely grunted his acquiescence as "K-P" pushed him out the front door. And so they set off towards the hub of the village.

'What's all this "K-P" nonsense? K for Klaus, P for Pichler, I presume – not very imaginative, is it,' grimaced Anton.

'Just a pet name, no more!'

Now was not the time to explain. Anyway his brother wasn't really interested. His despair, for that was what it was, was consuming all his energies.

'By the way, where's Freddie, Anton? I didn't see him in the paddock.'

'Sold!'

'Oh!' replied a surprised Pichler. 'And the cart?'

'That as well!'

For half a kilometre after that exchange, they walked in total silence. One brother reacquainted himself with the sights of his childhood. The other brother – downcast – was content to reacquaint himself only with his toecaps. As Gasthof Durstein hove into view, Anton suddenly stopped and placed a heavy restraining hand on his brother's shoulder.

'I'm in the shit, Klaus,' he declared, 'really, *really* in the shit!' And then it all came tumbling out.

A year ago, as autumn was coming to a close, his barn burnt down along with a lot of feed and most of his tools.

'Thank God it was some way from the house or that would have gone up as well,' he added.

What with winter on its way, he had to get it rebuilt and pretty damn quick. His herd wouldn't last long if it was forced to overwinter outdoors. The replacement cost amounted to more than he could lay his hands on. There was no other option. He'd gone to a reputable broker – at least he'd thought he was a reputable one. The terms were more than reasonable. There was only one little thing that had worried him. If he defaulted on the payments for more than one-quarter then the farm was forfeited.

'What the *entire* farm? No, that can't be right Ant! The farm's got to be worth at least ten times the cost of rebuilding a ficking barn, even with a hefty interest rate.'

And so it was! He'd read the contract thoroughly, of course he had. He just hadn't expected – ever expected – to be in a position of not being able to keep up the repayments.

'I would have been fine if the herd hadn't caught something really nasty at the beginning of this summer. I wasn't sure what it was. First off, they had that facial tear-staining. You'll remember what that looks like, they are forever blinking. It was obvious it pained them in direct sunlight. Of course that happens from time to time, but I've *never* seen it affect the whole damned herd. And then, all bar two had the most god-awful hacking cough. It didn't feel right – the time of year, the coughing *and* the watery eyes. I had words with the "wise-men" in the village, but they weren't much help. You know what it's like. You ask five different farmers, you get six different answers! Anyway I wasn't that worried at the time.'

He paused taking a deep breath to gather himself for the next bit. There was clearly going to be a next bit.

'Anyway, the coughs all disappeared within a week and the eyes responded well to salt water bathes. Three weeks later and they were all as right as rain, every single one of them. It was just as if it had never happened. Of course it's the devil's own job to persuade people to buy your milk once rumours of any kind of disease get going. Our sales really hit the floor. It's not as if the people around here aren't spoilt for choice when it comes to dairy.

So we had the village elders up to see for themselves. They gave us a pretty hard time, but eventually they were happy enough – clean bill of health. Sales very slowly started to pick up. Mama and I thought it was all over – just one of those inexplicable things nature throws at us from time to time. We've established a rock solid reputation for quality over the years, right back to pa's time. That in the end would have saved us, but for…'

Anton began to stammer. Klaus saw him clench his fists and take another deep breath to steady himself. The worst was yet to come.

'And then one morning, not two weeks ago, I came out to the field to bring them in for milking. Three-in-ten were on the ground as still as stone, no obvious signs. They could have been sleeping, but they *weren't'*.

'Dead?'

'As dead as our dear old papa! As dead as this farm! More have died since. I can't sell the carcases for meat. I can't afford to feed them come winter time – always assuming any of them are still alive by then. No, there's no way back for me from this.'

'Anton, I'd really like to be able to help you out, but we're pretty strapped ourselves...'

'Oh, I know that Klaus. *That's* not why I invited you to stay. You thought it was mama didn't you? Thought so! No, it was me. I thought you'd like to see the old place, one last time before, before…'

'Did you bring in the local cow-doc, get a professional opinion?'

He just shrugged his shoulders significantly. That gesture said it all. What'd be the point – still be dead, wouldn't they!

And then Klaus Pichler witnessed something he'd never expected to see, not in a million years. Not from his brother, not from that tough old sod, not from that hardy son of the soil. Anton just flopped down onto a bank by the roadside, put his face in his hands and wept. He used to joke to Anna that "Anton really loves his farm". Now for the first time, he really understood just how true that was.

Anton walked past the "Rest" without even noticing.

'Have you been to see this agent, the one you signed the contract with?'

'Hardly! The sod's office is in Munich. I will write though, see if I can't get some kind of extension on…'

'Which is when?' interrupted K-P.

'End of October!'

Those were the last words spoken for nearly an hour. They wandered aimlessly around the village and finally began their doleful return to the farm, sans beer. No, that's not correct – Anton walked in a fog, but K-P… K-P was thinking.

'I don't believe it! You're actually on time. The beer not to your liking?'

Anna couldn't see their faces but she sensed the mood almost immediately. Anton brushed by without uttering a word to either women. K-P took his wife's arm and led her outside.

A bystander witnessing their little scene would have seen a couple in their early thirties – both standing. The man seeming to talk almost non-stop – the woman merely nodding, only injecting briefly. After a quarter of an hour, he finally stopped – they hugged and returned indoors.

The dejected farmer looked up to see his sibling's face close to his own.

'Anton – don't *do* anything – don't *say* anything. Not for now anyway. I'm going to Munich tomorrow first thing. I'll need to sort out some timings and I'll want the address of this agent. Oh, and one other thing you must do, big brother. I can see a Schnapps bottle up there on the top shelf. Get it down and pour all of us a bloody big glass each. Don't despair, brother. We're not finished yet.'

The next day:

Pichler knew he'd need a bit of luck to pull this off in a day. The Garmisch coach ran on Wednesdays and Fridays – today was Monday! It had taken both of them a good hour the previous evening to convince old Willy. Firstly that his horse and trap would only be gone for the day. Secondly that it would be perfectly safe left at the stable next to the railway station. The clinching argument was the money on offer which would keep the old devil in Schnapps for a month! Well, perhaps not a month, but certainly a fortnight!

He set off before dawn the next morning. Willy's horse, the misnamed "Blitzen", Pichler was beginning to think, was unimpressed by the hour. He made his feelings abundantly clear on the subject! However, with some gentle encouragement from the man seated behind him, he slowly warmed to the idea of a steady trot. He, Pichler not Blitzen, had his passport (rarely without it) and his timetable book (*never* without that). He also had several packages of food, the latter thanks to Anna's efforts the evening before.

He was in a buoyant mood as he covered the first few kilometres. The dawn start should give him ample time to cover the thirty odd kilometres and catch the daily train from Garmisch to Munich Starnberg. He was just starting to settle into a comfortable rhythm when, ten kilometres out, he spied a tree trunk lying full across the road. He had time to rein Blitzen in and so avoided actually hitting the blasted thing – just. With a great deal of huff and puff interspersed with the foulest imaginable language, he managed to pull one end over to one side of the road. It left a gap just big enough to allow the cart to pass. Meanwhile, an oblivious Blitzen contently munched away at a patch of grass doing his upmost to ignore the noises emanating from the man. Pichler checked his watch –

twenty minutes lost, damn it. He leapt on board and urged Blitzen to pick up the pace and thank God, the beast did without argument! In those twenty minutes, his relaxed mood had changed to a fretful one. Could he still make it?

An hour later, Pichler consulted his pocket watch as the station hove into view. They'd done it! The heroic efforts of his steed would be rewarded. The horse would spend the day taking his ease in a nice, warm stable with plenty to eat – just as he'd promised old Willy he would. For the man, the day had only just started.

'I should return sometime this evening, but just in case, can you look after Blitzen tonight?'

The stable lad was delighted. He'd never stabled a horse called Blitzen before. What a steed he must be. He didn't object to the generous fee Pichler had put into his hand either.

The hundred kilometres to Munich's Starnberg station proceeded without incident. He was outside the station cab rank at just after eleven to find waiting for him – absolutely bugger all. It was called Starnberg-Munich but to be truthful, the good citizens of Starnberg were barely on nodding terms with the city. Munich itself had been the capital of a kingdom but Bavaria had, since the turn of the year ceased to be one. It was now a state within the newly created German Empire and the locals weren't at all happy about it!

With some twenty five kilometres separating him from his destination, the Military War College, Pichler had no option but to wait. And it was absolute agony! Eventually a cab did appear, serenely trotting up the road as if driver and horse had all the time in the world. By half-one he was there!

'Is it possible to speak to Major Meindl?'

Pichler closed his eyes and prayed while the Desk Corporal ran a finger down the page of the duty ledger.

Poldi Meindl had been an Oberleutnant in the 4th Infantry Regiment, Bavarian Army Corps and was an old friend. They'd first met when he had been seconded to Pichler's unit during the 1866 war as their liaison officer. Bavaria had allied itself with Austria against the Prussians. Now of course he was working for the opposition.

'Who shall I say wants 'im, sir?'

Pichler's sigh of relief was almost audible. The Corporal rang a bell to call an escort. After a few minutes march, he stood outside a door bearing the name he sought.

'What the bloody hell are you doing here, K-P?' said the officer in the dark blue jacket as he stood up, grinning from ear to ear.

'I like the uniform, Poldi. Very smart, though I thought the cornflower blue I last saw you in, was much prettier!'

Ah – 1866, when armies still went to war in parade ground uniforms. Now everybody was wearing dark blue, a lesson perhaps from the recent trans-Atlantic blood bath. Except the British of course, who insisted on persisting with the red they'd been wearing for the last three centuries. It hid the blood apparently. Pichler preferred Austrian-white. If he was injured he wanted every bugger to know about it!

'So was I, prettier before, I mean,' replied Meindl, lifting the patch which covered the opaque eye beneath. 'Mind, the scar's not *too* bad. Hasn't put Christina off me – child number two is currently in the barracks, awaiting imminent discharge. Hear you've joined the club at last. I was beginning to worry about you.'

'How dare you, sir,' smiled Pichler in mock-disgust.

'Well, don't you leave it too long before getting yourself a couple of sprogs, will you my boy. What were we talking about? Oh, yes this uniform thing. I'd have to say that it does grate a bit having these Prussians lording it over us. However there *is* an upside. This dark blue works wonders in galvanising the locals into action. They're terrified, do you see. In case we might actually *be* Prussians.'

On any other day, Pichler could have chatted away all day in this fashion. He and Poldi had had this type of rapport since almost the first minute they'd met. It happens that way with some people. This *wasn't* any other day!

He explained and the more he explained the deeper the frown opposite became. Meindl looked at his watch.

'We'll have to go right way – I know the street, it'll only take fifteen minutes by foot. But before we do… Sergeant!'

The man who appeared looked like all the other Sergeants Pichler had ever encountered – beefy, sullen and utterly dependable.

'Saah,' he exclaimed as he saluted the Herr Major. He turned to look at Pichler debating whether this man also warranted a salute.

'No, don't salute *him*, S'geant. He's not an officer anymore and when he was, he was one of Franz-Josef's lot, who we used to support but don't anymore.'

It's a difficult trick to pull off – being able to joke with the rankers yet retain their respect. Poldi had that gift. Most of his troops actually liked him. In Pichler's experience that was what counted when the shrapnel started flying.

'Didn't we used to have a cadet called Streidle here until very recently?'

'Sah?' replied the man, somewhat surprised by the question.

His officer frowned at him and he got the message. 'Yes, Sah! Did his basic wiv us – then transferred off to officer training in Berlin for the final brush up n' polish, just like a lot of 'em, after January.'

Pichler asked the relevance of this inquiry as the pair of them stepped it out towards Prinz Rupert Strasse, the offices of Streidle and Partners. The explanation made him smile – clever old Poldi.

***

'Well Gentlemen, this really is most irregular. In business, one expects to receive due notification of any visit,' stated Herr Streidle. He glanced somewhat perplexed at the impressive looking Major, adding 'especially if it is of an official nature.'

He was a flabby, bald man of small stature and advanced years. He wore thick glasses which hinted at weak eyesight. However these physical short-comings in no way diminished his self-confidence. The office was otherwise empty with no obvious second desk. The "Partners" in Streidle and Partners may have been somewhat of an exaggeration.

Pichler introduced himself as the deputy head of the South Bavarian Agricultural Collective. Anton had told him of the existence of this organisation. Apparently they acted as a specialist broker for farm insurance. Rather a pity Anton hadn't taken advantage of it – or of *any* insurance broker come to that.

'Well, Herr Streidle,' he began, 'we have received several complaints from our members regarding, hmmm, how should I put it – sharp practice.'

Streidle sat back in astonishment, whether feigned or genuine, Pichler was unable to discern.

'Whatever can you mean, Herr Müller? I'm sure I know nothing about such practices. In fact I find the whole idea quite extraordinary.'

'I believe you have arranged loan contracts, both here and over the border in the Tyrol region. My understanding is that the penalty for defaulting on payments is quite disproportionate. That is to say being many times the value of the original loan.'

Pichler, or Herr Müller, glared at the little man as hard as he could. This induced a perceptible squirming in his seat, but no dent in his defiance.

'It *is* true, I have acted as agent for a number of agrarian concerns, but I reject any suggestion of impropriety.'

'I shall need the names of these concerns, if you please. I have a list of all the complainants received by our head office. I wish to ensure that our list is complete.'

Pichler opened a file and extracted a list of farms, though it was in fact a page torn out of Poldi's army list for 1862. His pen hovered meaningfully ready to tick-off names.

'Oh really sir! You cannot expect me to divulge confidential information. That would be enough to get me dis-barred!'

He smirked, signalling that the contest was over and he had won. Emboldened, he turned to glare up at Meindl, who had not, so far, uttered one word nor availed himself of a chair.

'And why exactly are you here, might I inquire, Herr Major?'

'Two reasons – firstly, Berlin requires an official presence on any matters which might potentially damage the reputation of the Reich. I'm here to note any such instances and report back. It goes without saying that it is vital that the *new* states within the Reich follow the high standards of propriety set in Prussia.'

Now as bullshit goes this was pretty much at the top of the scale. In normal times nobody would have swallowed it for a moment. As if the army hadn't got better things to do! However, these weren't normal times. The inhabitants of all the newly incorporated states were desperate not to upset the new man. That new man? A certain Kaiser Wilhelm or even worse, a certain Otto von Bismarck. The next lie was far more plausible.

'As for the second reason; you might prefer to discuss this in private, assuming Herr Müller has no further questions…'

Herr Streidle was too smug for his own good. He'd become far too used to squashing all the "little" men who crawled into his office, desperate for his help, if indeed it could be called help. Basking in his recent trouncing of this glorified farmer, he casually waved the Herr Major to continue.

'It's about your son!'

Poof! The balloon of pomposity burst. The story Poldi unfolded was pure fiction but the collapse of the man was unexpected. Perhaps there might have been more than a grain of truth in it afterall. At least, that was Pichler's view!

'I was hoping to be able to write to Berlin', Poldi continued, 'assuring the disciplinary panel that we in Munich have had no reports of any such, er "practices". Issue a clean bill of health so to speak. However, I now feel it is my duty to inform them that there may have been some element of impropriety by the father. Such a shame! A very promising lad he is, or perhaps was until this thing happened. But then Berlin are such sticklers for protocol.'

The pair of them left twenty minutes later. They'd got all there was to be gotten, though that fell far short of what Pichler had hoped for. Still, there was no doubt in his mind now that some kind of sharp practice had taken place, if not outright criminality.

Meindl's parting shot visibly shook the man.

'Do NOT reveal the contents of this meeting to anybody. In fact, this meeting never happened. Is that clear?'

Would that be enough to deter the little swine from getting in contact with his sponsor though? And there *had* to be a sponsor, an organiser… a mastermind.

Transport back to Starnberg was courtesy of the army. Meindl waited with him for the half hour delay until the Garmisch train departed. The station buffet was small but the beer was much appreciated.

'Any use, K-P?'

'Yes, it's helped clear up a few things.'

'You didn't get any actual names of the farmers he's short-changed. It all seemed a bit vague to me. You didn't even try the bank!'

'We know he sets the contracts up but he's clearly just following instructions. We know any monies come directly to him and he then pays them into the bank just opposite from his office. And that's it! The money would have gone into a holding account. Once that was done, the bank would deal directly with the recipient. He wouldn't have been privy to that information. However, I am certain that he has had a part to play in this scheme with Anton. He didn't exactly deny this, did he?'

'Do you think he's lying about the little we did squeeze out of him?' asked Meindl.

'No! He's just a tiny part in a far bigger machine. Whoever is running this has lots of little cogs distributed all along the border. Each cog is pretty much in the dark when it comes to what the axle's up to.'

Boarding the train, Pichler was sad that he couldn't stay for longer – Poldi was a good friend. He must come back in the spring with Anna. She and Poldi's wife Christina could visit the places of interest to them. The two men would concern themselves with the important things in life – that is Poldi could reacquaint him with Bavarian beer. And they could drop in on the farm on the way home – if... Ah, but that was a very big if.

***

As his friend commenced his journey back to Seefeld Meindl climbed aboard his ride back to the college. He did so with a heavy heart, the same heavy heart he'd had from the moment K-P had first mentioned the name of Streidle.

His query to his Sergeant, "Didn't we used to have a cadet called Streidle here until recently?" was entirely disingenuous. It was purely for K-P's benefit. He knew damn well they did without having to look it up in any records.

Major Meindl was, amongst other duties, the college's pastoral officer charged with looking after the welfare of the young cadets. Some of these were born for the army; not so Cadet Jürgen Streidle! Now that he'd met the father, Meindl wondered what Frau Streidle looked like for surely young Jürgen had inherited few of his father's characteristics. Mostly this was a good thing. He was taller and his eyesight was good; in fact he usually scored highly on the shooting range. But this was his sole martial skill. The young man had inherited none of his father's over weaning self-regard or confidence; even a smidgen would have sufficed. His problem – he was painfully shy and for a potential officer destined to command men in battle, that was terminal. The lad had somehow endured several years of merciless bullying from his fellow cadets. Eventually he turned to Meindl in desperation a little over a year ago.

It took many meetings before they eventually arrived at a plan, but the first and the last interviews stuck in Meindl's mind. The first one was the most distressing – for both parties.

'Why ever did you join the army in the first place, Streidle?' Meindl had asked.

'My father was most insistent, sir!'

It had seemed barely credible at the time but after today, it made a lot more sense.

The final meeting was more agreeable – they had a plan.

'Just keep your head down for the next seven months. You'll then be eligible to apply for an honourable discharge,' Meindl had told him, adding 'no disgrace in that… the army's not right for everyone.'

The young man frowned. Seven months? It seemed like an eternity.

'Look, try the occasional drop of Dutch courage, if you're desperate,' said Meindl adding, 'did it myself from time to time.'

This was true, though the time to time Meindl was talking about was during two bloody wars. Still, the lad didn't need to know that bit.

Initially all seemed to be going well. One day, officer cadet Streidle presented Meindl with a carved wooden fox. It had a comical face but in a good way, for it was a toy, intended for a young child – Meindl's child.

'What's this for, Streidle?' he'd asked.

'A thank you, sir – for all your help!'

Meindl was proper chuffed. It's nice to be appreciated.

'It's really good,' said Meindl and he meant it.

'It's what I want to do, sir, when I get my discharge, work with wood, that is. It's when I'm at my happiest.'

But this was only a brief interlude of calm in the troubled life of young Streidle. Very soon thereafter, he graduated from the odd nip to a daily diet of exotic narcotics at a quite alarming pace. Meindl moved him onto duties which would keep him clear of his fellow cadets and more importantly the armoury. It was touch and go but they *almost* made it. "Discharge-day", the day when he could apply for release was just a few weeks away – and then Berlin intervened. He wrote to the CO there, explained the position and was confident of a result. After all, what on earth was the point of the army spending time and money training up an officer who was likely, nay guaranteed, to fold under pressure? None was the answer. The Berlin CO wrote back rebuking him for his "molly-coddling", promising that "we in Berlin, know how to knock these young men into shape". He took the letter home to Christina, who was similarly disgusted.

Streidle, in Berlin, alone, friendless, without even Meindl's sympathetic ear, well, it was only a matter of time before he did something silly. And with his predilection for drugs, that something silly could turn out to be something fatal.

Of course, K-P was unaware of all this. He probably thought it was something to do with "the love that dare not speak its name". In a way, Meindl would have preferred it if it was. There was this man in his regiment, one of the most courageous men he'd ever met… until he met his end at the hands of a French sharpshooter. He managed his private life by exercising extreme discretion. Everybody assumed the woman he lived with was his wife. Nobody suspected that she was his sister. He certainly didn't!

K-P probably thought he'd pulled a rabbit out of a hat on the spur of the moment with his story to Streidle. Christina would laugh at the very idea; "I love you with all my heart, Poldi dearest, but you are probably the least imaginative man I've ever met". He couldn't in all honesty disagree.

Homeward bound:

For some reason, the train from Munich to Garmisch completed the journey far more quickly than the same train on the same track had, earlier that day. And there it would sit until needed first thing the next morning.

Why the rush then? Obvious really! The sooner it was tucked up for the night at Garmisch, the sooner the driver and conductor could get off to their suppers. All that suited Pichler to a tee, although his own supper would have to wait a good few more hours.

He scurried around to the stable where the lad was sitting, patiently awaiting the return of his charge's master. He looked a little disappointed to see Pichler. Blitzen didn't look too happy either! Perhaps he and the horse had become friends during the course of the day.

'I popped 'round every hour, just to see as if he was all right 'n that!'

'Good lad!' said Pichler and transferred another coin into the hand of its grateful recipient.

It was a good evening for driving – even Blitzen wasn't unduly put out. The sky was clear and the moon, when it decided to make an appearance was nearly full. That was all he needed to make a safe if somewhat slower journey along a road he'd travelled along that morning. As he got closer to home he saw the same tree that had incommoded him about twelve hours before. He gave forth a torrent of abuse as he passed by. The tree decided to ignore him completely. Around nine that evening he finally walked through the front door of the farmhouse, utterly exhausted.

Anton leapt up like a spring that had been coiled up all day awaiting news of the "miracle" conjured up by his younger brother. He flopped back down when he'd received it. He then got up without a word, not even a "thanks for trying, Klaus". He was through the door in the next minute heading for old Willy's place to return Blitzen and the trap. He also carried two bottles of Schnapps which Pichler had brought from the station buffet at Munich for the old fellow. At least somebody was happy that evening.

It was a relief for Anna and Klaus to bid farewell early the next morning. Anna hugged both mother and son, departing with a whispered word in Anton's ear.

'You can trust your brother, Anton. Believe me! There's a lot more to K-P than the eighteen year old boy who left to join the army. He just needs a little time, that's all.'

Anton *almost* smiled.

Barely a word was exchanged until they pulled away from Salzburg. 'Sorry!' said Pichler. They had planned to overnight there. Anna had never been anywhere west of Vienna before and well, it was Mozart's birthplace and she did love her Mozart.

'I'll make it up to you,' but she just squeezed his hand by way of a reply.

Pichler very nearly did overnight in Salzburg – alone. At every stop between Innsbruck and there, he'd leapt off the train in search of a local newspaper. There'd been a queue at Salzburg and he only just made it, grabbing the carriage door handle as the train started to chug off.

When you can't see out of the window, it's nice if somebody paints a word picture for you; like your husband for example. Instead, the only sound was the turning of newspaper sheets complemented by occasional scribbling.

'Oh, look, K-P, there's lots and lots of deer in that field!'

And he *actually* did – look that is, before realising that this was a signal to put the dratted newspapers down and talk to her.

'This is our longest trip since the honeymoon in Trieste.'

'Yes it is,' replied Anna. 'The hotel Neptune; how lovely it was. And only a few years old! I like old but it's nice to go somewhere modern for a change. Do you think we shall ever go back?'

'Of course we will, though not this year!'

'No, not this year,' replied his wife.

The University, Pressburg:

A very large map adorned one wall of Pichler's "little corner". There were five pins, each one a best guess of a business caught up by this nasty little scheme. One pin was located a little north-west of Innsbruck and on its flag was written "Anton".

It had taken the whole of yesterday, trawling through all the accumulated local rags to come up with even five pins. A pin about twenty kilometres east of Innsbruck contained the symbol "+". One farmer had taken his own life shortly before his farm had gone up for sale.

He was a bit more hopeful that his other effort would come up trumps. He'd written a dozen or so letters to regional farming collectives or associations. Most wouldn't reply but one or two just might.

He'd spoken to Max about the symptoms as described by Anton. Max muttered a few vague ideas before pointing him in the direction of Herr Professor Dieter Hochwald. Hochwald was the odd-ball of the Department of Veterinary Science. Like so many of the departments, the centre was in Vienna; Pressburg was an offshoot – a place to stick the "second-raters". Max had warned him what to expect and Pichler wasn't to be disappointed.

'Well, Pochla, I'm not really that kind of Veterinarian. I don't treat livestock or sickly doggy-woggies. I'm a researcher!'

That figured thought Pichler – putting him in front of a bunch of students would be a recipe for disaster.

'From what you've told me, I would say it's the usual case of an incompetent farmer – probably didn't look after the grazing properly. That's at the root of most of these diseases, you know. Common enough with these yokel types, no science at all. They just follow what their father and grandfather and great-great grandfather had always done, all the way back to the 17th Century. Now if there is nothing more I can do for you, Herr Poklum, I must get back to my research. Good day!'

Pichler learnt all he was going to learn before Hochwald even opened his mouth. He'd knocked and hearing nothing walked straight into his office, an office that turned out to be in part, a laboratory. It was the furtive way the man covered up an in-progress experiment with a single large sheet. It was done with such proficiency that Pichler was convinced that he did this whenever anyone knocked on the door of his inner sanctum. This was a man who was clearly up to something.

'I glimpsed an anatomical drawing of a cow on his desk. He wasn't as quick as he might have been. A bit odd for a man who doesn't treat livestock, wouldn't you say Max?'

'Hmmm,' muttered Max. 'Pick up any strange smells on entering, did you?'

Pichler nodded.

'Thought so! Who uses their office for stinky experiments when there's a perfectly good lab within walking distance?' Max paused. '*Unless* it's to keep it away from prying eyes? A second visit perhaps – when he's out of his office?'

Pichler nodded. Great idea - but how to do it?

'Ah,' began Max. 'That reminds me, I need to have a word with Hochwald about a vital matter. Can't remember for the life of me what it was but I'm sure I'll remember when I see him. Perhaps I'll treat him to tea in the senior common room. Do him good to get out of his office for a bit.'

Pichler couldn't really see how that was going to help.

'Oh by the way, I don't think I ever mentioned it. It used to be *my* office when I was in the Chemistry department a few years back. Not sure I ever returned the key.'

K-P could only grin. Max you devious old sod, he thought, which was one of the many things he liked about him.

***

One association replied almost by return. It concerned a farmer just north of Innsbruck who had experienced something very similar to the circumstances described in Pichler's letter. It told him nothing he didn't already know.

A day later, he had a letter from the Vorarlberg, the region which lay on the western border of the Tyrol. This wasn't from an association but from the wife of the man whose farm was targeted. The association had written to her asking if she wished them to reply on her behalf or to write to Pichler herself. She was now living with her sister in St Anton, just widows together. She told her story. It contained little useful information. Her husband had taken most of the details to his grave. It was mostly a letter of despair. The description of how she had found her husband's body hanging from a beam in their barn was almost too much for Pichler to read. The worst of it was he could no more help this poor woman, financially speaking that is, than he could help his brother Anton. But God, it made him so angry… and so sad!

He got another letter and an irritatingly smug one at that. "Their members" it said, "would never put themselves in such a position". They were all "fully insured with only reputable companies who always honour any claims". It then went on to outline the details of their own comprehensive insurance scheme as if he gave a ****, the sanctimonious bastards! He crumpled their letter up and binned it before extracting it after just a moment's thought. He un-creased it with the palm of his hand and popped it inside his sparsely filled brown card file. It wasn't much but you should never bin evidence no matter how insubstantial. Max had taught him that!

He looked at his wall map. The replies from the farming guilds had added precisely – nothing!

A chat with Slota:

Ján Slota had first encountered Klaus Heinrich Pichler back in '67 when he'd first become Max's assistant. But it wasn't until the summer of 1870 that he'd had the opportunity to see K-P in action.

Ever since that time, the rascal would pump him for whatever information he could squeeze out. In the beginning Slota regarded it as something of a compliment. *He,* a mere Sergeant had been singled out from amongst all the officers of the Pressburg police department. A more obvious choice would have been his immediate superior, Inspector Hodža. But that was some time ago. He'd long since figured out the reason. It was because he was far more indiscreet. Mind you, that wouldn't have been hard as far as the inspector was concerned. When it came to leaking anything, "tight" and "duck's arse" were the apposite words to best describe Karol Hodža.

Not that Slota minded being taken advantage of in this way, not a bit of it. They were both after the same thing – protect the innocent – nab the thieving, murdering, raping and so much more… bastards! Sadly, the "bastards" were all too often not bastards in the literal meaning of the word. They had lineages dating back centuries and as such were almost untouchable regardless of the evidence. Pichler had fewer constraints than the regular police. As an ex-military man, Slota understood the role of the irregular forces in any conflict. Putting some ammunition their way was all in a good cause.

'So what are you after this time, K-P?'

He listened for the ten minutes it took for Pichler to put him in the picture. No real leads then! But the modus operandi was not unheard of in Slota's extensive experience. It had all the hallmarks of a "nob-job", police jargon for a crime devised and managed at arm's length by an aristo. Only aristo's had enough cash to provide the initial "hook", loans in this case *and* the patience to wait for their investment to show a return. The "roughs" didn't operate this way. They didn't have the spare cash to do so. With them it's all "threat today, pay-up tomorrow… or else".

It could be an Empire-wide scheme, explained Slota, though he corrected himself almost immediately. No, not Empire-wide; *not* from the Swiss border in the west to the Serbia border in the east. And *not* from Bohemia in the north to the Adriatic. That required too big a circle of influence to be feasible, unless F-J was running it, which seemed unlikely.

Pichler broke into a snigger at this point. Slota was the only person he knew who regularly referred to his Imperial Majesty, the King-Emperor Franz Josef as "F-J". Luckily, walls had not, thus far grown any ears.

'He'll probably confine himself to the Austrian Crownlands, but not the eastern provinces where the Polacks and the Ruskies live. In fact as all the rackets you've uncovered so far are in the Tyrol you can rule out Bohemia and Moldovia.'

'Why?' asked Pichler.

'Too many cultural problems, unless you're a real multi-linguist. Wouldn't rule out the "olive-eaters" though! Remember K-P he needs to set up agents, perhaps for every one or two schemes. I'd guess no more than that. Too risky otherwise – too many eggs in each basket. That means he's got to know what he's dealing with if he's to find the perfect combination of financial competence, dishonesty and fear. That's one reason why I'm banking on it being a "nob-job". The roughs will break your arm, but the aristo's can ruin you, financially and in every other way.'

'How many schemes would you guess he's running, Ján?'

'Weeelll, assuming each one nets around about the same return he'd get from pinching your brother's farm, I'd say at least four in any one year.'

'In any one year, you don't mean to say…?'

'Ooooh, yes I do! He'll have been up to this caper for years, decades even. It's his regular income, do you see? And one job a year wouldn't keep him in champagne and ladies underwear for more than a month or two, bearing in mind that the type of ladies in question don't come cheap.'

The University and Home:

Pichler had to admit it as he shuffled back to the lab, Slota's reasoning was mainly soufflé, all air and no substance. But despite that the profile he'd sketched out made complete sense to him. At its centre a member of the nobility who was extremely well-connected, at least in the Western half of the Empire. He was probably operating out of Vienna or somewhere nearby. But that was all theory. The chances were it'd turn out to be a scheme cooked up in Warsaw and run from a gipsy camp in Romania but in the absence of anything better…

As he passed Hochwald's office he noticed the lights were out. God was that the time? Had he pocketed Max's spare? Yes he had and it worked a treat. He was in and the door was locked behind him in a thrice. Still, Hochwald might have just popped out for a minute, so as quickly as he could Pichler worked his way around the room. Most of the equipment had been locked away and he didn't have a key for that. Likewise most of the paperwork he'd seen earlier was no longer there, almost certainly away in locked drawers. In fact, given the unkempt appearance of its owner, the room was implausible tidy, implausibly so for somebody with nothing to hide. That left the blotter, a trick he'd been taught by Slota. He untucked the top sheet, folded it away and made a few ink blots on the previously pristine sheet that now lay on top. He hoped his theft would go unnoticed.

Once outside, Pichler pulled out the blotter and held it up to a street lamp. It was difficult to make anything out, save one indentation. Never without a pencil he lightly shaded the area to reveal "R – 53". He shrugged – meaningless – and headed off home.

As he strolled past the main University building, the one where all the guest lectures took place, a poster caught his eye.

<u>Triumph in the Adriatic</u>

Count Eugene von Wittenburg, the owner of the ketch, the "White Swan" will describe his recent success in bringing the prestigious Trieste to Lissa trophy home to Pressburg against stiff competition from other parts of the Empire and abroad.

All welcome.

Talk starts in Lecture Theatre Number 1 at 1600 on the 22nd. Late comers will not be admitted.

He might as well give it a go. He had nothing else to do. It's not as if his investigation was going anywhere!

At home, Pichler mentioned to Anna that he might well be a bit late getting home on the night of the lecture.

'That's all right,' she replied. 'I'll be doing stew… again!'

They'd moved into her Aunt Emma's house, the one Anna had shared with her Aunt for years. Pichler wasn't sure it was a good idea, given the recent associations, but Anna had insisted. She knew the layout of the house, where everything lived and didn't feel she could cope with a new place, at least not just yet. Pichler shuddered as he recalled the scene. He'd found Anna tied to a chair with cigarette burns up and down her arm. Worse still – not two metres away lay her aunt. The sight of her stove-in cranium would stay with him for ever.

For an academic, Pichler was an extremely practical fellow. It must have come from all those years on the farm and then the army. With Anna reinstalled in the house on Rösslgasse, the first thing he did was to fit a narrow "roadway" of different types of carpet all around the house. She probably didn't need them. He knew that; and she was too polite to say. After all, she'd lived there for years. But what of a new house… and he was determined to move to somewhere with a garden, eventually. How would she cope then? So if nothing else, it was an early experiment.

The first time she'd "seen" it, she slipped off her shoes and investigated each room, nook and cranny with occasional squeals of delight. It was true her delight was more down to her appreciation of his thoughtfulness. She didn't need them. But then again how would she manage in somewhere entirely new? There did have to be somewhere new – she did so want a garden, eventually. Two peas in a pod!

Despite his best efforts, it was clear. It couldn't go on forever. She would need help eventually, what with him out most of the day. But that would be her decision and *only* her decision. Pichler knew all about being patronised! The long and short of it was that for the present, stews would continue to be *very* popular in the Pichler household.

During his musing, Anna was thinking about the forthcoming lecture, wondering whether she might be interested before deciding she wouldn't!

'You've always been interested in boats, even though to my knowledge you've never been on one. I don't know why you didn't join the navy rather than the infantry.'

Pichler smiled. She was right. It was just something about them, majestically sailing up and down the Danube; he could watch them for hours.

'All the other ranks are either Italian or Croatian so that would have been a bit of a problem. Anyway, I'd only have ended up on one of them large ocean-going jobs and that wouldn't have suited me one little bit.'

She hadn't heard a word; she was deep in thought.

'That name vaguely rings a bell… but I can't remember where I heard it or if I've imagined it. Hmmm. K-P! Toddle along "squidgy" road until you get to the tall cabinet. Three drawers up from the bottom, right-hand side, you'll find a very smooth box with two holes in the lid.'

'I'd far rather see you get it yourself,' he replied.

It was their usual game. It gave him pleasure to see how well she managed and she… well, she just wanted to show off. She faultlessly navigated her way back to the chair and pulled out an envelope. Job done! The next bit was beyond her. 'Take it!' she said.

'You know we were talking about the hotel Neptune, well I'm pretty sure that the brochure we kept as a souvenir is in there. See if you can find it and read it out to me.'

'Built in 1869, the hotel stands on the site of the old Neptune boatyard after which it was named. The boatyard ran into financial difficulties two years before when it had insufficient funds to complete the building of the 'Roc', a 15m ketch named after the mythical bird. The client withdrew support for the project and the yard collapsed shortly afterwards unable to pay its operating costs. A year later the site was purchased by the present owner of the hotel.

And who was that owner of the hotel? It didn't say on the brochure.

'Well, I'm sure I've heard that name before. Maybe I'm wrong, or maybe it wasn't Trieste. Still, it was nice to be reminded of the Hotel Neptune. I do hope we go again, one day.'

Bavarian War College

Major Poldi Meindl's usual day for meeting his immediate superior was Friday. Today wasn't Friday. He wondered what the occasion was because as far as he knew everything was going swimmingly. He was about to be sadly disillusioned.

'Ah, Major Meindl… take a seat. I'm afraid we have a bit of a problem.'

'We do, sir?'

'Yes we do… and the name of that problem is Jürgen Streidle,' replied the Herr Oberst.

Meindl could see the file sitting open on the Colonel's desk.

'I've read your notes on the interviews… quite a few weren't there?… and your recommendation to Berlin that his transfer should be deferred. Ignored naturally! You can't tell these Prussians anything.'

'I did my best sir.'

'Indeed you did. Well, the reason I've called you in this morning is this telegram,' said the Colonel sliding the message across the desk.

'Is he…?'

'No, Meindl, not dead. He's in the infirmary and will be transferred to Munich as soon as the doctors give him the all clear. It goes without saying that he has been discharged with immediate effect, although you'll be relieved to know, not dishonourably. It seems his fellow cadets have behaved badly leading up to this… er, "event"… and it is not something the army want banded about.'

'I don't doubt that for one minute sir but I don't suppose they were being any more spiteful than young men normally are. It was inevitable,' replied a deflated Meindl on hearing this news.

'Well, as the college's pastoral officer, I leave it to you to inform the family. I don't suppose you've ever met the mother and father, have you?'

***

It was nearly time to shut up the office. He was feeling a bit happier today. Perhaps less annoyed would be a better description. He'd worked himself up into a right old lather the evening of the day that those two impertinent fellows called into his office… *and* without any appointment. The civilian he'd batted aside with ease, but the officer, the one with the eye patch… what right had he to threaten him, blackmail him even, using his son's good name as the "ransom"? And that final remark – threatening him yet again – telling him that he must not reveal the contents of their meeting… or even that this meeting had actually taken place. It didn't strike him at the time but on reflection that all smacked of them being up to something entirely unofficial, perhaps even illegal. He'd had quite enough of dealing with bully-boys like these two. He'd been bullied all his days at school. But not now, not now he held the whip hand over others. And those others were paying… paying for all the torments inflicted on his younger self, both literally and metaphorically.

After two stiff brandies that evening he'd wrought himself up to write a letter to the War Ministry in Berlin. He didn't know the Major's name but he was obviously based in Munich, probably at the military academy and with his eye patch, he'd be easy enough to pin down. He wanted an official apology – his letter demanded one – it was his right, God damn it! The letter was completed, signed, sealed and only wanted a stamp. Had he known the postage rate for Berlin, it would have gone in the post box that same evening.

Come the morning, his first concern was a blistering headache. He was not a great drinker and they were *very* large brandies. He left for the office, the letter remained on the mantelpiece.

By lunchtime, with no clients to see and a morning spent in sober – nearly sober at any rate – reflection, he had decided *not* to send the letter. What good would it do… really? No, it was better to rise above it. He was clearly the victim of a "fishing trip" and the anglers had only caught a few sprats thanks to his dissembling. As for his boy… well, what could he have done to warrant censure? The boy's mother had on occasions expressed some concern that Jürgen showed so little interest in girls. He himself was a little at a loss to know how to make him more outgoing. He'd not get very far in business without more get up and go. That was the reason why he'd urged him to go into the army – that would toughen him up. Actually he'd done more than urge him, practically had to frog march him down to the college recruiting office. Still, no regrets, it seemed to be working out well.

As Herr Streidle went to lock up a man appeared. He was wearing a very smart coat and hat. Streidle, ever on the lookout for new clients, decided that it wasn't *quite* closing time.

'Come in sir. Welcome to Streidle and Partners. How may I help you?'

The man did not answer. The only sound came from the proprietor as he saw the eye-patch.

'How dare you come into my office? If you don't get out immediately I shall call for the police.'

Instead of answering the irate fellow, the man unbuttoned his coat and reached inside. Without a word, he pulled out a small object, placed it on the desk and sat himself down.

'What the devil is this?' demanded Herr Streidle.

'It's a wooden fox… a toy made for my first born,' replied Major Meindl.

The man was nonplussed but sat himself down opposite nonetheless, picked it up and examined the toy.

'Why are you showing me this? Why should *I* care what toys you buy your child?'

'I didn't *buy* it… it was made for me… by your son!'

As the college's pastoral officer, Meindl was very experienced in breaking bad news gently. For this man, shock tactics were necessary. This wasn't out of any feelings of malice. It was the only way to bring some compassion to the surface of this deeply unpleasant man. He handed the telegram over the desk.

Streidle went white, deathly white.

'Will he be…?' he stammered, his eyes welling up.

Meindl now treated the man kindly, as he would any cadet. He'd seen it all – from the heartbroken ones because his girl had found a new love to the devastated ones because they'd failed the leadership skills test for the second time.

'He'll be fine. He was found in time, but only just. Jürgen will be released from the army without a stain on his character or reputation. As soon as he has recovered, a matter of days not weeks, he will be sent home. I suspect his last few days will be a happier memory than he has experienced up to now. His fellow cadets will know that they had a part to play in him resorting to this desperate action and will try to make it up to him as best they are able.' Meindl saw a ghost of a smile appear on the man's face. 'As must you sir!'

Streidle, much to Meindl's surprise, at last recognised his failings as a father.

'You are right, sir. I should never have forced him into the army. My wife told me he wasn't right for it but I wouldn't listen. But what must I do now?'

The contrition was genuine, no doubt about it and Meindl surprised himself by actually warming to the man; he was human after all.

'Don't distress yourself Herr Streidle, Jürgen's life is not over. In fact it has only just begun.'

'What do you mean, sir?' asked the man, not aggressively as before but almost pleadingly.

Meindl explained how he'd come to acquire the wooden fox, the plan he and young Streidle had worked out. The plan but for Berlin's intervention, could have avoided all this… "unpleasantness".

'Just look at this fox, Herr Streidle, look at it carefully. Carved on any old bit of wood he found lying around, with duff tools I'll be bound… and even then, only able to work on it when he had a bit of privacy from the jibes of his classmates. Despite all this, it is a fine piece of carving is it not? The lad has talent. Just think what he could achieve with some tuition and the right tools. Are you not in a position to assist him with this?'

There was a long pause. It seemed probable to Meindl that Jürgen's father was already churning through a list of suitable contacts whose help he could enlist to that very end

'Indeed I can and I most certainly will! Whatever the boy wants… *Whatever*!'

And that was the job done. Meindl's hand was taken in both of Streidle's hands and warmly shaken… and for some time, but there were no further words; none were necessary.

Pressburg police station

'You don't seem to have made much progress, old lad,' said Sergeant Slota.

'Up until yesterday evening, I'd have agreed with you Ján. However this morning, I got a *very* interesting letter which was forwarded to me by the recipient. See what you make of it', said Pichler.

'Hand it over then,' said Slota.

Major Meindl
Munich War College
Delivered by hand

Dear Major

Having found out your name, I wanted to write to you to express my gratitude. Your help in this matter has been...

'What's this all about?' asked Slota.

'Skip to the last two paragraphs,' replied Pichler.

... Regarding that other matter on which you and your colleague originally came to see me, I must confess that what I told you at that time was not entirely correct. I do not use the bank opposite my premises. In fact I do not use any bank. I arrange to meet each debtor at a mutually convenient location and they pay in cash for which I issue a receipt. The payments are then collected by a courier at my office and he would issue me with a receipt. I truly do not know to whom the money is delivered. Of course this is highly unusual business practice and now I bitterly regret ever getting involved...

Slota skipped the rest of that paragraph and moved onto the final one.

I can never repay your kindness to my lad, but perhaps this may be of some small help. I have checked my files and can find no paper records which give the full name of the money lender. All letters were signed with initials only, namely EvW.

Yours with eternal gratitude...

'EvW,' said Slota. 'E von somebody or other. See, told you it was a "nob-job" didn't I? Have you got anything else for me?'

Pichler showed Slota the blotting paper.

'Ho, ho, R-53, eh? Well *that* does mean something. Just a minute!'

Slota disappeared into Hodža's office and was back in less than a minute.

'Right, the Inspector's happy for me and you to take a little stroll along the river.'

***

A thought occurred to Slota as they walked along the bank of the Danube.

'This business about paying in cash at – what did Streidle say in his letter – a "mutually convenient location"... It all strikes me as a bit of a rum do. Didn't your brother mention any of this to you?'

'No! And fool that I am I didn't think to ask.'

'Well, why should you, K-P? Surely it was down to him to say something?'

'I think I know why he didn't, Ján. He was just too plain embarrassed to admit that he'd signed up to a deal which had "iffy" written all over it!'

Slota grunted. That sounded reasonable to him. He opened his mouth to comment further when he noticed the first one. He pointed at the placard which said "R-11". At berth number 11, there was moored a rather nice houseboat. Slota smiled as he saw the light dawn on Pichler's face.

'Don't worry, odds on this side, evens on the other bank so only another twenty odd berths before we get there. And don't ask me what the "R" stands for – didn't know when we were investigating EvW three years ago – still don't!'

Pichler was fair galloping to get there his leg notwithstanding. Poor old Slota was out of puff by the time they'd arrived at R-53.

'What's she called?' asked Slota.

'The "Heron" and there's nobody aboard,' replied Pichler. 'Shall we?'

'Best not,' replied Slota. 'Laws of trespass and all that!'

Pichler was surprised. Sergeant Slota had a reputation for bending the law when it suited him. 'But we need to identify the owner,' said a perplexed Pichler.

'Oh, I know *him*. We had him in our sights a few years ago – for underage sex – never managed to snare the bastard though. That's why I didn't connect him with this present caper.'

'Come on, Ján, what's his fucking name then?'

'Count Eugene von Wittenburg, that's who!'

At the Lecture:

The first few rows were taken up by dignitaries from the university, the nobility and assorted officialdom. Pichler was ten rows back. There were two people on the stage. One, centre stage in all his finery was the Count. In one corner stood a rougher looking fellow whose sole job was to carry the various items the Count was using to illustrate his talk around to the members of the audience. This was so they could inspect these more closely and more importantly from the Count's perspective, admire his achievement *even more.*

The Count was so full of himself that Pichler found it almost embarrassing. Not so the first few rows where fawning was clearly going to be the order of the day.

Eventually the "rough" reached Pichler's row. Pichler sighed and tutted as the man's master had just come out with one especially pompous remark. He was barely aware of the fellow as he handed him a piece of ripped sailcloth. At that moment, the two men's eyes locked. Pichler saw, much to his surprise his own disgusted look replicated in the other man's face. This was followed by a wry smile. And that smile might just as well have been spoken such was the clarity of its message – what a complete and utter Prickchen the man is!

Thereafter Pichler paid very little attention to the Count's talk. This proved to be much less interesting than he'd hoped, consisting mainly of photographs of the great man accompanied by much boasting. Instead his eyes were fixed on the Count's assistant, who was directed at intervals to repeat his trips around the auditorium with scant acknowledgement and no thanks. Was it his imagination or was the man carrying out his master's orders with increasingly bad grace with each successive trip?

At the end, the Count commenced his deep bow before the applause had even started. As at the beginning he made no reference to the man. He offered no thanks. This would have been beneath his dignity, quite clearly. In fact, the only communication was a passing cursory wave. This meant nothing to Pichler but his servant nodded so it must have.

The front rows clustered around the Empire's latest sporting hero like eager schoolboys. They needed to be quick for the Count was already striding towards the exit. It didn't look like he had any intention of staying for the customary hospitalities. Clearly a man as important as this was a man on a mission. The nature of that mission would become apparent as Sergeant Ján Slota would later describe.

Pichler wandered down towards the lectern where the man, muttering and swearing to himself all the while, had filled one crate and was working on loading up the second one.

'Phew!' expounded Pichler, 'that lot looks a bit heavy. Can I give you a hand?'

The man stopped what he was doing and glared at the fellow aggressively. Was the bastard taking the piss? Pichler's honest, smiling countenance convinced him otherwise.

'Well that's proper 'ansom of you, squire. You could save me a trip. Here, I'll takes this 'un – a bit heavy for a land lubber. You do t'other.'

Once both were deposited in the locker room, the fellow stood fully erect, easing his back and supplied his unexpected help mate with an explanation.

'I'll load 'em into his carriage tomorra. We're off to Vienna for a repeat performance. Then, oh somewhere else… Prague, maybe. Anyway, he needs 'is carriage tonite soes he can get to his 'ouse boat.'

'Where are *you* staying?' asked Pichler.

'Oh, he's given me a coin or two to find some doss house. Anyways, least I can do is stand you a beer – wadda yer say?'

'Only if you let me stand you one right back,' replied Pichler.

Well thought the man, this one's a right regular gent.

Pichler had learnt from Hodža who owned the Neptune hotel. His initials? "EvW"! He was pretty certain that Dr Hochwald, the "cow-vet" had visited berth R-53 in order to deliver something to the houseboat "Heron", owned by a certain… EvW.

It was all starting to add up. But a written statement was crucial to finally nailing this bastard to the floorboards! And this man, his servant might, just might be persuaded to provide one.

Pichler found a dark corner in a tavern not far from the lecture venue. The man slumped down heavily and looked up at him expectantly. Pichler it seemed would be buying all the drinks this evening and by God, could that man drink. He'd downed his first Stein before Pichler had even got past the froth level. By the time Pichler had returned with two more, the fellow had more or less emptied Pichler's glass. Pichler affected not to have noticed as the man continued to talk – and not only could he drink, he could talk as well.

He'd been a foreman at the Neptune yard since he was a lad. He knew all there was to know about the place, but even he had no clue how the building dock sluice gate had been left open that night. The sea cocks were yet to be installed, so what with it being a spring tide, the dock was flooded up to the gunwale of the yacht they'd so nearly completed. The night watchman should have spotted the water rushing in and closed the sluice gate but he didn't. In fact when they all turned up for work the next morning, he was sleeping the sleep of the dead.

'Course, he was sacked on the spot – drunk on the job, though that was 'nother thing – Old Giovanni didn't drink, ulcers you see.'

'So, a right-off then?' asked Pichler.

'Nah! Yer'd think so if yer know nuffing 'bout boats, but the timbers was all fine – already been oiled, d'yer see. Nah, it was the furnishings that was buggered. Silks, finest quality carpets, cushions… all from China them was. Bit odd, we all thought. I mean… it was supposed to be a racing yacht not a tart's palace. Anyway, Signor Maldini, he was the boss, well, he'd bought all that lot on tic.'

'Tic?' queried Pichler.

'You know – payment on completion of the order. Well the Count…'

'Count who?' interrupted Pichler, playing the innocent.

'Aint you been listening? Him what's been droning on all evening! Where was I? Oh yes. The Count pulls outta the contract. We've got a boat on our 'ands nobody wants and a load of pissed-off Chinkies wanting their money. And that's the end of the Neptune boatyard.'

'So how did the Co…'

'Well, that's the funny bit – suspicious you might say, if yer got that turn-a mind. The whole lot – damaged yacht, site, all the yard fittings – all goes up for sale. And who d'yer think pops up to buy the whole kit and caboodle? And then he immediately decommissions the yard – all the machinery, workbenches, tools, all sold on? All the blokes sacked… 'cept for me. The land, now that made sense but to buy the yacht – with no boatyard to repair it – what's that all about? Anyway, turns out that he had no intention of replacing all the furnishings. Fact is he has me stripping out everything bar the bit you need to win races. Tell you summet else an all – she's a bit lighter now than he's declared on the entry forms. So he has me adding a bit more lead down in the bilges – encased in wood so they looks like ordinary stores. Now he's got a yacht that can carry a bit more sail than the rest… so he wins races. If any of the race committees ever found out…'

'But it can't just be more ballast. The Count must be a better sailor than the other skippers, wouldn't you…'

The guffaw interrupted Pichler.

'Don't make me laugh! Him? Couldn't tie a bowline if his life depended on it, which of course at sea, it sometimes does! Na, professional crew for him every time chum!'

So that was how the Yacht "Roc" morphed into the "White Swan"; almost jolly enough for a fairy tale, if it hadn't cost so many men their livelihoods.

The garrulous fellow was on a roll now. The tale of how his "friend" the Count had acquired der "Reiher" was a similar story. She had been built on the Donau, a few kilometres down river from Pressburg. There was a single boiler which supplied the steam for the yard's machinery; winches, hoists, that type of thing. It was the explosion of that boiler that had started the chain of events. Nobody knew how it'd happened. It'd never given any trouble in the past. It wasn't even that old. There was extensive damage to the yard and as a consequence, a bit of a delay in completion… not that much, a couple of weeks in fact, but it triggered a penalty clause. The client… you'll never guess who it was… renegotiated a revised and naturally heavily discounted price.

'What is the "Heron?' asked Pichler as if he didn't know – what the lawyers call "not leading the witness".

'His 'ouseboat. Now that *is* luxurious. No lack of fine finishing on 'er and no mistake. He keeps 'er on the river… at berth 53, if you fancy seeing how the other half lives.'

'Well, thank you so much for telling me such a fascinating story. Who'd have thought it, eh? It was a lucky thing for me that I happened to see the poster for the Count's talk *and* that it was being given in Pressburg,' said Pichler.

'Lucky be damned!' said the man. 'You couldn't very well have *avoided* seeing a poster. They're posted up everywhere as soon as he gets into town. I should know as it's me what has to stick the fuckers up. He's doing dozens of these talks; three in Vienna, one here, three in Trieste, one in Prague, one in Buda and a few other places I can't remember. He'd be doing one in the South Tyrol if it weren't so bleeding far from the sea. In fact you can't keep the bugger down… loves the sound of his own voice, does that one!'

Pot and kettle was the expression on the tip of Pichler's tongue. Instead he said – 'You ought to write this tale down somewhere. It'd make a tremendous newspaper story.'

The man shrugged his shoulders and laughed a coarse laugh. He suddenly seemed a lot more sober.

'Right then – I must be off now, chum. Gotta find a place to lay me head. Enjoyed chatting to yer. Ta very much for the beer.'

Pichler opened his mouth as if to forestall his exit. The man glared at him, his genial expression replaced by one of pure thuggery.

'Now mind, sonny, if yer ever repeats a word of this, I'll say I's never seen yer before in me life. Got it?'

Pichler cursed as he watched the man's back disappear out into the street. He felt as if he'd just unwrapped a Christmas present, one he'd set his heart on for weeks… only for his mother to tell me that it was Anton's not his.

Pressburg police station:

Sergeant Slota grimaced as he pushed the small of his hand onto the base of his spine. It didn't really help much.

'The old trouble, Ján?' asked Inspector Karol Hodža, to which Slota nodded and grimaced again.

'Worth it?'

'Yes and no sir! To me personally – yes! I'm even more convinced that he's guilty of the charge we tried to get him on three years ago. Legally – not one iota of progress!'

Slota had arrived at the Heron's mooring about the same time as Count Wittenburg was winding up his lecture at the University. He'd agreed with Pichler that he would keep watch to see if the devil was up to his old tricks. A hedgerow provided just the cover he needed some ten metres from the boat and so it was to prove. He could not only see the two of them arrive about an hour later but he could hear most of what was said. He didn't like the way he had his hand firmly clasped around her upper arm. Most whores know their business and don't need to be dragged anywhere; this was different. She didn't look sixteen, he wasn't even sure she looked *fourteen.*

The man spoke; 'just get on board, now! No more whining or it'll be the worse for you.'

Just for a second she looked over her shoulder directly into the hedgerow, not that she knew Slota was there. It was a half-wild, half-pleading look… a heart rending look! Her thoughts were as obvious to him as if she had spoken them. Should she fight or should she run? It was all he could do not to break cover and punch the man in the face. He restrained himself for two reasons. Firstly, getting the evidence was paramount. They had to put a stop to this, not just tonight, not just for this little one but for all the others and nights yet to come. And the second reason? Once he'd started punching that arrogant face, he wasn't sure he could trust himself to stop… He didn't fancy ending his career swinging off a rope at Pressburg's jail. After less than half an hour, the pair reappeared at the deckhouse door, the man's face blackened by anger. He threw her down the gang plank and she stumbled just missing the stone quay. In a second she was off and running, or at least trying to.

Slota caught up with the bewildered creature after just a few hundred metres. He wasn't as fast as he used to be but she was barely capable of walking in a straight line, let alone running.

She froze the instant she heard the Count's footsteps just a few metres behind. Oh God, no! But then she saw it wasn't him – it was another. But it *was* still a man.

'Wait, police' he had called waving his badge as he did so. 'Don't run, you're safe now, child.'

She paused. He got a little closer but then stopped as he looked at her. For the first time since *he* had chosen her from Frau Winkler's selection of girls, she noticed her appearance. Her arms were red where he'd pinched her and her mouth was bleeding, a memento of that slap. She brought her hand to her left eye. It seemed to be swollen.

'I'll walk you back to your home – no need to worry anymore,' said the man.

Home! Where was that – Frau Winkler's menagerie? Or back to the streets where that bitch had found her, telling her tales of fine houses and kind gentlemen. In the next instant she was off and poor old Slota gave up the chase after just a few minutes. He could only watch as she disappeared into the darkening night.

He bent over double, trying to recover his breath. Age had not just caught up with him it had overtaken him and was now waving back at him from afar. Then he saw it, something shiny lying in the grass; a little silver broach. Virtually worthless, but it was something the Winkler woman gave to all her girls, a symbol of her affection for them perhaps. "Ha", he grunted as he bent further over to retrieve it.

The Inspector said not a word during Slota's report, only turning his back on him as he reached the end. His Sergeant knew what this signified as he'd seen it umpteen times before. His anger subsided and back in control of himself, Karol Hodža turned and faced his Sergeant and spoke.

'No evidence at all then? Just this girl, who we may never find and even if we did, she'd never give evidence, *and* if she did, the Count's chum on the bench wouldn't believe her. Just the word of an honest police Sergeant against that of a lying, but ennobled Count! No doubt which one would prevail, is there Ján?'

Slota merely shrugged.

‘Do you think he could be the bounder K-P’s been after?’

‘I don’t think it sir, I know it! The Count’s man told all to K-P last night, but he won’t…’

‘Sign a statement to that effect?’ interrupted Hodža.

Slota stood up. The seat had become just too uncomfortable to bear any longer.

‘But it fit’s everything we’d expect, doesn’t it, sir? He *has* to be getting his money from somewhere; we just couldn’t explain from *where* back in ’68.

‘Look Sergeant, as far as the Department is concerned the von Wittenburg case is closed. However, if you can be of any help to K-P, then please do so. I suggest another one of your drinking sessions with Max’s young protégé. Put him in the picture but stress that we’ve been here before and getting enough evidence to convince a judge is all but impossible. I feel he’s on the road to disillusionment so let him down as gently as you can.’

‘Will do, sir,’ replied Slota.

‘Oh and have the first round on me,’ said the Inspector.

Slota smiled as he took the note. That would do him and K-P for the entire evening and might even run to a sausage or two each. It was the Inspector's way of giving his Sergeant his blessing for any off-the-record action which Slota might deem necessary. Of course, if he ever heard of such actions then a disciplinary hearing would be certain to follow. After all he *was* an Inspector in the Pressburg Police Department. That was *if* he ever heard of anything. Hodža was pretty sure he wouldn't; his hearing was getting dreadful these days.

At the clap-clinic

Sometimes even the nobility have to pay for their pleasures and when they do, medical skill is only marginally more important than discretion. Discretion was Doktor Grunebel's watchword. If he could, he'd probably advertise the fact but that would rather defeat the object.

Not that Slota thought for one moment that his "friend" the Count had caught a dose from the young thing he'd seen the other night, quite the opposite. The swine had more likely been infecting the virgins and whorehouse novices for years. He'd hung around outside the auditorium at the start of the lecture… seen the villain close up as he strolled into the theatre. He didn't exhibit any obvious symptoms but syphilis was like that. Symptoms come and go and it was only at the latter stages of the disease that sufferers exhibited strange behaviour. So there was no help for it but to watch the comings and goings outside the Herr Doktor's office. But even as he formulated this plan, Slota realised this was far too random. Oooo! What was that? A strange itching in his groin. Oh dear me he must have something nasty. Better call on the good doctor.

Doktor Grunebel noticed immediately that the man in front of him looked several cuts below the standing of his usual clientele. The dedicated medical practitioner that he was, his first thought was – could he pay up?

Slota wasn't much of an actor, but he was a damn good policeman and a scary one as well when the need arose. The need had just arisen! Out with his warrant card and out with a demand to know whether Wittenburg was a client and "don't give me any of that crap about client confidentiality. We've got enough on you to put you out of business… permanently."

That might not have worked in most cases but it did today. The reason – the doctor's face was the reason.

'Tell me about the bruises, Herr Doktor.'

Wittenburg was a patient all right, but not a very patient, patient and the doctor had the evidence written all over his face – literally. Out it all came and it was gold dust. But it proved to be only fool's gold. Try as he might, Slota could not get anything written down, save for the notes in his own notebook. Without a written statement, it was the same old story – one man's word. Still confirmation of Wittenburg's link with the pox doctor was useful, though to whom? That wasn't exactly clear… apart from a blackmailer, that is and even Slota couldn't justify stretching the law that far… more's the pity!

At home with the Pichler's:

Both the Pichler's were deep in thought as the afternoon drew to its close; one was sitting at home, the other was sitting in a cab as it made its way through the early evening traffic towards their home on Rösslgasse.

***

Anna had long since accepted her lot in life. It wasn't *so* bad, but sometimes, only sometimes you must understand, she wished she was able to do the things that sighted people took for granted, things which were impossible for her.

It was Doktor Sazonov at the children's hospice who had sparked off this particular train of thought. Once a week for the last two years, she had visited the sick children bringing with her, her stories. Sometimes these stories had lived in her head since she was a young girl. Other times she would work out the framework in the cab ride there and make up the rest as she went along. These were the ones she enjoyed the most, adjusting the story to suit the reaction of her young audience. Today had been one of those and she'd decided to make it a "scary".

These were always the most challenging. With no facial expressions to guide her, it was judging her audience that was the problem. She could easily tell if they were bored. Bored children don't sit still; first they fidget, then they chatter. But in any scary worth its salt, there ought to be prolonged periods of absolute silence. They should sit there totally enthralled until… she would unexpectedly clap her hands together and shriek. When she did, all the children screamed and then giggled – this one had gone particularly well.

There was always a member of staff sitting in, in order to look after the children naturally. Quite why the second or even third member had to be there…? Today Doktor Sazonov popped in, just as the evil witch had been cornered by the good fairy and was about to be turned into a rabbit, a black rabbit naturally. What other colour could it be?

'You know, Frau Pichler, I really think you ought to get your stories transcribed.'

Anna frowned; 'Why do you say that Herr Doktor?'

'So they can be published dear lady, of course. There is only one of you and there are so many sick children in so many hospices dotted around the Empire.'

It was she had to concede an idea which she had been tinkering with for some time. Perhaps if Aunt Emma was still alive… no, even if that were so her eyesight would not have been up to it. She put her hand to her face and rebuked herself sharply. Stop… stop… stop! Nice thoughts… only nice thoughts.

After a while the nice thoughts came. Tonight he would finish reading the play to her – the Merchant of Venice. It amazed her to think that this two hundred and seventy year old play was still being performed.

Would the Jew get his pound of Antonio's flesh? "They" – the Venetians were partly to blame for his behaviour, she thought. Were Jews treated in this way today – no, surely not!

***

Pichler liked working at home. Anyone who'd seen his cramped so-called office at the University would have understood why. Max didn't mind, just as long as he got the job done. He always did. Somethings he felt he was getting quite a few other people's jobs done at the same time. Around three, he thought he'd earned his daily crust from the university and it was time to start his other one.

It was funny how his masters at the university would happily pay him only two-thirds of the going rate but expected him to work full-time hours. The other third was paid by the Pressburg police department as proposed by the man himself. Proposals from the Emperor weren't suggestions and any of his subjects who treated them as such were destined for a very short career. The "Emperor's Detective", he snorted at Max's abbreviation of his official title, which was somewhat grander. This he knew for a fact; he had the certificate to prove it.

Pichler closed his eyes to consider the wealth of documentary evidence which he'd spread out across the full length of his kitchen table.

On count one: fraud, sabotage leading to the acquisition of the yacht die "weisser Schwan" and the Hotel Neptune.

He had bills of sales and proof of ownership documents which linked von Wittenburg to the hotel and the yacht. He had a signed statement from a former employee of the boat yard who later became a member of his crew. The statement also included an allegation of falsification in respect of the yacht race for which the Count had been so recently lauded throughout the Empire.

On count two: fraud, sabotage leading to the acquisition of the houseboat die "Reiher"

Pretty much the same documents as per count one.

On count three: fraud and sabotage in the acquisition of farm Pichler at Seefeld im Tyrol.

He had the statement from Streidle, the Munich agent explaining his role in the scheme, witnessed and signed by a Major in the new German army. Next to that was a transcript of the conversation he had with his brother. Completing this impressive array of damning evidence was a signed confession from Hochwald, the disreputable chemist at the university, admitting to developing, supplying and even delivering the potions which were used on Anton's stock.

On count four: *sexual and physical abuse of a minor.*

He had reached the far end of the table. Here lay two police statements; one from Maria Libaski, a fourteen year old Polish girl (sexual assault) and another from a Doktor Grunebel, a local physician specialising in the treatment of sexually transmitted diseases (assault). Last of all, there was a report from the Pressburg police detailing their investigation into the Count's activities, dating from three years ago and a request for sequestration of his financial records.

He opened his eyes. The kitchen table was bare, completely and absolutely bare! He had nothing! And yet to his mind, there could be little doubt as to the Count's guilt. No – that was wrong! There was NO doubt, none whatsoever.

***

'That was delicious – you are clever!'

Pichler, like any man, was always happy to receive plaudits on his culinary efforts. Several times a week, he was the chief cook and bottle washer. He couldn't do cakes or any fancy stuff but if it was a case of frying, he was your man. He had been since the age of about ten; too puny to help with the heavy duty farm work, his early efforts in the kitchen freed up his mama to help papa and Anton. And later in the army of course where he became the master of the one-pan meal for ten, invariably cooked over a camp fire!

Tonight it was fried fish, fried potatoes and green beans all washed down with something suitable and a bite of cheese to follow.

He closed the book. 'Well, what did you think of that?'

'Wonderful. It was simply wonderful! Oh, I should so adore seeing it performed!' replied Anna. 'And wasn't Portia clever, the way she led Shylock on, boxed him into a corner, but ever so slowly. He didn't realise what was happening, did he? And then *just* when he thought he'd won… the coup de grace!'

Anna ran her fingers across the glass-less watch that hung at her waist. The winder was at three o'clock, the setter at twelve. She felt for the little hand.

'Nearly eleven!' she stated. 'I'm ready for my bed.'

Pichler looked at the mantelpiece – five to the hour it was.

'I'll be up later – I've some thinking to do.'

'Well, don't sit up all night. I know what you're like.'

He knew now that he'd never get any signed statements. The Count had exercised just too much control over his minions for too long for *that* to be possible. Once fear takes root in a body it takes much more than normal levels of courage to fight it. Some people might say foolhardy levels of courage. Slota had told him so.

'You've made a lot more progress than the Inspector and I did. However the hard truth is that we were never closer than a mile away from getting the swine before a judge. To be brutal old son, all you've done is cut that to about half a mile. The sod's untouchable and unaccountable – an unaccountable Count you might say, though in his case I'd spell it without the "o"!'

So without a shred of evidence that would stand up in court, what were his options? Should he just let it go, let him get away with it all and see Anton and all the other poor souls completely ruined?

It was all too infuriating for words. He knew he had his man, knew it with absolute certainty. But knowing it and proving it are a chasm apart.

He dozed off and dreamt of the Count. There he was, pompous, pontificating, arrogant, self-confident, *over* confident even. He woke up with a start to find an unfamiliar name lodged in his head. It was the name of a character in a play written by a long dead playwright – a character who was pretending to be a lawyer – but not just any old run of the mill lawyer. No! One who was a "wise and upright judge", according to the old Jew!

A journalist calls:

Herr Stammer arrived at the Count's house situated in the fashionable end of Pressburg. He was not particularly impressed. It was not dissimilar to the two houses either side – one a family residence, the other a firm of solicitors. But then the Count had many other residences, two of which could even float.

‘Good morning, sir,’ sneered the lanky fellow as he gave Stammer the once over.

‘I wonder if the Count would be able to spare me a few moments of his valuable time?’ smiled Stammer.

‘May I ask what this is about, sir?’ asked the Count’s man servant.

‘Of course, of course, do forgive me. My name is Stammer, Otto Stammer. I am the features editor of the Pressburg Leben. Perhaps you’re one of our readers?’

The man effected a blank expression. Undaunted, Stammer pressed on.

‘Here is my card. We are interested in writing a series of articles on notable residents of the town. We would very much like the Count to be the first to feature in this series.’ He smiled encouragingly, hoping that his explanation would at the very least merit an interview.

‘Very well, sir. Please wait here!’

Stammer took a hasty step back as the man made it clear that the door was about to be shut, with him firmly on the outside. The man proceeded up the stairs at a leisurely pace and knocked on the door of the Count’s study – no reason for him to hurry himself for the likes of a journalist, was there?

The man relayed all that he’d just been told.

‘What did you say his name was, Raeder?

His man handed him the card which the Count perused at some length.

'Find me a copy of Pressburg Life in the rack over by the corner.'

It wasn't a journal that featured on his regular reading list, not unless there was something about him in it. He opened it to the inside page and there he saw…

Editor – Fritz Segler

Features Editor – Otto Stammer.

'Very well Raeder, show the fellow up.'

Stammer recognised the Count lounging in his chair and smiled engagingly but did not receive any greeting in return, other than a…

'Well?'

'Thank you so much for agreeing to see me, Count. I am very grateful for…'

'Yes, yes! Just *get* on with it!'

'Well, Count let me begin by admitting that I have a confession to make.'

The Count sat up in his chair, his expression changing from boredom to anger in a flash.

'What the devil do you mean? Have you entered my house under false pretences?'

'No, no, no, Count, I do assure you. Please, forgive my clumsiness. What I mean to say is that we *are* planning a series of articles on the Empire's great men – such as your good self – only *not* in the Pressburg Life. No indeed! It is to be a far grander project than that and if I might add,' Stammer leant forward conspiratorially at this point, 'our patron is none other than the,' he almost mouthed the words, 'the *Emperor*!'

Stammer noticed that the Count looked neither angry nor bored anymore.

'I didn't want to speak out of turn in front of your man, but with you, sir, I may be completely candid.'

'Go on!' replied a somewhat mollified von Wittenburg.

'As you may know sir many people, including his Majesty, are greatly concerned about the tensions which exist between the Empire's various ethnic groups. It is imperative that these should not spill over into any form of violence.'

The Count nodded sagely at this point.

'To that end, my Editor suggested to our proprietor, some months ago as it happens, that perhaps the nobility were the glue that could bind these groups together. It seems that all this has recently reached the ear of his Majesty. We are given to understand that he has smiled on the proposal.'

'Which is what exactly?' asked the Count, all ears now that a certain gentleman's name or perhaps it was rather the title, had been mentioned.

'It will be an entirely new publication to be called "All the Emperor's Men". It will feature a series of articles on the lives of the great men drawn from all parts of the Empire. Hungarian nobles will read of Bohemian nobles and Croatians of Polish ones.'

'I see! And you want me to feature as the first of these great men?'

'Indeed we do, Count. Your name has been floated before a certain Royal gentleman and he has given it his provisional blessing.''

'And what exactly do you have in mind?'

'Well, sir, I was fortunate enough to attend your excellent lecture a few days ago so I already have a good deal of copy. In hopeful anticipation that you would agree, my editor commissioned me to conduct a series of initial interviews.'

'Interviews?' interrupted the Count, almost as if he didn't like the sound of that.

'Amongst people with whom you are acquainted, my dear sir,' responded Stammer. 'For background information, you understand. Just imagine what would happen if we were to uncover any skeletons in your cupboard after we'd formally proposed your name to his majesty.'

The Count shifted uneasily in his seat.

'You don't have any skeletons in your cupboard, do you Count? Ha, ha! Of course not… the very idea!'

The Count nodded throughout this explanation. This all seemed most satisfactory. Then a frown flickered across his face.

'I would retain full editorial rights?'

'Naturally, Count. Nothing would be published that you were not entirely happy with.'

The Count smiled for the first time. 'Raeder… Raeder…!' he bellowed.

The man appeared somewhat flustered. God, what had he done wrong now?

'Some Madeira for my guest and myself.'

The nobleman spoke without interruption for a good half hour, ignoring any attempt by Stammer to interrupt his flow with a question. Finally, he ran out of steam.

'So who *have* you interviewed about me thus far?'

'Well it is quite a long list actually sir, surprisingly so in fact. Your reputation has preceded you over most of the Western half of the Empire.'

The Count beamed at the journalist.

'Well then, let me see. I had the pleasure of talking to your man, not Herr Raeder, no, no. I mean the gentleman who assisted you during your lecture. *What* an interesting fellow! In fact we partook of some libation during our little talk. My goodness, can that man drink! I wouldn't dare to imbibe so deeply myself for fear that it would loosen my tongue. Who knows what indiscretions I might commit?'

Stammer laughed at this own joke – the Count didn't!

'Excellent Madeira, Count,' he added raising his glass before continuing. 'Tell me sir, could you enlighten me – what exactly *is* a yacht rating declaration form? Your man rattled on about it at some length and I must say it all sounded rather salacious. I never knew boats could be quite so interesting.'

The Count opened his mouth as if to say something but closed it immediately as it was now Stammer's turn to hold forth without interruption.

'Then I met another chap, a Herr Streidle. He lives in Munich you know, well of course you do. And who else was there? Oh, yes, I have spoken to two doctors; a Doktor Grunebel who I believe you've had occasion to consult very recently.'

Stammer paused to study the Count's features with obvious concern.

'You are not in any discomfort at the moment, are you m'dear sir? Please say if you are and we may continue some other time.'

Rather than offer any comfort, Stammer's solicitude served only to irritate him further, which was obviously the *last* thing the journalist had intended!

'Now where was I? Oh yes – Doktor Hochwald up at the university. An odd fellow but a dab hand at "treating" our bovine friends. Yes, I understand his work has come to the attention of the Vice Chancellor. Oh dear me… I *do* hope my letter to the VC does not cause any unpleasantness for the good Doktor.'

The Count made to rise from his chair but was stalled in mid-pose as Stammer continued through his list. There was a farmer in the Tyrol with a startling story to tell and a young lady who he'd so recently entertained on his houseboat.

'I should say sir,' whispered Stammer conspiratorially, 'I interviewed the young lady in an "establishment", if you know what I mean. A quite amazing place – some of the ladies asked to be remembered to you. I only hope my wife never finds out I've been to such a place – she might get entirely the wrong idea!'

Stammer concluded his speech with an angelic smile, a smile that was altogether too much for the Count to stomach.

He rose to his full height and lunged – there was no other way to describe it – across his desk in a desperate attempt to throttle the journalist. Expecting such a move at any time in his diatribe, Herr Stammer was able to step smartly back.

'If you ever, *ever* print this pack of lies, I shall sue you for every penny your lousy rag is worth!'

The redness slowly drained from his face as he calmed down. His snarl became a smile – something had just occurred to him.

'Finklestein… he's the owner of the Life, isn't he, hmmm?'

Stammer was instantly stilled.

'Oh, you gave me quite a fright there for a moment, you young rascal. Let me explain. The Herzog von Finklestein is one of us, by which I mean one of *me,* not one of *you*, you pathetic little scumbag. Whatever you may think you have, he won't print it.'

Stammer did exactly that. 'Bbbuut, I, I wi…will bring a private pro..pro..sec.ution!'

'Ha! The police will do nothing; their betters simply would not permit it. And for why? Well, you see, my fine fellow, it's like this. The Empire, this magnificent edifice four hundred years in the making, is really no more than the most enormous social pyramid. At the tip, the very tip, so far above your level that it is lost in the clouds, is a club; a very select club. At its top sit the Imperial family, all those Emperors and Empresses, those Kings and Queens, Crown Princes and Archdukes, the very ones you common folk are so willing to don smart uniforms and march off to die for. Below these exalted ones are the aristocracy; the Dukes and Duchess', the Counts and Countesses. Second tier we may be but we are the cement of this "club". We mix with our betters all the time. Indeed their Royal Highnesses' pleasures would be greatly curtailed without the social diversions – I may say intercourse – which we "aristo's" provide.'

'Do you deny that you sent a man to burn down farm buildings, infect the livestock and cripple the business of a number of farms in the Tyrol?'

'I *could*, but I *won't*!'

'Well then, do you deny that one of your lackeys deliberately flooded the dry dock at the Neptune boatyard in Trieste – causing extensive damage to the yacht that *you'd* ordered – allowing you to engineer the collapse of a family business – one that dated back to the 18th Century?'

'My, my, you *are* a tedious fellow. Do you intend to list all of my misdemeanours? Well, let me cut to the chase – guilty on all counts!' He even smirked as he said it.

Stammer's anger mounted. He could hardly believe his ears – the nerve of this rascal. But he'd admitted it – he'd admitted it all… and that was all he needed to hear! Confirmation and… vindication for what was to follow!

'Let there be no misunderstanding Count. You are content for me to make these facts known to the press?' replied Stammer, who was stammering no longer.

'The press! Good God, weren't you listening, you imbecile? The newspaper proprietors are in the club, aristocrats to a man. Do you think their editors print whatever their fancy dictates? They print what they're told.'

'Forgive me,' replied Stammer with apparent sincerity and worryingly for the Count – calmness. 'I was referring to the back-street press, some call it the gutter-press. You know the sort of thing, tens of thousands of leaflets distributed on the street corners of every city in the Empire, freely available to the working classes.'

'And who's going to pay for all this, eh? You? You don't look as if you can even afford a decent suit!'

'Now *there* I have a surprise for you. I'd rather anticipated your reaction and as you may have already guessed... my editor has no knowledge of my presence here today.'

'And your surprise is...?' said the Count, rather unsettled by the man's coolness and no, he hadn't realised this villain was pursuing his own agenda. He did now, though!

'My friends have been in contact with organisations who have no love for the Empire and who would jump at the chance to heap a bit of – in your case *a lot* of – calumny onto Austria's so-called ennobled classes. Indeed, you'd be surprised just how many there are; wealthy irredentists, revolutionaries and fellow travellers, not to mention foreign powers. Impossible to sue these people I should imagine. You'd have to find them first!'

'But that's illegal!' he boomed, the irony of such an accusation completely lost on him.

'As you say, sir, it is illegal – completely illegal. Obviously *I* wouldn't dream of deliberately handing this scurrilous hearsay to such despicable anti-monarchists. Like you sir, I am first and foremost a patriot.'

The Count squirmed awkwardly at this. It was probably the first time in his life that anybody, anywhere had accused *him* of being a patriot.

'But things do get left in some odd places don't they sir and goodness knows how we'd ever get such sensitive information back under *our* control.'

Our control. OUR control! Damn it, the swine was talking as if they had a common interest. The anger sparked a defiant response.

'Very well, you villain. Go ahead. Yes. Go ahead. Distribute your catalogue of tittle-tattle to the great-unwashed. Do you think anything will come of it? Do you *really* think his Majesty would ever give credence to such piffle?'

'Oh, I know the charge of abusing a young prostitute would cause you little harm,' answered back Stammer, his disgust evident in every syllable he uttered. 'It might even enhance your reputation amongst the "chaps", which is to both your and their eternal shame.'

'Yes, I'm sure you right on that score,' sneered the Count, confident once more as he sat back in his chair, a lascivious sneer spreading over his features.

'But swindling his Majesty's subjects, I suspect for many years, is an entirely different matter. You have been enriching yourself at the expense of his hard-working, Kaiser-treu people, the very bedrock of his Empire, the people he relies on to fight his wars.'

'Oh yes, he won't be at all happy to hear about any member of the ruling class being associated with such accusations, I will concede that much. But I will simply deny them. He'll believe me and that will be the end of the matter. After all, we have broken bread together, not to mention some very fine wines on numerous occasions – all, I might add, at my expense. Same club, do you see?'

'But are you *entirely* sure that his Majesty will simply take your word for it? The Emperor will surely want to make enquiries…'

The Count guffawed – this *was* proving to be a most entertaining morning.

'Of course he will *ask*. He'll ask a chosen few, discretely of course. Some will genuinely know nothing. Others will have their suspicions, but will *say* nothing.'

'But what if the Emperor has his own trusted men, men he can rely on, perhaps not people of your station Count but…'

Stammer paused and appeared to think for a moment.

'What about this rumour of an Emperor's detective – a commoner who has done the Emperor good-service in the past and well, the Emperor might order him to investigate… he might be listened to…'

'Ha, ha ha. Complete hockum, my poor deluded fellow. Emperor's detective, indeed! I've heard this rumour too – one legged blighter, isn't he? – which only adds to the implausibility of the whole thing. Complete poppycock – no such fellow. D'you *really* think that his Majesty would bestow so great an honour on one such as this? Mind you, just as well for me and my friends. An incorruptible person from the lower orders, one who has the ear of the Emperor! The establishment would never survive it,' and he laughed heartily at his own joke.

Pausing to wipe his eye, using his monogramed handkerchief naturally, the Count sat back in his chair and reached for his hand bell.

'Well thank you *so much* for the entertainment you have provided me with today. D'you know, you really ought to consider a career on the stage. Why don't you? I'm sure the "chaps" as you call them and I would be only too happy to patronise you – we might even throw some coins in your direction – what d'you think of that idea?'

Stammer paused but a second before reaching down and opening the briefcase he'd brought with him. It contained instructions to the agents that only required the Count's signature and their addresses to be added. And a confession – *that* would also need the Count's signature. *And* there was one last item, one encased in a glass covered frame.

'What's this, a picture of your disgusting family or those of one of these men I have ruined? Are you playing your last card, trading on my sympathy? This grows tiresome – *you* grow tiresome, now…'

The "picture" crossed the desk.

'YOU?" exclaimed the Count.

Picher stood, put his left leg on a nearby stool, lifted his trouser leg just a fraction and tapped his leg firmly three times with a glass paper weight snatched from the Count's desk.

There had been many "shots" fired during their battle but the dull thud of glass on wood spoke louder than any sounds that had come before.

The Count slumped in his seat, for reality had finally struck home. And it was a very unpalatable reality. With this rascal whispering in the Emperor's ear, a full acquittal seemed unlikely, no… impossible.

He was right about one thing; the Emperor himself might be damaged by association if this ever reached the ears of the great unwashed. No, he was safe from public disgrace. He would probably be permitted to keep his houses, his boats and most of his money.

But privately… if the King-Emperor believed, *really* believed he was everything the pamphlets said he was *then* he was finished. Whatever might be said in public, he would be black listed, shunned, a social outcast.

And that meant – no more invitations – no more impromptu Royal visits – no more hunting trips where his opinion of the Hungarian renegades or of the Polish situation would be sought. And worse! This cold-shouldering would not go unnoticed by his peers. He would disappear from their inner circle as quickly as his boats if they were to be holed below the waterline. And that was exactly what had just happened!

He looked up at the now standing Pichler and just nodded; deflated… dejected… diminished! Pichler moved to the window and waved at the rather stocky gentleman standing on the pavement across the road.

'Raeder!' called Pichler in his best military voice.

'Ah, Raeder! I presume you've been listening all this while. Go downstairs and answer the door. It'll be the police. Then come straight back here.'

The man's face was a picture of confusion. Answer the door, but nobody had…?

KNOCK-KNOCK-KNOCK! And he was off!

'Now Count, I'm afraid I must trouble you for your pocket book,' continued Pichler.

'My pocket book? What the devil do you want *that* for?'

'Well, you *surely* don't expect *me* to pay for digging you out of the very deep hole you are currently sitting in?'

At that moment Pichler heard the steady plod of Sergeant Slota proceeding along the landing, followed by an extremely agitated Herr Raeder. It was likely that he'd been on the receiving end of some very sharp words from the Sergeant and was now on his best behaviour. His nervous face appeared in the doorway.

'Ah, Herr Raeder! Wait outside the study until I call for you,' said Pichler. 'You are then to collect up ALL the files which the Count will request when I've finished instructing him. Give these to the Sergeant and find him a comfy chair and a desk so he can address some envelopes.'

The man nodded obediently and turned away but was stopped by yet another command.

'Oh and Raeder, the Count and the Sergeant will need pen and ink… plenty of ink.'

It all took another three hours, even with Slota's help. The telegrams were the first to go off – fourteen in all – the addresses coming from the Count's surprisingly compact but highly informative "black-book". They all said the same thing!

"URGENT – Special loans contracts – Cancel all outstanding repaymts – Ack receipt by teleg – Rep to Pressburg police stn immed – FAO J Slota – Confirm lets in post – EvW"

The letters of confirmation only required topping and tailing, though Pichler insisted that they be sealed as well.

'I am to cancel *all* the outstanding payments? My God, you'll ruin me,' whined the Count.

Pichler leant over to reach, somewhat theatrically, into his briefcase, where the "picture" it's job done, now reposed. The Count waved to signal his acquiescence.

His final show of resistance was to pretend he'd lost his seal. An icy stare between Pichler and the Count's man was sufficient to galvanise the latter into action. That search proved to be *extremely* brief for the fellow understood that he was as deeply mired in the slurry pit as his master was.

The confession, which was soon to find a home in Slota's bottom drawer at the station, took rather longer. The Count hummed and hawed over each phrase to begin with, but after ten successive "just sign it, Count", he gave in and did just that.

While Slota wrote, Pichler read through the "black-book", making a few notes and nodding at some familiar names. At one point Slota stuck his head around the door.

'I'll take the little book shall I? I can put it next to its new friend,' by which he meant the recently signed confession.

'Fancy a drink, gentlemen?' he smirked at the Count and then left without waiting for an answer.

Pichler wasn't surprised and couldn't begrudge his friend. Policemen never get them all – or anything like – but when you get a big one, well, it makes the whole job seem worthwhile again.

The Count stood up as if to go. Pichler glared at him and he promptly sat down again. Slota needed time to get the telegrams off. Pichler wasn't taking any chances that this particularly slippery eel might try to get to the telegram office first.

In the hostile silence that followed, Pichler set to musing. It wasn't total victory. True, he and Slota had cut off this source of income. He might have to sell his boats or hotel to get by. But he would still be free to circulate within the social circles of the elite, still be free to try his hand at other unscrupulous schemes.

Pichler wondered whether the same thought had occurred to the scoundrel or even that he might attempt to thwart today's efforts. Time for one last salvo then as he stood by the study door…

'I'll be watching you Count… and so will the Pressburg police department. Now don't you go forgetting, they have your signed confession under lock and key which is exactly where it will remain, providing…'

The Count looked up. Just for once his expression was a humble one – a wholly novel experience for him. He'd been beaten. But then again, the Empire was a very big Empire and Buda-pest was particularly pleasant at this time of year or so he'd been told.

On the pavement outside, Pichler looked up at the room he'd spent the last few hours in. It was the only card he had to play. But he swore to himself that he would never abuse the certificate entrusted to him by his Majesty in this way, *ever* again. Well… hardly ever!

He walked to the post office, where he found Slota waiting for him.

'All telegrams and letters safely despatched. I don't think I've ever had to lick so many stamps in such a short period of time,' said Slota smacking his lips as he spoke.

‘Good job, Ján,’ said Pichler. ‘I couldn’t have managed without you.’

‘My pleasure! And now, Herr Pichler, I must arrest you on a charge of attempted blackmail of one of the Empire’s most beloved aristocrats.’

‘Are you open to a bribe?’ grinned Pichler. ‘Bearing in mind how thirsty you must be after all that stamp-licking.’

Slota’s grin was even broader than the one he’d treated the Count to, just a short time before.

As they walked, Slota remembered one other thing.

‘By the way, I posted that letter to your journalist friend in Innsbruck? You’ve got ‘em tucked all over the Empire, haven’t you, K-P? Ex-army pals you can call on for all sorts of favours. Didn’t have anything to do with this little escapade, did it?’

Pichler just grinned. ‘A *large* beer is it then, Ján?’

Seefeld:

The “Rest” was packed that night. Everybody was talking about the front page of the Innsbruck Reporter. And a decent length article it was as well. Apparently the Reporter had had a tip-off to be on the lookout for a poisoner cum arsonist, name of Hans Schmidt. He wasn’t from around here naturally. Of course with a name like Schmidt it was bound to be an alias so little chance of catching the swine, but at least the police had the incident on record.

But the real news was that Anton was completely blameless for his barn catching fire and for the death of so many of his cows. The farm had been sabotaged by "friend" Schmidt. He'd been targeted because like most of the farmers in the village, he had no or only minimal insurance. There was some hint in the article of a firm in Munich having their sticky fingers in this pie. All those in the "Rest" that night agreed – only what you'd expect from those big-city Bavarian types.

Some brandished letters that they'd just received from the Tyrolian Farmers Association, outlining some reputable brokers who were offering very reasonable premiums and warning against the dangers of using non-approved agents. Anton had not received his yet, but had received a different letter and it was a far more significant one. It was hard to describe the relief. The loan repayments had been cancelled and he was in the clear. Gott sei Dank!

For once Anton's mother had been tempted out of the house and sat next to her son nursing a small glass of white wine. And why not!

'It's almost unbelievable, Anton. How *could* such a wonderful thing be possible?'

'I don't know mother, I really don't. I can only surmise that some more lucrative financial opportunity arose for the rogue who so nearly brought us to utter ruin. Perhaps small beer like us were more trouble than we were worth. We'd already repaid more than we'd borrowed. Maybe he'd made enough out of us to move onto some other unsuspecting honest fellow.'

Frau Pichler stared long and hard into her half empty glass of Riesling. The thought had been bothering her ever since she'd read the letter.

'You don't think Klaus could have had something to do with it, do you, Anton?'

'What, you mean freeing us of our debt… and discovering that we'd been sabotaged. No, mother! I really don't. He's just a teacher after all. The very idea is preposterous, simply preposterous!'

THE MERRY WIDOWERS

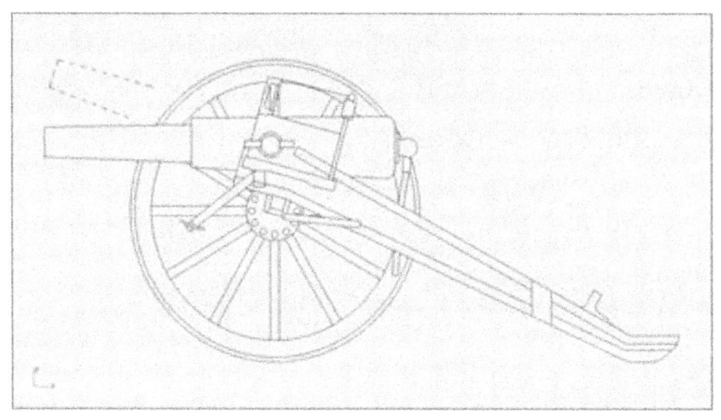

Josef Grün – 1914

German military intelligence, Berlin, 1867:

'It has been approved, approved by the great man himself.'

'The Kaiser, you mean, sir?' replied the Colonel.

'Higher than that Erich,' said the General, pointing theatrically towards Heaven as he spoke.

'Sir, do you mean the *Chancellor*?' which received a nod of affirmation and a broad smile.

'Listen Erich, he's *very* enthusiastic about us keeping as close an eye as possible on the Austrians. We may have just beaten them in the war, but that doesn't mean they aren't capable of causing us a good deal of trouble in the future. And that close eye means embedding our people at the very heart of government. And since we can't place then in the actual seats of power, the next best thing is to embed them in a more literal sense.'

'Did you mention the possibility that we might need to create, how should I put it, "vacancies" that our ladies can move into, sir?'

'I really don't think we need to trouble the Chancellor with the minutiae, do you Erich?'

The Erste Division Club, Vienna, 1872:

The "Erste" was the premier club for the Empire's most senior governmental officials. It was established during the reign of Josef the Second in 1788 and was founded according to rumour on the site of a much earlier masonic lodge. It was a serious club for serious people. There was also a "zweite" club for more junior officials. It bore a less pejorative name and was an altogether much jollier place to spend an evening.

Maximillian Kasselbaum was rather surprised to receive an invitation to dine there. He *had* been to the "Erste" numerous times before but not for the last three years. Even more surprising – the invite was from the *same* man who'd invited him previously. That man was one Christian von der Osten. They weren't close friends, more like colleagues, although even that wasn't completely accurate. They were men whose paths had crossed at various stages over the last three decades. They'd first met up in the mid-forties. Kasselbaum was a recently qualified army surgeon, considered to be a very promising specimen by those around him. Von der Osten on the other hand was a rather staid junior officer who seemed destined for a career in army administration. And so it was to prove. But the man had used what talents he possessed to good effect. He'd reached the position of right hand man of the Minister for Munitions. Whatever papers the Minister saw, von der Osten had seen them first. In most cases, *he'd* written them.

The "First" had a reputation for always employing the very best chefs in Vienna. It also had a reputation for poaching such culinary geniuses from rival clubs. For this reason alone it was adored by its members. It was despised by everyone else – for the very same reason. Perhaps it was only this that made Max look forward to the evening with such eager anticipation. It certainly won't have been the company. Von der Osten was what one would call a "dull-dog". He would drone on about the minutia of his job for most of the evening, barely pausing to ask how life was treating his dining companion.

Originally, Max had salved his conscience about not going "halves" because he was the one doing the travelling. He'd assumed that he'd pay when von der Osten visited his club in Pressburg. But this return visit never happened despite many offers. In the end Max considered that he was paying for his supper as a listening companion – even if his attention was apt to wander.

But all that was before the break. They hadn't fallen out, nothing like that. It was the accident that had transformed this functioning civil servant into a tragic, self-absorbed shell of a man. His wife had been on her way to meet him – it was their twenty-fifth wedding anniversary of all things. The restaurant was booked, a cake prepared, though he, busy man that he was, intended to come directly from his office. She didn't mind, she was used to him after all these years. He arrived to find a crowd gathered around a cab, one fellow trying to restrain a terrified horse, another comforting the cab's driver. A waiter had come out of the restaurant and tactfully placed a large table cloth over the body. The accounts of the driver and the few passers-by who'd actually witnessed the tragedy were confused and contradictory. The verdict – accidental death – did nothing to lessen von der Osten's grief.

And that grief penetrated to the heart of his very soul and never lessened its grip thereof. He continued to work and he continued to serve the Minister just as he had previously. Inside he was dead, as dead as the woman he'd loved for a quarter of a century. Max had tried to offer him comfort. So did all his friends and associates. The widower, though, would have none of it. Had he not had his work to sustain him, Max was in no doubt – he would not be alive today. With that depressing thought in his head, Max looked up to see his host arrive. He steeled himself. How was he to get through the next two hours? What in God's name would they talk about?

'Ah, Max, my old friend! Goodness me, you have aged since we last met. What *have* you been up to?'

Max was too stunned to speak. This was the last thing he'd expected. He stared at von der Osten trying to convince himself that it really *was* von der Osten.

'Er!' was as much as he could manage.

'Well, let's not dilly-dally old chap. Roast beef and red wine beckon. I could eat a horse. Waiter!'

The conversation was totally one-sided. Von der Osten did *all* the talking. Max didn't even get to ask "and how's the Minister treating you these days?" Just as well. The subject of work never came up, not once. Not the Minister, not his latest ingenious plan for reorganising the ministry, nothing! It was all "Viktoria this" or "Viktoria that". How clever she was, how beautiful she was, how widely travelled she was, how lucky *he* was. And then out came the photograph.

Max's head was starting to spin and it was nothing to do with the Claret. He looked at her photograph many, many times. He didn't have any option – the fellow kept pressing it back into his hand as he pointed out yet another feature of this goddess's face.

Sitting in his Viennese hotel room that night utterly exhausted after this two-hour verbal bombardment, Max set to thinking. The whole affair was odd. Not that after three years of mourning, von der Osten should want to move on. No, it wasn't that. He had been transformed into a kind of giddy schoolboy. The sainted Viktoria looked at least fifteen years younger. She wasn't what Max would have called a beauty, handsome was a better description. But if she'd been sixty with a wart on the end of her nose, he'd still have reckoned her a good catch for a man like von der Osten.

He was bald, short-sighted, round shouldered and in normal times just about the most tedious creature to have ever walked on God's earth. Of course younger women *do* fall for older men, but not men like this, surely. He pictured them walking arm in arm through the Stadtpark with von der Osten blissfully oblivious to the amazed looks emanating from passers-by.

Was he being cruel? After all they say love is blind. Maybe he was, but he'd hate to see the old boy's heart broken for a second time. Was she after his money? Hard to believe – he was comfortably off but hardly rolling in it. So if it *wasn't* true love and it *wasn't* for money, what the devil *was* the explanation?

The Imperial Security Service, Vienna:

1867 was a watershed year. Out went Francis the First's Austrian Empire of 1804 – in came the new Austro-Hungarian Empire. Out went the old Habsburg colours of black over yellow – in came any number of variants of red, white and green. Even the Emperor's position changed. There was now to be an Emperor in the west and a King in the east, though not the *entire* east. The isolated land of Galicia to the north of the Hungarian crownlands, bordering Russia was also part of the Western crownlands. The fact that Franz-Josef sat on both thrones only added to the fun. Other European nations looked on with bemusement.

For old Napoleonic warriors like General Erich von Ulmnitz, the loss of the old Schwarz-gelb standard was a sore one. Apart from that the Austro-Hungarian compromise of 1867 had worked out pretty well for him. Although the Imperial Security Service was based in Vienna and *in theory* responsible for both halves of the new Empire, in practice this wasn't the case. Von Ulmnitz now need only concern himself with the Austrian half. Well that was easy. All he had to worry about was the Tyrol, Salzburg, Carithia, Carniola, Küstenland, Dalmatia, Styria, Lower and Upper Austria, Bohemia, Moravia, Silesia and far-off Galicia. He didn't need to bother himself with the Hungarians, the Slovakians, the Serbians and the Romanians… just the Germans, the Czechs, the Italians, the Slovenes, the Poles and the Ukrainians.

Though his title was Director General, von Ulmnitz was a good few rungs down the ladder from being the top dog. Fortunately for him, most of his – in his view "so-called" – superiors were the type that liked to delegate. General Erich von Ulmnitz was the grateful beneficiary.

Over the years he'd been able to plug most of the gaps in the leaky old tub that was the ISD. The problem with rotten apples in the service was not finding them. They usually gave themselves away at some point in their traitorous activities. The problem was knowing what to do with them *once* they'd been identified.

They could be publicly tried and executed but that only served to alert their masters. They would immediately instruct their other subversives to dive for cover, leaving von Ulmnitz to have to start all over again.

"Accidents" were always an option but for a mass outbreak of the "disease", this approach attracted too much attention. The last thing he wanted was to alert his opposite numbers in Paris, Berlin and St Petersburg.

Von Ulmnitz's solution was what he himself had termed the "three-cell" structure. This involved no more than three men working together in an office which only they had access to. These men didn't know what the other cells were up to. Three such cells constituted a "triangle", each controlled by a senior officer. He knew nothing beyond the activities of his own triangle. And von Ulmnitz? He knew everything!

The beauty of this scheme was that any rotten apple could be safely left in place. He'd be totally unaware – as would his two, *hopefully*, loyal colleagues – that he'd been rumbled. The cell would then be redesignated with a "D" in the DG's files – as in "D" for disinformation. In this way he could funnel any codswallop he liked through a D-cell without anybody being any the wiser. The "anybodies" here were of course those "nice" gentlemen in Paris, Berlin and St Petersburg.

All in all, he felt paying the wages of a single cell was a small price to pay for the havoc he could wreak amongst the Emperor's enemies. Cutting off a hand with an infected finger was vastly preferable to cutting off the entire arm.

The key to making his system work was the "gang of five", his five trusted men each one a Colonel. One man was placed by von Ulmnitz in each of the five principal cities of Prague, Trieste, Krakow and Lemberg and of course Vienna.

The monthly meeting was almost over. No internal traitors had been found now for over a year. Excellent, the system was working.

The development of a new suicide capsule for the ISD's own people was going less well. The old style glass phials from thirty years ago were still in use by field agents. These worked *only* if it was obvious that there was no way out *and* there was enough time to break the phial. Many agents had heard those terrifying words "We have you surrounded, give up and you'll be well-treated" – terrifying because the translation was "give yourself up and we'll torture you for several days before executing you".

But if the man was arrested on suspicion only, then most seasoned agents would try to bluff it out. By that time the phial would have been discovered and removed.

They'd tried several new approaches to date. One was to plant capsules under the skin. In theory this method would allow some breathing space for the agent to decide if the game was truly up. Some phials were so thick that a hammer was needed. Others so liable to fracture that many piglets were sent to that great pig sty in the sky well before their time.

'Carry on working on it, Oberst Kaminski,' said the DG as he closed the meeting.

'Oberst Hajek, a moment of your time if you please.'

Colonel Alexej Hajek had been expecting this.

'So then Alexej – where are we?'

'The lady's name is Eliska Novakova. She is thirty eight years old. Her husband, one Jan Novak was a design engineer at the Skoda works near Plzen. He died three years ago as a result of an explosion, for which she blamed the company. Her father was an instructor at the Prague Military Academy, teaching mainly ballistics theory to artillery officer cadets. He died in 1862. The lady did not attend any finishing school. However I understand that nevertheless, she is something of an accomplished socialite. She is reported as having exceptional powers of recall *and* a mathematical brain that would put most of us to shame. Furthermore it seems likely that her father will have filled the inquiring mind of the young Eliska with a working knowledge of ballistics. I believe, General, we would be most wise to assume that all of this is true – at least until we know better.'

General von Ulmnitz nodded throughout Hajek's report but said nothing. He was silent for several minutes after he'd finished. Hajek made to ask a question but the General halted him in mid-sentence with a slight lifting of one finger.

'Did a certain Frau Rubach come up in the course of your investigations, Alexej?'

'Viktoria Rubach! Yes, General. Apparently she and Frau Novakova attend the same social events,' replied Colonel Hajek. 'Why do you ask, sir?'

Von Ulmnitz answered that question with one of his own. 'Are the two women close, do you know?'

'I believe not, sir, but will make further enquiries.'

'And how is the liaison between Dvorak and this Novakova woman progressing?' asked the General.

'Well sir, as you know, General Dvorak lost his wife some years ago, cancer of the breast I seem to recall. He was devoted to her and wore the locket she'd given to him when they married always close to his heart. Nobody was more surprised than I to learn that Frau Novakova's likeness now occupies her place in this treasured locket. Furthermore, my "spies" tell me that Novakova has been telling anyone who will listen to expect a happy event in the very near future.'

'I see! That certainly seems serious. Well, as the General is on the "Hercules" steering committee, we cannot afford to ignore this romance. It may be entirely innocent but she does seem eminently well qualified to winkle out any secrets from the man. Of course that in itself does not signify evil intent. Some women collect secrets just for the pleasure of having them. He is not a key player after all, not actually charged with any technical or develop-mental responsibilities. When did he formally retire?'

'Er, three years ago when he reached the age of sixty.'

'You mean he is twenty five years her senior! Please tell me he is a veritable Adonis and she is as plain as a pikestaff!'

'No, sir. Almost the contrary in fact!'

'Now Alexej, you *do* have me worried. We need to watch this one like a hawk. Can the General's man be relied on to be our ears?'

'We've hit a snag there, sir.'

'The problem being…?' asked the DG.

'It's Protek, the General's old servant and I do mean old, sir. His memory is not up to much. Even if we were to brief him only with the absolute minimum, he's bound to let the cat out of the bag. As your "inside" man, he'd be next to useless.'

General von Ulmnitz grimaced, his face creasing into a dozen lines. Then a smile appeared. He explained and followed this with a list of arrangements that he required Hajek to put in place by two days hence.

'And what should I tell your man when I get to take him in hand, about this Novakova woman, I mean, sir?'

'As little as possible,' replied General von Ulmnitz. This was *not* the answer that Colonel Hajek was expecting.

That ended the meeting, for the General had some arranging of his own to do.

Pichler's house:

Anna was silent. She'd listened to everything her unexpected guest had put to her, nodding her acquiescence at intervals.

'Of course, it's mainly because I don't want you to feel lonely. I appreciate that it must be difficult for you to cope without a *little* bit of help. Frau Neuburg is very accomplished,' von Ulmnitz glanced at the piano before adding, 'a soprano of some merit, I believe.'

Anna smiled a fraction – this was the General trying to be as tactful as he was able.

'And of course, Sergeant Slota will drop by from time to time to check all is well.'

'Ah,' paused von Ulmnitz. He had hoped she wouldn't ask this but it was inevitable. 'Two to three weeks at most, but we'll get him back to you as soon as we can.'

To the "where" question, she already knew the answer… "probably best I don't say".

And that was the deal done. But his last request was rather unexpected. She was to say nothing of this conversation. She was to give K-P no hint of it. She was to wave him goodbye in as normal a manner as she could before he left. Anna nodded. She kept her last thought to herself – where *was* he leaving for?

On the Train to Prague:

Anna had been in something of a strange mood last night. After dinner, she'd handed him a note. She'd *said* it had arrived by courier a few hours before he'd got home. But there was something about the way she said it that left him unconvinced. Anyway, however it had been delivered the letter itself was obviously genuine, written in von Ulmnitz's typically forthright style. He was to present himself at the station buffet at Vienna's Hauptbahnhof, not later than eleven hundred hours. He was to sit outside and wait. In due course he would be approached. The man would ask him if he was Waffenmeister Siegmund Flichner. He was to reply in the affirmative. All would be explained in due course.

He could tell straight away that the man striding purposely towards him was no civilian. He had "one of von Ulmnitz's inner circle" written all over him. Names were exchanged and Pichler was almost marched to the Prague train. They boarded it with only a few minutes to spare.

Colonel Alexej Hajek said nothing until they'd left Vienna well behind them. Their compartment was a sealed type, that is to say no corridor. Pichler was glad he'd emptied his balder shortly before he'd been approached. The Colonel started to speak and he didn't stop for nearly an hour. As far as the subject of madam Novakova was concerned, the Colonel was remarkably tight-lipped.

'Is that all clear, Waffenmeister Flichner?' he asked.

Pichler could hardly say no. Hajek had gone over it from start to finish, twice! So he lied!

'All clear, sir!

Flichner was to report to the Prague Military Academy for a crash course in ballistics and field gun command. The latter was something he'd seen often enough on campaign but never actually had to do. Well, you don't tend to… do you… not when you've served your entire career in the infantry of the line!

'*Remember*, Flichner, this is by way of a refresher course, it being some time since you were invalided out of the artillery arm. Take this manual and absorb as much as you can this evening. At o-eight-hundred hours tomorrow, report to the gunnery range. Then straight off to Professor Glichen's office for instruction. This manual covers the basic theory of ballistics – it's all pretty straight forward. You'll need to be up at six for breakfast. That'll give you an hour or two to go through it.'

As the train pulled into Prague, Flichner was given a kit bag.

'Your uniform's in there. It's a bit old because it's the same one you were discharged with in '67.'

Pichler suppressed a smile as Hajek spun his fiction with total conviction. The uniform he'd *actually* been discharged with in '66 was infantry white not this mucky brown.

'I'm sure you can smarten it up a bit. You'll find the necessary paperwork in one of the pockets. So I'll say goodbye for now – can't be seen together, d'you see! I'll find you sometime during the day tomorrow. And take this.'

Flichner opened his mouth to ask "what's the money for" but the Colonel anticipated… "for a cab".

Flichner, who had not the faintest idea where the Academy was, was duly delivered at the guardhouse after a short cab ride. Of course, he knew where it was *now*! That had been the point hadn't it? After all as a newly enlisted Kanonier, he'd have made the trip dozens of times, wouldn't he?

He'd expected a "who the bloody 'ell are you, chum?" from the guard. Instead his papers were briefly inspected and he was nodded through to a location in the main building.

On arrival at said room he was surprised to see a notice affixed to a stand. The notice said "Interviews for the post of Instructor (practical) – Wait to be called". After only ten minutes, he was. Directed through by an orderly, he sat himself down and looked up at the interviewer – Colonel Alexej Hajek. Whatever happened to "I'll find you sometime tomorrow?"

'Well, Flichner, I'm sorry to have to tell you that you have failed in your application to be an instructor at the academy,' and then he grinned. 'However, you have been successful in obtaining employment at the home of General Dvorak.'

Colonel Hajek proceeded to fill in some of the gaps that he'd omitted on the train journey briefing. Flichner wasn't to know it, but even then this was a long way, a very long way short of the full story! He had one burning question. He didn't like the answer.

'Two weeks, sir? Two *weeks*!'

'It might be longer, but rest assured Frau Pichler's welfare has been fully taken care of. You need have no worries on that score. Do *not* try to contact her for any reason. From now on you are a single man. You must "live" your cover every minute of the day from now until we tell you otherwise. I'll leave you alone while you sort yourself out. You'll be collected in half an hour.'

And with that closing remark Colonel Hajek left, closing and locking the door behind him.

What the hell was he supposed to do for half an hour? Flichner got up, took a turn around the room and nearly tripped over the kit bag he dumped there only five minutes before. Inside he found an artillery uniform – mucky brown as expected – a clothes brush, blue army trousers, a cap and a pair of boots. After a few minutes judicial brushing he felt it was "good enough" and sat down to put on the boots. One boot didn't feel quite right. He stood up to inspect himself in the mirror on the far wall. As he walked towards it he discovered that one boot, his left, had a thicker heel, causing him to limp rather more than usual.

'Bloody hell,' he said out loud.

He'd worked damn hard on compensating for his lost leg and now he was limping like a cripple again. What the hell was Hajek playing at? He didn't have much time to dwell on the subject as he heard the key turn in the lock.

'Flichner?' asked the head that appeared around the door. The head received a confirmatory nod.

'Hello, Sarg. I'm Grotchen. I'm to give you a bit of a tour on route to your "hotel". Actually it's the punishment cell where we puts the naughty lads, but it'll be nice 'n quiet. First things first – has you had any scoff?'

The food in the NCO's mess wasn't half bad. The stop off at the latrines was even more appreciated.

'Pick what you want for yer tea n' all, whiles yer here. I'll have it sent to yer quarters around sixish.

That Colonel told me you was to be left in peace once I drops you off there.'

The tour took two hours. They must have seen every ficking room in the ficking Academy, at least once. Flichner's new friend kept asking him how they got to this room or that room, usually one they'd visited at least half an hour ago. It was almost as if he was being prepared for an exam.

'Don't ask me why I'm asking you all this crap, Sarg? I'm just following orders. Was' the matter, you got memory problems, had a bang on the 'ead or something since you was last here?'

They examined half a dozen different guns. When Flichner asked for a "refresher" on the gun crew commands, his companion was only too happy to oblige. They discussed uniforms, artillery ranks and regimental engagements from the seven weeks war of 1866 and the Danish campaign. He was finally deposited in his "cell" with a parting remark of "Nothing wrong with your memory chum. Good luck with the interview for instructor, sure you'll walk it". Flichner had the distinct impression that the man knew no more about why he was here than he did. The cell turned out to be a lot closer to a hotel, albeit a very, very cheap one, than he'd originally steeled himself for. The presence of two bottles of beer on the window ledge no doubt helped!

The following day had gone pretty well so far starting with a very satisfying breakfast. The army in peacetime is pretty good like that. "Take what you want but eat what you take" is the rule and he bloody well did. The gun crew exercise was a breeze. What with the demonstration and the manual firmly fixed in his head the night before, he was damned nearly faultless. His years as a non-commissioned officer made the command of men second nature even after all these years.

And so onto the next step. He knocked on Professor Glichen's door, sat down as he was invited to do and started to read the piece of paper he'd been handed.

"A field gun set at an elevation of 20 degrees has a muzzle velocity of V m/s. The target range is 3800m and the target is at the same height as the muzzle. Neglecting air resistance and deriving all equations from first principles, estimate the required value of V. Estimate the flight time and the maximum height of the trajectory. Discuss the effect of air resistance on these values."

The *one* thing he hadn't had time to do was to review the folder on so-called "basic" ballistics".

The Professor stood with his back to his new student and stared out of the window, as Professors are wont to do. After ten minutes he turned and looked over the candidate's shoulder to gauge his progress.

'Hmmm. I've seen worse!' he said with a smile.

Flichner had drawn a roughly curved trajectory and purely from his experience had written "10 seconds". After some thought, he then added "extra drag means reduced range". He thought about completing that bland statement with an exclamation mark but thought better of it. Mathematical equations and derivations were notable by their absence.

The last of these numerous experiences in the field had started with a puff of smoke coming from the Prussian lines. It ended by shattering his left leg… and removing the head of the man standing next to him. Pichler, the man he had been until this morning, had taught himself many different subjects in his time. Kinematics wasn't one of them. He'd never needed it – in the infantry or anywhere else, come to that. That is until today.

By noon he had it, or at least it wasn't the complete and utter mystery it had been two hours earlier.

'Shouldn't worry too much, old chap. It's the type of thing we teach the first year cadets. But once the shooting starts there's not a lot of time to worry about cosines. That's why we tabulate it all. Anyway, I'm informed you're here to get the "gist", so here's a few problems for you to try. I've popped the solutions on the reverse… should you need them,' he chuckled.

After another self-indulgent visit to the mess, he repeated yesterday's tour, but this time on his own. He walked slowly, burning it firmly into his memory, as if he really *had* spent two years of his life here. He found a wall with some pictures on it. As far as he could tell the place hadn't changed much in fifty years. He should be on pretty safe ground if required to describe the academy as it had been a decade earlier. Then an hour spent in his cell, trying the Prof's exercises. He needed to get these firmly fixed in his noddle or it would drift away like a summer's breeze.

'All right, Flichner?' asked Hajek as he pushed open the cell door without knocking.

'Sir!' replied Flichner, casting his paperwork onto his bunk and standing to attention.

Hajek smiled inwardly. He remembered how General von Ulmnitz had regaled him with a similar story of the younger Pichler. "You'll never get the soldier out of this lad, Hajek – bloody good job considering our present predicament!"

By six they were in a carriage, just the two of them. Prague stood twenty kilometres behind them. Plzen, the site of the Skoda armaments factory lay seventy kilometres ahead.

'No doubt you're confused about the heel piece!'

'Not at all, sir. You want me to exaggerate my injury… so the "lady" might be less inclined to suspect me. 'However, sir, I shall need my own shoes back.'

'Why so?' asked Hajek.

'So I may follow the lady in a disguise, should the need arise, sir.' He paused for a moment.

'About this lady, sir? Seems a lot of trouble to go to – all this artillery training. I mean to say, she's not a spy is she, sir?'

Colonel Hajek cheek flinched but he said not a word. He was the one asking the questions. And he did so for the next fifty kilometres. He'd had his doubts about bringing in an academic for this job but, so far, it was beginning to look as though the General was right!

'Oh, one vital thing I haven't mentioned thus far, Flichner. General Dvorak believes that you are the genuine article. It is essential that you keep up the façade at all times, even when you're out of the old man's sight. You're a replacement for his manservant, a rather doddery fellow who was a liability for this assignment. Now listen, here's your cover. You came to my attention as a servant at the "Imperial Army Club" in Vienna where I am a member. You've been there since invalided out of the army in '67. Consequently you will be expected to serve the General and his lady at table.

Now as an ex-officer you'll be very familiar with regimental mess from the *receiving* end. Unfortunately we haven't had time to include any training on how to serve at table. The General didn't seem to think this would be a problem. I'm not sure I understand why but… Er, why are you smiling Flichner?'

General Dvorak's house, Plzen:

'Damn good meal, erm, erm..'

'Flichner, General,' added Hajek helpfully.

'Yes, Yes, Frichler. Good man! Better than my cook in fact. Might have to let him go now you're here. What do you think, Hajek old man?'

General Dvorak paused for a moment.

'Can't have you serving at table wearing *that* thing though! All right for serving a field gun but no damn use here… not when my dear Eliska comes to dine. White – that's the colour. We'll get you one eh, Hajek. Soon as possible!'

'When do you expect Frau Novakova, Herr General?' asked his dining companion.

'This Thursday, since you ask, Hajek.'

Sergeant Flichner bowed – the General didn't notice – and left the dining room, empty handed of trays, but with a great deal on his mind.

Two days later, the Vltava River, Prague

The two men walked at some pace, side by side.

'That's your whites, I presume.'

'It is sir, though it's a long way to come for a white jacket,' replied Flichner.

'A good excuse for us to meet up, away from prying eyes,' responded Colonel Hajek.

This was to prove a very detailed briefing about "Hercules", the code name for a hybrid field and siege gun.

'You know what these guns are, Flichner?'

'Yes, sir. The elevation can be increased to well beyond the few degrees necessary for a field gun by means of a special siege mounting.'

'Indeed. Well, there are one or two special features about Hercules. Even I don't know what they are… something about the range. By the way, could you derive the angle that gives the maximum range – mathematically I mean – ignoring air resistance, of course?' asked Hajek with a sly smile on his face.

Flichner considered this for a moment. Then he smiled back – yes, he *could*!

'Don't bother old chap. I'm a cavalry man myself. I wouldn't understand a damn word of it.'

So much for his earlier comment in the train coming here – "it's all pretty straight forward", he'd said, the cheeky rascal!

That was the end of any levity. Hercules was in the development stage but trials so far were proving to be very promising. The gun was light enough to be towed by a team of eight and at some speed. The range far exceeded that of similar Russian or German guns. That was the beauty of it. Yes, there were bigger siege guns capable of providing a bigger punch and greater range but these were in fixed installations like the fortress at Lemberg in Galicia. Lose the fortress, lose the gun. But mobility was the future of modern warfare. Having a gun that could do both was something both the Empire's neighbours would very much like to have.

The development team were located in Plzen. There was a twelve man steering committee which met at least once a month at various locations, mainly Vienna and Prague. General Dvorak was a member. The General himself was an ex-artillery man. He'd served in Italy in the war of 1866. After he'd lost his wife, he also lost interest in life, but this appointment had perked him up no end. His wealth of practical experience was essential given that most of the other committee members were theoreticians.

A thought struck K-P. A conversation he'd had with Max just before all this blew up sprung into his mind.

'Is Herr von der Osten on the committee, sir?'

'Why the devil should you ask *that*, Flichner?' the surprise evident in the Colonel's voice. 'Matter of fact he is. He's there to keep an eye on the costs. No point developing this damned gun if we can't afford to manufacture it in sufficient numbers to make a difference.'

After a few more exchanges the two men parted, one to return to his office, he had a progress report to make. And the other? He had to see a man about a formula!

Professor Glichen's office:

'Thanks for seeing me again at such short notice Prof.'

'My pleasure! Always happy to see a keen "student",' replied the genial fellow.

'It's about those formulas you gave me. Well, I tried 'em on the old Lorenz rifle we had back in '66!'

'Ah-ha,' replied Glichen, who had a feeling where this was going.

'Well, back then we used to reckon on about 200m effective and about 600m on maximum sight setting. Well the formula gave about twice that! Can't work out where I'm going wrong.'

'That's because you *aren't* going wrong! Do you remember the rider in the first question I gave you, the bit about "neglecting air resistance"? Well therein lays your answer. The real shell trajectory is not parabolic at all – it falls more rapidly. Here let me sketch it out for you.'

All this had little to do with his assignment. The only point of studying this stuff was so he could bullshit with confidence should the need arise. His cover wouldn't have lasted five minutes if he couldn't. No, it wasn't that. He was just interested or as Slota would say "that's bloody academics for you!"

'So how do you calculate the real range, Prof?'

'With enormous difficulty! You see it depends on so many variables; the projectile's weight, its shape, its surface area to volume ratio and roughness, any rifling. I could go on, but the most reliable approach is to apply an empirical factor as a multiplier.'

Flichner's gormless look was the signal for further explanation.

'Find an artillery piece which is basically the same as the one you're designing. Calculate the theoretical range of the real one, then fire the real one and see how far it *actually* goes. Now divide the real range by the theoretical range and that is your empirical factor.'

'Which you can use as an indicator to predict the range of your new design!' declared Flichner.

'Exactly so, my boy!'

'So really, sir, it's a type of efficiency factor, a factor that cannot exceed one. However the closer the factor is to one, the more efficient a gun is!'

Prof Glichen beamed. He could do with more pupils like this one.

This Thursday at the General's home:

When Pichler started his studies under Max's tutelage, he only had his war pension and a little bit of savings. He needed to work as well as study and that place of work was Café Lakatos. Initially he'd been a waiter on the outside tables – later on he was the cook's assistant *as well* as an outside waiter. He could already cook simple stuff so Café Lakatos simply extended his repertoire.

Having just served the happy couple with their coffee, Flichner bowed and made himself scare limping away towards the door. As he reached it, she spoke.

'Herr Flichner. Thank you so much. The entire meal was superb. I can't remember eating a better one.'

'T-t-thank you, madam,' replied the servant, blushing slightly at such unaccustomed and effusive praise. His embarrassment made the lady smile even more.

This little piece of theatre played itself out on another three occasions with little change until on the fourth one…

The first glimpse of daylight:

Flichner came rushing into the lounge as fast as his limp would allow him. She stood over him stroking his brow as he sat slumped in his chair.

'Flichner, thank God you're here. You must get the General up to his room, while I call for a doctor.'

He managed to heave the ashen faced man up to the first floor landing by pure huff and puff, but once there he had to pause for a breather. He heard the front door open and saw her walk down the steps onto the pavement.

'Here you, yes *you* boy! Come here! Quickly!' she shouted.

It took him a further few minutes to manoeuvre the limp man onto his bed, loosen his clothing and return to the lounge. She was not there, nor was she in the hallway or outside on the front steps. Then he looked in the direction of the General's study. The door was ajar and he'd *never* seen that before.

A flustered Frau Novakova was pacing back and forth, wringing her hands as she did so. She looked up as the door behind was swung fully open.

'Madam,' asked Flichner in surprise. 'What are you doing in the General's study?'

'Looking for some pills – there must be some – perhaps for his heart. I'm sure it's his heart. Oh Herr Flichner, *where* is the doctor? He should be here by now. Curse the boy! I must go to him,' she cried and almost ran up the stairs, leaving Flichner in her wake.

When he arrived he found her stroking his brow. At that same moment, the General opened his eyes and momentarily searched the room, unsure of where he was. As he struggled to prop himself up, Flichner rushed to his other side to assist. In a few moments more, his colour had returned and it was as if nothing had happened. He smiled up at the concerned face of the woman and the tension written thereon, Flichner observed, melted like snow in June.

'Thank God,' she declared, adding 'a doctor has been sent for.'

'No need for a doctor,' declared the old warrior. It seemed to Flichner as if the attentions of Frau Novakova were all the medicine he required.

'I must stay tonight Herr Flichner… in that chair. I can't leave him… you know… just in case he has another attack.'

So Herr Flichner made up a suitable chair with a few cushions and left them to it.

There was nothing else he could do at present save watch out for the doctor. His mind turned towards the incident in the study. Where had she got the idea from that it was something to do with his heart? Had they ever discussed the state of his health? Not within his hearing. And to take it into her head to search for pills that may or may not have existed. And why in the study? Surely these would be in a bedside cabinet or even a medicine chest if they were anywhere. In her position he'd have asked the General's manservant, which was him. It didn't make any sense.

As quietly as he could he slipped into the study and his eyes swept the room. Reasonably neat with no books protruding from the bookcase, there was nothing to suggest she'd been poking around where she shouldn't. When he'd surprised her by his sudden appearance at the study's door, she'd been pacing the room, not looking at anything. The desk itself was almost devoid of the normal clutter one might expect, if his own desk at the university was anything to go by. In fact apart from a few pens, a blotter, an ink pot and some sheets, the only other occupant was a rather thick encyclopaedia.

So on the face of it, the General had left his study door open. Was it normal for him to lock it? Flichner didn't know the answer to that one. She must have wandered in, in her distracted state. So that was the explanation, nothing sinister after all.

He *almost* missed it – a corner of blue paper protruding a mere fraction from the encyclopaedia. Bloody hell, General! What are you doing man – bringing this kind of thing home? And not only home but *not* even under lock and key?

It clearly said "Project Hercules" right next to the three centimetre high capitals "TOP SECERET". He ran to the study door and locked it. As he unfolded the blue print, he could hardly believe his eyes; profile view, plan view, side elevation – all fully dimensioned. On the right hand side, just above the title block, there was a full technical description – weights, calibre and ranges (estimated it said) for various elevations. In fact just about everything an engineer would need to build a "Hercules".

Never mind him bringing it home, how the devil did he get it out of the Skoda works in the first place? For a moment the thought crossed his mind that the General was a spy. Hajek had told him that the General was to know nothing of his own undercover mission, so that certainly fitted.

Then the pfennig finally dropped. If not the General, that left only one other person. Why the bloody hell hadn't Hajek mentioned any of this before? Did he *really* have no inkling?

So, had she found it and seen it? Suppose she had! Did it mean anything to her? Hmmm, difficult to say – suppose it did. All right then, did she have time to study it?

His mind ran backwards.

How long could she have been alone in the study? They'd only been separated for say, five minutes at most. Allow two minutes for her to find a boy and give him instructions. No! Assume there *was* no boy. She could have just opened the front door, shouted something and headed straight here. Right! Call it four minutes in the study, less thirty seconds as she heard him coming down the stairs to hide the plan and do her pacing up and down act. And of course, surely it wasn't just sitting there on the desk in full view. Although maybe it was! The General had been lax about everything else. Hmmm, call it two minutes of actual study time.

He concentrated on the plan for two minutes, waited a further five and checked what he'd retained – not much was the answer! At least not much that was reliable. He got all sorts of numbers mixed up in his head. No, it just wasn't possible! She couldn't have gleaned more than the vaguest impression of Hercules. Still, she might try again.

He wasn't going to burn it in the study grate. There wasn't a fire going and it would only attract her attention. It was essential that poor, old lame Flichner should retain his cover, now more so than ever. Fortunately as the cook he had an oven that would do the job discretely.

***

The next morning he brought tea for them both. The General looked completely recovered. Indeed it was the lady who looked exhausted. For some reason and regardless of the normal social hierarchies, she decided to join his manservant for breakfast.

'I can't *keep* calling you Herr Flichner – not after our shared experience of last night. And I *won't* call you Flichner – that's altogether too feudal. What is your Christian name?'

'S-s-s-siegmund,' was the stuttered reply and he blushed, a very deep hue in answering her.

'I think we should be friends, Siegmund. As you cannot fail to be aware, the General and I have become very close in the last few weeks. Perhaps you won't be calling me Frau *Novakova* for many more weeks.' And with that, she lightly touched the man's hand with a single cool finger.

The way she asked him to teach her "something about artillery" was a masterclass in stage craft. He couldn't help but admire it. He would have considered it to be entirely reasonable had it not been for the incident in the study. She began by explaining her reason. The General, it seemed, was fond of reminiscing about his long military career over the dining table. She found it fascinating, she told him. Yes that was the word she'd used, but she was so convincing that he *almost* believed she meant it. What she really wanted was to be able to follow his stories in more depth. She even suggested the topic –

ballistics! Now that would have rung alarm bells in any normal conversation, but she wasn't the only actor on the stage.

'Yes, madam. Ballistics would certainly help you follow the General's stories,' said Flichner earnestly. Pichler on the other hand was on the verge of pissing himself. Ballistic theory could only have been a faint and distant memory for the fellow. Flichner told Pichler to shut the fuck up!

'Of course, I can't hope to follow all the technical terms that the General uses, but I would so very much like to try. But be gentle with me, Siegmund,' she said coquettishly. 'My ability with sums is limited to ensuring that my dressmaker is not taking advantage of me.'

'V-v-v-very well, I'll do my best, though it's been m-m-many years since my days at college.'

So Professor Glichen's newest pupil was put to the test. For somebody who professed no knowledge of mathematics she showed an uncommonly high level of interest. Occasionally she'd interrupt his scribbled workings with exclamations. "Oh, that's so clever" she'd say or "what does that funny little squiggle mean?" usually interspersed with girlish giggles.

Then Flichner had an idea. Errors started to slip into the equations. He would add an occasional, "as I say, it's been a long time, madam. I might be getting some of this wrong!" At one point he had the strongest impression that she was itching to grab a pencil off the kitchen table to make a correction.

'Thank you very much, Siegmund. I now know my range from my elevation. I'll be able to follow the General's discourses more easily. Though I must confess I'm still not sure I know the difference between a "sin" and a "cos". Unless we are talking about original "sin", that is,' a remark that caused the poor man to blush once more – as it was intended to.

As he watched her depart to check on the General, he was reasonably confident that he had played his part without arousing her suspicions. What he couldn't understand was why she'd insisted on putting the "play" on in the first place.

A park bench in Plzen:

Berlin rarely allowed their agents to select their own code name. They were too likely to come up with something which could give them away. But sometimes Berlin did! The schwarze Witwe, she'd chosen. Not only was it the name of an infamous spider, it seemed apt given that widows or at least widow*ers* were central to the operation. She wasn't sure if von der Osten's and Dvorak's previous wives had been dispatched by Berlin. She didn't intend to ask; it was what it was! Her mission was to obtain the technical specification for the Hercules gun. And that mission was progressing splendidly.

The man sitting next to her was the least likely looking spy master one could imagine. He was old, he was grey… he was fat… and obviously partially lame. Anybody observing his progress to the bench would conclude as much. And it got worse! Judging by the thickness of the glass in his lens, he must have been as blind as a bat. He was nonetheless, one of Berlin's most feared men.

'Tell me then of your progress, my little arachnid.'

'The General is being most helpful, unintentionally so, of course,' she smirked. 'It's amazing what a "good" woman aided by a little cognac can coax out of a man. He'd brought a drawing home – strictly against regulations of course. It wasn't too difficult to locate it. I was able to study the engineering drawing of the gun at some length. The next stage is for me to get sight of a Hercules round, close up. Would you be able to arrange that?'

'We are working on a scheme which will allow you to attend the first demonstration of Hercules.'

'How is that possible – civilians at a military test?'

The little man emitted a coarse laugh.

'Firstly, this is Austria-Hungary. They do things differently here. Secondly, you're not the only one who has an Austrian official wrapped around her little finger. Wait and see!'

She nodded with a smile. 'And do you have the information I requested the last time we met?'

'On your little friend, you mean? Oh yes, he is everything he claims to be. Our inside man at the Academy has checked his records; date enlisted, date discharged, reason, that is amputation of his left leg. Oh and that other thing you were interested in – he has never married, though the relevance of that escapes me.'

'It might have been a useful pressure point. After all, that type of thing is common enough, isn't it? All those men huddled together, with no female companionship for weeks on end.'

'It *might* have been, did you say?'

'Yes, it *might* have been but it isn't now. I have a different pressure point. I think he might be a little in love with me!'

'So you're sure he's no danger to the mission? Berlin thinks it is suspicious that he only entered the General's employment so recently, though the explanation of servant illness is certainly plausible.'

'No. He is the same man who studied at the Academy. I darn well stubbed my toe in the process of checking the "falseness" of his left leg. And he's clearly studied the theory required of any artilleryman, though obviously he's not retained all he was taught,' she laughed as she recalled his "lesson" from a day ago.

'So no worries that he might present a threat to us in some way?' asked the spy master.

'None at all! In fact, he's more likely to be an asset than a danger, did he but know it. In fact *there* he is, do you see? Just over by that tree. If I were to wave to him he'd run a mile. And that's happened once before. He follows me around like a little lost puppy. Rest assured I am in complete control of the mission.'

The day of the test firing, Plzen:

Quite why there were two ladies in the officials' stand was a complete mystery to all and sundry, but two there were. One was sitting next to the Minister of Munitions and his assistant. The other sat next to General Dvorak. As one soldier said to another, "if I'd 'ave know that was the game, I'd 'ave brought my old lady down… 'n the kids."

The gun had been coupled up to the team of eight horses. It was raced up to the far end of the field, uncoupled, slid into position and a blank round was fired. It was then re-coupled and raced back to the end where the officials were.

The elevation was adjusted to what looked like just a few degrees. A live round was loaded.

Bang!

After a few seconds, the shell smacked into the target – a brick and wood construct built especially for the purpose. The target disintegrated in a huge shower of dust and wood fragments and when these had settled there was not a trace of it to be seen. The General, the Minister, his assistant and one lady were delighted. The other lady also joined in the applause but only after she'd finished counting the flight time.

The siege mounting was brought out. In less than five minutes, the gun crew had uncoupled the horses and run the gun up onto this mounting. The barrel elevation was now around forty degrees. A blank round was fired – more applause!

'Why didn't we see a live firing just now, my dear?' she asked of General Dvorak. 'I so wanted to see the shell fly into the air.'

'Well, you see, dearest, we only have a limited test range, about 1500 metres I believe. Anything more than a few degrees of elevation would cause the shell to go sailing over the range and into residential Plzen. I don't think that would make the army very popular, do you?

She smiled her understanding.

'Why my dear, are you trying to find the gun's range? You're not a Russian spy are you, you naughty little monkey, because if you are I can't really let you have a closer look at the gun, now can I?'

And they both laughed and were right to do so – the very idea indeed. Of course she wasn't a *Russian* spy.

Military Intelligence HQ, Berlin:

'Well Erich, didn't I tell you she was good?'

'Indeed you did sir.'

'She'll be in in a moment. I've brought in Haplin, the department's expert on military ordnance.'

When all four were eventually seated, the General began his summary.

'We know that Hercules is a big project for our southern neighbours. We first received intelligence from our inside man in the Skoda works. He's a Slav so take what he said with a pinch of salt – you know what these irredentists are like. In any event, he was dismissed shortly after contacting us – drinking on the job apparently which is never a good idea when you're dealing with explosives.

We know it is much more than a replacement field gun for the Imperial and Royal army. It simply has to be given that it's been five years in development and the expenditure is simply eye-watering. We know *this* because we have a little bird embedded in the ministry, code name "Eule".'

The lady looked up in surprise. Who was this woman coded named the owl?

'Ah agent Black Widow, you surely don't think you are our only placement within Franz Josef's three-ring circus. She is a little further advanced along the… hmmm… matrimonial pathway than you are. You may know her as Viktoria R. I believe you frequent the same social gatherings.'

Frau Novakova, die schwarze Witwe, nodded her agreement.

'We know that the range of Hercules, both carriage-mounted and siege-mounted, outstrips that of our own guns by around thirty per cent. And that lady and gentlemen is of immerse concern to the Kaiser. If the Austrians have come up with some technical innovation that makes this possible, then we need to know about it. So let's see what Oberst Haplin has made of madam's sketches.'

There were three items before them; sketches which the "widow" had made with the aid of the General's illicit blue print; an engineering drawing which Haplin's trusted draughtsman had made from her sketches; a drawing of the Prussian army's standard field gun, the C64, for comparison.

'Well, I'm an ex-infantry man,' said the General but I can't see any differences between these guns. What about the shell?'

'I saw one up close, General and it looked pretty standard to me,' said the widow.

'So your conclusions are…?'

'Hercules is a bog-standard field gun, no more, no less!' said Haplin.

'But *how the devil* can that be so?' exploded the General. 'They've spent a fortune on it, I can't… just a moment. What's this say here, Haplin?'

'It says "estimated" sir. It means the drawing madam saw is a pre-production design,' replied the Colonel.

'But you've seen the gun in action, have you not, madam?'

'If you're asking about the maximum range, which is the only difference between theirs and ours, no sir –

I haven't, only a low elevation shot. This was deliberate. That data, I imagine, is top secret and for all his influence, General Dvorak would *never* had got permission for me to attend if there was any possibility of the range being revealed.'

'Tell me, er… do either of you know how this range is estimated?'

Haplin explained how data from a similar gun was central to such preliminary estimates.

'So this range reduction factor is… typically about what, Haplin?'

Oberst Haplin started on what was almost certainly going to be a very technical, *very* long-winded explanation. He didn't get very far.

'Just the number, Herr Oberst.'

'Sir, for a gun of this type, we'd use around 0.5-0.6, say 0.55.'

'Or perhaps…0.57?' asked the lady, somewhat mysteriously.

Puzzled looks followed and the attempted question from Haplin was stilled by the lady's most unladylike, "be quiet!" Even the General obeyed her command. After five minutes of calculation, which Halpin observed she'd repeated three times, the silence was broken.

'I don't believe it… I simply don't believe it.'

'Madam, what is it that…?'

She stilled the General once more this time with a raised hand, instead passing her calculations over to

Oberst Haplin. After a few moments he nodded his agreement.

'General, you did say the range is around 30% more than our own gun, did you not?'

'Indeed!'

'I'm sorry to have taken so long to work out seventy five divided by fifty seven. The sum is a trivial one; the implications are far from trivial.'

It looked like the brain of this old infantry man was about to explode. Her explanation of the anomaly could be postponed not a moment longer.

'The range is *not* thirty percent larger. It is in fact about the same as our guns. This is not a technical mystery but a typographical error. Somehow and I have no idea how, the range reduction factor has been transposed. 0.57 magically became 0.75 and the gun's range was over-calculated by around 30%.'

'Is that possible?' declared the General, turning to glare at Colonel Haplin.

'Not in a well-run design office, sir. Such a mistake would have been spotted by the most junior draughtsman. However in producing the submission for budgetary approval, there is some degree of editing. That's usually done by the administrators who wouldn't have a clue what the number *should* be. And General, for some guns firing very heavy shells, air resistance may not be as critical, so 0.75 is not an *impossible* figure. Somewhere along the line, the range was erroneously recalculated. Of course once the official submission document was in being, it would have been very problematic for the designers to backtrack – even though it wasn't their mistake. That would account for why this project has run on for so long. The designers have been desperately trying to make some idiotic clerk's error a physical reality.'

The General's reaction was a great surprise to the other three. He burst out in a great and sustained laugh.

'Oh, I do so love the Austrians! We've see this type of thing before with their bureaucracy, haven't we Erich? Frankly, I find it all *too* believable. And the upshot is that they have spent a lot of time and a lot of money working on a weapon that offers them no advance on our own C64. Well let's not disturb them in their vital work.'

Colonel Haplin was dismissed. The next mission did not concern a "big-gun" expert, leaving just the three of them.

'An excellent result, my dear madam! I couldn't be more delighted, eh Erich? Had you found some technical explanation then we'd be chasing down this thing for months, maybe even years. In the meantime the Austrians would be getting closer to a production version and even large-scale integration into their army. As it is, I can pull resources off this dead-end onto other areas of concern, resources in this case being your good self.'

The widow was relieved. The General was happy!

'Forget about field guns,' he continued, 'the future lies with rapid fire, multiple round infantry weapons. This is an area where we are ahead of every nation save perhaps the British. I can't see us going to war with that Empire – at least not until the French are ready and that won't be for decades. Come with me if you please.'

As the General held the door for the lady to leave, he felt a restraining hand on his shoulder.

'Is it safe for madam to see this, General?' whispered his adjutant.

He paused to allow "madam" to get a few paces ahead and then half-closed the door.

'Has she not proved herself on project Hercules, Erich?'

'Indeed she has, sir.'

'And where do you think we could find another with the technical knowledge and… how should I put it… her feminine guile? No, I'm certain she may be relied on to deliver on this project just as she has on Hercules.'

With that they left the office and headed down the corridor until all three of them stood opposite a door with three locks.

'Erich, if you please! The top lock is yours I believe.'

The room was empty save for a single bench with a large sheet covering something.

'You expressed an interest in this type of weapon on one of our previous meetings. Wasn't it something your husband was working on at Skoda before his untimely death? Something he took to the authorities who completely failed to see the potential of his ideas.'

The sheet was removed and the widow's eyes opened wide. She saw a full-size gun, some photographs and three sheets of blue prints.

'You can see that there are no writing implements in the room and I would ask you for your handbag if I may. Please examine everything you see before you. Take as long as you want. When you are ready, please push that bell switch and we will return and unlock the door. Bis später, gnädige Frau.'

***

Back in the General's office, there were only two more items of business. Firstly, the General presented a tiny broach to the lady. It was given to all his female agents, though never before after just one mission. But then she was no ordinary agent.

It was called the "Auguste medal" named after the Kaiser's wife – a pretty thing with a cornflower blue enamel base and a central white letter "A. In shape it was not unlike the Eisenkreuz awarded to the armed forces, though a fraction of the size.

Secondly, the General outlined her mission. She was to return to her role as General Dvorak's new love and to continue to infiltrate the Skoda factory. The aim; to see what progress, if any the General added with a smirk, the Austrians were making on their own version of this war changing weapon.

'If you can repeat your "Herculean" task of convincing General Dvorak to smuggle out any drawings, then please do so,' said the General. 'But frankly I don't think they've reached this stage. Learn what you can and then report back.'

'And the affair, General… after I return to Berlin? Am I to continue it beyond…'

'I think when you return, the affair will have run its course. Don't worry. We will move the General on to a new "posting",' said the General, although he wasn't specific about the nature of this posting.

Naturally she was delighted to be given such an important job for the Reich. She had told the General so, though that much was obvious from her countenance alone.

Sad news received at Berlin:

'Do we know it was her Erich, I mean for certain?'

'This was sent to her Aunt in Prague as her next of kin. The Aunt posted it on to the box office address the widow gave her.'

They both looked at the heat-distorted tiny broach, the cornflower enamel largely gone and nodded – damn shame their shared thought.

'An accident do you think or did the Austrians actually discover what she'd been up to and take the appropriate action, Erich?'

'Gas leaks are common enough, sir, especially in the run down hotel she broke her journey at. We've had a man view the building or what's left of it. We can't get hold of any autopsy plates, assuming any were even taken but we've no reason to believe that she'd been compromised. The Czech General seems to be genuinely heart-broken. His man servant is no longer living there. He's got a job at the Academy in Prague. I should think he was glad to be out of the whole sorry business. I can't imagine what it's like in that house of grief.'

'Yes, you're probably right. How many cuckoos do we have in the field?'

'Five in all excluding the "widow" sir. Two are sleepers awaiting a suitable nest. Another two are only at the very beginning of infiltration. The fifth one is the Minister of Munition's assistant's paramour.'

'Right, let's not take any chances – pull them all out.'

'*All* of them, sir?'

'Yes, the Austrians probably haven't twigged what we've been up to, so let's put it to bed for a few years. We can always resurrect the cuckoos when the circumstances are right and Erich… good job, well done!'

The ISD HQ Vienna – The technical office:

'Does that look right? I'm worried the ammunition feed is not quite right,' asked the technician.

'No, that's exactly right,' replied the agent.

'And the technical specification; muzzle velocity, cooling system and capacity, rate of fire, bullet and overall gun weight, range,' he asked pointing at the table he had created in one corner of the blueprint – 'Have I recorded that all correctly?'

The agent peered and checked each figure as the technician had asked.

'Yes, all correct. You've done an excellent job, Herr Bruchler.'

***

Oberst Hajak and Pichler sat on the window side of the table in von Ulmnitz's office. Pichler didn't know whether his adversary had been assassinated or if her death was accidental. He only knew that she *was* dead. He felt the same way about her death as he had about all the enemy dead he'd seen on the battlefield. You couldn't be pleased, only sad; sad that those – whose patriotism was every bit as fervent as his – had come to this. At that moment von Ulmnitz strode into the room shattering Pichler's melancholy in an instant.

'Well, gentlemen, thank you for all your hard work over the past fortnight. The Prussians – damn it, I *keep* forgetting to call them Germans – now believe that the Hercules is a horse that will not run. No doubt they are rubbing their hands with glee. And to be fair it was a smart piece of espionage on their part. Perhaps I should introduce you to their principal agent.'

The door opened and in she walked. Pichler wasn't sure at first. The hair was at least two shades lighter and worn slightly differently. She was perhaps a fraction slimmer but there was no doubt… it *was* her!

'Good morning, gentlemen,' she declared smiling at the assembly before her.

'Please take a seat, Frau Novakova,' said General von Ulmnitz extending his hand to indicate the seat in question.

There were a few moments of stunned silence – the General *should* have been the one to break it – he wasn't!

'You're not called Novakova, are you madam?' It was Pichler who spoke.

'No, Herr Flichner, I am not.'

'And your husband didn't die in an explosion at the Skoda factory, did he? In fact, your husband isn't dead at all, is he?'

She looked at the General, unsure as to how much information she should provide to Herr Flichner, although that certainly wasn't his real name.

'You're correct,' interrupted the General. The lady's husband is a serving officer in the Kriegsmarine. He's temporarily on secondment on

Imperial business in South America. I expect "temporarily" to last at least five years.'

Another silence endured. Pichler frowned. And then it all became clear.

'The General placed you with the Germans, didn't he? You didn't need to read that plan you found in General Dvorak's study – not that you had time to do so – because General von Ulmnitz had already given you all the information which you then passed onto the Germans. In short you were never working for *them* – you were always working for *us*!'

Pichler finished by glaring at the General, who had remained stony-faced throughout.

'I had a feeling that this, older men in positions of power suddenly becoming appealing to younger, attractive women was a bit fishy…'

Die Dame bowed her head in acknowledgement of a back-handed compliment. Pichler failed to notice – he was on a roll.

'…how is the Minister of Munitions' assistant by the way? So Hercules was just a ploy – designed to smash this little game the Germans were up to. Surely not – there has to be more to it than that! There's something we're after – something the Prussians have but we don't – *but* which we'd very much like to have. They've developed something, haven't they General? And you have it now, don't you General? I don't know how, but you do… don't you… *don't* you?'

The General smiled benevolently. Pichler on the other hand had lent halfway across the table and was glaring fiercely at him. He'd allow him a little bit of leeway. That was only fair. He was a smart fellow and more than that, he was *entirely* correct. It might be some time before Pichler would forgive him for being kept so completely in the dark. That's why he'd allowed him to meet die Dame. It was right that she should explain at least the *part* of the story he could be permitted to hear.

'Don't be angry with the General, Herr Flichner – or with me. I know we've both abused you horribly but don't you see I needed to "live" the fiction the General and I had invented to fool the Germans. They had to believe that I'd acquired the solution to Hercules through my own resourcefulness. I couldn't very well have said "this nice Austrian General gave it all to me". You are right, I did not have time to view the plan, let alone memorise the information. My memory is excellent but it's not *that* good. And if the Germans approached you then anything you did let slip would only have corroborated my story. Your ignorance was my protection.'

She looked at Herr Flichner to see how he was taking all this. His expression gave nothing away.

'I can't tell you how helpful it was to have you following me to the park in Plzen where I met my contact. You gave him further proof that I was under suspicion by Vienna. It did my credibility no end of good, I assure you. Yes, your lurking presence helped me on both occasions. We used the *same* park bench – you used the *same* lime tree. I was able to point you out to my Berlin minder. But please believe me, your life was never in danger. I convinced them that you were just, well how should I put it? – rather enamoured of me.'

'*F-f-five* occasions!' stuttered Pichler with a glint in his eye.

She frowned good-naturedly but it was still a frown. Hmmm! That stutter… and this time he wasn't blushing, not even a teeny bit. The *little rascal*! Who was playing who? With a half-smile still on her lips, she replied.

'Five? No, just the two surely!'

'Twice when I *wanted* to be seen; then a few more times when I *didn't*. You may recall the road sweeper perhaps?'

'Ah – I *do* remember *a* road sweeper. He had problems getting his pipe to stay lit, as I recall.'

Pichler smiled benevolently as he put an imaginary match to an imaginary pipe bowl.

'Dear, dear me, General! I seem to be losing my touch, do I not? Time for me to retire, wouldn't you say?'

The portion of the story that was fit for Pichler's ears having now been told, the General decided it was time to bring this part of the meeting to a close.

'Well, thank for your services on this occasion, Herr Flichner. No doubt we'll meet again – very soon!'

Pichler wasn't so sure about that. He'd had quite enough of General Erich von Ulmnitz. He said nothing, stood up and pushed his chair back.

'Goodbye, madam. I wish you and your husband every good fortune in your new life in Argentina.'

Pichler had not the foggiest idea where in South America this new life would actually be spent. It was a fair guess though for a naval man and in the unlikely event he *was* correct… it would give them all something to think about.

'Goodbye, Herr Flichner,' said the lady, reaching out to take the hand he had extended towards her.

'We shall never meet again, nor know each other's real names, but I'd like you to know how much I have enjoyed our "duel" over the last two weeks. You did very well, but it was a game you could not possibly win. You only saw one side of the coin, while I could see both.'

Pichler had almost reached the door before being halted by von Ulmnitz's parting shot.

'And Colonel Hajek; you have never heard that name. Is that clear?'

Brought up on a farm and having risen through the ranks, Pichler was *normally* deeply respectful of his betters. Perhaps it was his encounter with Count von Wittenburg. Maybe it just that he was dog-tired after the last couple of weeks of being mucked about.

'Colonel Hoovic, sir? Not sure I recall the name. You don't mean the young lad who brings you your post, do you sir?'

With that he left von Ulmnitz's office heading back to Anna just as fast as his legs would carry him. He couldn't see for he had his back to them. *Had* he seen he would have observed an officer biting his lip in annoyance, a lady stifling a snigger in her handkerchief and a General…? Yes, what *about* the General? His face was unreadable… as it so often was!

***

Project Hercules was indeed a Trojan horse, though it offered some modest improvements. Was it that much better than Krupp's C64 field gun? Probably not!

Certainly the Minister of Munitions was right to be so concerned about the never-ending drain on his budget. The siege mounting was probably a white elephant from the beginning.

Right at the outset, a junior officer had suggested that portable ramps could increase the elevation by about thirty degrees. He argued that that was probably good enough for all practical purposes. The technocrats didn't agree! How could such a simple, cheap solution possibly be superior to their wizardry? And so the project rumbled on. Then a certain General von Ulmnitz got involved. *Some* of the money the Minister thought was being spent on project Hercules *was* being spent on project Hercules. A lot more wasn't!

General von Ulmnitz was right to be so concerned about these new multiple-round weapons. The French had their mitrailleuse and had even used them – against the Prussians in fact. The Americans had their Gatling gun. Both had their technical problems and they both needed to be carriage mounted – hardly portable! Every major power was working on them and nobody was sharing anything. What von Ulmnitz really needed to know now was how far these other Empires had progressed.

'Arr, Herr Bruchler, do come in,' said von Ulmnitz in response to the light tap on his office door.

'The Krupps M1872, General,' replied the draughtsman before making a rapid exit.

'Is it everything you'd hoped for, General?' said the lady. 'I do hope so. Our German friends gave me as long as I wanted. I wouldn't like to think that their error has gone unpunished.'

The silence lasted a good ten minutes as both she and Hajek shifted uncomfortably in their chairs. And then he stood up and offered his hand.

'I wish you bon voyage, madam,' was all he said but the ear to ear grin said so much more.

Alone in the room, von Ulmnitz had one more magic trick to pull off. There would be no difficulty convincing the Minister that using Project-Hercules as a cover for a radically different weapon had always been part of the plan. Whether he could convince the Minister to take credit for this was less certain… but he rather thought he could!

The Pichler's house:

It had been wonderful to have Charlotte staying with her for the past two weeks. It was just like when Aunt Emma was alive. In fact it was better. Charlotte was a much livelier companion, though she ought not to think that, she knew.

They both sat slumped in armchairs after many hours spent cleaning the house from top to bottom. It had been the most thorough clean the old place had had for simply ages. K-P was due back tomorrow and as much as she wanted him back home, it was a shame Charlotte had to go. It had been fortunate that her husband's ship was on a flag-waving trip to the Far East, but the SMS Elizabeta was due to dock early next week. As they say, all good things must come to an end.

'You know, Anna, you must get a housemaid, really you must.'

'I don't *need* one. K-P's happy with what I can do and we don't have the money to throw around.'

'Listen, my girl, use your common sense. Do you really think he's going to come home from work and start dusting? Don't you think he knows how inadequate that would make you feel if he were to do that? *And* you can't just live on stews in the winter and cold-plate in the summer.'

'I want to be a proper wife to him,' replied Anna through pouted lips.

'*He didn't marry you for your domestic skills for heaven's sake*!' responded Charlotte who was starting to lose her patience.

Anna folded her arms, frowned and sank her chin deeply into her neck. It was the beginnings of a category one sulk. But Anna, being Anna didn't stay that way for more than a few moments.

'Flipping good job he didn't,' she replied and the laughter from each chair settled the matter.

'Look, Anna. You know Ursula Friedstein has three daughters. Well the youngest, she's sixteen and the baby of the litter. Amelia will never be a great beauty and she'll never be a great wit. To add to that, she is painfully shy but could, with the right encouragement, be so much more than she is at present. It's not that her mother doesn't love her, it's more a case of her not really knowing she's there.'

'What could *I* do?' asked Anna.

'Well, for a start you could "pay" her by improving her piano skills which are quite dreadful and improve her Hungarian which is similarly…'

'Dreadful?' smirked Anna.

'Indeed. But mainly you could just take an interest in her, something that she's in desperate need of. If she just gained a fifth of your determination and a smidge of your sense of humour, she'd be an altogether more rounded person… *and* a better marriage prospect. Like it or not, Anna, that is the way of the world for many women like Amelia and you'd be doing her no favours by letting the current situation pertain.'

'Very well, Charlotte – I will *think* about what you've said,' replied Anna with some reluctance.

'You do that, dear! See you next Thursday for Kaffee und Kuchen. Good. Goodbye then.'

Anna got up and led her friend to the front door, a route she knew so well that outstretched hands were not required. They kissed and she heard the retreating steps before closing the door. But the door was open again within seconds.

'Charlotte… Chaaarlootteeee!'

'Yes, my dear.'

'Yes… Yes, you're right. I will!'

Two months later, the Senior Academic Club:

Max didn't expect to be invited to dine again at the Erste Division Club at the personal invitation of von der Osten. After reading today's copy of the Pressburg Tagesblatt, he knew he'd never meet him again *anywhere*. It had ended as he'd expected it would. Once he'd heard the news a few weeks ago that the man had resigned – *been* resigned in truth – there was only one likely outcome. Already something of a liability for a good number of years prior, he'd ended his career as a walking disaster. The body had been fished out of the river at the ancient town of Tulln an der Donau. It was a peaceful spot, totally out of keeping with his frame of mind, as he pined for the loss of his beloved Viktoria.

Max never knew why the lady had decided to fly the nest – a strangely appropriate expression, for the lady known in Berlin by her codename die "Eule" – the "owl".

A peaceful scene, a few kilometres out of Prague:

General Dvorak closed his eyes as he bowed his head. Though they had known each other for such a short time, he knew she was the one. He'd never forget his wife Rosa. She'd always be in his heart. But Eliska would have lessened the pain, he felt sure.

He looked down at the small brass plaque he'd laid by the gravestone. It would tarnish soon enough, of course it would. He would return next year on this same day and lay a new plaque. And would do so every year thereafter, until his own time came.

A man's height below where the mourner stood, the ill-fitting lady's dress looked out of place on the wasted corpse it adorned. Too many nights on cold pavements in all weathers, too many evenings spent in oblivion imbibing the coarse alcohol that made her life tolerable had finally done for her.

Her penultimate place of rest had been the Prague city morgue. A stranger had come to claim her as his own. Perhaps she might have taken comfort from the attentions of the kind gentleman who now mourned her passing, she who had never known any kindness in her travesty of a life. Perhaps it might have gladdened her soul that she, now at rest, could offer some form of solace to another.

THE MISSING WAR PLAN

Josef Grün – 1917

Wahn POW camp, near Cologne, March 1871:

Capitaine Jules Altorf had been in the camp ever since the disaster at Sedan in early September. Strasbourg had surrendered at the end of the same month. This hurt him even more. Altdorf's village stood but a short distance north of that great city. The conflict continued on and off for the next few months, with French successes being few and far between.

By the beginning of March, it was all over, but not before France had been subjected to a succession of grievous humiliations. The first of these was in mid-January – the acclamation of the King of Prussia as Wilhelm the First, the first Emperor of a unified Germany. This was held in, of all places, the Hall of

Mirrors in the Palace of Versailles. Meantime Paris itself was under siege. The last of these was on the first day of March when the triumphant German army paraded through Paris. To rub salt into their wounds, each of these indignities were gleefully reported to the POW's by their guard. The "fat Sergeant" they called him or Feldwebel Fritz Arntzen as it said in his pay book.

Arntzen was a reservist – most of the POW guards were. He'd never fired a shot in anger. Not that that stopped him from sneering at brave men who had. On one occasion, Altorf tormented beyond his endurance, very nearly brained him. Only the intervention of his fellow officer Paul Lebrun stopped him doing murder.

'Ach, so gentlemen. And how are we this matin? Alles gut Ich hoffe? So then soon we all go home, eh? I hear a rumour… Some of you will go to fight your brothers who have set up a… wie sagt man.. oh, ja eine communion.'

'Commune, you dolt!' muttered Lebrun under his breath.

'Ja, Ja… We will make a little hole in the iron ring we have around your not so gay *Pah-rhee*. Then your *brave* army can march in and slaughter your own civilians. Isn't that kind of General von Moltke? So then…'

He proceeded to read through a list of names. Altorf was not amongst them.

'Er Sergeant.. ?'

'Oh yes, Kaptain Altorf. *You* are not going back to *France…* because your home is now in *Germany*. The new name for Alsace und Lorraine will be Reichsland Elsaß–Lothringen. So you see, mein Herr, you are going to be a German subject. Isn't that wunderbar für Sie?'

And with that, he waddled away, laughing his stupid head off as he went.

Berlin, Old Palace, December 1872:

'So you have the maps for my approval, do you, Chancellor?'

'Majestät,' nodded the man, a man known across the Continent as the "iron" Chancellor. The first map, a map of Central and Eastern Europe was unrolled before his sovereign.

'So what am I looking at here, Bismarck?'

'This, like the other two maps, is entirely hypothetical in nature. All three have been developed by our General Staff here in Berlin. Perhaps you have heard the term "war-gaming", Majestät?'

The Kaiser nodded.

'This is the one your Majestät will shortly hand to Tsar Alexander. You will see,' he added pointing at the map, 'a series of arrows. This set start in European Turkey. They run through Romania and then cross the Russian frontier between Odessa and the Hungarian border. They represent the lines of advance of an entirely hypothetical Ottoman invasion force *into* the Tsar's Empire.'

'And these straight lines, the ones entirely within Russia?' asked the Kaiser.

'These lines, Majestät are the most likely Russian defensive positions,' replied the Chancellor.

'To counter this invasion, eh? Yes I see. So no doubt who is the aggressor here!'

'Exactly so Majestät!'

'And these arrows, the ones crossing the Hungarian-Romanian border into the Ottoman Empire?' asked the Kaiser.

'These show the advance of the heroic forces of Emperor Franz Josef. You can see they are heading towards the port of Varna on the Black Sea. We've assumed in an effort to cut through the Ottoman lines of communication. This would be of most help to their Russian ally.'

'…And this will happen as you've shown it here, only if the Tsar and the Emperor are bound by a mutual assistance agreement, yes? Oh yes, I like it. I like it very much. So I suspect will Tsar Alexander. What are these squiggles around the edges, Bismarck?'

'These Majestät are the initials of those members of the general staff who attended the planning meeting where this scenario was discussed.'

'I see. And this empty table at the bottom; is it awaiting my signature?'

'Indeed it is Majestät. If the map meets with your full approval, perhaps you could kindly initial it. In the space here,' he pointed, 'and date it here,' he pointed again. 'It can now be stamped with the Royal seal. It will be returned to the central safe until such a time as your Majestät should request it.'

The Kaiser smiled and then nodded at the second map. His Chancellor proceeded to unroll it. This map was identical to the first one except this time the Ottoman arrows crossed into Hungary. The straight lines were the *Austrian* defensive positions. And the arrows running *from* Russia *into* the lands of the Turks marked the advance of the Russian troops.

'Here the Russians are coming to the aid of the Austrians, eh? Because of their agreement! This is the one I should give to Franz Josef!' smiled the Kaiser. 'Excellent job, Bismarck. I will happily initial and date this one as well. If these two maps don't convince these two old protagonists to get around the negotiating table then nothing will. These maps are just the nudge they each need. Though perhaps I'd do well not to let the Emperor see the Tsar's map and vice versa,' at which remark, the Kaiser chuckled to himself.

'Our forces don't seem to figure on either map though, Bismarck, which begs the question where does Germany come in?'

'We guard both their western flanks from the French, Majestät!'

'Quite so, quite so! And the last map?'

The German Emperor noticed a slight hesitancy on the part of his Chancellor. His frown was enough to galvanise him. The third and final map was unrolled. Again it looked virtually identical to the other two with its set of initials around the edges, except…

'I must emphasize, Majestät, that this third map predates the current rapprochement… a time before an Austro-Russo-Germanic allegiance was thought to be remotely possible. It is no longer valid.'

There were two sets of arrows on this one – a confused mixture of Austrian and Russian arrows facing each other along the entire Galician border. Here Austrian and Russian forces were heavily engaged one with the other, though it wasn't clear who had invaded who. To the west, four arrows emerging from Nuremberg, Leipzig, Dresden and Breslau were shown proceeding south into Bohemian and Moravia.

'So we are attacking Austria to help the Tsar, is that what these arrows are showing, Bismarck?'

'They *could* be Majestät. The Russian railway gauge is incompatible with our rolling stock so the mass transportation of German troops *through* Russia to the Galician front is not feasible. The best way to assist the Tsar in this eventuality would be to open a second front against the Austrians in Bohemia.'

'You say *could* be, Bismarck?'

'Indeed Majestät. *If* the intention was to assist Austrian *against* the Russians, then the best strategy would be to transfer German troops directly through Austria and Hungary to Galicia. Not only are we moving through friendly territory but the railway gauge is compatible.'

'But we would also need to set up defensive positions on our side of the Russo-German border, would we not?'

'Most certainly, Majestät.'

'But these defensive lines are not shown on the map, are they?'

'Noooo, Majestät, regretfully they are not.'

'So there are two completely different but equally plausible interpretations of this map. The first applies in the case of a Russo-German pact – the second in the case of an Austro-German pact.'

The Kaiser thought for a moment. This in the hands of either Emperor would be the death knell of any aspirations for a tripartite alliance. Germany would at best be accused of duplicity and deemed untrustworthy. God's teeth, the other two might even gang up which would be worse than the present position. He looked down – undated – un-initialled. Thank God. He thrust it back at his Chancellor.

'Take it… for God's sake, take it Bismarck. Put it back in your safe and don't ever bring it to me again.'

A small village outside Lemberg, February 1873:

He'd first noticed the pair of them the week before. They'd been standing by the barracks gate as if they were waiting for somebody. He felt their eyes boring into the back of his head but when he turned around, they'd gone. It was the following week when they approached him... asked him if he was interested in earning a little money. He looked around at his hut where he now sat, no more than a hovel really. Then he scoffed – of course he was – who wouldn't be in his position! They headed off in the direction of the village and talked. Their hut sat a few kilometres beyond the city walls. Mending shoes didn't pay well enough for them to afford to live inside the city.

He was tempted. It didn't seem they were asking him to do that much. He'd only be away for a week, maybe ten days at most. What's more he'd earn more in those ten days than he could in a year repairing shoes. As the three of them approached the west gate he was almost convinced – but not quite.

"It's too late for you to walk back home and that's our fault", one of them had said. "Here, let us take you!" He couldn't remember ever having been in a covered wagon before let alone a coach of this quality. They said not a word to him during the short ride to his home… and that was clever, he could see that. They were giving him time to mull over their proposal.

'Well, if you're *really* not interested, we do have a few others we can talk to,' the man had said.

Nonetheless they would like to make him a small present, compensation for his time this evening. He looked at the coin – a *small* present!

'A pity for your wife and son though!'

He'd asked what they meant by this. A hotel, for her and the lad, in town, all costs found, they'd replied. And some pocket money as well so they could both enjoy themselves. They'd be safe and sound until his return. He'd been able to do so little to brighten her hard life, despite working all the hours the good Lord sends. How could he deny her this? And so the deal was done.

It began a few days later. They'd arrived first thing this morning in that lovely coach. The look of joy on his wife's face, the pure excitement of the lad removed any lingering doubts. There'd be money in his pocket and the experience of a lifetime for her. What they were asking seemed to disturb his conscience less and less with each passing minute. It wasn't as if he was being asked to harm anybody, was it?

This bed would be the first thing to go, they'd already decided that. *And* a new roof, one that would keep the rain and the snow out all the time – not just when it felt like it. "And some new clothes?" she'd asked hesitantly – "of course" was his reply. The two men would be back shortly and then his mission would begin. They'd only said "Hungary". He was content with that. Bag packed there was only one thing left to do.

They'd taught him to read and write in the army. He couldn't manage long words but he could write this. Once done, he put it in a small leather pouch, one of his few treasured possessions. And then he hung it on a hook on the wall-side of their bed. Nobody would see it there – certainly not those of his neighbours who might use their absence to have a poke around. He drew a chalk mark on the door frame. She'd know what that meant. She'd know he'd left her a note – just in case. He'd arranged with the men to bring him back before they collected his wife. He'd remove the chalk mark and the slip of paper before she returned. She'd never have to know!

The shrine to the Virgin Mary of Seven Sorrows
One week later:

Sergeant Ján Slota had arrived at the university at just after two o'clock.

'Fancy coming to a murder scene?' he said adding, 'you'll be sorry if you don't – this one's a strange 'un!'

There was a police wagon waiting outside the building with two officers sitting astride the box seat.

'Get a move on K-P,' shouted Inspector Hodža from inside the wagon, 'it'll be dark by five.'

The wagon set off at a furious pace. Both the driver and his colleague bellowed furiously at any pedestrians who were too dozy to notice that this was a police wagon in one hell of a hurry.

'An attempt has been made on the life of the Empress!' said the Inspector.

Pichler's jaw dropped.

There wasn't a great deal to tell. The attack had occurred this morning on the Buda to Vienna road, just five miles east of Pressburg. Her Majesty was returning to Vienna from one of her frequent visits to the Hungarian Crownlands. The assassin had fired two rounds, or so the captain of the escort had reported. Both missed it seems, though they wouldn't know for sure until the coach had been inspected. The driver had whipped up the horses at the sound of the first shot. Three of the escort went off with him, the other three set off in search of the assassin.

'What's first, sir?' asked Slota once they'd arrived at the scene.

'There are three of us and three of the escort guarding the body. We'll do one each – see if they tell the same story. But keep it brief for now. We'll do a formal interview later if needed.'

The two policemen, having secured their wagon took over the "guarding" of the assassin – not that he was going anywhere.

Pichler got the youngest of the Hussars. He looked as if he was barely into his twenties. He fair bubbled over in his enthusiasm to get his story out. They saw a man taking cover behind a fallen tree trunk. He had a rifle pointing in their direction. Without a thought for their own safety, all three rode off at the gallop, side arms drawn. He insisted on showing his revolver to Pichler. “It’s a Gasser M1870, only recently entered service, sir”, he told him.

‘When did you open fire?’ asked Pichler.

‘The moment we saw him, sir!’

‘Which would be from, what… about twenty metres?’

‘Oh no, sir we saw the villain much early than that!’ replied the young Hussar with evident pride.

‘And you fired how many rounds?’

‘What me personally, sir? Well, I didn’t fire at all. Afraid of hitting the other two who were in the lead, as you’ll understand sir.’

‘Well thank you Hussar. We’ll be in contact via your CO if we need to talk to you again. Oh, let me have one of your bullets, will you.’

Slota, Hodža and Pichler gathered together around the body which was still lying as described by the young Hussar. His torso was sprawled over a fallen tree trunk, rifle still pinned under his arm and his head was slumped to one side.

‘How many?’ asked Hodža.

‘Two!’ replied Slota.

‘None!’ answered Pichler.

‘So with my man that makes four in total!’

They all looked at each other. With an army made up of marksmen such as these, how the hell did Austria manage to lose to the Prussians in just seven weeks?

'I bet there's not a mark on him!' said Slota. 'You know what we foot soldiers used to say about the cavalry and their side arms – they only use them when they're too close to swing their sabres!'

The other two laughed, though there was an element of truth in it to be sure. To make a kill shot, at some distance on a moving horse was difficult enough. When the target is small – just his head and shoulders visible – it becomes very, very difficult. When only four shots are fired it becomes… well ficking inconceivable. The odds of any of these finding its mark were just too great.

Slota carefully laid the body out, while Pichler took the rifle. The chamber was empty! His younger self, an infantryman, rebelled at the very idea. The first thing you did in action when you'd just fired your rifle was to reload.

'Any sign of what killed him, Ján?' asked the inspector.

'Not that I can see sir and a bullet wound to the upper body should be pretty obvious.'

'Ján,' said Pichler, 'have a feel in his pockets, see if you can find any unspent rounds.'

While the Sergeant was doing this, Pichler looked on either side of the trunk around where the body had previously been. It was common practice for soldiers to lay out a handful of rounds on the ground or even on a handily placed trunk as in this case. It saved having to waste time delving into an ammunition pouch. Slota shook his head – no bullets!

‘Any idea about the rifle, K-P?’ asked Hodža.

Both he and Slota had been demobbed in 1848, while the much younger Pichler had been a regular “white-coat” up until ‘66. Of the three of them, that made Pichler the “expert”!

‘Breech load, single shot; looks very much like the Prussian Dreyse needle-gun; rate of fire of around six to ten, in the hands of a proficient marksman, I’d say.’

‘But it isn’t?’ asked Hodža.

‘No, I don’t think so,’ replied Pichler as he turned the weapon around in his hands. ‘Hello, there’s a manufacturer’s plate screwed onto the butt. It looks like it might be in Russian. It *is in* Russian *and* there’s one word in English, “Berdan”.’

The name meant nothing to the two policemen.

‘Hiram Berdan! I read about him somewhere. He was the man behind the Union sharpshooter regiments, in their civil war and he invented this jobbie!’

‘Tell me, K-P, as you’re our resident military “expert”, do you think, from this tree, *you* could have hit one and possibly both of the leading hussars?’

‘Well, Karol, I was never a great shot but I’d have to say that I would almost guarantee it. Not only that, I could have got all three. Reloading the extra rounds needed to bag all of them would take about eight seconds each – plenty of time! The three Hussars had to respond to the first shot then gallop back to here all in plain view. I'd get the first at about fifty metres, the second ten seconds later. The third would probably turn and bolt but I reckon I'd get him too.'

'And hence make a clean escape!' replied Hodza.

'If I had any ammunition left!' declared Pichler.

'As you say… *if* you had any ammunition left!'

At this point Slota joined them again.

'I've found where two of the Hussars' bullets hit. Come and have a look!'

One vertical trunk to the left of the body had a gouge at a height of about a metre. A trunk on the right was similarly damaged. Slota had dug out the bullet. Where the other two bullets had found their mark was a mystery, but it wasn't in the assassin's body, that was for sure. Pichler handed Slota the unspent round taken from the young Hussar.

'*That's more like it*, much more like the cavalry we know and love,' said Slota, comparing the two rounds.

Pichler frowned, opened his mouth, closed it, frowned again and spoke.

'This whole set up is wrong!'

His explanation to the two policemen ran as follows. There was only one reliable way to conduct this type of operation and that was to use two marksmen.

Position one at the front where a road block could be set up moments before the carriage appeared. Position the other at the rear. Then eliminate the escort by firing from both front and rear simultaneously. Lastly either pepper the entire coach at close range or send a man in to fire through the coach window directly at the intended victim. This wasn't what had happened.

'Our man,' began Slota, 'appears to have been on his tod, firing blind into coach which had already gone past him. How could he hope to hit one person when he'd no idea where they were sitting? Doesn't tick any of your boxes, does it K-P?'

Any further discussion was halted as one of the two constables came up to Hodža.

'Morgue wagon's arrived, sir.'

'Very well, constable, just ask him to wait will you. We're almost finished here.'

'Yes, sir. Can we release the three Hussars, sir? They're getting a bit twitchy!'

'Anything else you want to ask for the present?' said Hodža, turning to Slota and Pichler. 'No? Fine! Tell them they can go constable.'

The constable had not covered three metres before he sensed somebody on his shoulder. A second later and that someone was striding past him. After a brief conversation with the three Hussars, Pichler returned.

'What was that all about?' asked Slota.

'I wanted to be certain that they hadn't interfered with the body. They hadn't! The senior man had dismounted and approached on foot ready to fire. The other two covered him with their revolvers. They could see that the assassin was slumped motionless over the tree trunk and his hands were well clear of the rifle. It was safe enough, they all agreed. If he'd been feigning, he'd have three bullet holes in him before he could have moved a muscle. They were hoping to take him alive for interrogation, but he was as dead as a coffin nail when the leader poked him.

Apart from that they stayed well clear until we turned up. Luckily for us, the young lad's old man was one of us, or I should say one of you two. He's a senior inspector in Buda. So he knew all about not messing with a crime scene and warned the others off. I told him his father would be proud of him. I think he was pretty chuffed with that.'

'Well good to hear,' said Hodža, 'but that helps us how?'

'The point is we know for sure that he wasn't killed by Hussars so it's either a case of murder or a case of suicide. Help me turn him onto his front, will you?'

He had to lift up the fellow's hair in several likely areas and pull it apart to reach the skin. He was beginning to think he was wrong. Worse still, Hodža now had his impatient face on… and then he found it; a tiny mark where a needle might have gone in. But it would have been so easy to miss. Without a word to the two professionals, he turned and started walking very slowly in the opposite direction to the road. Slota was only a step behind him as he knew what was going through Pichler's mind. Hodža on the other hand was rooting around in the long grass with a stick – he didn't want to stick himself!

'Got it!' he called fifteen minutes later. They were too far away to hear. 'Oi! I've found IT!'

Pressburg Police Station:

If it had been just any old "Johann Bloghs" who'd been the subject of this assassination attempt, General von Ulmnitz's could have stayed in his nice warm bed. It wasn't – it was the Empress. So he'd had no option but to drag himself away on this frosty February morning at the ungodly hour of five. He had to be somewhere. Four hours later, he was.

'Only it wasn't an assassination attempt, sir!' began Hodža. 'Her Majesty was in very little real danger. We doubt either of the two rounds fired came within even a few metres of the carriage. If they had it would have been entirely unintentional on the part of our "marksman". You see, General, the assassin wasn't really the assassin, more like the victim.' He then went on to explain.

'Let me see if I've rightly understood you, Inspector. A man fired two shots using a standard Russian infantry rifle, these being the only two rounds he had in his possession. He had little chance of doing anything other than bringing the escort crashing down on his head. Immediately or at least very soon after he'd fired the second shot, an unknown person stuck him in the back of the neck with an as yet unidentified poison. This was the cause of death. This person then left unseen by all, heading deep into the forest. Excuse me if I'm being particularly obtuse here, but have you asked yourself this question… WHY!'

The desk reverberated under the impact of the General's clenched fist. Silence prevailed.

'Come on then. Let's inspect the body,' ordered the General disconsolately. This case was going to be a "pig"– he could feel it in his bones.

The basement morgue used to be a source of great irritation to the police surgeon on account of its poor lighting. But that was some years ago. Since then the walls of the room had been retiled in gleaming white and numerous gas lamps installed. Now there was barely a dark cranny left to be found. Sadly nothing could be done to enlarge the morgue. There was scarcely room for Hodža, Pichler and the General to fit in – impossible if the other two had been of the General's build.

The General pointed an open palm at Pichler and then at the corpse, inviting him to make an examination.

The corpse laid out in the morgue was that of a man in his late thirties to early forties. It was difficult to be certain for the body stretched out on the slab before Pichler bore all the hallmarks of an exceptionally hard life. The hands for sure were those of a manual worker, not those of a professional assassin. The face was definitely Slavic. His muscle tone was good – his teeth were not – peasant class then. His skin showed the effect of many hours spent labouring in the sun and the wind. His arms were mottled in that tell-tale way that wind burn produces.

‘Karol, could you give me a hand?’ indicating to the inspector that he wished to turn the body over.

He shaved off some hair. The entry point of the needle was even less obvious than it had been at the crime scene. They, whoever *they* were, hadn’t intended anyone to find it! Had the Hussars actually hit the fellow, Pichler wouldn’t have even gone looking for an entry point in the first place.

It was impossible to know if death had been instantaneous, but it can’t have been long after. The Hussar’s evidence told him that. It was a minor detail. It was the poison which had killed him. However one point was beyond dispute. He couldn’t have injected himself, thrown the syringe far enough away that it took Karol a quarter of an hour to find it and then neatly rearranged himself back on the tree trunk. There had to have been an “accomplice”, though that wasn’t the right term. Accomplice implies somebody who was there to help commit the crime, not kill the shooter.

‘Sorry, General the corpse tells us no more than we already knew,’ said Pichler. ‘But there can be only one logical reason why he was killed. After he’d gained our attention by shooting at the Empress, his body… and his rifle had to remain in place.'

Von Ulmnitz glared at him.

'So they could be found, General… by *us*.'

'Are... you… telling… me,' said the General pulling himself up to his full height, 'that this was some sort of attention-seeking exercise, the sole purpose of which was for us to recover *this*?'

He pointed at the corpse, before adding 'is that really what you are telling me, Herr Leutnant? Well, is it?'

'I'm saying, General, that it is a distinct possibility sir!' replied Pichler without flinching a muscle.

Hodža, responding to Pichler's request, helped him turn the corpse so the body was once again lying face up. In the process of doing so, and somewhat distractedly, the Inspector looked at the face of the dead man once again.

'He does look *very* Slavic indeed, doesn't he? I mean Russian, rather than Bohemian or even Polish. Wouldn't you say so K-P?'

For answer, Pichler walked over to the bench and picked up a pair of scissors. Was it possible? It was a long shot, a really long shot, but he'd be a fool not to try while the body was still in a fit state. But where? It *could* have been anywhere on the body, but it was usually the least obvious place that the man could think off. Where was that? Of course! Taking small turfs of pubic hair in one hand, Pichler sniped away until the flesh was visible. He was a bloody hairy bugger but it was worth it.

'Inspector, could you write this number down please?'

Pichler read out the seven figures and then stood away from the body.

'Well?' said the General. He was slightly irritated. Not so much by the time all this was taking. No, it was the fact that *he* of all people didn't know what the hell was going on.

'General, if you care to look up that service number in army records you will find his name and regiment. However I for one would be heartily surprised if it doesn't turn out to be a Ruthenian one.'

'What are you on about, K-P?' asked the exasperated Inspector.

'Remember, Karol I served in Galicia in 65/66 right up until I got dragged back west when the Prussians invaded. I got to know their little ways, one of which was to have their service number tattooed on their body.'

'Yes, I've heard of that practice going on in some of the Eastern regiments. It's so if they get killed and mutilated beyond recognition, the authorities would still be able to inform the next of kin,' interrupted Hodža. 'Though, they usually had it done on the upper arm – never heard of anybody tattooing themselves down there before.'

And he winced at the very idea.

'True,' replied Pichler. 'The thing is, these boys had a tendency to go AWOL, for weeks on end, especially if their wife was about to give birth. Very family orientated these Ruthenians. Well, think about it. There you are wetting the baby's head when up pops the local gendarmerie on the lookout for deserters. They might check your arm, but…'

'Yes, I get your point, K-P,' replied Hodža.

'So,' started the General, 'they've grabbed our attention. Hmmmm, how likely are they to have known about the hidden tattoo?'

'Highly unlikely, sir. Most officers would be totally ignorant of the practice. I only know about it because one of my chap's tattoo got badly infected. They asked me if I could "acquire" something suitable from the company M.O.'s store. I don't know why, but they seemed to trust me.'

'Gentlemen,' began von Ulmnitz, 'I must pause the discussion at this stage as I have some urgent matters to attend to. Inspector, may I have the use of your office for one hour, after which time perhaps you could both meet me there. And I shall need one of your constables to be on station within earshot.'

***

Von Ulmnitz wedged himself into the Inspector's chair. It seemed to him that Pichler was entirely correct. The people that they were up against were completely ignorant of the "privately" concealed service number. The only way they would know would be if the man himself had chosen to reveal its existence. And why should he do that? So, the forces of law and order had been given a break and he wasn't about to waste it. The first telegram was sent to Oberst Franz Keppler at Lemberg. Regimental records were held in the principal city of each province, not centrally in Vienna. For Galicia that meant Lemberg, one of the two principal fortress towns which guarded the Empire's Carpathian flank with Russia. Keppler was a member of his inner circle and would have no difficulty in understanding von Ulmnitz's own code. It wasn't a high-level cypher, just good enough to prevent its contents being understood by any casual observer. The next telegram went to the ISD Vienna and the final to one to the Wienertagesblatt newspaper, both in Vienna.

His next job was to formulate a cover story for Pichler. He was the right man for this one! Von Ulmnitz had been reluctant to use him back in the summer of 1870, but he was glad he had. And *that* was the hour spent!

"Knock-knock".

'Come in, gentlemen. I am expecting to receive a number of responses to my enquiries over the next few hours. In the meantime, Herr Pichler this is your cover story. I will pick up a letter this evening from the Editor of the Wienertagesblatt and give it to you tomorrow morning. The editor, do you see, has just commissioned one of his reporters which is you by the way, to obtain material for a special feature. It will be called "A view from the Carpathians". You will be accompanied by a Ukrainian speaking colleague, who I'm in the process of identifying. The paper will contain a short announcement of this forthcoming piece, just to add credibility to your cover. If you've ever read the paper, you'll know this type of article is not untypical of the "happy-Empire" nonsense that editors occasionally pump out. Your name is Klaus Kahpeh and this is your first assignment since joining the Vienna Daily from the Innsbruck Reporter. You'll be entered on the staff roll of both papers by midday tomorrow. I hope you will be able to poke around without attracting any undue suspicion but if you do and some nosey individual decides to check your cover story out, then I think this precaution will keep you safe.

Pichler nodded; it was only what he had come to expect from the General. Some called it the "intelligence game". But it wasn't a "game"; get it wrong and lives are lost, his in this case! There was no such thing as "overkill" when it came to cover stories, especially ones put together as quickly as this one.

'I've asked my office to come up with a native Ukrainian speaker, but frankly I'm not holding out much hope. Ideally I'd want the pair of you to step off the train at Lemberg together. You understand, in case any undesirables are watching out for you. However if push comes to shove you may have to use a local…'

'Actually, General, I can suggest somebody who works here in Pressburg!' interrupted Pichler.

'Go on!'

'Danilo Bondarenko. Mid-twenties; his mother's German, his father's Ruthenian and he has an uncle living in Lemberg *and* it was his home town as a boy.'

'And you know him from where?' asked the General.

'He took a law degree. I taught him one module. He graduated last summer and has been working as an intern at Wallenstein, Pytror and Kauble, the law firm on the Rettenstrasse. I don't think they pay him, so I can't imagine he'll have any problem getting the time off.'

'But is he up to the job?'

'He is that!' stated Pichler boldly while thinking "rather him than some unknown bod from Lemberg".

'Very well... CONSTABLE!' bellowed von Ulmnitz, following up his bellow with a set of instructions to the same poor sod who'd already spent the previous hour running around like a blue-arsed fly at the General's behest.

'Inspector, be so good as to have the three telegrams I'm expecting to be sent to the Army Club. Herr Pichler, I shall expect to see you there for dinner at six. Draw expenses from the Inspector here. And lastly get me a cab.' With that the General was on his feet and out the door.

'He's like a human whirlwind, isn't he Karol?' said Pichler.

'Bloody good job he is Herr "Kahpeh". Your life may just depend on him being so,' replied Hodža.

Pichler's home:

'So Anna, Amelia, I'm likely to be away for a week, possibly more.'

'Oh, how lovely K-P,' interrupted Amelia. 'Where are you going?'

Anna touched her arm.

'We never ask that question, dear,' she said to the girl, 'Hush-hush!' which excited Amelia even more than if Anna had just made up somewhere.

'What time will you be back this evening, my dear?' asked Anna.

'Not late – "vonU" will want to be back in Vienna tonight.'

He didn't enjoy being away from home for any length of time, but it was a godsend that Anna had agreed to take on a servant – at last. Servant though was a poor description of the relationship his wife had developed with Frau Ursula Friedstein's youngest daughter Amelia. They were more like a pair of sisters; one younger and gauche, the other older and wiser.

Amelia's confidence had come on in leaps and bounds over the last few months. So had her accomplishments. Musically, her strong point was singing rather than playing. Anna was able to convince one of her inner circle, who just happened to be one of Pressburg's foremost music teachers, to attend one of the "sisters" regular afternoon sessions. The result? Amelia was taken under a second wing.

Frau and Fräulein Friedstein did not get on especially well – which is to say not at all well and it was getting worse. One evening, as her day's work had come to an end and she was on the point of going home, the poor girl burst into floods. Of course, Anna told her, she couldn't stay overnight, despite her sobbing, *not* without Frau Friedstein's acquiescence.

Anna and Pichler had walked Amelia home the next evening to discuss a permanent boarding arrangement. Frau Friedstein had readily agreed to Anna's proposal with a rapidity which thoroughly disgusted her, causing her to rail against the woman for the whole of the walk back to the Pichlers'.

The army club:

'So, Herr Bondarenko, I need you to sign this form,' said von Ulmnitz.

He looked hesitantly to the man sitting to his left, 'Just sign it, Bondo – I had to!' replied Herr Kahpeh.

'Good! You are now in effect a government employee, albeit a very temporary one. I've cleared your absence with your employer, handed him a sizeable sum to cover your time which I understand he doesn't even pay for anyway. If you make a success of this my lad I shall write him such a glowing report on you that I would expect an immediate improvement in your circumstances. Your contact in Lemberg, Herr Kahpeh, is an Oberst Franz Keppler and he is to be the *only* point of contact, but don't contact him unless you really have to – he's probably being watched. Coded messages can be sent to Vienna only via the Colonel and only if it is *absolutely* essential. Now then, I have received the Colonel's response; our corpse now has a name; Gemeiner Artim Koval, ex-19th infantry (Lemberg); released from full-time service six years ago and now a part-timer in the reserve. He rose to the rank of Sergeant major but was reduced to the ranks in his last year; drunk and disorderly. Koval's home is in a small village three kilometres west of the city walls, called Bozac. I'll meet you at Vienna station at nine tomorrow morning with some further items you are going to need. And that gentlemen, only leaves me to settle the bill and for you two to go home, pack for at least three days and get a good night's sleep.'

'Well,' said Bondarenko, 'this wasn't the kind of day I'd expected when I was sitting down to my breakfast this morning. Still, I'm not in the least bit sorry.'

'Do you need any money?' said Pichler.

'I only graduated last summer, I don't get paid and am living off my old man's generosity! Of course, I need money.'

'I meant tonight!' said Pichler with a smile and with that they parted company.

Eastward bound:

There was no scheduled service from Vienna to Lemberg only a military train which departed from the military depot, situated some five kilometres to the Northeast of the city. Pichler had taken this journey seven years before and it was truly memorable but *not* in a good way.

Bondarenko's experience of trains was rather limited so he really enjoyed the first part from Pressburg to Vienna. They had shared a compartment with a family of four and an old gentleman. The family included two younger children, probably no more than five years old and almost certainly twins. They brought out the five-year-old child in Bondarenko! He started it…

'The train's moving… here it goes… are-you-ready… chuuufff – chuff – chuff – chuff – chuff…… wooo-a-wooooo!'

And the children followed suit enthusiastically as did their mother. Their father, the old gentleman and Pichler all smiled benevolently – at least for the first ten times they'd heard it.

Von Ulmnitz was waiting at the platform with a briefcase and a small box. The former he handed to Pichler, the latter to Bondarenko. They had no time to look at these as he hurried them out of the exit and onto a waiting cab, with a "good luck".

The cab deposited them at the entrance to the military depot in double-quick time. They had no problem in finding the right platform and the right train – there was only one of each. As they walked towards the train they were greeted by an "All right then Gents?" It was the train marshal. They were escorted to the only wagon that had a roof and four sides; all the rest were flat tops loaded with stores, ammunition and ordinance. The marshal pulled open the sliding door and pointed at two wooden benches, a pile of blankets, a box of provisions for the journey, which was reassuring large and the stove in that order.

'Now, you've both gotta flint, ain't yer?'

Picher pulled his out of his greatcoat pocket and waved it at the marshal while Bondarenko looked on, totally mystified.

'Good, 'cause it you let that thing go out overnight, the next terminus you see won't be fortress Przemyśl, it'll be eiver the pearly gates or somewhere a lot hotta than you'd like. You've plenty of grub. Feel free to use the bucket when standing at a station, cos there ain't any stations on this route. Whatever you do, stay on the bleeding train if it stops. It'll eiver be taking on coal or water or clearing the line. It's liable to go off without warning and that'll be the end of you, this time of year.'

The military train, like the train they'd been on earlier also had a rhythm of its own; not so much chuuufff – chuff – chuff – chuff – chuff…… wooo-a-wooooo!, more like…Clang – clang – ter-werk – clunk – THUD – Christ, my fucking back!

After a good number of hours of this, young Bondarenko looked thoroughly miserable and probably wished he was back at his desk.

'I reckon it's time for some grub, Bondo!'

Bondarenko smiled. Pichler only used contractions of his students' surnames. When asked, he explained it was all to do with social equality, but "Bondo" thought it was more likely that he couldn't remember names. The offspring of the Count von this or Herzog von that didn't like it. Not one bit. They complained to the Dean who hauled Pichler in. "You *must* use their full titles, Herr Pichler, really you must". Each time he would promise he would do his best, use the same excuse that his war injuries had affected his memory and never attempt to do anything different. Eventually the Dean got tired of giving him the same lecture and the ennobled sons, well… they got to rather like it.

The box contained potatoes, Würste, onions and lard, two metal mess tins, two spoons and an enormous frying pan. And that wasn't all. Underneath that little lot were further goodies. Pichler thought he'd save these for later – it was a long journey. So Pichler peeled, chopped and fried and within twenty minutes, each tin was piled up to the rim. Bondo thought it wasn't right, he was the junior – he ought to be doing this. Though he was glad he wasn't – the motion was getting to him, making him feel distinctly queasy in fact. Strangely this nausea evaporated the moment Pichler shoved a loaded tin under his nose. Ten minutes later Bondo was asleep, snoring his head off with a hint of a contented smile on his face.

Pichler opened the briefcase; a single sheet of instructions which he pulled out, took only a few moments to read and even less time to turn to ash in the stove; an ordinary looking brown envelope contained an impressive looking authorisation certificate, not to be used unless under extremis; a commissioning letter from the Editor of the Wienertagesblatt, *his* editor (apparently) which outlined the scope of their assignment.

What else was there? Oh yes, a notebook, embossed with the words "Reporter's Notebook", just so Pichler got the general idea; a map of the city – in German; a wad of notes – expenses for the use of.

Then he opened the box Bondo had been given and found a small box camera and a note. Pichler had never seen one as small as this. He removed the lens cap and then searched for the plates – there only seemed to be the one. What was the point of lugging a camera around, even a small one just to take one picture? Puzzled he turned over the note. It said "Just for show – doesn't work. Get the young lad to wave it around as if he knows what he's doing." Clearly it was *just* a box which the old boy had had knocked up by the backroom staff at ISD HQ in Vienna overnight. The old rogue!

***

It was many hours later and there wasn't a bit that didn't ache on either of the men, but at last, they were nearly there. Bondarenko peered into the box – bread, jam and milk. Well why not? It might be some time before their next meal.

The village of Bozac:

When they got to Bozac the next day, much to Pichler's joy, they discovered it wasn't a small village at all; it was a tiny six house hamlet. The chance of strangers paying a visit and not being observed by at least two of the other households was next to nil. It's the same the whole world over – the smaller the place, the more observant, not to say downright nosy are the inhabitants.

'You'll have to pay him again for the return trip *and* at twice the rate, K-P,' observed Bondarenko.

It embarrassed him to say so, but the avarice of some his own people knew no bounds. In this case, he was referring to the driver of the dog cart that had brought them here.

Pichler had no intention of being stuck in this dump for a moment longer than necessary. Anyway he'd already decided to spend as much of the General's money as necessary, so he pre-empted the situation even arising.

'Here's something for you to buy yourself a little food and drink with. I'm sure one of these houses will be more than willing to provide some sustenance while you wait. After all we can't have you hanging around in the cold. And *of course*, we'll pay double the rate for the return. I expect it'll be so much harder on the dogs going back. Translate will you, Bondo?'

The man was dumbstruck. Why it should be any harder for the dogs when it was exactly the same distance back to Lemberg, he had no idea. The fact that he didn't have to haggle for ages to screw the return rate up to double pleased him immensely. Then it struck him… maybe he could have got the fellow up to two and half times. His old woman would give him hell if she found out. Perhaps he'd stick to the "it took me best part of a half hour to persuade him to…"

'Wait outside!' Pichler instructed his companion.

The home of the Koval's was a poor affair. The roof was sparsely turfed and several gaps could be seen between the wooden slats in both roof and walls. How could a family survive a Carpathian winter in this? He poked one of the gaps and noticed a thread of wool was attached. Inside it was clear that previously, perhaps only a week earlier the ramshackle hut had been lined with woollen rugs. He stuck his head outside and saw faces in the two huts opposite pull smartly out of sight. He reckoned he had a pretty fair idea where those rugs now resided – and the roofing turf for that matter.

There was little left in the hut that could further his investigation; just a rickety old bed and a few stools too dilapidated to be of interest to his former neighbours. No evidence remained to indicate what might have happened to Koval's wife and child. It only remained to question their former neighbours.

As he'd expected, they all knew "nothing about nobody". It was hopeless. A wasted journey!

"Bondo? Bondo! Where the devil are you man, I'm freezing my bits off out here?'

There was no answer, so Pichler went back inside Koval's hut to get warm. It was only marginally better than standing outside. A few minutes later and he heard, 'Sorry… I'm on my way,' but by this time where Bondo was or had been was of no interest. The pouch was wedged between the wall and one of the bedposts – small wonder that he hadn't seen it the first time. Pichler found a rolled up slip of paper inside.

'I'm here!' said the young face at the door.

'What have you been up to?' demanded Pichler.

'Tell you later!' was the reply, uttered with an authority that would brook no argument.

'What about you K-P?'

'Tell you later,' he replied with a smile.

Their hotel back in Lemberg:

'I was inside with the old woman in the hut directly opposite. She told me that two men had turned up at the hamlet late one evening a couple of weeks ago, in a posh coach of all things. Naturally every one of the neighbours had their noses pressed right up against their windows. And who did they see get out but our friend Koval. Anyway, the coach…'

'What day of the week was this?' interrupted Pichler.

'She said she wasn't too sure, but thought it was Tuesday. Shall I go on?'

Pichler nodded.

'So she was on the lookout and when the coach turned up again about a week later, there she was – nose to the window again. The wife and lad got in and off they went leaving friend Koval behind twiddling his thumbs until it returned sometime later and off he went never to be seen again.'

'What was it *you* were looking at when I came to the hut?' asked Bondarenko.

Pichler removed the note from the pouch and handed it to the young man.

'Can you translate it?'

Bondarenko frowned. The scrawled letters were hard even to discern; the grammar was awful.

'God knows where he learnt to read and write!' was his opening remark.

Pichler said nothing, confident that Bondo would make something of it.

'Not sure if he's ever heard of punctuation, but here goes, word for word…

Darlin Nadia/ I do what must – keep you + boy saff/ If I no return you this life I wait you in next/ Men odd – When fink I no hear – They speaked tongue I no no

… and *that's* the best I can do, K-P. I think saff means safe and "no no" means "didn't recognise". What language would he have never heard before?'

Pichler was ahead of him. It couldn't have been German. All the officers spoke that. It was unlikely he'd not heard any Polish or even Hungarian given his years in army. Russian was similar to his native tongue, leaving what – Czech, Serbian and the other Slavic languages perhaps? But would any of these have sounded *so* different to his ears? Three candidates *did* fit the bill; English, French, Italian but they all sounded equally improbable.

'So what's on the list for tomorrow?' asked Bondo.

'Our editor has arranged for us to attend a gathering of Lemberg's social elite, to be held at the Grand hotel at one,' said Pichler. 'I will make a short presentation outlining the scope of my forthcoming article "A view from the Carpathians". After that I'll work my way around the tables to interview the good and the great. *You* will be taking photographs.'

'So I can have the morning off exploring my old stamping ground, can I?' asked Bondarenko.

He took Picher's silence as a "yes"

***

Earlier the next day, before venturing out on his solo exploration of his home town, Bondo spent the hour straight after breakfast practicing in his hotel room. He'd take a photograph, carefully remove the plate and making sure it had a black cloth over it at all times, place it in his bag. Next he'd rummage around and find another plate (actually the same plate) which was covered with a similar cloth (the same cloth) and slip the "new" plate into the camera. So pleased was he with himself that he intercepted Pichler as the latter was leaving his room.

'What do you think, K-P? Convincing, eh?'

'Have you ever seen a photographer at work, Bondo?' said Pichler.

A rather deflated Bondarenko had to admit he hadn't.

'Neither have most of the people you're going to be photographing this afternoon, so your little charade will do the job nicely!'... which brought a broad smile to the young man's face.

***

Come the meeting, Bondo duly followed in Pichler's wake, taking photographs as directed. He embellished his morning's performance with much posing of the subjects, interspersed with "tutt-tutts" about the poor lighting. Pichler had a job keeping a straight face. None of the audience had the faintest inkling that this was all for show – but then they'd probably never seen a camera like this one before. A few even voiced this thought…"Amazing what these clever fellows in Vienna come up with, isn't it my dear?"

At some tables, Herr Kahpeh would say… "My boy will call on you in the next few days to discuss an agreeable time for an in-depth interview. Just think the whole of Vienna will read about you". And the "boy" duly wrote down their addresses. There would be much disappointment amongst the elite of Lemberg society in the coming days.

By evening back in their hotel the pair of them had done such a sterling job that nearly a dozen invitations to visit this event or that had arrived during the course of their dinner. Pichler reviewed each one and with a "no", handed the invitation straight back to his colleague. After several more "no… no… no's…" came a "yes – this one!"

***

'Why did you like the look of this invitation, K-P?' asked Bondarenko, 'and come to that where did you disappear to straight after breakfast? I'd hoped that you might like to accompany me on my trip down memory lane.'

'I was playing a hunch. I went to the Barracks! Tuesday night is drill night for the reservists, one of whom is or was until recently Private Koval. And right opposite the barracks, is…'

'Tonight's meeting place!' replied the younger man triumphantly.

***

Thanks to a little local knowledge – Bondo's local knowledge – they arrived at the hall in quick order via a series of short cuts. The bill sticker on the door read "Galician Plebiscite – the people's right to choose". The hall probably had room for several hundred persons, but Pichler estimated that it was less than a third full. The audience was split roughly half and half and the rough-half looked *very* rough indeed. The smooth-half wore suits and were gathered closer to the stage where stood a single lectern.

The two journalists weaved their way from the back to the front with cries of "press, press!" Initially they encountered oaths and black looks, but these turned to "make way for the gentlemen of the press" once they were in the land of the suits.

The speaker for the evening arrived a few moments after their arrival at the front of the hall. He was a tall, good-looking man of around forty, wearing a suit that definitely wasn't made in Lemberg, or even in Galicia come to that. Pichler looked across at Bondo as the man began his address and the returned-look said "not from around here!"

The fellow spoke in a mellow tone. The people, he said, were entitled to decide their own future.

Some might want to continue to be part of the Austrian crownlands though the accompanying scowl made it clear to the audience that *that* would be the *wrong* answer.

Some might wish to be part of the Hungarian crownlands. That also merited a scowl.

But the right-minded ones, he suggested by a smile, might see their future as an autonomous, self-governing enclave, with the Austrian Kaiser to the south and the Russian Tsar to the north.

He smacked his hand down on the lectern declaring that there *must* be a plebiscite to decide this. They had sent envoys to the Tsar asking him to guarantee a free and fair ballot and his Imperial Majesty had agreed to this. He went further – even offering to send observers from the Tsarist army to ensure that this happened.

There was much nodding and murmurs of approval. Pichler silenced these by raising a hand.

'Ah, the gentleman from the press. And which paper do you represent, may I ask?'

'We are from the Wienertagesblatt, sir.'

'Vienna, eh! And you have a question for me?'

'Yes, sir, if you please sir. If the people vote for an autonomous enclave such as you have outlined sir.'

'Yes…?' the mellow tone has been replaced by something rather more menacing.

'Do you intend to allow free-passage of either the Russian or the Empire's forces in that event?'

The speaker had no intention of responding to that thorny question. Instead he turned to his audience.

'So, this is *exactly* what I've been talking about comrades. This is "Vienna" dictating what we may or may not do – yet again. It is *exactly* why we must push on, as hard as we have to – to achieve our objective.'

The crowd responded with a chant "Pleb-is-cite... Pleb-is-cite ... Pleb-is-cite" mildly by the "suits" but raucously by the "roughs". A friendly voice spoke in Pichler's ear.

'You need to get out – NOW! Through that side door – quick – GO!'

By the time they were out in the side street, half a dozen roughs had broken out of the hall and had spotted them. "Get 'em!" they yelled. Bondo was away like a hare and Pichler notwithstanding his physical disadvantage wasn't far behind, but they *were* being gained on. Bondo stopped for a second and lobbed his camera and plate bag at the pursuing mob and on reaching their trophy they paused to kick seven lumps out of it. None of this was seen by the young man who rushed by his former teacher, turning right into a narrow side street and turning right again into an even narrower ally. Pichler followed as close as he could, hoping to God that Bondo knew where he was going.

The next thing he knew a hand had reached out and grabbed his collar, yanking him into a recessed doorway. And there the pair of them hid, jammed into the corner as far as they possibly could, making not a sound. One group of roughs missed the first turning – the next group missed the second turning – the last few made both turnings but sped pass the two shadows concealed in the doorway.

After what seemed like ages, Pichler chanced a whispered question.

'Safe to go?'

Bondo's answer came as music to his ears.

'Yes, safe to go!'

***

There were around two hundred people carrying banners each bearing a single word – "Plebiscite". They occupied the entire width of Lodlov Street and extended along it for about a dozen shop fronts. Facing them were thirty soldiers armed with rifles and out in front of them, a single officer. He looked no older than Bondo to Pichler, who was observing the gathering from the top of the town hall.

Never without it, Pichler examined the crowd through his pocket telescope. He found them to be neither roughs nor suits, but poor wrenches that as likely as not, had no conception of what a plebiscite actually was. He worked his way towards the rear of the mob. No it wasn't a mob! The people were shuffling along as if in a daze. Such chanting as there was was half-hearted at best.

And at that point he spotted the roughs – a good dozen of them, each armed with a pistol. He knew what was about to happen, knew that he couldn't do a damn thing about it. The shots were fired and people started to fall, but only at the rear. The mob, for it was *now* a mob – a terrified mob – charged forward towards the as yet undischarged rifles of the soldiers. He closed his eyes and waited for the sound of the first volley. But it didn't come.

'Cavvvaaalry break!' it was the young officer.

'Opeeeen… break!'

The soldiers split into two thin columns and rotated through ninety degrees, pressing themselves close to the shop fronts on each side of the street. As the last of the crowd passed through this gap…

'Cloooose… break!'

The soldiers reversed the manoeuvre blocking further passage but the street in front of their rifles was now empty of all save bodies and discarded placards.

'What just happened?' asked a startled Bondo.

Pichler explained; when the cavalry return to the safety of their own lines after making a sortie on the enemy, it's generally thought to be a good idea if they don't mow down their own infantry in the process – hence the command "cavalry break". It would have been so easy, understandable even for the young officer, confronted by a mob running towards him, to panic. But he didn't and he'd saved dozens and dozens of innocent lives in the process.

***

Oberst Keppler, General von Ulmnitz's man in Lemberg, had conducted the interviews of all twenty-two of the demonstrators they had detained. They were easy enough to round up as they stood cowed behind the ranks of soldiers who had provided the "break". They all told exactly the same story; a man had come to their dwelling late last night, given them a Kreuzer coin and instructions as to where they had to be and at what time. Had they made the banners? No – they'd been given them. Did they understand what a plebiscite was? The blank looks needed no verbal response.

***

As they set off for what they thought would prove to be their last job in Lemberg, they ran into the Lieutenant they'd seen earlier that day. Bondo observed their little scene as Pichler advanced towards him; an outstretched hand offered by a man the officer didn't know, accepted and words exchanged; broad smiles from both men and a final parting handshake.

"What did you say, K-P?'

'I told him I'd seen his action today and if I had the power I'd recommend him for an exemplary commendation to his senior officer.'

He talked as they walked and parted with "see you back at the hotel, Bondo. Good luck!"

Pichler had done all the hotels, boarding houses and rental agencies in the eastern half of Lemberg. It sounded like an impossible task but being foremost a military town, there were only twenty such places. This was a gamble. There were probably many more places where one *might* stay, providing the one in question was not adverse to lice but those types of places were of no use to Pichler. The law said guests must show some form of identification and for foreigners their papers would also show their nationality. Only reputable inns that followed the law and kept a record would be worth trying. Anyway, judging by his smart attire, it was unlikely that the man they sought had ever had any close acquaintance with such tiny creatures.

Pichler's net was empty and back in the hotel he consoled himself with a beer while awaiting Bondo's return. He had just ordered a second when a bedraggled wretch flopped down in the seat opposite. The waiter returned with the beer on a tray. Pichler gestured for him to place it in front of the new arrival and immediately dispatched him with an order for two more.

'God, you look like you've been dragged through a hedge backwards!'

Bond grabbed the beer and didn't replace it on the table until it was two-thirds empty.

'I had to run between virtually every place. Do you know how many inns and hotels there are in Western Lemberg?'

Pichler shook his head innocently and in truth he didn't know as he'd stopped counting at fifty before handing Bondo his "half" of the list.

'Just one thing before I start K-P. Why did you tell me *not* to ask about Koval's wife and child at the same time as I was asking after this chap from the meeting?'

Pichler took a deep breath, knowing the effect his words would have on Bondarenko.

'Because they're dead!'

'How can you know that K-P?' replied an alarmed Bondo.

'They were taken off in the carriage – you remember telling me that. Think about it – they couldn't be allowed to live; they were never going to meet Koval on his return because he was *never going* to return. I don't suppose, assuming they were promised money that there was ever any intention of paying anything beyond a small "tempter". No, it pains me to say it but I expect their bodies will be found somewhere between the city wall and the village and probably not until the thaw has arrived.'

Bondarenko looked down at his feet. If this was the world of applied criminal science, then maybe life as an articled clerk was not so boring after all.

'I'm sorry to upset you,' said Pichler, 'especially as from your face when you entered, I rather thought you had some good news for me.'

'Oh, yes I have. I've found him!' he declared triumphantly. 'The manager's description matched. His name is Louis Martin, from Paris and he left Lemberg this morning by coach.'

Pichler smiled as Bondo grasped the second beer the moment the waiter had set it down. It wasn't as good as the younger man supposed. Even with his limited French, Pichler knew that Martin was the equivalent of Schmidt. Of course it was always going to be a false name; he'd known that before they'd started. Monsieur Martin had been speaking fluent Ukrainian at the meeting yet he was not a Ruthenian. He had to have some Russian blood in his veins, but was he a friend of France and an enemy of Russia or vice versa? He remembered Maggie telling him a little about the Russian exiles in Paris. What did she say – were they Jews forced out by a pogrom? He couldn't remember – a job for Pressburg that one – go to see Maggie. The address on the man's papers would have been a fake. In fact the *only* things he could be sure about was that he *had been* in Lemberg, it *was* the man at the meeting and now… now that man had bolted!

'Where was the coach heading, Bondo?'

So that's where they were going – to Krakow in Western Galicia where neither of them spoke Polish but at least there was a better chance of getting by in German.

'Next one's in three days, K-P,' added Bondo anticipating the "boss's" next question.

Pichler hadn't really expected this newly discovered stroke of luck to last much longer. He put his hand in his jacket pocket and his fingers rested on the large wad of cash so generously donated by the General.

'What's your philosophy on a juicy steak and a bottle of red wine, Herr Bondarenko?'

'In general, Herr Kaypee, weighing up both sides of the argument, I would consider them to be fiching marvellous,'… and so they were!

***

The next day Pichler tried to ascertain the origins of the Galician plebiscite movement. He tried the military police, he tried the local newspaper and he tried asking the people living around the area of the meeting hall – all to no avail. So if this was a one off event what was it all for? Perhaps the sole aim was to create some unrest amongst the population and indeed that might well have happened but for the actions of one very smart lieutenant. Pichler left Bondo to his own devices, giving him time to look up his uncle.

The opening conversation at dinner that night was, for once, not about the case.

'Did you meet your uncle?'

'No, 'fraid not. The poor soul died about a month ago.'

'I'm sorry to hear that.'

'I'm not,' replied the younger man much to Pichler's surprise. 'I spoke to his neighbour – it seemed he was in a lot of pain, a "screaming in the night" type of pain – there was nothing the doctors could do and so it was probably a relief to the poor old fellow.'

'How old was he?'

'Fifty-five!'

'That's not old, not these days,' responded Pichler.

'Depends how you look at it, K-P. My mama used to warn me off skating on our local pond at either end of the winter. She'd tell me "Your father's brother" – don't know why she never referred to him as my uncle – perhaps they weren't that close. Where was I, oh, yes, she'd tell me… "one day he broke though the ice and fell in when he was seven. If your grandma hadn't been so close at hand that would have been the end of him – don't let it be the end of you my lad". Mothers, eh! So in a way he was granted a gift – a gift of forty eight years! What did you manage to find out?'

Pichler could tell that despite his stoic exterior, he was keen to move onto a different subject. Pichler wasn't keen to dwell on his fruitless day either so decided to make a review.

'Of course, we don't *know* they were French. They could equally as well have been Russian, given that for the Russian aristocracy, French is a second language. In fact when you think about it, that's far more likely; how many French people speak Russian?'

'*They*?'

Pichler frowned. This was not a question he would expect from one of his star ex- pupils.

'How was Koval able to hear a conversation in an unfamiliar language?' Pichler asked, glaring as he spoke and then stopped himself. Good God… he was turning into Max!

'Right you are, K-P. There are two of them.'

'*At least* two of them – he only said *they*. My best guess and it is only a guess, Bondo, is three – Monsieur Martin, his able lieutenant and a third man for the "nasty" work. That's probably sufficient to achieve what we've observed here and a good number to fit into a single coach… assuming they are *all* in the same coach.'

'The one currently on its way to Krakow, yes!' replied Bondo.

Pichler nodded.

'I would expect it to make a stop at Przemyśl. Maybe that's as far as they're going,' said Pichler.

'It doesn't!' replied Bondo. 'I checked that out earlier. The route takes it well north of Przemyśl. So Krakow's got to be their destination.'

Pichler smiled; some certainty on one thing at least.

'Well done, Bondo!'

Then he frowned. Did this mean that they were leaving Przemyśl untouched? It didn't seem likely.

Przemyśl and Lemberg were the two principal military towns in Eastern Galicia. Stirring up Krakow made sense as well. It was the capital of Polish Galicia and so *had* to be a target… but to leave Przemyśl alone? Maybe they'd be coming back – maybe there were several three-man cells – maybe….

Pichler shrugged. The travails of the last few days were starting to take their toll. Both men were struggling to keep their eyes open the moment the last mouthful had disappeared… and then they were wide awake.

'BBooooooooooooooooommm!'

'What the fick was that?' exclaimed Pichler.

Both men rushed outside their hotel to see a plume of smoke rising into the night's sky. Bondo headed off in the direction of the smoke until a firm hand restrained his progress.

'Hats, coats, gloves *and* a flask – catch!' demanded Pichler flinging him his room key in the process.

He'd been at too many night time crime scenes where hanging around, shuffling feet and getting bloody cold were the order of the day. The young man flew up the stairs and was back in less than five minutes.

It was the Ruthenian-German society hall that had been hit. All the ground floor windows had been blown out and the walking wounded were milling around in a daze. The army had arrived a few minutes before Pichler and Bondo and already three corpses had been laid out and tactfully covered with military greatcoats. There would be more, Pichler felt sure, before the night was much older.

'Good idea about the coats and gloves, K-P,' said Bondo as he stamped his feet. 'What do you hope to find once we're allowed in, always assuming we aren't frozen to the pavement by the… hang on. We're being waved at.'

An officer was indeed waving at them, a Colonel no less.

'Let the press through, Sergeant!' he exclaimed.

The dust had settled. The damage gave a pretty clear picture of the scene and where the bomber would have been sitting.

'I don't believe it!' declared Pichler. 'Even fanatics don't *deliberately* blow themselves up!'

'Unless,' began Bondo, 'they're doing it to keep their family alive!'

'Good point,' replied K-P, 'though of course, they won't be – keeping them alive – not if the Kovals are anything to go by. Who the devil are these people and what in God's name are they trying to achieve?'

Bondo shrugged his shoulders. If he knew the answer to that one, he'd be a Professor by now.

Bondarenko left first; he'd had a bad chest infection as a child and all this ficking ash everywhere was going him no good at all. Pichler stood around for one last look. As he turned to leave he came face to face with the Colonel.

'Can you make any sense of all this, Herr Kahpeh?' he asked.

'Ah, Colonel Erich Koda, I assume,' replied Pichler with a smile.

The Colonel smiled. 'My-my, the General *has* brought you up well, young man. Were you trying to trick me into owning to that preposterous name? Franz Keppler's the name… as you know full well, *Herr Pichler*!'

They shook hands.

'It should be safe to talk here.'

Keppler related the outcomes of his interviews with the demonstrators; Pichler told everything that *he* knew.

'Very well, I shall code that up and inform Vienna – not using the old boy's own code but a proper military cypher.'

Pichler was convinced – only the genuine article would refer to General Erich von Ulmnitz und Waldsee as the "old boy" in front of a mere Unterleutnant like Pichler.

Days later, Krakow, Polish Galicia:

The first stop was the police station to report the disappearance of his cousin Louis and provide a description naturally. This produced no immediate response from the officer on duty, who duly took the details down and promised they'd do what they could but… "You have to understand, sir, Krakow is a very big city and…"

Next stop – a hotel.

'Get me the local papers will you. I want to see if anything's happened at Przemysl,' said Pichler.

A selection of papers was hanging on a rack at the far end of their hotel's lounge. Bondo wondered if he was brazen enough to grab the lot, decided three would be enough and returned to their table. K-P barely acknowledged this; he was clearly in introspective mood and so he decided to go for a walk around Krakow city centre, a place he'd never visited before. He'd set out to see the sights yet he wandered past the historic Cloth hall, the large covered market in central Krakow's Grand Square, barely noticing it. K-P wasn't the only one of them in deep thought.

As far as this Galician "field trip" was concerned, Danilo Bondarenko had to admit… it had changed his outlook on life – the body count alone was responsible for that. He was also learning, learning just how frustrating the real world of investigation could be. It was a bit disappointing as well. He'd rather hoped for a bit more "detecting" and a bit less "translating" and now they were in a Polish speaking province, there wouldn't even be much call for that.

***

Nothing happened the next day. The trail had gone cold – positively glacial. It was time to go home. At the start of the return trip, Pichler seemed to be on the verge of spelling out his conclusions to Bondarenko, but to the young man's dismay he then thought better of it and clammed up for the rest of the journey.

Pichler was mindful of his dismay but von Ulmnitz had given him firm instructions before they left *and* in no uncertain terms.

'Keep as much as you can to yourself, Herr Pichler. Don't you go entering into any long discussions of your pet theories! You can save those for my attention. It's not fair to involve the young lad any more than we must – for his own safety.'

As they neared Vienna Pichler suddenly became more communicative.

'Well then Bondo, we won't get any privacy once we get off this god-awful cattle wagon, so now's a good time. Let me see what you've come up with.'

Bondarenko pulled out a single sheet from his pocket and handed it to Pichler, who proceeded to compare it with a single sheet taken from his own jacket.

'Oh, I say Bondo. This is excellent, truly excellent. Here take a look for yourself.'

The two sketches of "Monsieur Martin's" front and profile looked remarkably similar as were the estimates of height, facial characteristics, hair colour, etc., etc. They may not know his true name or his actual address, but by God they had an excellent description and that would prove to be extremely useful – no more than that – critical!

'The only trouble I'm going to have, Bondo, is convincing the General that we did this completely independently.'

'Come on, K-P. When have you ever known any of your students to cheat in an exam?' replied Bondarenko which brought out broad smiles on both their faces.

Berlin, Old Palace:

'This is unforgivable, man – quite unforgivable!'

The "iron" Chancellor was in danger of melting under the withering glare of the man seated before him.

'Majestät,' he stuttered, almost lost for words. 'It should have been impossible for it to have been taken out of the secure vault, let alone removed from Staff GHQ!'

The "it" was the third map, the one that Tsar Alexander and Emperor Franz Josef must never be allowed to see.

'Could we claim it was a fabrication, Bismarck?'

'The other two maps are already in the hands of the Tsar and the Austrian Emperor?' asked the Chancellor.

The Kaiser nodded glumly.

'Then no – a definite no is the answer, your Majestät. As you have seen the plans are very similar, with initials around the edge. There are no other plans missing and without a template how could a forger produce anything convincing.'

'But I didn't initial it… or date it… so no Royal seal!' said the Kaiser, clutching at a straw that his Chancellor blew away in the blink of an eye.

'A Royal seal has also gone missing so…'

'So then, is it the case that the thief has only to date it and forge my initials and to my fellow Emperors it would appear no different to the one each of them holds?'

'Indeed Majestät and so it should for it is just as genuine as the others!'

The Kaiser put his head in his hands.

'We can't allow any more of our young men to make the ultimate sacrifice, Chancellor – we just can't. Nothing must get in the way of this agreement you have worked so hard to achieve, the… the… what did you call it?'

''Die Dreikaiserbund, Majestät!'

'Yes, indeed; the League of the Three Emperors. Well, I want this agreement signed before the end of the year, Bismarck. You must do everything you can to prevent Franz Josef or the Tsar from seeing this stolen plan – that is your highest priority.'

With his marching orders duly received, the Chancellor bowed and left. Once outside the Old Palace he lit one of his infamous cigars, drew heavily on it and thought of his next step, step being the operative word. He'd be stepping alright, he'd be stepping his foot right up the arse of the person or persons who had allowed this most sensitive of plans to see the light of day.

***

The Chancellor had better news to report to his sovereign the very next day. The hares he had set running the moment he'd learnt the map had been stolen had now returned.

'We have the man's name, Majestät. Hauptman Altdorf is an adjutant serving on the General Staff. He's been in post for eighteen months and gave every appearance of being a meticulous and reliable officer. Three days ago, he was asked to collect another map by a senior member of the General Staff who shall remain nameless for the present. This officer had all the necessary protocols required to access the plan but rather than collect it himself which he ought to have done, he sent Altdorf in his stead. Altdorf left the vault with one map rolled up outside the other and the Sergeant responsible for checking "in's and out's" merely asked Altdorf to open the roll out a little until he could read the title block. Somewhere between the staff officer's room and the vault, Altdorf, we must presume hid the second plan away. Two hours later he left the GSHQ complaining of severe stomach cramps and has not been seen since.'

'Do we know why he did this, Chancellor?'

'Majestät, Hauptman Altdorf was previously Capitaine Jules Altorf of the army of the Emperor

Napoleon. He is an Alsatian! You will recall your Majestät, that it was at your Majestät's pleasure that officers from Reichsland-Elsass should be "accelerated" into important positions in the Reich Heer in order to facilitate integration.'

The Kaiser peered over the top of his spectacles at this hint of a rebuke coming from his inferior, albeit that he knew him to be the second most powerful man in the Reich. He decided to ignore it.

'And what steps have been taken to recover the plan?'

'We believe that this is a plot which has its roots in Paris – only the French have so much to lose if they are denied an alliance with preferably Russian but failing that then Austria. Kaptain Altdorf will have left Berlin by the fastest possible route. It seems unlikely that he will have remained within the Reich by returning to his home in Strassburg. However we have covered both eventualities as far as we are able by sending two teams, though with a three day head start… '

'Would he not have gone directly to Vienna?'

'No, Majestät – that is highly unlikely. I very much doubt he will be the courier. His part will be over once he has delivered the package to the Deuxieme Bureau in Paris.

The imperative for the French, Majestät is to deliver the map directly into the hands of the Austrian Emperor, unseen by any of his intermediaries. If any of his minions saw it before him and realised the threat it posed to the stability of Europe, then they might well destroy it. He would never see it. The Emperor is well protected so getting him on his own won't be easy. Organising all that will take a little time.'

'Very well, Bismarck. Do whatever you must.'

'Majestät,' replied his Chancellor, who bowed low and turned on his heels.

ISD HQ, Vienna:

The Emperor and Chancellor of Germany weren't the only ones who had maps on their minds. Erich von Ulmnitz und Waldsee pondered one which was not dissimilar, except it stretched as far west as the Bay of Biscay. He did his best thinking alone *once* he had gathered all the data. It was just him, him and a Napoleon brandy.

Pichler's and Keppler's reports told the same story – a small scale and totally manufactured plot, trying to suggest that the province of Galicia was about to break away. A so-called attempt on the life of the Empress, demonstrations which fortunately didn't lead to large-scale civilian deaths, a plebiscite, some acts of terrorism – it all smacked of a small group of activists, certainly less than half a dozen, trying to stoke up something which simply wasn't there to be stoked. It wasn't exactly amateurish but it didn't have the feel of any state-sponsorship, or if there was any, it was all very hands off. Pichler's initial hypothesis was right – it was one big diversion aimed at diverting their attention east when the real threat could be coming from the west or in other words France.

Pichler and his lad had heard one of them speak at that meeting in Lemberg. Bondarenko had said something very interesting to Pichler; he'd told him he thought it might not have been Russian-Russian. When Pichler asked him what he meant, he said and Pichler had written this in his report… "as in Russian spoken by a foreigner".

The French being behind this made perfect sense. They'd rebuilt their defences since 1871 but weren't yet ready to launch an offensive to recover the lost provinces of Alsace and Lorraine. In the meantime they had to prevent the Germany Empire entering into any alliances with Russia or Austria. In fact if all three signed up to a pact then France would have no allies, just as it did in the 1870-71 war and little chance of reversing that outcome.

Von Ulmnitz took another sip of his brandy, replaced it on the table, picked it up again and this time took a huge slug! It seemed to help.

So if disruption was their game, then how would these few incidents in the far north east further their cause? Such treaties are founded on the trust between the signatories, in this case the three Emperors. Were these people acting as agent provocateurs, trying to further increase the bad blood that already existed between Franz Josef and the Tsar?

Well if that was their game, they hadn't reckoned with General Erich von Ulmnitz he thought with some satisfaction aided, it must be said by another visit to his brandy glass.

The Emperor trusted him and had every reason to do so. It was unlikely that these "incidents" were of sufficient magnitude to attract the great man's attention… and if they ever did von Ulmnitz would apply the appropriate "velvet coating". An assassination attempt on his consort would be "a drunken local tenant, your Majesty, who had had an argument with his landlord and decided to take it into his head to fire off his shotgun at the first passing coach of quality". The plebiscite demonstration would prove to be a "peaceful protest about bread prices – nobody injured…" And so on.

How then could the Emperor even learn of such unfriendly actions perpetrated – allegedly – with the approval of the Tsar?

No, these pinpoints were for *his* benefit. They knew he'd filter any information reaching the Emperor, knew he'd be distracted by all this Galician nonsense and that could only mean one thing – they had a bomb – a political bomb – one that is primed and ready to go, or it very soon will be. And another thing – this bomb had absolutely nothing to do with Galicia which was one enormous red herring!

Von Ulmnitz looked at his glass. It was empty. He made it a rule never to have a second one but then sometimes, rules are there to be broken. And anyway, he had to work out a way of keeping the Emperor well away from that explosive message, document, certificate, photograph or whatever the hell it was.

Strassburg:

Two men were stationed outside Altdorf's last known address just two hours after the telegram had arrived from Berlin. Of course there was no knowing where he actually was. He might not be at this address – he might be somewhere else in Strassburg. He might not even be in the Country – he could be halfway to Paris! Regardless of all that, they had to start somewhere.

His rooms were situated in a three-story building, sited within a half-hour walk of the station. He used it whenever he returned home from Berlin, which wasn't very often these days. He had had to leave the familial home of his youth. They wouldn't talk to him there, wouldn't even say his name, not since he'd turned traitor and signed up with the "occupiers" as most of his village referred to the Reich.

"Their loss" would have been the general opinion amongst his army colleagues in Berlin. He had fitted in exceptionally well at HQ and was even courting a nice Berlin girl. Nobody would have believed he could ever be a traitor. But that was the view of three days ago and a lot of things had changed since then!

'Got it!' said one man to the other, holding the key aloft.

'Good, let's go, but *quietly*!'

They crept up the two flights of stairs to the second floor and edged along the corridor to room seven. It was still not light outside. If the swine was in, he'd be asleep and in for a very rude awakening. The key was turned so, so slowly. Both men winced at the slight "clunk" made as the latch was slid back.

They stood away from the door and looked at each other. The corridor was dark enough not to silhouette them as they became framed in the doorway. One man nodded and his compatriot eased the handle down and inched the door open.

The room was dimly lit by the early dawn light. The curtains were not drawn, he couldn't be there! The door was opened a head's width. Nothing stirred.

'Empty!' mouthed one man to another. God damn it!

The door was pushed wide open, allowing both men to step into the room, caution thrown to the wind, apart from their revolvers of course, which each man held close to his body.

'What the f..'

He was there. And… he was dead!

'Light the gas, old man.'

He lay on his back, his face pallid, his eyes wide open and staring straight up at the yellowing ceiling. Neither man was medically trained but both had seen their share of dead bodies, both on and off the battlefield.

'What would you say… two days, maybe three?'

'About that, yes.'

'Go and bang up the caretaker; see what he knows.'

There was nothing on the body and nothing in the wardrobe or drawers. All the room contained was a small case in which his Hauptman's uniform had been rudely stuffed and his travelling clothes which were strewn across the floor by his bed. A search of the pockets revealed… nothing!

He must have changed out of his uniform as soon as he could, probably on the first west-bound train leaving Berlin. He most likely would have changed trains at least once; he might not even have made the final leg to Strassburg by train. He was not to know how long it would take for the theft to be discovered and there was a chance he'd be recognised at Strassburg station. The man started as he heard footsteps coming towards the room, then relaxed – it was his colleague.

'He thinks our man arrived two days ago! The old boy wasn't entirely sure as it was sometime during the night. He banged on the door the next morning but got no response and he hasn't seen him leave the room since.'

'So that's it then; one dead body and no sign of the plan. We may as well get back and tell them to call off the other search teams. Otto won't be pleased!'

His colleague wasn't listening. He was standing by the grate with a poker in his hand.

'Come and have a look at this. The swine was burning something, look!'

'The plan, do you think? There's a decent amount of ash here and he wasn't lighting a fire for the heat; see all the logs are still stacked up on one side, unused.'

'Could be, could be... Holy Mary. Look *what I've found*!'

The corner of unburnt paper was triangular in shape and was singed along the long edge. The two shorter sides were undoubtedly the two edges of something much larger – there were four sets of initials written along the bottom.

'What do you think these signify?' asked one – his colleague responded with a shrug.

Small though it was, the fragment was large enough to include a part of a title block.

'That doesn't say what I think it says, does it?'

'It most certainly does! What was that you were saying about dear old Otto?'

Old Palace, Berlin:

Dear old Otto stood before his Kaiser, a smile on his face for the first time in days. He'd almost skipped into the room.

'I take it you have good news for me, Chancellor.'

'Indeed, Majestät. The map never left the Reich.'

Important men rarely need to hear the full details and his Chancellor decided not to overburden the gentleman seated before him. There was no need to make mention of Altdorf's final note; it was enough that *he* should know of it!

'And the men responsible – I mean to say *our* men at General Staff HQ?'

'They will be reassigned, Majestät.'

The Kaiser asked no more questions on that front, but it didn't stop him thinking to himself; what a shame we do not have colonies like the English – somewhere very hot, very dry and infested with insects, though one final question did spring to mind.

'This Altdorf fellow – I believe there was talk of him citing a stomach problem as the reason for his rapid departure from GSHQ. Might that have been genuine do you think?'

'Who can say, Majestät?' replied the Chancellor.

***

Well he could for one, thanks to a Strassburg postmaster who recognising the address passed the letter onto the appropriate authorities, who then telegrammed the contents to Berlin! It was the man's final note in this world that was the final proof he needed, the proof that the ashes in that grate in Strassburg were indeed the remains of the third map.

It was barely legible, for the man was dying, struck down by the illness that had started sometime earlier in Berlin. It was to his family, a plea for forgiveness and remorse for having deceived them for so long. But at the end, he wanted them to know; he was never Berlin's man – he ended it with "la liberté pour l'alsace". In a way, the Chancellor admired the man. If he couldn't complete his mission then he could at least destroy the plan. That way the Germans would never be completely certain as to its fate. And he would have succeeded but for that tiny unburnt fragment… and this note of course.

A small yacht in mid-Adriatic:

The least obvious and hence the safest way to get to Vienna from Alsace was by sea. He'd started by taking the train to Nice. From there… a pleasant cruise to Genoa and then over land by train to Venice. Next a private yacht across the Adriatic to the Austrian Küstenland, rowing himself ashore under the cover of darkness. Finally to Vienna by the Graz train, arriving at a northerly bound platform rather than the other direction as might be expected.

Nobody in their right mind would anticipate such a time consuming journey. He was probably being over cautious, he knew that. After all the Austrians had no idea who he was or even that *anybody* was coming who meant their Empire no good. Still, time was on his side. He didn't *need* to travel through the lands of the German Reich, so if he didn't have to, he preferred not to!

He would meet up with the two of them in Vienna at the agreed venue in two days' time. That was where he would pick up the uniform. He was rather looking forward to it. Their army wasn't much good – he'd fought them in Italy in '59 so he should know. Their uniforms though… well, they were very pretty.

The third man, the one who'd gone to Galicia with Philippe and Nicolas as their dogsbody, had been sent back to Paris. His German simply wasn't good enough. There were farmers in rural Bavaria who spoke better German than this man, handicapped as he was by his heavy Alsatian dialect. No wonder the German soldiers couldn't understand a word his people said as they "liberated" the province in 1870.

***

It was a shame about Altorf, but what else could he do? It was crucial that Berlin believed that the map was no longer in existence. This would give Philippe, Nicolas and himself a clear run and au revoir to any alliance between the three Eastern Empires.

He'd been there to meet Altorf off the Strasbourg train when it pulled in close to midnight a week or so ago. The platform was almost deserted and they were able to enter Altorf's rooms completely unobserved. He'd brought a bottle of Chablis with him and late as it was, he could see the pleasure that gave the ex-Hauptman – not just because it was wine, but because it was *French* wine – he was home, at last! He was relieved to see him drain his glass in one go – not a very French attitude to such an excellent wine perhaps, but the best way to take your poison, if that be necessary. A momentary look of confusion flashed across the Captain's face and he was dead before he even hit the floor.

There was no option the bureau had decided; the fragment of map and the body must be found by the Germans. The Germans must also receive Altorf's letter – the icing on the cake so to speak. Which they would, thanks to a very patriotic postmaster – a postmaster who spelt the city of his birth as "Strasbourg"… definitely not "Strassburg"!

Still, it was a shame nonetheless; mais c'est la guerre!

Vienna, the Schönbrunn:

Vienna had a number of splendid gardens which offered the populace a glorious opportunity to get away from the hustle and bustle of a big city without actually leaving it. Some liked to stroll while others like to ride, on horse or in the comfort of a carriage. His majesty the Emperor Franz Josef was no different from his subjects in this respect. Despite the onerous demands on his time, he would usually find a brief interlude during each day to enjoy a short carriage ride. Though it had to be a short ride – the Hofburg or the Schönbrunn could never be more than ten minutes away… just in case.

That was their best chance. They wouldn't have to negotiate the barrier put up by his army of minions. Dressed as senior officers, they would march up to the carriage, salute and then hand him the "parcel", a parcel that required his urgent attention. They would be challenged; of course they would, probably by the one or two officers who were acting as escort. But it wouldn't be more than two for the Emperor liked, just for once, to be able to enjoy the garden as any other private citizen.

Would he look at it immediately? Of course he would! The next thing… he'd bark out an order to the driver. That order? That order would be to get him back to the Hofburg or the Schönbrunn as quickly as possible.

As they watched him drive off, they would probably smile at each other. Why? Because the "bomb" had been successfully delivered, that's why.

It had all seemed so easy when the idea had been proposed by Paris. Franz Josef, they'd told them, was as regular as a metronome. While "It" was on its way from Venice, they had used the time productively to conduct a few dummy runs. It wouldn't hurt and might even help if the Emperor noticed the two smart officers who delivered such impeccable salutes as he rode by. It should have been as easy as shooting fish in a barrel; but it wasn't!

'When's he due in?'

'In about an hour, God damn it!' replied his colleague. 'We've got to do *something*!'

'Try him,' said Nicolas, pointing at an official looking type who was standing by a half open door at the Schönbrunn with a clipboard.'

'Guten Morgen,' began Philippe.

'Yes sir, how may I help you?' replied the official.

'Well, I know it's a bit of cheek, but we're both on leave from our depot in Salzburg. It's our first time in Vienna and all the chaps from the regiment told us, "You *must* see his majesty when he takes a carriage ride around the city". Well we fully intended to do so and have been hanging around the garden in the hope of catching a glimpse… for a couple of days in fact, but no luck so far.'

The official nodded sympathetically.

'Well you won't see him gentlemen because he is not in Vienna at present. At least not officially – he's preparing for a trip which will take him outside the capital for a few days. And he's given orders that he's not to be disturbed!'

The two officers looked so crest fallen, that the official felt quite sorry for them. 'Just a moment,' he said before disappearing inside the building.

'Well, mon ami, we are well and truly fu… Hang on, he's coming back,' said Nicolas.

'Gentlemen, I've checked with my superior and I am permitted to provide you with details of his Majesty's movements. After all you are both senior officers in his Majesty's armed forces and not foreign agents…'

He laughed as he said this and they smiled back.

'So I can tell you that he will be leaving for the Royal residence at Pressburg tomorrow morning. He will be there for three days. It's only a short train journey so if you are dead set on seeing our Emperor…'

'Will he be out and about in his carriage?' asked Nicolas.

'No, I doubt that! But he is fond of strolling around the castle grounds. I believe that there is an opportunity for the general public to see him, from a distance naturally. Sometimes they set up a special viewing stand located outside the walls for that very purpose.'

'Thank you so much, you have been very kind,' said Philippe.

'My pleasure Gentlemen. Good day to you.'

The two gentlemen stepped off in the direction of the station.

'You were saying, mon ami, something about us being truly fu… ?' said Philippe with a broad grin.

Vienna, the Hauptbahnof:

The Graz train had just pulled in.

'Philippe! Look over there! Him in the grey coat.'

'I think you're right – it *is* him. Quick, get your pipe out.'

The nameless man approaching them took a step to one side so that his fellow passengers from the train could pass by unimpeded. Taking out his pipe from his top pocket and lighting it, he saw two men, one of whom had just lit his pipe, turn their backs on him and head towards the station exit.

Walking down the entrance steps, he saw them again.

'Quick, get in!' urged Nicolas.

Within seconds the carriage had pulled away at some speed.

Philippe banged on the coachroof, pulled down the window and stuck his head outside.

'Not so fast, you idiot! Do you want to get us stopped by the police?'

'There's been a change of plan,' said Nicolas, but did not elaborate until they'd driven past a road sign that said "PRESSBURG 60 kM".

Pressburg Castle, the next day:

Three men smoked their pipes and leant against the wall at the bottom of the ramp which led up to the castle. They chatted away without a care in the world, the very picture of idle young men with nothing better to do.

At the top of the ramp was the main entrance to the castle, guarded by two soldiers. One was fairly short, fairly stout and fairly old; the other was younger, thinner but no more impressive. These were

Landwehr which is to say reserve troops. And not very good ones at that, judging by the way they were slouching. It was surprising to see troops of this poor quality being given responsibility for the Emperor's safety, though of course they had no reason to expect any trouble.

Occasionally one of the three loafers would step away from the wall and go for a very short stroll.

'If I stand here, I can see right into the courtyard,' said Nicolas.

Philippe and the "man" each effected a bored look as if to say "who cares, it's just a castle", though of course they did care – very much so.

It was hard to imagine that such an important personage as the Emperor was currently in residence. In fact, were it not for the Imperial standard which could be seen flying from the west tower, one could be forgiven for thinking that the rumours to that effect were somewhat misplaced.

'You *are* sure he's definitely in there, Nicolas?' asked the nameless man.

'That's what we're here to find out.'

At that moment an officer came striding towards them from within the castle, ramrod back and every inch a regular. The two sentries must have sensed him coming for in the next moment they had adopted regulation "at-ease" stance, ready to snap to attention. Too late – he'd already seen them. Philippe smiled as he could see the two sentries flinch under a veritable stream of abuse. The officer, having delivered a suitable admonishment, proceeded to march down the cobbled ramp from the entrance in their direction.

'Oi, look out, we've got company,' said Nicolas.

After some twenty paces, he abruptly halted and turned his head to the left as far as it would go. Then very deliberately, very slowly, he rotated his view, examining the street before him until he had completed a one-eighty survey. Totally ignoring the three idlers, he nodded to himself to indicate all was well, about-faced and marched back up the ramp. They watched him disappear through the entrance but not before he'd taken the opportunity to give each sentry an icy stare for good measure. After a few moments both sentries shrugged their shoulders at each other before resuming their preferred pose of two dozy layabouts masquerading as soldiers.

'Right… if we lounge around any longer, we might arouse suspicion. I'm away to buy a paper. Then I suggest one of us sits in that café opposite while…

'Hang on, something's happening!' whispered Nicolas.

Unmistakable – mutton chop whiskers, white jacket, red and white sash. In front – two soldiers, each man carrying a rifle over his shoulder; behind – the same. The party of five took only a few seconds to cross the viewing aperture which the main entrance afforded, but it was enough.

'What time is it?' asked the nameless man.

'It's bang on ten!' said Nicolas and then grinned. 'It's old Herr Metronome.'

Later that afternoon, a very smartly dressed man walked up the ramp and addressed a few words to the same two guards. They shrugged their shoulders so he reached into his pocket and handed them something shiny and that seemed to loosen their tongues.

***

'I asked for wine,' said Philippe.

'This is the local equivalent; you're not in Paris now old friend and that's why *I'm* drinking beer,' replied Nicolas.

'So then, he does this at ten and four according to the Landwehr's finest. There's no reason to delay, so finish your drink and we'll meet back here at a quarter to. Nicolas and I have to get changed.'

***

The carriage waited down one of the many side streets that ran off the main road leading to the castle. Two officers sat anxiously inside, the driver's seat was vacant – but not for long.

'I've just seen that same Hauptman march halfway down the ramp and do the same visual sweep up and down the road that he did this morning. The Emperor *must* be about to enter the courtyard,' said the man who leapt onto the driver's seat. "Go!" he heard from within.

The carriage pulled out onto the main road and trotted sedately towards the castle.

'You have your pistol ready in the briefcase?' asked Nicolas.

It was the same type of side arm which was issued to officers in the Tsar's army.

Philippe nodded. If they were successful, Philippe would merely reach into the briefcase, extract the map and give it to the Emperor. If it looked like they were about to be arrested, he was to pull out the pistol instead and kill him. This would mean their own deaths, but at least the death of Franz Josef would disrupt any progress on treaties – the provenance of the murder weapon would see to that! It was a price they were both willing to pay – for France!

The carriage pulled up at the base of the ramp and two army officers got out. The driver remained where he was.

'Best foot forward, Philippe. Remember, I'm the Colonel, you're the Major.'

The two men marched up to the gatehouse, stern-faced, except for the tiniest of smiles as they saw the same two guards from the morning. They got to within three steps before either of these dolts reacted. The old one nudged the younger one and they came to something resembling attention. A document was thrust into the face of the younger man, who glared at it in the same stupefied manner they had come to expect.

'Musím sa opýtať dôstojníka, pane.'

'Was sagt der Idiot?' asked the Colonel of the Major.

'Sir, he's speaking Slovak, I think he's saying he needs to ask an officer.'

'Sehr Gut. Los!'

The young guard seemed to be momentarily confused then he understood.

'Ja, mein Herr. Sofort!'

He shot off, well limped off would be a better description, disappearing out of sight.

'It's him!' he had time to say before returning to the gatehouse.

'Entschuldigen, mein Herr. Bitte, bitte!'

And they were in.

It was a nervous wait. The Major chanced a look over his shoulder and was relieved to see both guards leaning up against the gate, chatting away quite happily.

Nicolas had decided that they would present the Emperor with the map the moment he appeared rather than wait for him to cross the parade ground – less time to be discovered. They already had the words prepared – "For your most urgent attention, your Majesty – vital for the security of the Empire!"

'Philippe – here he is. Are you ready?'

They marched forward. The Emperor saw the two men and presumed that these were messengers from Vienna – was he never to have a moment's peace?

‘So, was haben Sie für mich, meine Herren?’

“For your most urgent…” was as far as the Colonel got before both men were each felled by a hefty blow from the butt of a rifle.

The man seated on the driver’s seat of the carriage, his revolver in his lap but concealed under a blanket, was becoming increasingly anxious. This was taking longer than he’d expected. The man glared at the gatehouse, willing them to return. Then he saw the two dozy guards walking purposely down the ramp towards him, only they didn’t look so dozy anymore.

Their rifles came up, “Stay right where you are!” one of them called out in German. He reached for his revolver with one hand and the whip with the other. His arm came up to fire but he never did.

‘Well done, K-P. Still got it in you I see!’ said Slota.

***

‘Well then Franz-Josef, my honoured sovereign, are the villains under lock and key?’ asked General von Ulmnitz.

‘Indeed they are, sir,’ replied the “Emperor” as he pulled off his side burns, removed his wig and once more became Leutnant Peter Rühigen, one of von Ulmnitz’s most trusted men from the ISD in Vienna.

‘In that case,’ replied the General, ‘we may notify his Majesty that it is safe for him to return to Vienna.’

‘Ah, the first of our merry cast of actors approaches,’ said General von Ulmnitz gleefully.

Inspector Hodža or rather Hauptman Hodža saluted the General. It had been twenty five years since he'd "escaped" from the army, but he hadn't forgotten how to do it, although he'd never worn an officer's uniform before all this.

'Christ, I'd forgotten how uncomfortable these trousers are!' he exclaimed; 'too many years walking around in baggy civi's.'

'Time for a changing of the guard, I think,' replied the General.

By six o'clock, they were all gathered in the officers' mess, more than happy to drink the local beer, especially Slota.

'Well Corporal Pichler – I'm glad to see you and Private Slota remained at your post throughout. Those posters you and your young friend, Herr Bondarenko came up with were very useful in the end. I'd hate it for us to have "brained" two bona fide officers.

'Yes, General,' replied the reserve trooper who had so failed to impress the three Gallic observers.

'One question General; how did you know that today would be the day?' asked Pichler.

General von Ulmnitz smiled seraphically but said nothing. Better for them to think he had special insights. The reality was more mundane.

He'd placed a man in the Schönbrunn, given him a copy of Pichler and the lad's drawing and description and an instruction

'If anybody turns up wanting to see the Emperor, see if one of them looks like this fellow. If one does… then spin him the "three-days in Pressburg" yarn and send a telegram to me immediately.'

The General didn't know it would be today, but he was sure it would be one of the three days. That was easy! The clever bit had been to work out how the villains could possibly contrive to get the Emperor alone and set the trap to catch them. It might not be good for the liver, but Napoleon brandy worked wonders for the little grey cells… at least it did for him.

***

General von Ulmnitz was confident that his plan would work, but not *so* confident that he was prepared to risk the Emperor's life. No, it was far safer for the great man to be three hundred and fifty kilometres due west of Pressburg, enjoying the tranquillity and frische Luft that the Kaiservilla at Bad Ischl had to offer.

And Philippe and Nicolas? They remain in prison just outside Linz, waiting to be traded for Austrian or Hungarian subjects engaged in similar activities and currently "guests" of the third Republic. However their wait is likely to be a long one. There are some important treaties that need to be signed before their existence can even be acknowledged.

Deuxieme Bureau, Paris

'So, the map never reached their Emperor, is that what you're telling me?'

'That is correct, sir. Our courier is reported to have drowned on route to the Austrian coast. He was seen safely off the yacht which took him from Venice, but he rowed himself ashore and they lost sight of him before he made land fall. His body was washed up near Trieste and was identified by one of our people a few days ago.'

'And our agents?'

'We have heard nothing of them, sir. They have not returned to the Franco-Russian quarter. There have been no sightings since they left for Galicia. We *think* that they boarded a train to Vienna at Cracovie, but that is the last we heard.'

'So, our plan has failed. It seems our quest for allies must go on.'

'For how long, sir? How long must we endure the shame of the loss of Alsace?'

'*Oh, Colonel,* we will wait as long as we must – fifty years if needs be. And we will not forget. We *will* be revenged.'

'And Capitaine Altorf, sir? Will he be receiving recognition for the service he rendered to France?'

The head of the Bureau said nothing, for there was nothing he could say. There are some brave souls who must remain "a soldier known only to God".

The League of the Three Emperors

During the course of 1873, the three Emperors of Germany, Russia and Austria-Hungary met and signed a series of agreements of mutual support. These culminated into what came to be known as the League of the Three Emperors. It was the first slab in the path that would inexorably lead over the next forty years to the greatest catastrophe mankind had ever known – they called it the “Great War”!

THE ITALIAN TENOR

The Aladdin Club, Trieste, May 1874:

There were many gentlemen's clubs in the Imperial City of Trieste, but the foremost of these was the Aladdin. The view from its dining room was spectacular, especially as the evening sun set over the Adriatic. *But* other clubs had equally impressive views to offer. The club employed a master chef from Rome and his dishes were never less than exquisite. *But* he was not the only master chef in Trieste. The luxuriant reading room took all the papers from the region and even some from Vienna though they were always a day behind. *But* then so did all the other clubs.

No, what made the Aladdin club a favourite amongst a certain type of gentleman was to be found two floors below. The floor even had its own name; "Klub Siebzehn-Vier". Here there were no views of the Adriatic and there were no newspapers. So what was the attraction?

It was here that the bankhalter would deal two cards to each player, drawn from a German pack. This consisted of ace, king, queen, knave, ten, nine, eight and seven, that is thirty-two cards in total. Ace counted as eleven, the royal cards as two and the others, ten down to seven counted as their face value. The aim of the game, vingt-et-un as they call it in France, is to obtain twenty-one. It's a simple enough game requiring a bit of skill and a lot of luck. There are various rules about who pays who but there is only one rule the uninitiated need to bear in mind – however well it seems to be going at the start of the evening, the bank always ends up ahead!

'Bank scores twenty one with two cards – all players must pay double the stake to the house… thank you gentlemen… thank you sir… and you Signor… thank y… ah, this is not sufficient. And I see you have exhausted your reservoir of chips. I'm sorry Signor you will need to withdraw from the game. I will inform the manager as to the extent of your losses.'

At that, the Bankhalter raised an arm and two men rapidly appeared at the table, one either side of the unfortunate punter. He was escorted to the manager's office in a very far from friendly manner. It wasn't the first time he had been required to make such a visit.

'This really won't do, Signor. The money you now owe the house has reached… let me see… the sum of…' He scribbled down a figure on a scrap of paper and passed it across the table.

The two men who had escorted him here now stood either side of his chair. Both leaned over to view the sum. Their muttered expressions of "phew!" on one side and "fick me!" on the other did little to ease his anxiety.

'Rest assured, Signor Regatta, I shall have sufficient Gulden to make good what I owe, very, very shortly. I just need a little more time.'

How many times had the intimidating figure of Signor Regatta heard that from the poor unfortunates who had sat in this same chair? If punters chose to gamble then that was perfect as far as he was concerned… right up until the point where they were "choosing" to gamble with *his* money.

'Shall we say, one week!' It wasn't a question.

The man opened his mouth as if to plead for more time but he knew such pleas would fall on deaf ears, so he closed it again.

'Very well, sir – one week it is!'

On the way home, he worked out what he could sell. He also worked out how much he could expect to come his way in the next seven days. Yes, these two would yield enough.

The University, Pressburg:

'Hello, K-P.'

'Good morning, Karol… oh and to you, Ján! What brings you two officers of the law to this centre of academic excellence, may I ask?'

'An invite,' replied Inspector Karol Hodža. 'How do you fancy a free ticket to see a full-dress rehearsal of an opera, one sung in Italian, no less?'

'Frankly, Karol, I'd rather saw my own leg off!'

'Bit late for that, I'd have thought,' chipped in Sergeant Slota.

'You *really* are a miserable old sod, aren't you K-P? What I can't understand is how you managed to convince an attractive and talented musician like Anna to take you on,' said Hodža.

'You mean a *pair* of tickets?' replied Pichler.

The Inspector nodded.

'Well, why didn't you say so in the first place... wait a minute, wait a minute! What's the catch?'

The catch? Of course there was a catch. Tickets for the Pressburg opera cost an arm and a leg. To be truthful the Opera house wasn't that much of a venue, at least compared with the State opera in Vienna. It was rather more of a music hall which tended to put on orchestral performances. However getting a touring opera company to visit was still a pretty big deal for the musical aficionados of the city. So why were the Pichlers' being offered free tickets?

'You'll be attending a matinee performance this coming Wednesday. All the performers, all the orchestra players will be there, singing and playing their hearts out, save one! He'll put in an appearance for the Friday evening show when tickets will be available to the general public. More on that later because I can see you're dying to ask me two things. Why you and why this rather "theatrical" arrangement?' Hodža paused, while Pichler's mouth opened and closed.

'The answer to both is security. This Meistersinger is apparently pretty hot stuff amongst the diva community so you might think he's too grand to show up for a "rehearsal". However, it isn't a rehearsal for them it's a "rehearsal" for us, i.e. the forces of the law. You see K-P, this fellow, Enrico Durando by name, is something of a rarity. He's an Italian who actually likes living in the Empire. He has a reputation for speaking out publically in favour of the status quo.'

'You mean he believes that the Süd Tyrol and Küstenland should remain part of Austria-Hungary. Phew, I bet that makes him popular with the irredentists,' said Pichler.

'Excuse my ignorance, o' learned ones, but what exactly is a ficking irredentist when he's at home?' asked Slota.

'Home is the right word, Ján,' answered Pichler. 'An Italian irredentist is an agitator who wants the return of all Italian-speaking districts, currently *outside* Italy – *to* Italy.'

'Agitators is one thing, but are they violent?' asked Slota.

'I wouldn't have said so… at least for the majority, but it only takes a few hotheads…'

'Well put, K-P,' interrupted Hodža, 'you're spot on. There have been threats against Signor Durando in the recent past. A public "execution" as they might term it, would certainly give their cause a huge amount of publicity. Now the city grandees would rather that *not* happen in our fair city so the purpose of the rehearsal is for us to carry out a security check. You know the sort of thing; areas a sharpshooter might use, places where bombs might be secreted. And to disguise what we're up to, this performance is being called a "dress-rehearsal" for the benefit of the good and the great, present company excepted!'

And that was that. The Inspector handed Pichler a fly sheet for the coming Friday – for which he was not invited – and the time he was to be there on the Wednesday.

As they left the younger man contemplating what he'd just been told, the two policemen discussed the collection and transfer.

'Right then Ján, instructions for Friday, though what I'm going to tell you will astound you.'

There was to be no police protection; no escorts from the train station, always assuming he planned to arrive by train, or back to his hotel. They were not to know, in advance when he'd be arriving at the music hall, when he'd be departing… until he actually left. Or how he was getting from A to B and the name of the hotel until he notified the police. It seemed, so the chief of Pressburg Police had informed Hodža, that Signor Durando did not trust the forces of law and order. He would also make his own arrangements for departure on the Saturday morning.

'What! No security detail, nothing at all?' said a suitably astounded Slota.

'Oh yes, he's agreed to us providing a guard in the hotel lobby, but that is it, my old friend. All you need to do is arrange for a man and his relief to be on call. When we receive a summons from the "great" man, they can keep watch in the hotel.'

Slota considered what he'd been told. He'd dealt with lots of celebrated personages in his time and it was true that they could be a bit eccentric, but this was quite extraordinary. On the other hand, Sergeant Slota was a man who always looked for the bright side of any situation, an invaluable gift for a serving police officer. If the whole thing went arse-up, at least they couldn't be blamed; he told the Inspector as much.

Haus Pichler:

'Oh that sounds absolutely splendid, dearest. However did you get tickets?'

When you're the Detective to his majesty the Emperor, there is only so much you should let on to your nearest and dearest. This was one of those occasions.

'The Vice Chancellor gave two tickets to Max and he didn't want them. It's not his type of thing.'

The idea of the VC giving *anything* away and to *Max* in particular, was so outlandish that Pichler wished he'd given his answer a bit more thought. However Anna was so excited by the prospect that she didn't seem to notice.

As he'd read the flysheet out to her, she scuttled off towards the piano seat where she stored her music. There was no order to the pile at all. It was only ever consulted if she needed help in memorising a particular piece. This of course could only be done with the aid of a sighted person. That person was her own music teacher, a good friend who'd been working with Anna for years.

Recently this lady had also started "working" with K-P. To say her pupil was slow on the uptake would have been rather unkind but wholly accurate. He was making some progress, though it was painful beyond belief – bless him. However she wasn't on this occasion looking for music. Reaching right to the bottom of the stool she found a dozen or so little booklets. She dumped the pile in his lap.

'So this thingy, Cosi fan tutte! What's it all about, Anna?'

Pichler dug through the synopses for the various operas in Anna's collection until he found it.

'Well, read it to me!' she said.

'I thought you knew it!' he replied mischievously.

…Two chaps were engaged to two sisters. This third fellow offers a wager to test their fidelity. They're on for this and so this Alfonso fellow tells the sisters that the two boys have been called away to war. Enter a maid – she tells the girls that while the cat's away the mice should play. Alfie bribes the maid to introduce the sisters to two "infatuated young friends".

'Don't tell me, it'll be the two lads, heavily disguised by wearing a different coloured hat?' said Pichler sarcastically which brought the inevitable scowl.

Anyway, the girls play hard to get but start warming to the two men after a bit more shenanigans. Pichler put the book down.

'That's just Act I,' said Anna. 'There's another one to go.'

Pichler managing to stifle an "oh God!" got up and returned with a glass of lemonade for each of them. He continued reading. The sisters decide they *do* like these chaps after all but choose the other's fiancé (*how* hilarious, thought Pichler, I think I'm going to wee myself). There was bit about an exchange of gifts – "Good God, do people pay money to see this?" thought Pichler though he struggled on manfully for Anna's benefit. Anyway, a bit more shenanigans, the sisters agree to marry the imposters, who then “return from war”. There’s a bit of a falling-out all round. Then a bit of a making up and finally Alfie tells ‘em all not to be such daft buggers in the future. Phew!

Anna smiled at him. ‘Yes, I agree – it’s not exactly a novel is it? But it’s all about the music. You’ll enjoy it once you’re there!’

Pichler had his doubts. He half hoped some mad irredentist *would* show up as it would liven up the show… enormously.

‘What does the title mean, wife of mine?’

‘Literally, it means “so do they all”, but it’s a slight pun and it’s usually taken to mean “women are like that”.’

‘Some women, perhaps!’ he replied which caused her to raise her glass in acknowledgement of the compliment he’d paid her.

Wednesday at the opera house:

Anna and Pichler were in the upper balcony. It was too far away to get a good view of the actors’ expressions but that hardly mattered to Anna. Nor Pichler who scarcely looked at the stage other than when “Alfonso” put in an appearance. Hodža had explained his role when he’d dropped by again, earlier in the day.

‘Look K-P, you’re there to identify any viable positions which might be feasible for a sharpshooter to get off a kill-shot.’

'What type of rifle are you thinking off, Karol?'

'He'd need to get it there well before the performance, I imagine. We're banned from upsetting the good and the great by searching them. But at least the Mayor has allowed me to insist that no outdoor coats can be taken into the auditorium. Anyway, we'll be looking for potential hiding places and they'll be locked or guarded just before the performance begins.'

'Not necessarily!' said Pichler. 'There are some pretty specialised weapons out there. Remember that air-rifle that was used in the "*affair*"?'

Hodža nodded, oh yes… the affair! The affair of the fraudulent birth certificate it later became called as Pichler's casebook grew. But this was his first and perhaps his most important case. Emperor Franz Josef would certainly agree with that. But for now, amongst Pichler, Hodža, Slota and Max, it was simply the "affair".

'You couldn't hit the stage with an air rifle!' remarked the Inspector incredulously.

'Who says it has to be an air-rifle? I know of one dealer in Buda who knows of a man. You know what I mean – no names, who not so long ago, tried to sell him a screw-on barrel. So barrel down one trouser leg and stock and breech down the other. I imagine most members of the audience sitting up in the gods will bring their opera glasses, perhaps of the telescope type.'

'You mean that would serve as his sight?'

Pichler nodded before continuing. 'It'll be at least a metre in length overall, so we can rule out a shot from the stalls. I think I'd notice if a muzzle suddenly appeared over my shoulder from the fellow sitting behind. And he would need a clean escape route.'

'So a box!' said Hodža.

'Two options for making the shot; either from a box or from a gantry. The box would be my choice as it would be easier to get away in the general pandemonium. That's the type of thing I'll be on the lookout for come Wednesday.'

Sat next to Anna, he could only find one box on each side, positioned at the very front of the balcony. There was a small wall light located two metres above the box. It was good enough to follow the performance with the written libretto as many opera buffs liked to do. However it was too high for the assassin to snuff out. He would check the lower balcony at the interval. It was the same, so having done that he informed Hodža that it looked like a definite no-go from either level.

'Thank you K-P. You've earned your ticket. Now take it easy and enjoy the second act.'

… and much to his surprise, he did! To say he had any idea what was going on, would have been an exaggeration. He'd pretty much forgotten the stuff he'd read to Anna. It's difficult to retain information you're not very interested in but he did like the tunes!

And since he'd got the tickets for free, he thought he'd push the boat out – dinner for three at the Karlhoff. Anna was already dressed up. He knew she would be. It was irrelevant that this was *only a matinee* – it was *still* the opera. So that just left Amelia.

He had written down the directions that she should give to the cab driver and the money. "Give him it all. I've added a small Trinkgeld. If he tries it on, ask him for his number. He'll want to know why you want it. Tell him your employer works for the police". Anna might be educating Amelia in the social skills but Pichler was teaching her the way of the world.

The Karlhoff was not the type of establishment regularly patronised by a glorified laboratory assistant like Pichler. However he had done the manager a favour a few months ago. He'd been assured of excellent service at a "very agreeable price" the very next time he dined there. Pichler hoped that that meant "agreeable" to him, rather than to the manager.

Anna had to be guided between the numerous tables but once seated she commenced to "see" the restaurant. Spreading her hands to the furthest extent of the cutlery, she worked her way inwards.

'Soup, entrée, fish, and main,' she said before moving onto the glasses. 'Water, white, red, dessert. My, my, husband dear have you been at the cards again?'

Requests to describe the room were interrupted by the manager tapping on a glass.

'Ladies and Gentlemen, I regret to inform you that our regular Wednesday evening recital has had to be cancelled, due to the illness of both the chanteuse and her accompanist.'

A waiter approached and took their order.

'A shame about the music!' said Anna.

'It is indeed, madam,' whispering, 'I believe the "illness" is also known as elopement.'

Both ladies were thoroughly enjoying themselves. After the first course, Amelia excitedly exclaimed, 'I expect you often dine like this at the University, don't you K-P? I mean when the Vice Chancellor invites you to, of course.'

Pichler made a mental note to cut the quips he regularly made to Anna at the expense of his esteemed leader. Amelia was apt to take them seriously.

Anna bent over and whispered to Pichler who nodding, got up in search of the manager.

The glass was tapped a second time.

'Ladies and Gentlemen, I am delighted to announce that we have two special ladies dining with us tonight. May I introduce the celebrated pianist, Frau Anna Pichler. I'm sure many of you will have heard her perform at the Pressburg Musik Verein under her maiden name of Kabos. And her new protégé, Fräulein Amelia Friedstein.'

After this announcement he turned to face their table and began to applaud and was followed by the rest of the diners.

Poor Amelia – she looked ashen. 'But, but, I can't…'

'Too late now,' said Anna as she grabbed the girl's arm. 'Off you go… point me at the piano.'

Pichler followed them as they made their way accompanied by another ripple of applause.

The manager made to offer Anna some music before realising that this wasn't going to work. So he passed it to a shaking Amelia instead.

Pichler knew his wife had been desperate to return to that aspect of her old life. And now she had Amelia at her side. She wasn't a substitute for András, her murdered brother, but a good friend nonetheless. "I know she can do it, K-P" she'd often say to him.

Looking at her now as she stood by the side of the piano he wasn't so sure. Would she even get the first words out? He stood behind the seated Anna and looked earnestly into her eyes.

'Don't worry about them, Amelia. Sing it to us… just to us!'

Yes, the start *was* a bit shaky… but thereafter… What do they say – a star is born!

After the encore, all three returned to their table, only to find a person was sitting there. He appeared to be drinking their wine, the cheeky beggar, thought Pichler. He stood as they approached.

'An excellent performance Frau Pichler, Fräulein Friedstein. Permit me to introduce myself. I am Count Zorban Weilieski. Perhaps you have heard of me?'

Pichler and Amelia looked blank, but Anna saved the day.

'Of course, Count Weilieski. You were the guest conductor at the Pressburg music festival, two summers ago. I was there – sublime, quite sublime.'

The Count was clearly delighted. Pichler had noticed in his limited dealings with "arty-types", that no matter how famous they were, they were *always* amenable to receiving plaudits.

'As you see, I have taken the liberty of ordering some champagne.'

"Never heard of you – probably will have forgotten your name by tomorrow – but for now, you are my best friend", thought Pichler as he did the honours.

'I very much enjoyed your performance. Naturally not full professional level. I would have to say that in all honesty.'

Amelia's chin wobbled.

'… but close. Oh yes, very close indeed! And with a little professional training for the young Fräulein…'

Amelia's chin recovered!

Of course, they both said yes to the offer to join the Count's list of semi-professional artists who provided musical entertainment to private gatherings – mainly in the privileged homes of the privileged classes. There was no formal payment as such, but a collection was made at the end of the performance, all of which was theirs to keep. Pichler didn't interrupt though he was dying to know what the Count was getting out of the arrangement. No doubt each hostess would be coughing up a decent amount, depending on the "star" quality of the musicians. Away, that really didn't matter and nor did any money Anna might receive.

The point was Anna was back, back playing before an audience and she could do this just as often as she felt like. As for Amelia; Anna's long-delayed decision to accept a maid into their house was the best thing that could have happened to the girl.

Friday evening at the opera house:

It only took a grey wig, some spectacles and a little grey face powder to transform Signor Enrico Durando into his elderly "travelling" companion, Herr Ludwig Mauer. The make-up had to be kept simple. He needed to be able to apply it in a matter of moments. Despite this it was surprisingly convincing, fooling even people who knew him. Herr Mauer always travelled light; one small bag was sufficient to meet his needs for a two venue tour such as this one.

The secret was never to be predictable. Sometimes he would take the first cab at the station rank, sometimes the third or fourth. Sometimes he would emerge with the masses and join the queue for a cab, sometimes he would hang back and wait for the crowd to disperse. And on occasions when he had reason to be suspicious, he would walk a few streets from the station and hail a passing cab.

When he got to the music hall he was no more impressed than he had expected to be, which was not very. Still a fee is a fee and he had the state opera in Vienna to look forward to. He marched up the entrance steps and on entry, as expected, found nobody in the foyer. He glanced up at the wall clock. It said a quarter to four. The orchestra would be waiting for him.

He was in an out of the rest room in thirty seconds – in as Herr Mauer, out as Signor Durando.

The conductor looked up as the figure in travelling clothes strode towards the orchestra pit. They'd all been sat there since just after two. It took considerable will power to transform his scowl into something resembling a welcoming smile. Not that it was worth the effort! The great man barely nodded in his direction, demanding of no one in particular to be shown to his dressing room. The members of the orchestra sat tight. Most were thinking of ways to launch "musical bombs" during this rehearsal. Fortunately the musical director of the opera house arrived in the nick of time and led Durando backstage.

Needless to say, after waiting a further quarter of an hour, their mood had worsened considerably. But being these were true professionals, they performed all of Durando's arias… with as much good grace as they could muster.

***

Hodža and Slota mooched around during the course of the evening trying not to look like policemen. He had a dozen men strategically placed around the auditorium. They'd been here since eight this morning. They'd searched the place when they got here. They'd searched it after lunch. They'd searched for the last time just before the audience started flocking in. If they searched it anymore, they would have started to wear through the carpets.

Hodža had watched the whole of the rehearsal – Slota didn't! He went in search of food!

'Any good?' he asked when he got back.

'Not my world, is it Ján? He ponced on… he sang… he ponced off. Not sure what all the fuss is about. More importantly is there any food to be had?'

Slota handed him a couple of rolls, adding "the buffet's closed now".

***

To say Durando was elated would have been an exaggeration. Mollified was the best that could be said. The standing ovation had been the only satisfactory thing about the whole evening. His dressing room was a flea pit. The supporting performers' timings were off. The orchestra was third rate and the conductor was clueless. And to compound their collective ineptitude, none of them had the decency to attend the traditional post-performance libations… with one exception – the fourth violinist.

‘Well my dear,’ said Durando as they reached the end of their second bottle of Champagne, ‘this really is a most dreary little place. My hotel is far cosier!’

‘What *are* you suggesting, sir?’ giggled the young lady.

‘I think you *know* what I am suggesting.’

‘What would my dear mama say?’ she sniggered, the second bottle having had the effect he’d always intended it should.

‘Well I won’t tell her if you don’t!’

Herr Mauer was destined to remain in the bag for the rest of the evening – only Signor Durando’s presence would be required tonight. He left her seated in the foyer as he hastily retrieved said bag. On his return he ran into another incompetent!

‘The Empire!’ he called to the man as he brushed by.

Hodža glared after the retreating figure. He watched him haul the inebriated woman to her feet and head off down onto the street. So Hotel Empire it was. He’d have to let Slota know.

‘Not that one…Leesss take thes one. It’s a nicer collar… hic.. I mean colour, hee hee.’

‘Very well my dear, whatever your heart desires.’ “What a nice man”, a bystander might conclude. He’d be wrong! The only desires that mattered were his own, as he pushed her on board the cab under the scornful gaze of Inspector Karol Hodža.

***

Inspector Hodža finally got to bed about an hour later. He was just drifting off when…

Bang – bang – bang!

'Why on earth is somebody knocking at this time of night?' asked his sleepy wife.

Dishevelled as the Inspector looked in his nightgown, it was nothing compared to the sweating, heaving, red-faced man that confronted him in his door way.

'What is it?' Neumann.'

'Sorry, sir. It's the Italian gent… he never turned up at the hotel. We thought he might have got waylaid, so we tried all the nearby bars… case he felt like a nightcap, sorta thing… and we've been to the music hall… see if he'd actually left, but it was all blacked out.'

'Wait here, Neumann. I'll be back down in a minute.'

'Will you be calling on Sergeant Slota, sir?'

Saturday morning, Pressburg police station:

'Well, Hodža… explain yourself!'

That was just *one* of the reasons why the Chief was held in almost universal contempt by the real policemen who served out of the station. Never mind that a person had gone missing; never mind that his life was in danger. The first priority was to ensure none of the mud stuck to him. He seemed to have forgotten what he'd told the Inspector just a couple of days ago…

…"Yes, well as you say Hodža, the fellow has decided to ignore my advice regarding security provision. The department cannot be held responsible in the event that something goes awry. Nevertheless we have our duty to perform so do your best Hodža. He is one of the Emperor's subjects after all".

***

It was a full twelve hours later that he met up with Slota to review the day's efforts. There were a few restaurants run by Italian families. Sadly there was not a single Italian speaking officer in the department. That made asking around for information that bit more difficult. Still it probably didn't matter. The chances that the irredentists would be using Italian names or indeed go anywhere near any Italian restaurants were pretty much non-existent. It was by no means certain that the locals would co-operate with the police even if they had. Who could say where their true loyalties might lie?

Another group of officers had been assigned to ask around the hotels, boarding houses and the like, just in case the paranoid Durando had given Hodža a false hotel name.

They could ask around at the same time. Slota had outlined the approach his officers were to adopt.

'You're to ask the landlord or hotel manager if he has booked in a group of three to four, Mediterranean looking men. They'd be in their twenties or thirties – probably, booked in since Wednesday – probably.'

Personally he thought it to be a complete and utter waste of time. He said so to the Inspector.

'Why would they send anyone who'd stand out from the crowd, sir? It'd make more sense to send people who looked exactly like your typical Pressburg resident.'

He also interviewed their only witness.

'What about the coach and its driver, sir? Do you think you could draw up a description?'

Hodža puffed out his cheeks.

'Go on sir, give it a go!'

'Black sides, black wheels, driver in a black coat wearing a black scarf… and it was dark.'

The Inspector sighed. This was hopeless. Then a thought struck him. 'I think it might have had red wheel rims, Ján.'

Slota shrugged. 'Not much help, is it sir?'

A small Gasthaus on the outskirts of Vienna:

Three men gathered around a corner table; they looked German, they spoke German but very, *very* quietly.

'So he'll have left Pressburg by now and should be here by just before the start of the lecture at three.' This was Angelo, the tallest and youngest of the three.

‘Good. You’ve agreed that he will find his own way to the University?’ This time Claudio was doing the speaking. He was the leader and without doubt, the most ruthless of the three.

‘Yes. It is his practice. He will be sitting in the audience and will not reveal himself until the lecture is already underway,’ replied the younger man.’

‘I still cannot believe that he was so foolish as to agree. No security, no protection. He’ll be a sitting duck. However did you manage it?’ asked the third man, the heavily built Marco.

‘I simply appealed to his vanity,’ smirked Angelo, ‘or rather my sister did!’

The lecture was entitled “Good Relations in a Multi-Ethnic Empire” to be given by Professor Klaus Ritter (of the University of Bozen). It was due to last just forty minutes. After all, he had to be at the state opera house by six.

The audience would be made up of the usual wishy-washy liberal elite. And a few invited members of the press corps would be there, ones who were sympathetic to the cause – Durando’s cause that is, not that of the three irredentists now clustered around this table.

Five minutes in, Professor Ritter would sit down and a member of the audience would reveal himself. He’d then speak for the rest of the allotted time. The audience would be delighted! They’d been hood winked by the Empire’s most celebrated advocate of their cause! They could look forward to a half hour of enlightenment. Sadly for them, they'd only get about five minutes' worth.

At that point, Marco would stand up and fire from just three yards away. He'd make quite a splash. A heavy calibre bullet through his head is liable to do that!

'…Though,' added Angelo, continuing his theme, 'his own sense of superiority and arrogance made the task that much easier. But for that even my beautiful sister would have had her work cut out to snare him.'

'Do we have our own press release ready just in case the authorities try to hush it up?' asked Marco.

'We do… but if they are able to hush *this* up, then Franz Josef is the Emperor of China. No, rest assured, Marco that won't happen. If we didn't need the publicity, we could have killed him a hundred times over. This way, publicity and buckets of it is exactly what we'll get. Viva l'italia!'

'Viva l'italia,' the other two chorused.

Pressburg Police Station, mid-day on Monday:

'Thanks for dropping by, K-P,' began Inspector Hodža. 'Ján and I thought it might be worth picking your brains. Perhaps Ján, you can bring K-P up to date.'

The most optimistic scenario was that Durando had stayed somewhere other than the "Empire". He'd arrived at Vienna safe and sound under his own steam and performed at the State Opera on the Saturday evening. That optimism was ill-founded. Replies to the telegrams sent to the Vienna police and the opera house confirmed that he did not show up.

'So he's either dead, foul play or accidental, we know not which *or* he's been kidnapped,' concluded Slota.

'And we've already had half the station out on the lookout at all likely places between the music hall and his hotel,' added the Inspector.

'How far apart are the hotel and the opera house?

'Just over a kilometre,' answered Slota.

'*If* he has been taken by the irredentists, he'll still be alive most likely. If he was dead, you've have found the body by now. He would be hanging from some public lamppost or dumped on the steps of city hall. Anywhere in fact where their action would get the notoriety that they crave,' said Pichler.

'What do you mean "if" – who else could it be?' demanded Slota who didn't relish the prospect of further complicating this case.

Pichler closed his eyes for a moment.

'You need to smoke them out, Karol. Let's just assume that it *isn't* them for now. We should lay a trap and see what drops out. It may not help you find Durando, but if they fall for it, then that rather confirms that they don't have him stashed away. You also might nab some undesirables in the process.'

'Go on,' responded Inspector Hodža. 'Tell me what you have in mind. ...'

***

"Signor Enrico Durando, the celebrated opera singer had, it is reported, suffered a mild heart attack while returning to his hotel after his stellar performance as Alfonso, in Mozart's Cosi fan tutte at the Pressburg opera house on Friday evening", so the press release began. "His condition has improved dramatically over the following two days and he is expected to leave the St Johann Hospital within a few days. Messages and flowers may be sent, care of the Senior Matron, St Hildegard ward......"

'Make sure it goes to the Viennese press as well Ján. We can't be certain where the buggers might be hiding.'

'Will do chief!'

The Green Dragon, Pressburg, Wednesday:

'Did you see him, face to face I mean?'

'No,' replied Angelo. 'It seems he's suffered a bit of a relapse. They've moved him to a special care ward – no members of the public allowed to visit.'

'Damn and blast it. It'd be just like the bastard to up and die before we can get to him.' Claudio bit his hand in frustration. Then another thought occurred. 'If we *could* get to him, steal him away... would he survive the shock?'

Angelo shrugged. What was he – a doctor?

'All right – this is what we are going to do. It's far from ideal, but I'm not going back to Italy with that shit still alive to peddle his opinions.'

The other two listened, nodding at intervals.

'Tomorrow evening then… when most of the staff have gone home!'

St Johann's, late Thursday evening:

Claudio looked at their chins – all clean shaven. Then their necks – collar and tie. Exactly as he'd told them. It just needed the white coats.

They'd entered carrying flowers, skipping through the entrance when the guard had been called away. They got as far as the second floor before being stopped by an attendant, who was about Marco's size.

'Visiting hours are over, gentlemen. The times are…' and that was as far as he got.

'In there Marco… and be quick!'

One of them was now suitably dressed. They passed a rack of coats and so attired the three medical men made their way to the special care ward, one of whom was pushing a wheelchair.

The special ward was smaller than they'd expected, containing only three beds. One bed in particular was surrounded by a variety of medical instruments – and something else – a sleeping body.

'Close the door, Marco. We don't want to be disturbed.'

There was a click as the door closed but they paid it no heed; nor to its sturdiness or even the shininess of its brass fittings on the outside.

'Quick get him into the wheelchair!' demanded Claudio.

'Fiiiiiicchhhhh! Quick get out!'

They made no impression on the door, no matter how hard they charged it. Then they searched around for some sort of battering ram – to no avail. Then they all reached into their pockets for their guns – the same guns that they had left back at their hotel. They'd *never* need them in a hospital, for heaven's sake!

'I told you we should have brought them,' screamed Marco, who had that moment seen a face appear at the small round window in the door. The face smiled and then moved to be replaced by a hand and in that hand, there *was* a gun.

The bundle of clothes that was the body in the bed had slept soundly through the entire fracas.

Pressburg police station, Friday morning:

'So it *wasn't* them, Chief!'

'Apparently not, Ján.'

'Did we learn anything?'

'No. They're just these happy-go-lucky chaps up to some larks. I think the attendant who they battered may have a different view!' said Hodža.

'He's identified them?' asked Slota.

'Oh, yes. That will get them banged up for a short period. Enough time for our friends from Vienna to arrive and cart them off for some less delicate interrogation.'

'So where do we go from here, now we know for certain that it's nothing to do with Italian nationalists?'

Inspector Karol Hodža had to admit – *that* was a good question – a damn good question.

Haus Pichler:

Pichler had finished the last of his marking – Gott sei Dank! He heard the key turn in the front door and got out of his armchair, fingers crossed.

He didn't even get the chance to ask "how did it go?" before young Amelia threw her arms around his neck before turning away and skipping into the kitchen to prepare supper.

'I take it the afternoon was a stunning success then?' he asked as Anna proceeded behind at a more leisurely pace.

'I think we were both a little nervous at first. Honestly dearest, the number of fur coats Amelia saw hanging in the cloakroom when we arrived was enough to intimidate anybody – not to mention the odd tiara. But it was a beautiful piano – puts poor Aunt Emma's old thing to shame.'

'Do you think Amelia will want to perform again?'

'Do, I! You try stopping her. We performed three pieces. Then there was a refreshments interval… during which she drank heavily of the admiration of the few young men who were there. I also allowed her a small glass of wine. I wasn't quick enough to prevent one of her new admirers from recharging her glass. But in the event it relaxed her and I must confess – though not within her earshot – that she sang the better for it.'

'It always works for me!' replied her husband though he was thinking of pre-battle nerves rather than bashing out the odd tune to a bunch of old biddies. It was as well that he kept *that* thought to himself.

'So the next performance is…?'

'I don't know yet,' replied Anna. 'Would you like to come?'

'Very much so,' he replied without thinking. On seeing her reaction, he managed to save the day.

'But… I've so much on… what with my day job and helping the Inspector. Would you mind terribly if I missed the next one?'

She brightened up.

'Not at all! I understand how busy you are.'

Of course she didn't want him there. This was about her… and Amelia of course. She *knew* that he *knew* that. Kisses on both cheeks was his reward.

'Amelia… Amelia,' he called, 'wine for the maestro, if you please.'

'But not for you, my dear,' called Anna after him. 'You've had quite enough already.'

Once the "wine waiter" had come and gone only to be transformed into the cook, Anna became rather conspiratorial.

'You remember the lead singer who performed last Friday,' she whispered. '… the one we didn't hear on the Wednesday… What *was* his name now? … Dorondu, wasn't it?'

'Something like that,' replied her husband, feigning ignorance of the fellow.

'Well, during the interval his name came up. One of the pre-interval pieces was "Der Liebe himmlisches Gefühl" by Herr Mozart. Of course you know it, don't you dear?'

'Loves Heavenly feeling – course I do. I whistle it every day on my way to work.'

For which he received a dig in the ribs.

'It's not an easy piece and we had to skip over some of the really tricky bits. Somebody asked why we didn't include some of the great man's Italian pieces. I said that Amelia's Italian wasn't up to it… are you all right K-P?'

Pichler, whose attention had begun to wander, perked up immediately.

'I am getting there,' said Anna. 'Anyway, talk of Mozart's Italian works naturally led onto Cosi Fan Tutte and from there onto Herr Durando. That was his name, I remember it now. Anyway, it turns out, if the rumours are to be believed, that he's something of a lothario. He's broken the hearts of a number of young ladies around Pressburg. Two of the mothers there had had what they described as "close calls" where their own daughters were concerned. There was even a suggestion he'd done more than break hearts, you understand what I'm saying… virtues were at risk.'

Pichler shook his head from side to side.

'Anyway, who'd have thought it, my dear? Just goes to show – you never can tell, can you?'

'Perhaps the police should be involved?' he suggested.

'Oh no! We were all sworn to secrecy. Anyway, it is enough that we have all been warned.'

And that was as far as Pichler could take this particular conversation – still… food for thought… a veritable banquet in fact!

Pressburg police station:

There was room for the three of them in Hodža's office but there was no room for optimism.

The Inspector began by reporting what he'd been told by Vienna regarding the results of their interrogation of the three suspects captured at St Johann's.

'They *really* don't know *anything* about Durando's disappearance. Yes, they were here to bump him off – they didn't deny that – in fact they was proud of it…

think they'll be some sort of national heroes when they get back.'

'*If* they get back home!' added Slota.

There was justice in the Empire of Franz Josef. There was also "rough" justice in the Empire of Franz Josef. When it came to cases involving sedition, well… he didn't like to think what their collective fate might be.

'Your ruse worked a treat, K-P. How did you come up with the idea of the self-locking door?'

'All I did was to suggest the catch be mounted on the outside. You see I got locked out of a lecture theatre a couple of weeks ago. I had a meeting to attend and I was running late, so I dashed out leaving my briefcase behind. I rushed back as the last of them was leaving and the little sod released the catch on his way out and closed the door, so I couldn't get back in again. Still, they'll be sorry. I'm going to revise their exam paper; no more Herr nice lecturer.'

'That simple, eh!' smiled Slota, adding 'apart from fitting a totally new door and fittings of the big and beefy variety.'

'Yes, Ján. Though I messed up on those fittings. I should have scuffed them up a bit, so they didn't look brand new. Luckily for us, they didn't notice.'

Slota smiled. Dear old K-P; never satisfied with anything less than perfection when he was in "detecting-mode".

'On the bright side,' piped up Pichler, 'it's more likely that Durando is still alive… and being held captive… somewhere.'

'We don't know *who* might have done this and until we do know, we have no chance of finding *where* "somewhere" is,' replied Hodža.

Pichler fell silent for a few moments, while the two police officers discussed their options, with it had to be said, very little success. Should he tell them what he'd gleaned from Anna's recent triumph? It was mainly supposition of course. Worse still it was only *his* supposition. It had all the makings of a wild goose chase. His introspections were interrupted by the realisation that the room had gone quiet and both men were now staring at him.

Hodža and Slota both knew; they'd seen it a dozen times before. Slota nudged his colleague.

'The great Prof's been at it again, chief.'

'Weellll?' asked Hodža.

So he told them.

'Hmmm!' said Hodža after a moment or two's thought. 'It's pretty thin pickings, but right now "thin" is all we have. And it could be worse – it could be a *lot* worse. If the man's predilections were for those ladies who walk the pavements, then the pool would be too big for us to even contemplate. As it is, we have a starting point, or at least we will have, won't we K-P?'

***

Pichler played the concerned husband to a tee.

'Thank you for your understanding Count.'

'Not at all my dear Pichler, not at all. I should hate to cause you a moment's concern. I should hate to lose the services of your talented wife and her young protégé even more!' and he laughed good-naturedly at his own remark.

'By all means, if it puts your mind at rest, do visit the addresses on the list. I can assure you that these are all located in very safe areas of the city. The two ladies will be perfectly safe travelling to and from without you needing to ride "shot-gun", as our American friends would say.'

As he left Count Zorban Weilieski's impressive mansion, his main concern was whether Anna would get too used to these kinds of surroundings!

***

'So,' said Hodža, 'a total of twelve. We'll try these. If they don't come up trumps, then we're back to square one.'

'What are we going to ask them?' asked Slota. 'We can't refer to Durando directly as Anna wasn't supposed to repeat what she heard at that soiree. After all this might prove to be nothing more than gossip, and that would leave the Department liable to legal action for slander.'

'Leave it with me, Karol. All I shall need is a pony and trap and Ján to accompany me – to make it official.'

Pressburg – The "Mansion" quarter:

Pichler looked skywards and grimaced. The sky was grey edging towards charcoal and that could only mean a rather soggy day lay ahead. The trap offered no protection from the elements so it was a case of lumping it.

He cast a sideways glance at Slota as the two-wheeler the Inspector had allocated them trotted towards the Bernstein mansion. He had huddled himself into his greatcoat and looked fed-up, bordering on miserable.

'So have you worked out your patter yet?' he asked.

'I'm going to play it by ear, Ján. Actually play it by ear is rather apposite, get it… especially in my case with my lamentable ability to read music.'

Slota just grunted. Pichler's weak attempt at levity was not helping his mood one bit.

He'd thought about putting a standard Spiel together as he lay in bed last night but rapidly abandoned the idea. It really was a case of judging the reaction of each house holder and then adjusting to suit.

The Bernstein mansion was just as he'd expected it to be; grand tending towards ostentatious but not *especially* large. These were where the self-made men lived. It was wall to wall financiers, captains of industry and senior officers. Of course, the houses themselves weren't that large, at least not large by the standards of the nobility. But land was cheap this far out from the centre and so each mansion lay in its own grounds. The minimum separation was measured not in metres but in multiples of shotgun range – an important consideration as there was nothing the nouveau riche liked better than blasting small furry animals to pieces – ideally without killing any of their neighbours. So "wall-to-wall" was a poor description of their proximity, hence a rather longer journey than Pichler ideally would have liked.

As the trap drove between the impressively ornate gates, the front of the house came into view. To make what was almost certain to be a fool's errand – and a wet one at that – more enjoyable, Pichler thought he'd play a little game; guess the number of columns supporting the portico. Two, obviously the minimum, would look "cheap"; five was vulgar. So three or four! Three it was.

'Good afternoon, sir,' said the butler, eyeing up the two men standing before him.

'Good afternoon. This is Sergeant Slota, Pressburg Police. My name is Pichler. May I speak to the master of the house, please?'

'In town, I'm afraid, sir. I can ask if the mistress will see you.'

They were shown into a decent sized room hung with large portraits, none of which either of them recognised. A middle-aged lady sat alone on a settee and smiled up at them.

'How can I help you gentlemen?'

Pichler repeated the introductions he'd given to the butler.

'Thank you for seeing us, madam. We are making enquiries regarding the disappearance of a young lady following the performance last Friday evening at the Opera House.'

'Oh dear! Who is it, is it someone I might know?'

An impossible question to answer – how the heck should he know all the young ladies this lady might know. Instead…

'We're keeping that confidential for the moment, but perhaps you could tell me whether you and your husband were present at the opera?'

They were! They'd never been known to miss a touring concert or opera or anything musical. Would they like some tea – they weren't given the option to refuse and three-quarters of an hour later…

'This is going to take all week if we carry on at this rate, K-P!'

On to the next one! Three pillars again this time. Pretty much the same result; yes, they were both there and no, they hadn't seen or heard anything and no, they weren't aware of any previous disappearances.

Three mansions later and Slota's mood had deteriorated to the down-right morose stage.

'This isn't getting us *anywhere*, K-P.'

'Yes, it is, Ján. We know these people are music lovers… they're all on Count Weilieski's list. We are almost certain that they were at the opera. Did you notice how confidently they asserted that but much less so when it came to not being aware of any previous disappearances.'

'Yeeessss! You mean they were lying.'

'I mean they were lying,' replied Pichler.

'Now if all twelve come up with the same responses, we've drawn a blank. But if we get something that doesn't feel quite right, then we could be in business.'

The penultimate mansion on their list stood before them. It was the master himself who came to the door – an unusual thing in itself. And in the doorway he remained! No invitation to "step inside" and as for their next cup of tea, well that would have to wait for the last house. It was a very odd conversation. The man's manner was brusque though that was understandable when a policeman stands before you asking impertinent questions. It was lucky for Pichler that General-Major Schwarzenburg did not know he was not being addressed by a bona fide policeman, but a mere Unterleutnant and a retired one at that. Pichler decided some more pointed questions were worth trying.

'We are conducting enquiries sir regarding the disappearance of a woman outside the music hall last Friday. Witnesses claim to have seen a man bundle a young lady – a lady of some quality from their descriptions – into a cab which then took off at speed.

We're just checking amongst such families to see if they have heard anything that might be of interest.'

'What type of thing?' asked the Officer in what sounded like a somewhat aggressive tone to Pichler.

'Perhaps you have heard some of your social circle discuss a mutual acquaintance whose daughter went missing at that time or perhaps even have knowledge of an earlier close encounter with the man. I have the description of him sir if I may read…'

Pichler got no further.

'I have heard nothing, nothing whatsoever. Now please be so good as to leave.'

'Very well, sir. But perhaps I may ask whether you attended the opera at the…'

'No! My wife and I seldom go into town and certainly not on a Friday evening. We are childless and we are *not* musical people. We have our books and that is sufficient. Now – good afternoon!'

They looked at each other as they drove out onto the road.

'If they're not musical people, what the buggery heck are they doing on Count Weilieski's list?' the pair of them chorused.

By the time the final house frontage was in view, Pichler had reached the "fick the number of columns" stage. The spitting had turned into heavy rain.

'Oh you poor things,' exclaimed the young woman who stood before them, even before he'd completed his own introduction.

‘’Slovan… get towels will you… and some tea… or would you prefer coffee?’

Anything hot would do thought Pichler and his shrug indicated as much.

She was a bonny thing and full of life. If what he’d heard about Durando was even half true, it seemed highly unlikely that any young woman could have come away from such an encounter undamaged. No, she couldn’t have known the man but he went through his script nonetheless. At each question, she would put her hand to her mouth or say something like… “oh, how terrible!”.

‘You should try the next house to ours!’ she declared.

Pichler’s heart sank. He didn’t think there *were* any other houses.

‘Yes, you should ask at General Schwarzburg’s house. It’s the middle one of the three in this particular area. But I should warn you, he is rather a morose gentleman.’

Oh really, *thought* Pichler. I hadn’t noticed. But he *said* ‘Why do you say this?’

The young lady brightened up at hearing this.

‘You mean, you *don’t* know? It was about two years ago that it happened. Their daughter took her own life. She was with child and the father had abandoned her. Of course we all knew but pretended to believe the General and his wife’s story that it was an accident. Very sad, very sad indeed! Since then the pair of them have become virtual recluses.'

'Do you know anything of the father?'

'Only rumour – some sort of itinerant musician apparently, a Latino some people said, but he might have been a Zigeuner. We had a few gypsies here around that time. Could *he* be the man you are seeking?'

'No, Miss. We believe that the man involved in that incident died last year,' lied Pichler with utter conviction, which was impressive given that it was the first he'd heard of this rumour…

…'Home?' asked Slota.

'Back the way we've come!' declared Pichler.

It was getting pretty dark by the time they reached House Schwarzenburg and that was their intention. Tying the trap up some way from the entrance and hoping to God that it hadn't been pinched by the time they got back, the pair of them set off in the direction of the coach house.

'We'll take one of the carriage lamps with us and light it once we're inside,' said Slota.

The coach house itself was clearly wide enough for two carriages which meant double doors. They couldn't chance opening these as they might be spotted from the house some hundred paces away.

'Try round the back!'

Pichler returned after a minute or so and gestured for Slota to follow.

The small back door wasn't locked – there was little to steal apart from the carriages themselves.

'Light it!'

Slota cupped his hand over most of the lamp allowing just a sliver of light to peek out.

'Look at this one, K-P! Doesn't look like it's been anywhere for ages, does it?'

Its companion on the other hand, clearly had. Pichler looked behind at the two large front doors. Neither had any windows or other openings – good – they could risk turning up the lamp.

'Yes?' he asked as Slota worked his way along the carriage.

'See this red trim along the wheel arches?'

Pichler nodded.

'Yes, this must be it.'

'So *now* what?' asked Pichler.

'To the station to see the Inspector. Then back here tomorrow with a half dozen of our lads and an emergency search warrant.'

***

The warrant took a little longer than they'd hoped. Further delay was caused by the Chief of Police insisting on leading the search since a person of note was involved. Hodža didn't mind a jot. He knew the Chief didn't like to get involved in anything resembling real police work but he might come in handy in smoothing the General-Major's feathers.

While he was doing that the three of them went to the coach house.

'Is it the same one, sir?' asked Slota

'Yes, I'm as certain as I can be,' replied Hodža. 'I've got the lads examining the insides for clues.'

As it turned out, no amount of smoothing by the Chief would have helped. Schwarzburg had only given Pichler a glimpse of how aggressive he *could be* when the situation demanded it. Threats were made to all and sundry – by the time he'd finished with them, Pressburg police station wouldn't boast a single officer above the rank of constable.

Hodža joined the Chief in the sitting room, his boss failing to get any kind of answer – straight or otherwise – from the General. Pichler stood by the window and was subjected to a series of angry glares until he could stand it no longer and walked out of the room, feeling the General's eyes boring into him.

'Maria… Maria,' boomed the General. 'Follow that man. Make sure he doesn't steal anything.'

To say that his wife was under his thumb would have been to put it mildly. She was a diminutive figure, with mousy coloured hair and the beginnings of a pronounced stoop. As Pichler passed into the adjacent room his gaze fell on a portrait of the woman who followed at his heels – at least he presumed it was her. It must have been done at least twenty years ago and it was like looking at a different woman – one for whom life had still held meaning.

Once inside, Pichler saw it… and everything changed. He walked over to the piano and saw the music. So much for them not being music lovers! He couldn't read a note and he wasn't sure what the title meant as it was in Italian, but he *could* read the composer's name. Anna's favourite – Mozart. So they had been to the opera or seen a poster at least. "Cosi fan tutte" he said out loud despite not meaning to.

He turned and as he did so he saw her nervously glance at the music stand on the piano. She knew that now *he* knew.

'What was your daughter's name?' he asked as kindly as he could.

'Marianne!' she replied and the tears that had begun some minutes before, now flowed in torrents.

He closed the door and they sat down together and she talked… and she talked and she talked.

'Where is he?' asked Pichler once the tears had abated.

For answer she pointed to the floorboards. Pichler returned to the sitting room where Inspector Hodža sat his hand on his brow in exasperation. Looking up at K-P he saw him waving.

'What's… where… where do you think you're going?'

The General got up to follow them but as he reached the music room, he was intercepted by his wife.

'They know, Manfred,' she said… 'They know!'

Pichler turned around ready to assist the wife, but no assistance was needed – it never had been. He saw the man take his wife in his arms and the two hugged each other for dear life. It was not *he* that had transformed the portrait into the woman he saw before him – it was *him*, the man sitting one floor below!

Hodža halted abruptly as he passed a small portrait in the corridor. It was of two girls, sisters obviously. One he did not recognise but the other was a younger version of a member of the Pressburg orchestra – a fourth violinist in fact.

The door to the cellar was locked but the key remained in the lock. As they walked down the stairs they heard the sound of a chair leg being scraped along the floor and a muffled cry. And there *he* was!

Once outside, Pichler looked at Hodža. 'What the hell are we going to do now Karol?' he asked.

'I asked the two of them what they intended to do with Durando,' replied the Inspector.

'And?' asked Pichler.

'They simply didn't know. They've not physically harmed him. He's only had bread and water but that won't have done him any harm.'

'You know Karol if they hadn't chanced upon that poster, I don't believe…'

'They didn't… chance upon the poster, I mean. The General and the young lady you saw at the last house were both telling the truth – the Schwarzenburg's have been living the life of recluses. His wife *was* a regular on Weilieski's soiree-circuit, hence her appearance on the list, but she hasn't attended any for the past two years.'

'Then how did they…?' asked Pichler.

'The fourth violinist! She's the daughter's cousin. It was she who told the Schwarzenburgs. Apparently they have regular sessions, just the three of them. The General is quite an accomplished baritone, or so his wife informed me.'

'Oh, that's not good news, Karol. That means you're going to have to charge the General, his wife, the cousin… and I suppose the servants. What a bloody awful mess!

'Apparently, the servants were kept in complete ignorance.'

'I can't believe that!' replied K-P.

'Oh, I have the General's word on it. It was he who drove the coach into town and he who manhandled our Italian friend into the basement… all by himself!'

'No!' replied Pichler incredulously.

'Well, I mentioned that an eye-witness could identify the driver by the blue scarf that he was wearing…'

'And, he said…'

'Yes, that was me!'

'But Karol, it wasn't a blue scarf, was it?'

'No, it wasn't, K-P.'

'What about the cousin…?

'Married, two children, lives in Pressburg West district.'

On hearing this, Pichler turned away, partly in anger, partly in sorrow. That it should come to this; half a dozen lives ruined on account of this man who… He turned back to face the Inspector.

'You know what, Karol. Had fate not dealt them this hand, I don't believe they would have done anything, I really don't. As it did, well, it just opened a wound, a wound that was, perhaps, just starting to heal a little.'

'I agree with you K-P. I suppose they'd have just let him go, in a few more days when common sense had finally prevailed. They're not murderers I'd stake my life on that. Still, you can't go around kidnapping people, so I suppose I'll have to charge them. Sod it to hell!'

They hadn't noticed the presence of Sergeant Ján Slota, who was standing just a few yards away, but he had heard them – every word. At that moment, Slota was brushed to one side by an irate Italian intent on browbeating his boss.

'Inspector, where's the Chief of Police. I demand these people be arrested. I insist that they be. I shall be pressing for the maximum penalty under the law. I've been imprisoned, abused, tortured even…'

Neither law officer responded being somewhat stunned by the fellow's complete absence of gratitude or any acknowledgement of his own guilt in the tragedy.

'You *do* know who I am, I suppose,' he glared at Hodža in particular.

'This way, sir,' said Sergeant Slota as he escorted the man at rifleman's pace – or as near as Slota could manage with his short legs – towards the open coach house. There an animated discussion could be observed to be taking place, though it was a "discussion" in which the shorter of the two men did all the talking accompanied by much finger wagging. The taller man was seated and after a while his attempts to interrupt became less and less frequent and his chin dropped lower and lower onto his chest.

Ten minutes later saw both men back to where they had left the Inspector who'd now been joined by his Chief.

'I've decided not to press charges!' declared Durando, as ungraciously as he possibly could.

Not that the General-Major and his wife heard this reticence. They embraced each other, only separating as the Inspector approached them.

'General… Madam,' he began. 'I know it's not justice, but it's the best we can do. I hope it will be possible for you to never to have to think of this man ever again.'

He didn't add any platitudes; "I'm sure it's what your daughter would want". What the fick did he know what their daughter would have wanted? She might have wanted to rip his balls off and watch him bleed to death! But the mother tried to smile a little and the husband took his hand and shook it warmly.

And that was that. Or it almost was.

'What did you say to the swine, Ján?' asked Pichler.

Slota gave him a mischievous grin, adding only 'need to know, K-P old son… need to know!'

'Herr Pichler!' called a booming voice. It was the General-Major. A superior officer had called and Pichler almost marched up to him as he invariably did. He took the offered hand as he looked into the older man's face.

No words were exchanged – no words were needed.

Hotel Schlossburg, Graz:

It was too far to travel from Pressburg to Trieste without breaking the journey and he hadn't been to Graz for simply ages. Tomorrow he would explore opportunities for future operatic endeavours, but tonight, ah tonight – he had other endeavours in mind.

She smiled at him fleetingly, as he, seated at a table for one, once again ran his eye around the room. When their eyes had met for the first time, he had smiled at her, but she had returned only a very modest glance before returning to the discourse of her husband – her much, much older husband. Now, she was waiting for him to look at her again.

As he saw her look back at the man seated opposite, her boredom was evident; he could hardly fail to notice it. Was her attitude exaggerated? Did she wish to leave him in no doubt as to her interest? He chanced a slight inclination of his head and to his delight, that gesture was reciprocated. This was going to be easy – perhaps too easy! Half the pleasure was in the pursuit but this hind was making no attempt to evade capture. So be it!

The couple adjourned to the lounge, the old fellow continuing to prattle away as he had all through dinner, oblivious to the scene that was unfolding before his very eyes. Tonight he would be wearing the cuckold's hat, though probably not for the first time if this was the care he took of his younger and, what would he say… *reasonably…* yes, definitely reasonably attractive wife.

The man slowly dried up with each successive brandy, until after three such, his "good" lady would need the assistance of a member of hotel staff in order to get him to their room. He saw his cue.

'May I be of assistance, madam?'

She smiled her gratitude, a smile that said, "For this and for later".

'Room 217!' was the only further communication that passed between them, until he heard a gentle knock-knock on his door.

He advanced towards her but she restrained him with an up held hand.

'You must wait my impetuous boy. I have ordered Champagne and we cannot let the boy see us. When he comes, I will hide behind the door.'

Normally, he would delight in the anticipation of the pleasure to come, but for some reason, perhaps all the strain he had endured over the past few days, he was anxious to begin. Then came the single knock and "room service" and his waiting was over.

The man who entered wore a suit; he looked more like a guest than a member of staff. Perhaps it was the manager himself. He'd noticed a few people who had seen him arrive then turn to their friends and he even heard one say… 'Isn't that Enrico…?'

'Signor Durando… your Champagne!'

He swung the door wide open taking care not to crush the object of his lust as she hid behind. She winked at him as he stood to one side to allow the manager in and indicated where the tray should be put … but then something unexpected happened.

Without a word, she sidled around the door edge and slipped out of the room without a word. His astonishment momentarily left him stunned; the blow on the back of his head, left him permanently so. He would know nothing of the large, strong hands that would soon close around his windpipe.

The manager closed and locked the door behind him and proceeded directly to the lounge, where he spied the young woman and her "husband".

'Thank you father,' she said squeezing his arm.

She knew she'd led the man to his death but it had to be done. She'd do it again if she had to. Anybody who crossed the "family" had it coming and welching on debts was second only to informing to the police. He'd had enough chances to pay up! Even so, the traditional punishment was garrotting but that seemed just too, too cruel.

The old man smiled back at her. He wasn't in the habit of being merciful but he'd indulge his own daughter on this occasion. She was not destined to ever become the head of the family and there was a limit to how ruthless she'd ever need to be. Not like her brother!

'All done?' he asked of the manager.

'All done Papa!'

THE PROMISSORY NOTE

I hereby promise to pay the lady who bears this note the sum agreed in respect of services previously rendered to the signatory.
Signed... Hagen

Giuseppe Verdi — 1923

Three months earlier:

Outside, all was peace and tranquillity. The grounds were a picture. The gardener was trimming the box, the cook was gathering herbs for this evening's dinner and the Count's manservant was taking the air. Normally he would be inside waiting within earshot to respond in a moment to his master's every wish, but not *this* morning. Inside, there was a maelstrom of emotions. How had it come to this? What had gone wrong?

The Count sat at one end of the breakfast table, the Countess at the other. It was a long table, but the distance between them was more than physical.

'How *could* you do such a thing, to me of all people? Aren't I enough for you?'

It was hard to explain how it had happened – it just had!

'And to write that note; what in God's name possessed you?'

'I… I… I don't know, I really don't! It didn't seem so unreasonable at the time, but in retrospect… I realise now… oh God, I'm so, so sorry.'

'Well, there's no option but to pay. How much is the bitch asking?'

The letter was pushed across the table.

'Good God, *that* much? Well, there's no help for it, it will just have to be found; that's the long and the short of it. Let us both just pray that that will be the end of the matter.

May 18th 1875 – Day 1:

'Good journey, sir?' asked the servant as he opened the carriage door for him.

"No!" thought Pichler, "Bloody atrocious actually, but thanks for asking all the same." Instead he returned a fairly non-committal smile.

Still he was here now he reflected, squeezing some life back into his aching buttocks as he walked towards the door the servant was indicating. It was about eighty-five kilometres from his house on the Rösslgasse to the Schönbrunn palace, the summer residence of his majesty Franz Josef. He'd been here a few times before, most notably in the September of 1870, but it always impressed him – rococo style with yellow walls, "Schönbrunn yellow" they called it. As to why he'd been brought here in such haste he had no idea but then he rarely ever did.

***

The day had started at just after seven, just as he was about to sit down to breakfast. Three sharp raps on the heavy front door sent Amelia scurrying to answer.

'Herr Pichler, if you please my dear,' said the man standing in the doorway.

The man of the house was off his seat and heading for the door before the third rap had started.

'Thank you Amelia. I'll deal with this.'

He looked their visitor up and down, noting that while he was in mufti his bearing gave the game away; quite obviously an army man. Pichler had had enough of these early morning visits to become something of an old hand.

'Do come in, Sergeant. I know you won't want to remain outside – a bit too conspicuous, eh! The coach'll be around again in about five minutes won't it; it's always best to keep it circling around the block for the same reason, isn't it?'

The Sergeant – for he was indeed a Sergeant – was somewhat taken aback by all this. He seemed to be having a conversation with this fellow but without actually being part of it. But then, this was his first such visit to Rösslgasse.

'Did they tell you how long I'll be required for?' asked Pichler.

'I'm to tell you, sir that you'll be required in Vienna for up to five days,' replied the Sergeant.

Most of the "lines" he'd been given by his superiors had been rendered superfluous by Mr "know-it-all" here, so he was determined get at least *one* phrase out intact!

In his early days Pichler would ask "what's this all about, then?" This afforded the man who'd come with the coach the opportunity to respond with a somewhat pretentious "I'm not at liberty to say, sir." This used to annoy Pichler. He'd served under the colours for eight years and he knew it was army-speak for "search me, chum – no bugger tells me anything". So he didn't ask!

'Anna!' called Pichler. 'The feather bag please.'

Anna was already on the landing for she was also an old hand at this game. In a flash she was on her knees scrambling under their bed, where there were three bags, pre-packed and ready to go – biggest nearest the headboard, smallest nearest the foot. She pulled that one out far enough to check that it had the feather "marker" threaded through the handle… just to be doubly sure… removed that and dragged the thing out from under. By the time she was downstairs with it, Amelia had thrown together a makeshift parcel and both women arrived at the door step simultaneously.

The Sergeant stared at the bag, which looked like an ordinary leather bag to him. He was a little disappointed, never having seen a bag made of feathers before.

A quick hug and as he stepped onto the pavement, he saw the coach turn the corner onto his street. Rather than wait, he walked smartly towards it, flung open the door before it had stopped and slammed it behind him once aboard. The Sergeant, being a little fellow had to grab onto the side rail and haul himself onto the driver's seat muttering a sarcastic "thanks for slowing up, mate!" to the driver. Pichler smiled to himself, which was *not* very kind!

It could be a tedious journey – too bouncy to write anything and trying to read made him feel a bit sick. Once he'd scoffed down any food, which usually took less than ten minutes, there was nothing to occupy him. It wasn't so bad if he could sleep… which he couldn't today because the thing was veritably rocketing along, so all that was left was to look out of the window.

***

'Good morning Herr Pichler,' said the official-looking man, checking his pocket watch to see if it *was* still morning. 'I'd tell you my name, but you *really* don't need to know it. It will be sufficient for you to understand that you are here at the *direct* request of his majesty and that I am his mouth piece. This way please.'

As they approached a door the man halted. 'Herr Pichler – let me inform you that you will not *see* the Emperor – you will not *hear* the Emperor.'

Pichler was taken aback. He hadn't expected to see the Emperor; why all the hoo-ha, why the need for all that "I am his majesty's mouth piece"? But he just nodded.

'Good!' said the official, who swung the door open and Pichler dutifully, followed him in, closing the door behind him. Turning around he got the shock of his life for sitting at the far end of the room was… the Emperor Franz Josef. He began a genuflexion but was pulled up sharp by a wagging finger from the official.

'Sorry sir, my imagination,' he said which *almost* but not quite, produced a smile.

'To begin, Herr Pichler, not only is his majesty not here, I am not here and *you* are not here.'

Pichler struggled to suppress a grin and only just managed it. This was surely all getting just a little bit silly.

'Of course not sir,' he replied, adding somewhat facetiously, 'and where am I sir?... just in case I need to find myself.'

'You are currently in the City's central library, researching information for your book.'

'I'm writing a book, am I sir?'

'*Of course you are* – kind of thing you academics are always wasting your time on, isn't it?'

The briefing began and Pichler soon understood why the official had indulged in his little game of charades, such was the extreme delicacy of the matter. The gentleman at the heart of the case was one Count Paul von Hagen, a deputy minister in the War Office and also the Inhaber, or Colonel, of a well-respected regiment of the line. He lived in Vienna with his wife, the Countess Inga and they were both regulars at high-society events, including those attended by the Emperor and Empress. On the surface a thoroughly respectable man; in practice, like so many privileged men of his class, he'd been tempted to stray beyond the marital bed. Nothing uncommon about that, thought Pichler.

Had he not mislaid his wallet, then the subsequent scandal would never have arisen – but he did! Sadly the absence of the wallet had not been noticed until the deed had been completed. The "lady" in question was a Madame Louise de Rousseau, a French national and a noted courtesan of the highest standing amongst the upper classes of Vienna. Normally, one might have expected such a lady to take the gentleman's word that he was temporarily embarrassed and that he would return the next day to make good the debt. After all, she wasn't a common street whore, far from it! But no! She had insisted that he should provide her with an IOU. He had visited Madame de Rousseau on numerous occasions, so he did not – one may presume – see any great issue in complying with her request. However, returning the next day, wallet in hand, the lady refused to accept payment *or* return his IOU. She told him that she would be in touch. And "touch-him" she had been doing at the rate of fifty Gulden a month!

'Clearly, Herr Pichler, you will have immediately grasped just how embarrassing this could be if it *ever* became public. And not just to von Hagen but to the War Office, the entire Government and perhaps even…' the official's glance moved in the direction of the man seated at the far end of the room.

'There may even be security issues, *if* this monthly demand for payments should escalate into demands for sensitive information. We cannot rule out the possibility given the Count's standing within in the Government and the fact that Madame is French. You may not be aware that the French are extremely unhappy with the alliances that the Empire has recently entered into.'

Pichler shook his head. Slota would have approved. "Always plead ignorance of anything and everything, my lad – especially when dealing with officialdom".

'We require this matter to be concluded within four days,' continued the official. A distinct cough emanated from the far end.

'… As I said, within *three* days. How you do it is up to you. We do not need to know. However you *must* do this alone – we don't want you bringing in any of your little friends from the Pressburg Police Department. You are to report here on the morning of the fourth day. Find yourself a hotel, nothing too pricey! Here are some expenses and your authorisation.'

Pichler cast an eye over this authority. Once he'd reached the part which said, "You are commanded to offer the bearer of this note whatever assistance he requires of you…" and noted the official looking seal at the bottom, he stopped reading. That was good enough for him.

'Any questions Herr Pichler?'

'Two, sir! I don't need to know the name of the regiment of which the Count is the Colonel but I do need an appropriate uniform, an officer's uniform naturally. Hauptman would do nicely. Can I pick that up tomorrow morning first thing, from… well *wherever* you'd like me to pick it up from?'

The official nodded his agreement. '*Don't* come here! You can pick it up from…' and he scribbled down an address, 'not before ten, though!'

'And, secondly, sir… and you don't have to answer this, I'm just curious. I'm based in Pressburg. This is all related to events in the capital, so why me?'

'You are the Emperor's detective, are you not?'

'I am, sir and very proud to be so but I can't be the only one, can I sir? I mean there must be men in the same boat living in Vienna.'

'I think, Herr Pichler that you may be in danger of underestimating the uniqueness of your appointment!'

And with that, Pichler was shown the door. Whatever happened in the next three days it was worth the aching arse just to learn that. He'd often wondered over the last five years and *now* he knew. Well bugger me!

***

Frau Brunner was always happy to see "young K-P" as she insisted on calling him, even though he was now in his mid-thirties. He'd stayed at her unpretentious little Gasthof in the village of Nussdorf a good number of times since he first visited the Capital back in the mid-sixties.

He much preferred it to Vienna and being eight kilometres away it was a lot cheaper. Of course, he was on expenses so he could have splashed out a bit but these big hotels were very impersonal and sometimes too full of themselves and anyway, they wouldn't be serving beer from the Nussdorf brewery.

'I *do* like to see a clean plate!' she said, smiling as she cleared away. 'One more?'

He thought not – he'd had two beers already and there was always tomorrow evening… and the evening after that.

And that was the other thing he liked about Nussdorf; he could walk along the Danube in peace and quiet, and a walk was just what he needed.

He wasn't sure at the time why he'd asked Herr "Smiler" – as he'd nicknamed the official at the Schönbrunn – for a Hauptman's uniform – it just seemed like it *might* come in handy. It was inevitable that he would need to meet several people over the next three days. As it was to be *just* him without any of his "*little friends from the Pressburg Police Department*" – patronising twat!... then disguises were going to be the order of the day. Luckily he had his "feather" bag with him.

One thing was blatantly obvious. There was zero possibility that he could sneak into Madame's room, discover the one piece of paper he sought and return home the hero. That was the type of thing that was only possible in cheap and *very* badly written crime novelettes. He'd been on enough police searches to know the reality. You went in mob-handed having cleared the place of any suspects or other people who might simply get in the way. Then with no attempt at subtlety whatsoever, you'd turn the whole place over, collecting everything you could in the hope that you might – just might – find some crucial piece of evidence.

Maybe he could "scare" the note out of her, turn up in army uniform and wave some piece of official looking paper around. He'd get that from the Viennese police… once he'd shown 'em his authority. What next? Yes, accuse her of spying for Paris. That might work. Of course she was bound to counter with a threat to expose the Count at the trial and… Ah! He had an answer to that one. It would be held in camera; national security, he would explain.

He walked on a good hundred metres, working out his script for the entire scene before juddering to a halt. What a complete load of old bollards! She might be a high-class courtesan now but chances are she'd been a common or garden tart in her early apprenticeship in the world's oldest profession and those ladies are nothing if not resourceful.

He stopped for a few minutes by a bench and as he tried to clear his mind, he watched the Danube flow past as it made its inexorable journey to the Back Sea. When he was a youngster, back in the Tyrol where the mountain-fed streams would fair race down into the valley, he would chuck a stick in and attempt to beat it to the next tree. Now he was in a different race; one it seemed he had no chance of winning, for he was getting nowhere. It was time to turnaround, to head for his bed. And that moment – when he'd abandoned all hope of a plan – was the very same moment that one popped into his head. He laughed out loud. Sometimes life really is like a cheap novelette!

May 19th 1875 – Day 2:

'Good morning, my fine fellow. My name is Hauptman Flichner… from the regiment. I need to see the Colonel about a matter which…' and here the Captain winked knowingly at the butler, 'I know he's *particularly* interested in.'

The Count's butler regarded the officer with admiration – tall, straight-backed, every inch a prime specimen of the Empire's officer corps. He especially liked the expansive sideboards. These had gone out of fashion with some of the younger officers but this fellow was obviously a traditionalist. After all if it was good enough for the Emperor then it ought to be good enough for these young whipper-snappers.

'Of course, Captain. Please come in. He's just got back from his post-breakfast constitutional. You'll find him in the summer house. Let me show you the way.'

The man pointed out the building which was set back some way behind the Count's house. It appeared to be a veritable den of tranquillity.

'Can I escort you, sir?'

'No, no. The Colonel is expecting me,' he lied.

He'd been given to understand that the Count was in his early fifties. The man seated before him looked a good fifteen years older. His skin had acquired that greyness that is not uncommon in the elderly but it was his eyes that were the most disturbing – deep set and red-rimmed.

'Who are you?' he asked without any attempt at civility.

As Flichner told what he knew of the matter, the man seemed to wilt, shrink even, into his leather arm chair as the retelling of his catastrophe was unfolded. When he limply gestured that the Herr Hauptman should sit in the chair facing him, it was with a resignation that said – What can be done? Nothing! I know *nothing* can be done!"

The stench of strong liquor from across the desk was almost over-powering, setting him to wonder exactly what type of "breakfast" the Count had been attempting to walk off this morning.

He spied the Count's empty glass, stood up and walked around the table. Very deliberately he picked it up and crossing to the farthest point in the room, he pointedly laid it down on a table.

'Now listen, Count! I want you to write this down…'

The letter was addressed to a woman. It said that he would offer her five hundred Gulden as a one-off payment in order to put an end to the matter. He'd learnt his lesson, the letter said – nothing must be in writing. She must open a safety deposit box and it must be at Rosenberg's bank on Großdorf Strasse. She may use any name she wished, but not her own naturally. Finally, she must do this today before four o'clock. The money would be transferred tomorrow before noon and on acknowledgement that it had been paid into the deposit box, she must agree to hand over the note to his representative, one Doktor Hass.

'But, but… I don't have five hundred Gulden or anything like and certainly not at a day's notice. This is madness!'

The Captain smiled at his commander. 'No, sir, it is not! But tell me, she *will* know your letter is genuine; she will recognise your writing of course – from the earlier note which is still in her possession!'

The Count's response was a stifled grunt as if the recollection of *that* note was just too painful.

'No, no. I don't understand what your game is Herr Hauptman. You're from her, aren't you? You're trying to trick me.'

Whatever the temperament of the fictitious Captain Flichner, Pichler was normally the most sympathetic of men, but even he finally lost patience. The old fool had landed himself in this mess and now he was lashing out at the very people who were trying to save him. He thrust his authority into the Count's hand and stood back while the seated man's eyes fixed on the text, at first disbelieving what they were telling him, then amazed that perhaps, just perhaps salvation was possible.

'But you intend *sending* her a letter, after you told me nothing was to be put on paper, that I'd learned my lesson.'

Pichler was on a tight schedule – when the Emperor said three days, he meant three days. There was no time to explain.

'Count – I shall not *send* it I shall *deliver* its contents verbally. Now please, leave it all to me. You just concentrate on doing one thing, for me.'

'Which is?'

'Be kind to your poor wife, Count!'

At which point, the Count broke down into a series of loud, sustained sobs which was the last reaction Pichler had expected.

***

He didn't have time to get to Nussdorf and back so he was faced with the rather undignified option of getting into his next guise in a toilet cubicle at Vienna's Hauptbahnhof. He had to improvise a bit and that, he was embarrassed to say, included filching one of the Count's overcoats which he'd noticed hanging on the coat rack when he'd first entered the house.

'And what can we do for you, sir?' asked Madame Rousseau's maid with a smirk. He didn't look like the kind of fellow who'd be able to satisfy Madame's demanding pecuniary requirements. In fact he looked like an accountant.

'Good afternoon, madam. My name is Hass, Doktor Hass. I'm here as the representative of a certain noble man with whom your mistress has had dealings. I have a letter from said gentleman which requires her immediate attention!'

'Well you just gi'it to me and I'll sees she gets it.'

'No, madam – I shall not. Please be so good as to inform your mistress of my presence.'

The maid was on the point of giving him some lip, but the ice-cold stare she encountered made her think better of the idea. She returned within two minutes and directed the fellow into the front parlour. Pichler glanced around the room. This was just like any other parlour in any other house; presumably not where her clients were seated while they awaited their "appointment".

'So, Doktor Hass; what can I do for you?'

'Thank you for seeing me madam. I have been commissioned by my client to offer a settlement which I believe you will find to be very much to your advantage.'

'Give me the letter then, I have other people to see today.'

I *bet* you have thought Pichler. Doktor Hass said…

'I regret that my instructions are to permit you to view the handwriting only – for authentication purposes, madam. My client is understandably nervous about allowing the letter to enter into your possession, in case it should not be returned.'

She tossed back her head and gave a coarse laugh that was at complete odds with her outward veneer of gentility.

'Very well; read on then… read on,' she said indicating that he should sit if he cared to.

Doktor Hass *didn't* care to!

However accomplished Madame de Rousseau might be in acts of seduction, her negotiating skills were far from impressive. She betrayed her feelings only too clearly as Hass read out the proposal; "I have won!" they said.

'Quite acceptable, though I do not need to open a new safety deposit box account. I have numerous such accounts already, as any lady in my "situation" must.'

'Are any of these accounts held at Rosenberg's bank on Großdorf Strasse?' asked the doctor.

'None! But why should that be an impediment? A safety box account is a safety box account, is it not?'

'No, madam, it is not! Five hundred Gulden is an enormous sum. Although my client has the funds, the bank is insistent that the transfer should be an internal one. You see, the moment it leaves my client's account, until you present yourself and sign off that you have taken possession, the bank are liable. It is a small technicality but it must be observed. The alternative is that transfer to a different bank, even a different branch of Rosenberg's would necessitate a three-week holding period… and that madam is the law.'

'I see. No matter – it is easy enough to open a new account and I shall do this straight away as the Count… I mean as your *client,* requests.'

'Excellent, madam! May I call around this evening to obtain the deposit box details? I have already arranged an interview with the manager of Rosenberg's for eleven AM tomorrow. He has assured me that he will be able to issue a letter confirming that the transfer has taken place. This will be delivered by hand in the early afternoon. I will then present myself here tomorrow evening and retrieve the note. Would that be satisfactory to you?'

'Most satisfactory! When will I be able to access the contents of the box?'

'At your earliest convenience. As I explained earlier, Rosenberg's will be anxious to relinquish liability. I shall tell the bank when I arrange the transfer that they may expect you to sign-off their liability as from… what should we say… the day after tomorrow?'

'Perfect!' replied the Cheshire cat.

'Until this evening then!'

***

His reception at Madame's house that evening had been very offhand and very brief. He was left standing on the door step, the front door fully shut on him, while the maid beetled off to see her mistress. She returned clutching a scrap of paper which was passed to him though a fractionally-open door, a door which was slammed shut the moment he had it. The writing was childish, probably written by the maid in order to hide any connection between her mistress and the account. No matter – it said what he needed it to; Fassbender, J. K. Number 1285430.

May 20th 1875 – Day 3:

The interview with the manager was a fraught affair. He really didn't want to do it and without the authority he wouldn't have. Even then Doktor Hass had had to jab repeatedly at the signature before he finally gave in.

He'd allowed forty-five minutes for the exchange, but it was an hour and a half later that he emerged from the bank, carrying the all-important envelope and a brown paper parcel, tied around with string. Strangely, he had had almost as much difficulty in prising that out of the manager as the letter contained within the envelope.

It was now getting on for one o'clock. He headed for the park and brought a sausage off a street vendor. Hunger can make a chap lightheaded and he needed to be at his sharpest for his next part in the "play". Not that he had any dialogue in this role; if he did have to speak then he'd have completely cocked the thing up.

***

'Madam, madam, the letter's just arrived.'

'Did you see who delivered it?' she asked, while noting that it was franked with a stamp bearing the wording "Rosenberg's of Großdorf Strasse, Wien".

'No, not actually seen 'is face, madam. I heard the knocker go three times, very loud it was n' all. Then I saw the letter being pushed through the letter box. I opened the door and I sees him strolling down the street as if he hadn't a care in the world. He was wearing one of them purple jackets, the ones with the yellow piping along the sleeve.'

'And he was wearing a hat?'

'Oh yes, madam.'

'Describe it!'

'Well madam, it was a funny thing. Didn't have a peak but it 'ad a yellow tassel hanging from the crown – proper daft, I thought.'

'Very good. You may go!'

Everything was as that Hass fellow had said it would be. She'd seen the bank runners wearing those self-same jackets and hats when she'd opened her deposit box yesterday afternoon. It was all going splendidly.

***

Pichler had to time his walk away from madam's place of business to perfection. The view of his back was all that the maid could be permitted to see, but it was critical that she *did* see that much! Face to face, he could hardly expect to pass as a delivery boy when he was getting on for twice their age and that was assuming the maid didn't notice his striking resemblance to Doktor Hass… which she almost certainly would.

The "package" safely delivered, there was nothing more to do other than return the uniform to the bank and pay the Count a visit so he could cheer the old soul up, and then… wait for this evening.

***

As he walked towards her house his confidence that the original scheme *would have* worked was undiminished. That it should no longer be necessary was a cause of unutterable sadness to him.

'Oh, it's you!' said the impudent maid. 'Suppose you'll want a come in then?' she added in as an off-hand a manner as he thought she was capable.

"Over confidence", he thought. That's cost many a General his victory laurels.

'Good evening, madam. I trust you have received the confirmation from the bank?'

'I have!' she declared triumphantly.

'In which case, I have come to retrieve the promissory note. If you'd be so kind…'

'Before I do, you must answer me two questions. Five hundred Gulden is an enormous sum, as you have said yourself, Herr Doktor. How is it that the Count *just happened* to have that sitting around in his bank account?'

'My client had recently sold off some of his land to a company that is intending to run a new railway line from Vienna to Brünn in Moravia. The Count's estate facilitates a significant short-cut for which the company was prepared to pay handsomely. He *had* intended to use it to fund another venture, but… how should I say… unforeseen circumstances intervened. And your second question.'

'*If* I had mislaid the note in the interim, would I still have access to the money?'

'Of course, madam! The money no longer belongs to my client. It is being held in trust until you present yourself and sign for it. By the way, I was true to my word – the manager is expecting to see you tomorrow.'

Doktor Hass could see that madam was greatly pleased by this answer and that worried him, as was evident from the expression on his face.

'But you have *not* mislaid the note, I trust,' said the good doctor with a smile, though it was a forced one.

'Indeed not!' she declared. 'Why the very idea,' and she smiled to see the look of relief on her adversary's face.

'I have however decided *not* to return it. I may still have a use for it,' and her delight at his distress was evident but then his distress turned into a sly smile.

'Perhaps you *cannot* return it … perhaps it never existed!'

The smug look vanished.

'Countess von Hagen… please come out now, I'm sure it cannot be comfortable for you in that tiny cupboard.'

The door creaked and out she stepped, not defiantly but shamefacedly.

'How did you know?' the words were out of her mouth before Madame de Rousseau could stop her.

The Count had inadvertently provided the signposts but he'd been too blind to see them. The first was his hesitation when Pichler had asked him if the note would confirm the handwriting on the letter was his own.

The second, his distress when Pichler had asked him to be kind to his wife as if the Count was the villain of the piece and the Countess was the injured party.

As Sergeant Slota would have said at this point – "you've had this arse about face from the very beginning, K-P, m'lad" and so he had.

The Count had learnt of the compromising letter *only* because his *wife* had told him of it… so there was no need for its existence. There was only one matter yet to be resolved.

The French woman pulled the Austrian Countess to her side enveloping her in a protective embrace.

'Why then did you give us the money?' she demanded with more than a trace of anxiety written across her features.

'You have the letter from Rosenberg's?' he asked.

She rushed to her escritoire and pulled open a drawer and there it was. For one moment she thought he might have stolen it. She was relieved. It would not last!

'The signature…' continued the doctor, 'does it bear the name of the bank clerk… and would that name be "Frankenheim" and would his initial be "J"?

She glared at him, struggling to comprehend the implication of his words.

'You… *you* wrote it?'

He smiled.

'There is… *no*… money?' asked the Countess, visibly shaking.

He smiled once again.

They flew into each other's arms and as Madame tried to kiss away her lover's free flowing tears, Pichler had the final confirmation, though the letter had left precious little room for doubt.

The vixen was wounded but had not lost her fight. She sneered at him, reading a message that was simply not there to be read.

'I can see it in your face. You are shocked to find two women such as we… we… the daughters of Artemis… So typical of the narrow minded men who blight our lives…'

Her rant might well have continued for some time had Pichler not put a stop to it.

'You mistake me madam if you think your proclivities offend me – they do not – "do as thou willst, but *harm no other*" has always been my motto.'

This was most definitely *not* what Madame de Rousseau had expected to hear.

'But you have harmed another haven't you and that is something you will both have to live with for the rest of your lives.'

Then sadly turning to the Countess he added 'Why-oh-why could you not *just leave* – the two of you. Why did you have to destroy a good man who, I believed loved you madam, a man who deserved *at least* honestly from you.'

All this was to protect *her* reputation. And now, at last, everything made perfect sense. He'd never fully understood until now why such a note, a note from a run of the mill noble man to a prostitute – should be quite *so* perilous, of such concern to those at the very top. Surely that kind of thing was common enough! But the suggestion that his wife, a Countess was… was… well, he'd didn't even know what the correct word was…. But he knew well enough the fate of those officers whose pleasures lay in that "other direction". Right or wrong – and who was he to judge – that sadly *was* the way of the world!

'Why do you say… destroy a good man? Where is Paul? Is he all right?' asked the Countess with real fear in her voice.

'Why, madam? Because he is dead, *madam* – that is why! And *you* have *both* been his executioners!'

Three hours earlier:

'Hauptman Flichner – how nice to see you again! You'll want the Colonel of course. Normally you'd find him in the usual place at this time of day. But after breakfast today he told me he had some work to do and he'd take his daily constitutional later on. I'm not sure if he's gone out yet, so you might be lucky. Anyway, you're welcome to try.'

Pichler tapped on the door of the summer house – no answer. Then he tried the handle – locked. Damn it – he'd missed him. What a shame. The news he bore was that he was about to be let of the hook he'd impaled himself on. And that would have bucked the old fellow up no end.

Still, he might just have nodded off. He walked around the corner of the wooden cabin to find no door on the side he was on. Onwards around the next corner – there was no door at the rear either. He had to duck to avoid knocking his head on the bottom of an angled wooden strut. Looking along the length of the rear he saw six of these struts, all equally spaced supporting a one-metre wide balcony.

'Oh, Christ!' he exclaimed.

He ran back away from the summer house and from there he could see the Count's body. It was gently swaying, suspended from a rope, a rope that had been looped over a joist of the roof ridge.

The cabin's construction and the balcony struts enabled him to hoist himself up and over the balcony rail. From there it was all too obvious how he'd managed it. The Count must have thrown the rope over the protruding joist. One end had been secured around the rail. And the other end? He shuddered to see the ligature which had tightened around the poor man's neck as he leapt over rail and at the same time ended his struggles.

Pichler stood back in some distress; the drop from the rail height might have killed him instantly, but somehow he doubted it. More likely death was by slow painful strangulation – surely the last thing the poor fellow could have intended. But then who knows how much rationality remains in a mind which has crossed this bridge? He tried to think positively; *perhaps*, the Count had taken up a metre or two of slack in the rope, clambered – somehow – onto the rail and then literally thrown himself towards the ground. Whether his conjecture was accurate or hopelessly misplaced, one thing was clear; there had been no foul play. This was an attempted suicide and tragically… it had been successful.

Whatever mission he'd been charged with by "he who must be obeyed", it faded into insignificance compared with this! This whole case had been about avoiding embarrassment to all and sundry, but how much worse for the Count and his wife, that he should have taken his own life…

Now everything was lost. There wasn't even the consolation – for the Countess that is – of salvaging the Count's reputation… not unless the powers that be decided to get out their own special type of carpet brush. His own duty, however, was clear.

Unable to face the climb down, he walked down the stairs to the Count's desk. There he immediately noticed that the bottle which had been nearly full yesterday was now quite empty. The key was lying there – he should have walked straight out and locked the door behind him.

And he would have, had it not been for the crumpled piece of paper lying on the floor beside the Count's chair. It was a passionate love letter of that there was no doubt; it ended… "To Louise with all my love, from your very own" but the "very own" was not *Paul*. It was signed *Inga.*

He spent the hour it took for the Viennese police to arrive consoling the Count's butler. The man had been with them for years and it was abundantly clear from the conversation that he had no inkling of what had been going on under his master's and mistress's – particularly his mistress's – roof.

The Inspector arrived with his Sergeant – the mirror image of Hodža and Slota, the Inspector being the stout one and his Sergeant being as thin as a rake.

They had both come across their opposite numbers from Pressburg and much to his surprise they'd even heard of him. There wasn't any hint that he was under suspicion and he was grateful for that as it meant he wouldn't be delayed in closing off this unfortunate affair this evening. His "imperial-authority" remained in his pocket; the fewer people who had to see *that*, the better.

He spent the hour or so before the meeting walking around the gardens of the Schönbrunn; he needed the time to think. You can't help who you love and neither should you be prevented from doing so. But to ruin the man into the bargain… was that really necessary?

Perhaps if she'd been honest from the start, told him that their marriage was over, then perhaps, an amicable divorce, a modest financial settlement. Perhaps he was in some way to blame. But to bleed the man dry! Who was the vampire in this affair? He had little doubt on that one.

Of only one thing was he absolutely certain; nobody, but nobody needed to die.

May 21th 1875 – Day 4:

'Congratulations on a job well done… and on time too, Herr Pichler,' said the Emperor's representative in the same room as before, though this time the "invisible" Emperor actually *was* invisible.

'But, sir… the suicide..?'

'*There was no suicide*, my dear man – just an unfortunate accident. I believe the culprit was woodworm!'

Pichler was confused and it showed.

'Oh yes, tests showed that the little perishers must have been nibbling away at the balcony stanchions for years… the Count leaned too far over the rail and, well… tragic, most tragic!'

Hmmm – a little more aristocratic scandal had been neatly swept under the carpet. He couldn't say he was surprised. He *was* surprised though by the immense gratification he felt. Normally such legalist malpractice would have appalled him, but not today. When all said and done, what would have been gained by telling the whole truth… and more importantly, what would have been lost?

By the mid-afternoon he was home. Anna came bouncing to meet him expecting his usual kiss. Instead he hugged her to his chest and held her there.

'What was that for?' asked a surprised but delighted Anna.

'That? That was for everything!' replied her husband, as contented with his lot as any man can be – as well he should be after the last four days!

The University library, Pressburg, three weeks later:

'You here again K-P? I suppose you'll want the foreign newspapers yet again!'

Pichler made a habit of regularly reading the main German language papers and those of the other peoples of the Empire. His Slovak was good after nearly a decade living here. He still struggled with Hungarian, despite having a Magyar spouse but it was improving under Anna's tutelage – even his Italian was good enough for the essentials of life, that is to say ordering food and drink.

But French – that was a definite Non! France had nothing to do with the Empire and he certainly couldn't conceive that she could ever be an ally – too much bad blood between them and Kaiser Wilhelm, who definitely *was* an ally. No, if he ever needed anything translated from French, he had only to pop along to Maggie's office.

'Italian papers today, is it?'

'The English language editions only, Helmut. Haven't the time to wade through the originals.'

He only intended to flick through these… really to see who'd died and who hadn't amongst the movers and shakers of that fairly new country that still coveted bits of his Empire – well not actually *his* Empire of course!

Then he found it – "woman found drowned at Ponte Vecchio". Apparently according to the Priest of the nearby Church of Santa Felicità, this foreigner had spent the entire previous night praying at the altar. He had spoken to her, asked if there was anything he could do, to which she replied "there is nothing anyone can do, now!" When he returned for matins, she was gone. The woman had yet to be identified but a pendant was recovered from the body bearing the inscription; *an meine Geliebte Inga von Ihre Paul.*

Paris, 1877:

The official entered the cell where she'd been imprisoned since the verdict was pronounced ten days ago; her crime – entrapment of a member of the French government for the purposes of blackmailing him into revealing state secrets which would be handed over to the enemies of France; her sentence…

'Are you prepared, madam?'

Her hands were tied behind her back; her hair had been gathered into a bun. She nodded and so the slow procession to oblivion began; two men in front, two guards behind. Then she saw it – the awesome blade, suspended some two metres above the platform, ready to drop at the touch of a lever. She had seen many pictures of such devices – what French school child hadn't? But to see it there – massive, threatening and so final…

The executioner stood to one side as she reached the level of the platform. She looked around; there were no dignitaries present, no members of the public, just a barren courtyard – she had expected nothing else, for her execution, like her trial would be a closed affair.

Ironic then that the man standing to her side should ask "do you have any last words, Madame?"

No… no last words… only last thoughts… thoughts of the one she had loved, the only one she had truly loved… and lost.

The University library, Pressburg, one week later:

It was a pity that Pichler never read the papers coming out of France for one headline from last week's *Journal-Pari*s would have interested him greatly; "Madame Louise de Rousseau executed for Treason."

And so the affair in which *nobody* needed to die had claimed its last victim.

Epilogue

Here I am sitting on the deck of the Steamship Goliath, staring out across at the distant horizon. The sea is calm and the sun is shining; God's in his Heaven and all is right with the world, especially *my* world. The only thing I need right now is one of those stewards in their smart white jackets to come around the corner, carrying a tray of drinks.

Some men are born wise; some are born rich. Me? I was born lucky. As I've grown older, I've come to the conclusion that of all the lucky men, lucky enough to be born lucky, I must be about the luckiest. For why? Well one reason is walking towards me right now, with, if I'm not mistaken two young'uns in tow.

'Ciao, Giuo. You arer staying outsider, eh?'

'I am indeed, my darling. Did you have a lovely stroll my angels?'

'Si, papa.'

'I'ma going to the cabin, the bambinos, they-ra getting colde. Don't be too a longe, eh!'

The other reason – I'll still alive and I probably shouldn't be.

Oh, my name? Giuo – that's just her pet name for me! I'm Giuseppe Verde – how do you do? Yes, I know what you're thinking, but no. You see I was Josef Grün for the first thirty six years of my life and well, I got rather attached to it. And now I think it's time I told you my story.

I was born in 1882 in Pressburg, an imperial city on the western border of the Hungarian Crownlands in the Empire that was Austria-Hungary. Don't worry, you won't have heard of it – it's called Bratislava now and may be found in the Slovakian half of Czechoslovakia. I know… it's difficult to keep count what with all these new countries springing up.

Anyway, my father served in the Pressburg Police force for some twenty years, but in 1890 he had the option to transfer to Bozen in the northern German speaking part of the Süd Tyrol and he jumped at it. I haven't seen Pressburg for thirty five years and I don't intend to ever see it again.

That was my first stroke of good fortune. When the Great War broke out in July 1914, Franz Josef's Italian speaking regiments were sent to the Serbian front and later to the Galician front. I got called up but was moved south to defend the Italian border. German speaking regiments were considered to be less of a risk, I mean of deserting. Not that there was much going on, not until May the following year when Italy entered the war on the side of the allies. The Trentino front was definitely the one to be on. Most of the fighting was much further east on the River Isonzo. By the time we mounted an offensive on our front, I was already a prisoner of war. I spoke pretty good Italian and was regularly sent out on trench raids which involved crawling close to their trenches and listening to their troops' gossip. I got too close on one occasion and by September 1915, I was in the bag. I thought my luck had taken a turn for the worse, but it was the best thing that could have happened to me.

Of the class of 1899, I was the only one to survive the war undamaged. A lot of my class mates were taken prisoner and on the eastern front that could be just like getting killed on the battlefield, only it took rather longer to die. The Italians were on the whole pretty decent, especially to me, as I could speak to the guards in their own language; we weren't that different really – none of us wanted to be there.

By the summer of 1916, the Italian government had signed up most of their young men, who were getting mown down like corn in their futile attempts to get into Austria via the Isonzo. They made *so many* attempts that they ended up having to give each battle a number rather than a name. I think they got up to twelve by the war's end. You'd have thought *somebody* in high command would have given *some* consideration to the detrimental effect numbering the *same* bloody battle ground was having on troop morale, wouldn't you?

Anyway, to cut a long story short, some of us were paroled and allowed to work on the land down in the south of the country. Parole – that means promising not to try to escape, doesn't it? Escape *from* three decent meals a day, a warming sun and beautiful women… *to* muck and bullets and almost certain death! Needless to say we never saw a guard from one month to the next, because guards would have been entirely superfluous!

I ended up living with the family; an older couple and their very fetching daughter. From day one, the old boy refused to call me Josef, so Herr Grün died and Signor Verde took his place.

You're asking aren't you? Well *of course*, I married the daughter and believe me, it was best thing I ever did. It was idyllic and we would probably still be there, not aboard a steamship heading for a new life in Australia were it not for one man; Benito Amilcare Andrea Mussolini. It wasn't so bad when the King first appointed him to be Prime Minister three years ago, but this year he declared himself el Duce and his black shirts were starting to show their ugly faces even in our little island of tranquillity. It was time to go!

So why am I telling you all this, you who may have lost so much more than I in those four years when the world went mad?

Sometimes, in the night, when all is still, my thoughts turn back to another century. Was it a kinder time? I'm not so sure, but it *was* a time of greater certainty. As a child I went to bed each night knowing that I would awake the next day to find my smiling mother and father waiting to greet me. And these thoughts bring me to my last stroke of luck, only this time it was not a "what" but a "who".

The "who" was my "Uncle" Ján, though he was not a real uncle, just a good friend of my father who, like him was a policeman in Pressburg. When I was young, before we left for the South Tyrol, uncle Ján would tell me about the adventures of Siegmund Flichner, the "Queen's Inspector". Set in a country called Ruretainia, he was a sort of special investigator who operated in the twilight world between ordinary police work and military intelligence; usually at the behest of the beautiful Queen Marianna, the regent of that Country.

I tried to find Ruretainia once on an old atlas my father kept in his study, but I never could. One day, just before we left Pressburg for the last time I asked uncle Ján if he'd made the whole thing up. I remember it as clear as day – he just smiled at me and winked.

I didn't see him for a couple of years after that, but just after his wife died in around '92, I think it was, he paid us all a visit. He *said* he needed the fresh Alpine air.

One evening, he asked me "did I remember what I'd asked him just before we left?" Of course I said "yes" at which point, without a word, he pulled out a rather tatty realm of paper tied together with yellowing string and handed it to me. I spent most of the night reading it as I suspect he knew I would.

The next day, we went fishing together, though fish was the last thing I was hoping to catch. Sitting on a bench together by our local pond, I fired question after question at him. I'll remember one thing he said with absolute clarity, I'll never forget it. It was the answer I'd been seeking for two years.

"*Of course*, I didn't make it up, young Josef. I don't have the imagination to do that. And even if I did once upon a time, thirty odd years in the force is enough to knock that kind of airy-fairy thing out of a chap. What I will confess to, officer is that I changed some names of people and places. All right, all right governor, I changed *all* the names. But that was just for the stories, when you was a nipper. The *manuscript* you have in your sticky hands as we speak is *exactly* as it happened!"

I wrote to him many times in the next few years, always addressing my letters to "The Queen's Inspector – Ján Slota" – I think it made him laugh. He answered my questions, and suggested who else I might write to, which I did. I knew he was manipulating me – he wanted his friend's story told. And do you know what? I enjoyed every minute of it.

I played "uncle Ján" to my fellow inmates during my time in the POW camp, telling them the same stories he'd told me, but with the real names this time. All from memory of course – the manuscript was back in Bozen. But I scrounged some pen and ink from one of the guards and I started to make notes – things I needed to check or find out… if I ever got the chance.

Of course at that stage, it was still largely a case of taking uncle Ján's word that the manuscript was true, although I never had much doubt. You must remember that I did some of my own checking back in the last Century. Still, I'd never met anybody who could corroborate it, face to face so to speak.

Then one day, a fellow junior officer interrupted me – "this chap Pichler, Klaus Pichler, you say? I knew a chap of that name… Yes K-P Pichler. Some rumour about him being the "Emperor's Inspector" as I vaguely recall". And d'you know what? That wasn't the only time I heard that during my time in captivity!

As soon as the war was over I went back to Bozen. There was something there I wanted. My old folks had died during the war. I knew that from letters I'd received whilst in the camp. Of course, the South Tyrol was now part of Italy and there was plenty of bad blood around. So I was Signor Verdi in the south and Herr Grün in Bozen.

The old place was much as I'd remembered it. No reason why it wouldn't be as the war was happening somewhere else. But there were new owners and they could have given me a hard time – but they didn't! In fact once I'd explained, they all got pretty interested, even helped me search for uncle Ján's manuscript. And guess what, dear reader… we found it, just where I'd left it. See what I mean… lucky again!

In 1919 Josef Grün went to the records office in Vienna. Vienna was a mess at that time – on the verge of civil unrest. There I met an old pal who agreed to send me copies of any relevant papers, as they became declassified. And they did become unclassified by the bucket load as nobody gave a damn about an Empire that no longer existed. These confirmed most of uncle Ján's suppositions, even the wilder ones.

The manuscript uncle Ján gave me has grown considerably in the last two decades under my tender care. You're asking me if this one's all true as well, aren't you? Thought you might. Mostly it is but I've had to use a bit of artistic licence here and there – you know, to make them into proper stories.

Why did I do this? Not for commercial reasons that's for sure. The chances are I'm the only one who'd ever read it. No, because the life of Siegmund Flichner, the "Queen's Inspector" was told to a young boy by his uncle as an adventure story. So it should be here as befits the real life of Klaus "K-P" Pichler – the Emperor's Detective.

I probably have enough for several books now. Will I ever get around to sending a manuscript to a publisher? Not in Europe that's for sure. People don't want to read about Empires, their Kings and their Queens and the lives of the many who died for them, especially as we now know just how futile it all was.

Perhaps in my dotage, if the world is not at war again, I might find a friendly publisher in Melbourne and try my luck – who knows, it's worked for me this far!

Giuseppe Verde
SS Goliath
28th September, 1925

PRINCIPAL PLAYERS

Hodža, Karol. Inspector. B. 1818,
Pichler, Anna. Amateur pianist. Pressburg resident of Hungarian extraction. B. 1841.
Kasselbaum, Professor Dr. Maximillian. Professor of Applied Kriminal Sciences at the University of Vienna at Pressburg. B. 1819.
MacPherson, Professor Margaret. Associate Professor at the University. B.1820
Pichler, Klaus "K-P". Ex 2nd Leutnant. Now graduate and Max's assistant. B. 1840
Slota, Ján. Hodža's Sergeant. Kriminal Department, Pressburg police department. B. 1821
von Ulmnitz, Erich. Director General of the State Security Service (ISD) – Based in Vienna.

THE RETRIBUTION WALTZ TRILOGY

If you enjoyed *The Case book of K-P Pichler, the Emperor's Detective*, then you might be interested in reading the full story on which it and the characters within are based.

Set against the backdrop of the geopolitics of central Europe in the late 19th and early 20th Centuries, *The Retribution Waltz* Trilogy begins in 1870 as the young Pichler comes to the attention of Emperor Franz Josef and concludes at the end of the First World War.

These are available in both e-book and paperback formats.

The Emperor’s Detective

The first two chapters

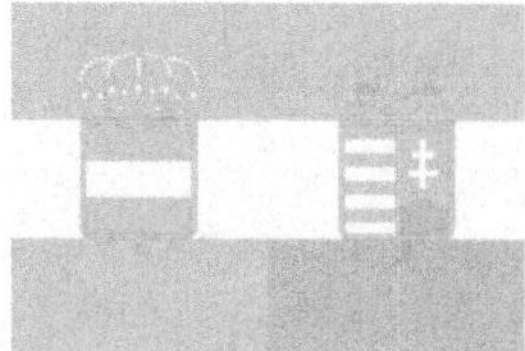

TODAY

It was quite impossible that this most wonderful day, the herald of so many halcyon days yet to come, could have ended thus. No – not impossible – for it did end so. What then...?

Late afternoon, Tuesday 19th July 1870, Pressburg Royal Palace:

'May I walk you to the servants' quarters?' the young man asked, ever hopeful.

'Best not,' she smiled unable to disguise her pleasure at the disappointment written all over his face.

'It's nearly a quarter to and you know I'm to be in before the hour strikes... and anyway, dearest, you're *supposed* to be a secret. I'd chance it if old Fürster was on his own but the head cow is always on the prowl on Tuesdays... you know what she's like!'

He started to smile but the grin froze on his lips as, staring into her eyes, he saw the depth of sadness written there.

'You'd best go or you'll miss your train,' she said hesitantly – but still she held his hand, so very tightly. Neither spoke, until finally, he shrugged his shoulders...

'Very well, meine liebe Sophie, I *suppose* I must be off then.'

His dear Sophie nodded resignedly, but his words and her approbation were deceivers both. He clasped her to him and they embraced, hugging each other for dear life with all the intensity of young love soon to be separated forever, for such as these, a week *is* forever. Reluctantly … they *did* part, each looking anxiously over a shoulder to see if any passing soul had chanced to witness their shameless display. But her bashful smile and his nervous giggle, the tell-tales of their embarrassment, were extinguished within the blink of an eye. At this moment of parting, neither could spare a thought for what others might think. He was her world and she was his.

A light kiss on his cheek, a ‘Bis nächste Woche’ [1] and at last the hands were free.

The girl watched as he walked down the cobbled lane away from the servants’ block, every now and again turning around, walking backwards for a few steps, waving madly as he did so. Then he caught his heel in a pothole and started to tumble. A gasp of alarm but in an instant he had righted himself and continued to wave and her gasp turned to laughter. At last he turned the corner and disappeared.

She waited.

She knew he’d pop his head around the corner for one last look – he always did.

---

[1] Until next week

'Gute Reise, Joachim,' she trilled at the grinning face that looked back.

And then he *was* gone.

Reaching into her vanity bag, a present from him of course, she pulled out a comb and mirror to repair the damage caused by their parting embrace. The neat light brown hair, golden-honey Joachim called it, readily obeyed its mistress's commands. She smiled – not even her darling mother had ever told her that – and not just honey, but golden-honey – and the gloom lifted a fraction. The seven days would pass, though painfully slowly, and he'd be back. As he would often tell her, "he was working for their future".

Slowly she walked towards the servants' quarters, a large stone building which stood close to the castle's perimeter wall. Herr Fürster had once told her that the wall had been there since the thirteenth century – what cared she for the past when such a future beckoned?

It had been a most beautiful day. Not the weather of course. It had rained on and off for most of the afternoon, but somehow, huddled together under his umbrella listening to the calls of the exotic birds, that didn't seem to matter. She couldn't remember a time when she'd felt happier, though there would be tears later this evening, after she'd finished her letter. It was simpler before – before Joachim had resigned his position at the Royal Palace. But she knew that he couldn't turn down the gilt-edged opportunity Count Urlov had offered him, even if it did mean they were now many kilometres apart and could only meet once per week for a few short hours.

They'd lost track of time and he'd missed his usual train back to Vienna. "Not to worry" he'd said – he'd get the next one and still be there in plenty of time to attend on his master at dinner. He'd insisted in fact. And still he wanted to see her right to her very front door… well as near as they could get without being spotted by the dragon – as if any harm could come to her now, inside the castle perimeter, the old silly!

* * *

Joachim Brauwald walked briskly along the road, wondering if he'd cut it too fine. He couldn't afford to miss this one. Even then he'd have to leg it all of the way from the Vienna Hauptbahnhof to Kopsaweg if he was to escape the Count's censure. As he walked he counted: Tuesday today, work over the Sabbath … the Count always entertained at the week's end, then Monday – a clearing up day and with luck, if he worked late into the evening … he'd be away to greet the dawn chorus and in time for the first train to Pressburg … just as he did every week. At that thought he began whistling a military march – it helped despite knowing that each successive stride took him further and further from his beloved.

* * *

The entrance to the maids' quarters lay at the back of the building, around a corner and a hundred paces along a narrow roofed-over walk way. Such light as there was came through a few holes in the roof – evidence of the ravages of time. It smelt of dank and mildew, and of much worse on hot summer days! Turning the corner she thought, just for a moment, that she'd seen two shadowy figures pull smartly back out of sight. She stopped and peered intently but could only see strakes of gloomy evening light shafting through the roof. She edged another twenty steps forward.

'Hello…?' she called out, unable to hide the anxiety in her voice.

Nothing! She tip-toed forward for a few paces more.

'Hello? Is there anybody there?'

Still nothing!

Now who was being an old silly, she thought.

* * *

Brauwald's exuberance had carried him right up to the entrance of Pressburg's Grand Station in no time at all. He raced up the last few steps to grab the heavy metalled door handle just a fraction of a second before the elderly couple coming the other way did the same. He swung it open and grinned enthusiastically as he held it for them to pass through. The old lady smiled, the old man thanked him and as he watched them amble down the steps he saw her whisper into her husband's ear which caused him to squeeze his wife's arm affectionately. He didn't need to guess what she'd said about him – it was written all over his face.

He looked up at the gold-gilded station clock. What a magnificent timepiece it was and if force of will could make the hands move faster, it would be Friday morning already. Friday – the day when his letter would reach her and hers would arrive at the Count's residence. They would both write this evening and post their letters first thing tomorrow. It was silly really, there was nothing to say – just a few hours had elapsed since they'd said their goodbyes. And yet there was *everything* to say.

* * *

With a quick look up at the threatening rain clouds, she stepped out to time her arrival at the side door so that she could slip in when Frau Uffer was most likely to be in another part of the building. She had her routine did Frau Uffer and all the girls knew it by heart. Oh she might have thought she ruled the roost but they could all run rings around her, the old witch. No, that wasn't quite fair. Most of the time she wasn't *so* bad, only whenever it came to timekeeping, she…

A scuffling sound stopped her train of thought and in that very instant her irrational fear returned. She glanced down – the walk way was a notorious meeting place for the local rat population – best not to dawdle. Striding forward purposely she grasped the side door handle and as she felt it's reassuring solidity, the relief swept over her in waves and she smiled at her own childish flight of fancy…

The rough hand smothered her mouth. It held something soft – soft and moist. Another man appeared from nowhere and viciously grabbed both her legs. She was transfixed by the face, his dark eyes and sharp, twitching nose – the face of a ferret.

She felt the breath of the other on her cheek and struggled to twist her head a little. Their eyes met just for an instant. Not a ferret, this one – a devil more like. Her eyelids became so very… very… and then the dark mist descended.

'Is she?' asked the ferret

'Yeah – she's out.'

Der Teufel [2] picked her up and threw her roughly over his shoulder, swinging her left hand against the coarse brickwork as he did so. The ferret scuttled ahead to check that the coast was clear. The wagon stood exactly where they'd left it, safe as houses round here. This was the castle district after all – not a place where any low-lives ventured.

'In yer go, me dove,' he said as he heaved the slender body onto the back.

'*Care…ful*,' said the ferret gripping her right arm as it looked for a moment as if his burly accomplice might pitch her clean over the other side onto the cobbles. The devil snarled angrily at this ill-advised rebuke and the chastised ferret sullenly scuttled to where the old nag was tied up. They didn't speak as

---

[2] The devil

they both mounted the box. They didn't speak as they drove down the hill towards the river, not until they had reached the old long abandoned pre-Josef wharves around the Danube.

'How long now?' he risked.

'She'll be a coming round in a few minutes,' replied the devil.

'Better do it now then,' ventured the ferret, chancing his arm once again.

'Shut your poxy trap. It'll be me what does it, when I'm good n' ready, you Dummkopf! Now pull down that back alley – stop there 'tween them two red brick rum-dives.'

The ferret sat where he was, transfixed. He saw the girl lifted from under the straw and dumped on the pavement. Then nothing! Waiting – waiting deliberately – until she started to regain consciousness. As she did so the ferret saw a small cushion pulled from a black frock coat, but saw no more, not the woman staring up at the man, her pupils enlarged beyond anything natural, as she tried to suck in the last vestige of air that he allowed to pass through the cushion. Nor the look she saw there – a look of pure pleasure. Only the noise as she struggled to get the word out.

'Wad she say?' called the ferret.

'Dunno! Jochan, or summit like that.'

The man on the wagon grunted.

'Don't matter now, do it,' he said shrugging as he watched the body being propped up against a wall, her legs askew, her eyes staring vacantly into space. The whole scene had played out in less than two minutes – two minutes to end one life and destroy one other.

As he was joined on the box, the ferret felt drops of rain and pulled his collar up. A dig in the ribs was his signal and the empty cart moved off through the darkening streets. The people they passed did not give them a second glance. Showing undue interests in the affairs of others wasn't something you did in the Zigeunerplatz – not if you knew what was good for you.

Chapter I – 'That's damned unusual, unheard of I'd say

Tuesday 19th July 1870, midnight, Pressburg, not far from the River Danube:

He gathered his well-worn coat tightly around himself. It wasn't a cold night but he felt chilled to his marrow nonetheless. It wasn't the first he'd ever seen and it wouldn't be the last. He cast his eyes towards the heavens in exasperation, exasperated that a loving God could permit such things.

Another man, who up until that point had been striding purposefully towards the star-gazer, stopped in an instant. He knew that gesture of old, knew exactly what was passing through the other man's mind, though he himself was never troubled by such thoughts. If the Almighty had decided to hand over the task of the smiting of the unrighteous to the Pressburg Kriminalpolizei Department... well then, that was just dandy as far as he was concerned.

Inspector Karol Hodža dropped his eyes to see the small set of ankles, the stockings which covered them were wrinkled and torn. Delicate shoes were still on each foot. The legs were askew, left in that all too familiar position. The throat showed where the fingers of her assailant had been applied. With a melancholic sigh, he took in the face. A nice face, not beautiful, but a face someone could easily love. He rather hoped for her sake that somebody had.

'Poor little cow,' he said out loud to no one in particular.

Hodža breathed another deep sigh and thrust his hands into his overcoat. People who didn't know – had never seen the sights he had – expected their policemen, like their doctors, to be inured to tragedy. He'd often heard them speak in this way – called him a "hard bitten so and so". How could they know the cost of days like this?

On the whole Hodža had enjoyed his thirty four years of service in the Police. And he'd done well, well that is for a Slovakian, not the most favoured of the Empire's dozen or so peoples. All subjects of the Empire were equal but as the old saying goes, some were more equal than others. Still, nights like this made him glad that retirement was only ten years away, maybe nine if he was lucky. Same job, so many years – of course he was going to get jaded from time to time, who wouldn't? No, it wasn't that. This was worse than the usual. It was the waste, he thought to himself, the waste of life and especially young life.

'Why did the bastard do it? If this was what he was after this part of Pressburg has a brothel every other alley.'

Hodža didn't turn – he knew the voice, angry as it was, as well as any he'd ever known. The man standing next to him was a good ten centimetres shorter, carrying considerably more weight and although a few years his junior had that lived-in face that made it difficult to guess his age. Hodža couldn't imagine beginning a case without this man, his friend, at his side.

'So, Ján …' he began.

Familiarity with one's sergeant was frowned on by the "gold buttons" back at Karlsstrasse but there was precious little chance of any of them showing up on a nasty night like this, especially when the state opera was in town. He'd seen a poster the other day – some nonsense about magic trumpets or flutes or something like that. He hadn't really been paying attention. It wasn't his world, was it!

'…what do you make of it?'

'Well sir,' (it had to be "sir" – somehow even after all these years, Ján Slota never felt it was quite right to return the compliment), 'it does look as if she's been interfered with.'

The Inspector nodded his agreement. Her dress had been pushed up above her knees and there was no doubt as to the terror she must have endured in her last few moments on this earth.

'Any clue who she might be?'

Slota stared hard and then shuddered visibly. For a fleeting moment the face of the corpse bore a passing likeness to his daughter-in-law. In an instant the image disappeared, but it upset him, upset him more than he could say.

'A servant would be my guess sir, probably a lady's maid to one of the toffs. *Maybe* she was on an errand and got lost but it all seems highly improbable. Frankly I can't think of a single reason why she would venture down to this shithole, especially on her own.'

Hodža paused to look intently at Slota. 'A lady's maid…?'

'See the dress? Definitely not skivvy standard, I'd say, but not quite top drawer either. Now look at the cuffs. Rather more worn than the rest of the dress – not that she did hard labour – look at her nails – but cuffs need more washing when you're forever helping madam with her bits and bobs. Hello, what's that? There sir, on the left breast, see it, just peeping out from under her lapel. That's not a cheap jewel even to my uncultured eyes. And that,' he said coming closer and pointing again, 'looks like a miniature crest in one corner, just below the flower?'

'Well I'm blowed! *But* Ján…'

'That's *just* what I was thinking sir. Why didn't he take the jewel? Around here you could shift that type of thing in a heartbeat, no questions asked. And why leave the body so exposed when the river's just a hop and a drag away?'

Hodža turned up his mouth in that characteristic way he had – what Slota called his senior officer's face. 'That's damned unusual – unheard of I'd go so far as to say.'

'Maybe, he didn't see the jewel, sir. You know – only one thing on his mind. After killing her, perhaps he just panicked.'

Hodža grunted. He wasn't convinced – not in the least.

'The scene's been marked up by one of our lot. The sketch-man's probably skulking in the Deerhound and there's no chance of getting a photographic plate at this time of night and with this lighting. It'd be as much use as a chocolate coffee pot and probably the same colour. We'll get the body moved and see if there's anything to be learnt from underneath.'

'Righto, sir, the morgue wagon's just turned up. Oi, you two – get your arses over here…come on, *shift* yourselves! So this sad slip of a thing's bound for Hartmann's slab then, eh sir? What a tragic end to a life!'

'Not quite Ján. He's still on sick-leave. Can't say I'm surprised. The poor sod's been doing this job for thirty-five years… bound to catch up with him sometime. No, I don't expect we'll see Hartmann back in harness again.'

'So it'll be Max then?'

'I'll send an officer to his apartment after we're done here with instructions for Max to come to the station morgue just "as soon as". Meantime, you can take that jewel and start making enquiries.'

As they walked back to the Karlsstrasse, Slota took a sidelong glance at his chief – "Jacob and Esau" as they were known by some of the old lags at the station, though anything less like twins would be hard to imagine. Hodža had sported a neatly trimmed moustache and sideburns ever since they'd both got out of the army together. He stood ramrod straight and was what most people call lean. His hair was a uniform steely grey, without any hint of the black it had once been or the white it was one day God willing, destined to become. Hodža was one of life's striders and they made an odd couple as Slota walked alongside, his short, staccato gait oddly out of place for an ex-military man. But these were just physical differences and in their line of work this wasn't what counted.

Wednesday 20th July 1870, 1030 hours, Karlsstrasse Police Station:

Hodža's office was surprisingly large given his rank. His desk was the length of a man and there was easily room for five chairs. True, one wall was completely covered with filing cabinets and shelving, but there was still room to swing a cat – two if Hodža felt like it, which he didn't, he being what Slota called "a bit soppy" when it came to the feline inhabitants of Pressburg. These days a mere inspector would not qualify for such lavish accommodation. He'd only got it in the first place due to his joining the criminal investigation branch long ago at a time when rooms were plentiful and bodies were not, although his last boss had foisted the branch records onto him, hence the filing cabinets.

Slota sat opposite him. He looked tired but then he'd been at the station since four. There'd been no report of a missing person but that wasn't too surprising. There was any number of reasons why Fräulein "Unbekannte" [3] had not as yet been missed.

'Is Max with her now?' asked Slota. Hodža was too distracted to answer.

'It just doesn't *feel* right, does it Ján? Just leaving the body there – to do the deed so publically. I mean, even the prozzies go around a back alley. What if anybody came around the corner? It wouldn't have needed to be one of our beat boys – the "tarts' militia" would have done a first class job of kicking the shit out of him. He'd never have got out of that alley alive. In fact I'm amazed he had time to even *do* the deed. The Zigeunerplatz is fairly busy at any time – even a Tuesday evening. It's got to be a good ten minutes work.'

Hodža paused and looked across at Slota. Slota had his eyes closed during all of this and for a moment Hodža thought the early start had finally caught up with him.

'Unless,' Slota's eyes suddenly sprung open, 'she was assaulted elsewhere and just dumped at the place

---

[3] Miss Unknown

where she was found. *That'd* be less than a minute's work.'

He saw the frown deepen on the inspector's face. 'Did we check her shoes, Ján?'

'Her shoes? You mean how wet they were?' said Slota nodding. 'Of course – and her coat. Give me *some* credit, chief!'

'I meant the *soles* of her shoes – for wear!'

With that each man got up and said not another word until they both stood in the evidence room and Slota had removed the shoes from their box. They'd each noticed that the shoes didn't look quite right at the time the body was found but now both could see *just* how wrong they were. They were looking at a pair of very smart shoes, most probably the best pair she owned and fine for the elegant streets of the city centre. But people didn't go walking the streets of the Zigeunerplatz in this kind of footwear or if they did, they could expect them to be scuffed to buggery!

If she *had* walked, walked any distance at all to the place where she'd met her demise, over the random coarse flagstones that constituted a pavement in the Zigeunerplatz – then those shoes would have been pretty roughed up – they just had to be! And they weren't – they were virtually unscratched. Carried from carriage to catastrophe – that was the only explanation.

She *must* have been dumped there – there in that *public* place and that meant a forint to a krajczár she'd been murdered elsewhere.

'Any joy on the brooch?' asked Hodža.

'Sami's looking at it as we speak. He fair snatched it out of my hand and then ignored me thereafter so I'm pretty sure it meant something to him.'

A pavement table at Café Lakatos, Pressburg:

The solitary youngish man, for he was not yet thirty, sat at a pavement table outside Café Lakatos on the Marktplatz, nervously chewing at an errant hangnail. He was of median height and average appearance. In short, he had stood in the middle of the queue on the day when good looks were being handed out. He possessed neither the manly angular chin nor the bouffant locks that are liable to set young hearts aflutter but nor did he have those over large ears or any other comical features which afford such amusement to the local street urchins. His hair was a commonplace brown, only marginally longer than that permitted in the Kaiser's Regulations and devoid of any indication that he had embarked on an early path to baldness. He did not sport such affectations as the eye-glass or long whiskers which were to be found amongst so many of his generation. You would pass him in the street and not give him a second glance, save for one aspect. His mid-brown eyes were as commonplace as his hair, but when you looked into them, you saw that they were kind eyes – they seemed to smile back at you. People looked and immediately liked what they saw – he didn't have to speak. If the eyes truly are the window to the soul then this was a man at peace with himself, though not so today – today he was a bundle of nerves.

Klaus Pichler stared at the empty Schnapps glass sitting on the table in front of him. He wasn't a great drinker – couldn't afford to be – but today was special. Subconsciously his hand moved to scratch his left calf – just couldn't stop himself. He looked at his watch for the umpteenth time in the hour since he had first sat down. It said 10.51.

* * *

Samuel Hochmaier knocked politely on Hodža's door. A tall, slender-framed man, he had the appearance of a rather timid clerk but the memory of an elephant. There was hardly any artefact he couldn't identify, given time, in this case very little time.

'Morning Ján… sir. Sorry it took so long. It's an award given by her majesty on her last visit to the Royal Palace. The men got a badge and the women got this brooch, at least the above-stairs staff did. That was back in sixty-eight.'

Hodža opened his mouth but his question was anticipated.

'Twelve altogether sir. I don't have the names of the recipients, I regret, but I imagine…'

'No, that's excellent work, Hochmaier – you've given us a good starting point for our enquiries. Ján?'

Slota got off his chair without a word and patted Hochmaier on the shoulder as he eased the pair of them out of the inspector's office. A moment later, Max occupied the recently vacated space.

'Here's the gist, Karol. She wasn't raped but she was violated – violated in a manner which I can only describe as unique, at least in my experience. Page three – last paragraph. I'll call back after lunch. Sorry to rush – I've an appointment to keep with a rather nervous young man of my acquaintance.'

* * *

'Mein Junge! Wie gehts? [4] I thought I might find you here.'

Professor Doktor Maximillian Kasselbaum, late surgeon of his Majesty's imperial army and Professor of Applied Criminal Science at the University of Wien at Pressburg, strode into view. As usual regardless of the season, he was wearing his old and increasingly moth-eaten bear skin coat from which derived the nickname "damp-dog" devised by the fine young minds of the faculty. It was mildly amusing in a banal undergraduate humour sort of way. Klaus knew better – damp-dog. Paah! If the man had canine traits it was those of a French chien de Saint-Hubert – the sleuth hound as they called it in his neck of the woods.

---

[4] How are you, my boy?

'To be honest Max, I've been sitting here trying to stoke up a bit of Hollander's courage.'

Today was results day, results that were due to go up at noon – pinned up under that archway through which he'd passed so often. He'd either get the degree he'd worked so hard for at a university he should never have even got into in the first place, or it would all have been for nothing – or almost nothing – he *had* met Max along the way.

For an academic, a profession noted for its ability to call a spade an "earth/mud or soil redistribution artefact of agrarian origin", Max was a man of relatively few words. He sat opposite and unfolded his newspaper.

'How many is that?'

'This is my first, Max.'

'You sir, are a bloody liar,' said Max beaming one of his infectious smiles. 'Now we'll just have the third or maybe... *fourth?*' Max paused just long enough to receive a slightly guilty acknowledging nod from Pichler, 'and then it's up to the castle for you.'

Max ordered top of the range, a luxury for Pichler. Tapping his front page he said 'Looks like the "horse-eaters" are getting themselves wrought up to invade the "Piefkes". Silly buggers! They'll fare no better than we did.'

Pichler nodded. To all South Germans they were the Piefkes – to the rest of the world they were the Prussians, the foremost military power in Europe, saving the French perhaps. As Max uttered these words, a troop of the Empire's finest and fittest – or at least those who weren't rich enough to avoid conscription – marched by. Max and Klaus both rolled their eyes upwards in perfect synchronicity as if to say "and there's *another* lot of silly buggers". They had both done their bit for König und Land and could speak with authority. Fortunately the Empire was at peace at the moment – this squad was off for training – in the infantry butts judging by the harnesses they were wearing. Max looked over the top of his spectacles.

'Let's just hope the bayonet practice dummies are not feeling particularly aggressive today, shall we?'

The Schnapps arrived and were duly despatched with military precision. 'So, K-P, that's it. Anymore and you'll be legless,' said Max. 'Time to go. Aaattention. By the left… to Pressburg castle …quick maaaarch!' With those words, Klaus's teacher and confidant dismissed his young friend and as he watched the fast disappearing back, Max smiled to himself.

* * *

Pichler had done this walk a thousand times but he was just as impressed by the castle today as he'd been in 1866 when he'd seen it for the first time. His mind drifted back to that October four years ago. Just out of the army and with no prospects in view, he'd seen a notice in town – places available at the law faculty.

Why not give it a go? What was the worst they could do – they could only say no? Perhaps not – the worst they could do was to arse-kick him all the way down the hill. And if they did? … well then so ficking what? What was that for a man who only three months ago had been facing the fearful guns of the Prussians?

The questions he'd prepared for never happened – they didn't even start! He had prepared a long spiel, "yes, it was true that he had no formal qualifications but eight years serving under the colours in all parts of the Empire, a facility for languages, an enquiring mind, extensive reading, this, that and the other – all this gave him an excellent prep…".. In fact he got no further with the admissions tutor than "Name? Right Herr Pichler, you're late! We were expecting you *two* days ago. Sign here please. Classes start on Monday at 0900. Here is your timetable. You have your digs sorted? Yes of course you do – right. NEXT!"

Well he knew universities were full of bright people but how in hades they knew he was going to apply two days before he did himself was a complete mystery. *Maybe* they'd had a recommendation from his old commander. He was a decent old buffer who'd handed him his discharge papers back in August. "Buck up, my dear chap. There's more to life than the army. You could consider becoming a scholar. Think about it my boy. Let me know if you need any strings pulling", he'd said. He must have done just that off his own bat – only explanation. So come the following Monday morning at 0900, there he was sitting in the lecture theatre, aged twenty six, an "old" man in a sea of fine and very young gentlemen. It was a bit of a strange lecture for law – all about human anatomy. No matter. It could have been on the Peloponnesian wars and Klaus would have been just as enthralled.

All was well for about a fortnight until the Under-Dean of the Faculty – unsurprisingly the medical school as it turned out – stormed into the lecture he was absorbed in, something about blood circulation he seemed to remember. The irate man frog-marched him into the corridor in a distinctly non-professorial manner and commenced bawling him out along the lines of… "What did he think he was doing, impersonating a genuine student, a person of no less a standing than the honourable Count (he stressed the title) Karl-Heinz Pichler". It seemed that the excessive demands of the Count's hectic social calendar had prevented him from putting in an appearance at the university until that morning.

Yes, there had been a cock-up. Fortunately it wasn't Pichler's but that of the admissions tutor who he came across waiting sheepishly outside the Dean's office. No question of him being allowed to continue in medicine and the Dean of Law made it quite clear that he was "certainly not going to have a medical school reject". Fortunately for Pichler, vacillation was usually preferable to decision making, especially if that decision did not reflect well on the University and so a week later, Klaus found himself the only student on the newly created Sonder Studium or "Special Studies" course – a hotchpotch of whatever courses Pichler could get himself accepted onto. "Turn up to whatever lectures you like, within reason – just try not to bother the genuine students and on no account waste the lecturers' time with questions". Fine by me he thought. He knew he was lucky to even be there. And he had catholic tastes, catholic in the sense of varied, not religious – he hadn't seen much evidence of God on the battlefield.

* * *

Back in the present and staring ahead, he saw Böhm, the head porter.

'Hello, K-P. They've just this minute posted them. Ready to face the enemy are you lad?'

The academics save for one or two, had little time for Pichler but all the ancillary staff, from cleaners to head porters, recognised "K-P" as one of their own – he liked them and they liked him back.

'You know the way lad … and the best of Slovak luck.'

When he got there, there were only two other students. One was in tears while the other seemed at a loss as to know how to console him. He wasn't surprised to see so few. Getting a degree for most of his cohort was a matter of supreme indifference – just so long as the old man kept up their allowances. He stared up at the archway ceiling with an intensity that suggested that its baroque architecture was the sole reason he'd come here. Slowly he dropped his gaze until his eyes fell by chance on the faculty of medicine and about midway down he came across a familiar name.

Pichler, Karl-Heinz aus Prag

Well what do you know? The dear count had passed. Never did a stroke of work mind, so he'd heard. What a lucky old *"count"*, though not so lucky for his future patients!

He trawled quickly through all the other faculties until he got to the 'S's. No sign of his name! And then he found it – on a separate sheet. Special Studies with just one name:

Sonder Studium

The following candidates have satisfied the examiners:

He took a moment to make the translation – *candidates* meant just him – *satisfied* meant passed!

Pichler, Klaus Heinrich aus Seefeld im Tyrol (besondere Auszeichnung) [5]

Bloody hell, he'd done it, he'd bloody well *done* it!! Maybe there was a God after all.

---

[5] Special award

1822 hours, Karlsstrasse Police Station:

The Inspector opened the door carefully – he didn't want to make Slota jump and besides he had two cups of coffee precariously trapped between his ribcage and one forearm.

'Wake up old friend, it's time to talk.'

Slota blinked and sat himself upright. He had nodded off in the time his chief had taken to nip across the road to Café Hitzle – another ten minutes and he'd have slid off the chair completely. Hodža reached into his pocket, pulled out a brown paper bag and slid it across to his Sergeant – a cheese roll – guaranteed to return the man to full consciousness in a matter of seconds. The man looked exhausted and it wasn't just the miles he'd tramped this day or the lack of sleep. Like himself, like Doctor Hartmann, Ján Slota only had a few more cases like this left in him. But Hodža had given him all the time he could spare.

'So Ján, your report first … and then I have something which will astound you.'

He'd arrived at the Royal Palace at two and spoken firstly to a certain Frau Uffer, the keeper of the royal household and matron of all the female serving staff. They checked the "pass-out and returns" book together for the previous evening and it was all present and correct. None of the girls had failed to report for duty this morning… as far as she was aware, though she'd been too busy to check on everyone and it wasn't unknown for a certain amount of "covering" to be done amongst the girls. Slota asked to see the lady who'd actually signed the girls back in – a *Herr* Fürster as it turned out. Herr Fürster was the general dogsbody, the only man in the residence. Well into his seventies, he was there to do all the little jobs that needed doing – repair a latch here, fix a tap there and was, so Frau Uffer had said, something of a father figure to the girls.

It was hard going. He was a kindly old soul but he didn't seem to grasp the fact that a woman had been murdered – seemed to think that this was about some minor breech of servant regulations. The Sergeant persisted, gently nudging him round to the awful truth. When the penny finally dropped Fürster's face dropped with it and he sobbed uncontrollably for some minutes.

'Yes, mein Herr. From your description, it can only be our darling Sophie. I did sign her in, even though she had not arrived by the five o'clock deadline. It wasn't the first time. Tuesday was her day-off, do you see? She always went to her parents' home on Hurdanstrasse. '

Hodža nodded. 'So *then* what did you do?'

'Went straight back to see Frau Uffer, chief. She'd had time to check around. One of the girls *had* covered for Sophie this morning.'

'What about friends outside the domestic staff … an admirer perhaps?' asked Hodža. It was the next obvious question of course. Slota blew out his cheeks.

'She went off the deep end when I suggested that – strictly against the rules. Apparently she wasn't especially chummy with all the other maids, just one or two. She kept herself very much to herself – just work – except for her Tuesday visit to see her folks that is.'

'Which is where you went next, right? How was it?' asked Hodža.

Slota grimaced. 'Gruelling – especially when I asked the same question about a man.'

The inspector nodded glumly. He could picture the scene – the disbelief – the anguish which grew as the hideous reality dawned – the clumsy attempts, no matter how carefully one trod to get information that might help bring her murderer to justice. He hated it – who wouldn't? One day, not in his lifetime of course, there'd be a justice minister enlightened enough to employ specialists to do this sort of thing – better still women. Yes, women. They'd be much better at it than old sods like him and Slota.

'I did get one bit of surprising information though. I asked what time she left their house. Half-eleven they both said and I believed them. She only had the morning free and had to be back at the Palace by noon, apparently. '

'Well that's not right, is it Ján? Not if Fürster's saying she was supposed to be in by five.'

'No, it's *not* right at all, is it sir. So what was she up to for five hours?'

Hodža paused for a fraction. ‘So what does your nose tell you Ján?’

Slota seemed to sniff the air, exactly like a mole. It would have been comical in any other circumstances.

‘I’d say that there is definitely a man involved. The housekeeper didn’t know, neither did the parents which they most definitely would have done if it was a female friend. There’d be no reason *not* to tell ‘em. The question then is how the ficking hell do we find him?’

‘Well one thing we won’t be doing is giving anything to the newspapers.’

Slota’s jaw dropped. Normal procedure was to release an edited version to the press. It wasn’t about gathering evidence – it was about warning the public, especially the most vulnerable, that there was a rapist on the loose.

Hodža read his mind. ‘She wasn’t raped Ján!’

The Inspector had expected to read the dry, depressing words of an autopsy report. He had turned to page three of Max’s report some hours ago but it still hadn’t really sunk in. Pinned to the page was a thin strip of ribbon, a marker put there by Max he’d thought. He moved it aside to read the text…

The victim was virgo intacta, though the hymen was partially disturbed. On examination it was found that a small piece of material (specimen A) had been inserted into the lower reaches of the vagina.

The writing was readily identifiable by anybody who'd seen the state of his hands as Max's scrawl. He'd preferred it when K-P was assisting – at least then it was legible. Hodža read this passage to Slota and then placed the ribbon on a glass sheet before handing it over.

Slota looked carefully at the specimen. It hadn't come from her clothing of that he was certain.

'You can touch it,' said Hodža.

Slota wasn't squeamish or fastidious but for some reason he couldn't really explain he felt awkward as he stroked the surface. 'Top quality dressmakers ribbon that is sir!' he declared.

'Yes! It is. And the colour?'

The Sergeant examined it once more, a stripe of black next to a stripe of yellow. He looked up perplexed, only to meet Hodža's steely grey eyes staring fixedly back at him.

'Oh for God's sake, sir, what the fick's that all about?'

'It's too early to say for certain. Tomorrow I've a job for you. Go up to the palace – see Frau Uffer again and see if you can get any more out of her now that she's had a chance to get over the initial shock. Talk to some of the other maids as well, especially the young lass who covered for her. See if *she* knows anything about an admirer. Lastly have a scout around the area – maybe you can pick up something. You never know, she might have been murdered close to the servants' quarters. Take Kreshall to do the search. He's young and has better eyesight.'

Slota hauled himself off his seat, clutching his aching back as he stood up.

'Shall I do you a dance as well, chief?'

Hodža laughed a dry laugh – for the first and only time that day.

Printed in Great Britain
by Amazon

87374025R00251